BLIND
LADY
BLUES

A Comedy of Lawyers, Monkeys, Bananas and Justice
by Michael Sadler

Michael Sadler (signature)

Cover design by Teresa Wilkinson.
Author photo by Ron Graber.

Copyright © 1998 by Michael Sadler

ISBN 1-892896-13-3

Published by:
Buy Books on the web.com
862 West Lancaster Avenue
Bryn Mawr, PA 19010-3222
Info@buybooksontheweb.com
www.buybooksontheweb.com
Toll Free (877) BUYBOOK

Printed in the United States of America
Published August-1998

I would like to thank my family and friends for their encouragement and support.

Ironically, I would also like to thank lawyers. Their profession provides a rich target for humor without which this book could not have been written.

FOREWORD

In this book I utilize the analogy of a monkey tribe to explore and illustrate the inherent defects of our lawyer system. The comparison of lawyers to the monkey tribe is indispensable to the theme of the book. I admit this comparison is unfair and possibly insulting. In the interest of demonstrating a sincere respect for civilized standards of conduct in the midst of lawyer reform I hereby apologize to any monkeys I may offend. I do not take liberties with the sensitivities of monkeys. Objective observation dictates that the common sense, dignity and humor of the monkey is superior to that of the lawyer. I am confident that monkeys will accept this book with greater amusement and insight than will lawyers.

It is hypothesized that if an infinite number of monkeys were seated before an infinite number of typewriters then all the works of Shakespeare would eventually be reproduced. It is never hypothesized that if an infinite number of monkeys were seated before an infinite number of typewriters that even one document suitable for litigation could be produced. The result of seating an infinite number of lawyers before an infinite number of typewriters is, of course, too horrible to contemplate. This properly illustrates the relative positions due both monkeys and lawyers in the echelons of honor and respect.

I declare this book is one of opinion, and only of opinion. There are no facts in this book, only opinion. There is no call to action in this book, only opinion. There are no reforms advocated in this book, only opinion. There are no ideas in this book, only opinion. There are no words in this book, only opinion. There are no pages in this book, only opinion. There is no book, only opinion.

This declaration of "opinion only" may seem like an attempt to avoid responsibility and accountability for the contents of this "book". While this is most assuredly true, necessity dictates that I make every effort to avoid the litigation which would result if I attempted to elucidate the truth about lawyers. As such truth might somehow be interpreted as unflattering, I fear that lawyers would swarm over me like soulless, perverse, blood-sucking vampires in a grade B movie. Therefore, to reiterate, there is no truth contained herein. However, I do swear to tell my opinion, my whole opinion, and nothing but my opinion. Lies have been told and sworn to be truth, I swear to tell my opinion and you, esteemed reader, may decide the truth. My desire is that any judgment made of my opinion be made in the public arena, not the lawyer arena. Any similarity of the sordid, disgusting lawyers described in this "book" and actual sordid, disgusting lawyers is merely unavoidable coincidence.

Similarly, in this "book" I have created an organization of corrupt, amoral and lethal lawyers called the Missouri Bar Conspiracy. It is a fictional organization and should not be confused with the Missouri Bar Association which is real. Also, the fictional national conspiracy of lawyers referred to herein as the the American Bar Conspiracy should not be confused with the American Bar Association, which is also real. I hope this is clear.

In a further attempt to avoid litigation, I would like to expound upon the application of the term "opinion" as it relates to this "book". Contained herein are several instances when the joyful contemplation of the extermination of lawyers is indulged. While such sublime musings are harmless to all acceptable life forms, lawyers may take exception or infer some type of inherent threat. I therefore declare that I am unequivocally opposed to any illegal and senseless slaughter of lawyers. If a legal and sensible slaughter of lawyers can be implemented, this, of course, would be an altogether different matter. Likewise, the torture, dismemberment, neutering, spaying, disembowelment, beheading, poisoning, burning, hanging, shooting, stabbing, strangling, barbecuing, broiling, boiling, roasting, stoning, bludgeoning, mutilating, drowning, asphyxiation, confinement, sacrifice, premature burial, retroactive abortion, enforced suicide, unauthorized scientific or surgical experimentation, exportation, skinning, or electrocution of lawyers, while popular topics of daydreams and social conversation, cannot be condoned until such time as it is legal.   Logic, fairness and procedure are essential elements to social progress. Anarchy is neither desirable nor beneficial to society. Our civilization could not survive the consequences if lawyers were considered fair game for each individual. There would be riots and violence such as this country has never seen. After all, in spite of the horrendous and burdensome increase in the lawyer population, it should be obvious that there are not enough to go around. Since it will not be possible for everyone to have their own lawyer, we must devise some way to share. Only by sharing can a society achieve enlightenment. Therefore, the elimination of lawyers will have to be postponed until such time as it can be accomplished in a manner which guarantees each citizen an equal opportunity for participation and enjoyment.

Having expressed the foregoing opinion, I must realistically assess the proposal as tenuous in the absolute. Just as there are always a few who cannot wait until the Fourth of July to shoot a few fireworks, and just as there are always a few who cannot wait until Christmas to open a present, there will be those unable to contain their enthusiasm until such time as the methodical genocide of lawyers can be accomplished. Enlightened patriots should view an occasional preemptive lawyer termination with the same compassion as we would a child who sneaks a fresh-from-the-oven chocolate-chip cookie. After all, we all like chocolate-chip cookies and just one will not be missed when the platter-full is served.

Legally, I am on thin ice advocating such compassion. I wish to remind the reader (and particularly the legal professionals) that I am merely expressing an opinion. Lawyers fight justice on a daily basis so that it is subjugated below the concept of legal. So I must remind anyone tempted to dispose of a lawyer, before the establishment of legal guidelines, that they are breaking the law and, regardless of public support, must face the consequences. If caught, they would face the full punishment applicable under <u>current</u> laws. They should definitely request a trial by jury.

Further opinion-only advice to such a patriotic perpetrator would be to consider the legal ramifications of "intent". Current legal doctrine recognizes that if an individual commits a crime the severity of judgment may be mollified if it can be proved that the individual did not actually intend to commit a crime. The ratio of success of this defense is usually proportionate to the ratio of money the accused can pour into the lawyer system.   Therefore, to use "intent" as a defense, a patriot should dispose of a lawyer in such a manner that it can be proved there was no "intent" to deprive the general public of vicarious participation and enjoyment. A good suggestion would be to keep it whimsical and public. Perhaps hanging a lawyer and briefcase from a busy intersection streetlight would appeal to the humor and sensitivity of a jury.

I, myself, am a reasonable individual. I would be quite content if lawyers were simply lined up against a wall and shot. I realize, however, that this may violate the aesthetic criteria of some Americans. As I am more concerned with the ends than the means, I am in favor of full contemplation and public debate of all options to determine the most creative and artistic method of lawyer eradication. I am quite confident that some method can be devised which satisfies and pleases everyone.

I must offer the following apology. Being from Missouri, and having experienced a Missouri lawyer (whom I will not refer to as corrupt for fear of lawsuits; even though he was disbarred I believe it was for screwing other lawyers not for screwing his clients), the Missouri Bar Administration (which I will not refer to as corrupt or self-serving, even though I believe it protects corrupt lawyers), and a Missouri Attorney General (whom I will not call corrupt in spite of the fact he was disbarred and sent to prison); I often speak of Missouri lawyers as if they were the worst possible vermin to infest any legal system. I do not mean to appear conceited by these references. Citizens of forty-nine other states, and many districts, territories, and protectorates of the United States; could offer good arguments to contest the assertion that Missouri lawyers are the worst. In the interest of avoiding trivial disagreements about exactly where the worst lawyers reside, I offer the following recommendation: whenever you read "Missouri" lawyer within these covers, merely substitute the disgusting lawyers of a state or region of your choice. New York, New Jersey, Florida, Louisiana, Texas, California, Nevada, Illinois and the District of Columbia will be among the many, many popular choices available. I do apologize for this concession on your part, respected reader, but the thought that there are worse lawyers than in the state of Missouri is simply too terrible for me to seriously contemplate.

Also, I wish to demonstrate one of the solutions proposed by this "book", which is that we must take a "divide and conquer" approach to lawyers. Most people speak of the lawyer problem only in general terms. We must isolate specific groups of lawyers and attack them in an organized manner. By reducing lawyers to a manageable group, such as Missouri lawyers, we can then proceed to propose solutions rather than merely complaining. More on this later.

Finally, I have been accused of portraying Missouri lawyers as scum with no redeeming qualities whatsoever. I must, reluctantly, admit that there are decent lawyers from Missouri (lawyer Quality Control has not been 100% efficient in eliminating ethics and morality from their profession). However, the good Missouri lawyers will be the first to agree with the problems and solutions outlined in this "book". I respectfully apologize to both of them for the tone of this "book".

So there is no confusion, I would like to clarify another important aspect of this "book". It is not my intent that any illegal acts be conducted or influenced by my writing. If I read about a justifiable homicide targeted at a lawyer, or of a grisly, gruesome, grotesque accident involving a lawyer, it should not be misinterpreted that I pop the cork on a bottle of bubbly and begin dancing, singing, laughing and making wild toasts. In my opinion, I am allowed to grieve in my own way. This should not be taken to mean I condone violence. I react with the same exuberance to front page reports of the demise of a lawyer as I do to their more discreet, but equally festive obituary notices.

FRANK SIXFEET

V

CHAPTER ONE

SOME WORDS IN ITALICS

Hey, I wouldn't lie to you.

If, at times, the contents of this book seem unbelievable, indeed, bordering on the fantastic, then I would be obligated to point out that you are judging my story by the yardstick of your own limited experience. This, I would remind you, is an exceedingly biased formula for evaluating reality.

If you persist with objections that I must have exaggerated my adventures then I am forced to remind you that the truth is often better illustrated through fables, anecdotes, parables and legends than by so-called "real life". I would further point out that all history, biography and other "real" records suffer a major defect in that all are tainted by the opinion, prejudice and ego of the chronicler. Therefore, I would maintain that my story is as real as anything you will encounter in any work of either nonfiction or fiction.

If you continue to criticize my narrative as an inflammatory tool to assert my own opinion then I would remind you that opinion is the basis of our existence. When we are young we are sustained by beliefs because we have too little experience and insufficient facts; when we are older we are sustained by beliefs because we have too much of both.

Finally, if you get snooty and declare that I am a fraud with delusions of grandeur then I would be forced to remind you that you are an idiot. I'm sorry, I didn't want to insult you but you started the whole thing.

I guess that ought to take care of the riffraff. I apologize for the foregoing, but I wanted to feel comfortable with the quality of my reader.

Now then, since you are still reading this I am convinced you are an intelligent and perceptive individual. I admire these qualities and assure you that your faith is not misplaced. You see, I have had some particularly interesting experiences which I will now relate. Since I know you to be a wise and enlightened reader, I'm sure you will be inspired with a few discerning, insightful thoughts during the course of my narrative.

I promise, without reservation, that you are about to engage in an enjoyable and rewarding experience. Hey, I wouldn't lie to you.

****

EEKIM

Eekim (pronounced eek-m, emphasis on the first syllable) first came to me as I sat on the sandy river bank bordered by a grove of banana trees. He walked from the trees with a small stalk of bananas on his back. Sitting not too far away, he ate a few while maintaining an almost reverent air of detachment. After drinking from the stream, he strolled over and plopped down beside me. This, of course, immeasurably impressed me. I did not look directly at him for fear of breaking the mood, but tactfully considered him from the corner of my eye.

My first impression was that he was a typical monkey. He possessed the tail, fur, ears and general features which I had come to associate with that species. There was a twinkle in his dark feral eyes.

"I bet somebody's pet monkey has gotten loose," I thought. "Maybe there's a reward."

But then, suddenly with a sigh, he looked directly at me

2

and sharply declared: "Bananas are good!"

This amazed me to a extent which far exceeds the usual definition of the boundaries of amazement. I simultaneously felt like I was falling, the world was falling, and that both the world and I were falling in exactly the same direction and at exactly the same speed. It was most extraordinary.

However, I quickly got a hold of myself and responded: "What could be better?"

This seemed to please Eekim a great deal and he chattered briefly but happily in a loud voice. Similar chatters echoed from the depths of the banana grove.

He was silent for a moment while alternately watching the river and glancing my direction. Finally, he said: "Monkeys eat bananas!"

"Monkeys are wise," I replied without hesitation. I said this rather smugly because I felt as if I was being tested in some bizarre monkey-Zen manner.

I realize (as I'm sure you, my perceptive reader, are also aware) that flattery is a double-edged tool which can be turned against the wielder. However, it pleased Eekim and he chattered once more into the trees. The echoing chatter was much louder and considerably closer.

Silence descended once more. A short litany of barking screeches came from the forest and Eekim looked quickly and accusingly at me. I felt my face flush with embarrassment. Feeling that my flattery was neither undetected nor appreciated I looked guiltily back at him. Silently I wished for an opportunity to redeem myself. I lowered my head and stared at the bright, hot sand in front of me. Heat waves wafted like elemental spirits from the sand and blurred my vision as if I was gazing through a paranormal kaleidoscope.

Eekim was silent for a long time. I feared he had quietly left but did not lift my gaze from the sand. Sweat formed on my forehead and ran down my face in small drips. I felt shamed.

"Bananas are yellow!" the simian voice announced.

Relief flooded through me as I realized I was to be given another chance! With effort I controlled my elation and concentrated on my answer. Sweat trickled down my back as waves of heat arose from the sand around me but still I considered. I wanted something profound and beautiful and simple. At last I said: "Bananas are yellow like the sun. But the yellow of the banana is the greater, for it can be admired and touched." On impulse I added: "Life is good."

Eekim joyfully chattered and was enthusiastically answered from the edge of the jungle. Critical screeching did not follow this time. I detected the dark forms of monkeys dancing just beyond the tree line and swinging through the branches.

"Bananas grow on trees!"

Although Eekim had a teasing lilt to his voice I could find no humor in the statement. I searched for an acceptable answer but my mind was blank. A breeze blew my hair and I felt the dripping wetness there. Eekim seemed impatient and in exasperation I blurted: "You want they should grow on rocks?"

Eekim and the hundreds, maybe thousands, of monkeys gathered in the shade of the jungle immediately burst into laughter. It was a heartfelt and appreciative response which conveyed acceptance and friendliness. I grinned with manic joy at this development. Sweat drenched the back of my shirt, rolled in rivulets from my armpits down my sides, and dripped from the soggy hair plastered to my scalp. Vaguely I considered that this experience might represent the first symptoms of sunstroke.

Nonetheless, I was determined to pursue further conversation with Eekim. I suspected that, having passed the initial tests, more substantial conversations could take place. I had visions of teaching the monkeys a more complete vocabulary so that complex concepts could be discussed. I was enraptured with the thought of a sophisticated exchange of ideas.

"The sun is hot!" said Eekim.

What? Another challenge? Feeling somewhat miffed at further riddling when my answers had brought such a positive response, I formed an eloquent reply. This monkey didn't know with whom he was dealing if he thought I could not quickly catch on to this game.

"The sun is hot in contrast to the moon which is cool, revealing the dichotomy of life, the Yin and Yang if you will. The sun is hot revealing the paradox of all things for, though it is the sun's heat which gives life, the sun's heat can also parch, dry and destroy life. The sun is hot to reveal the balance necessary for all life."

"Yea...right..." Eekim spoke slowly. "But what I mean is we, particularly you, should get out of the sun." With a pedantic tone he added: "You should avail yourself of some of that balance you mentioned by getting yourself out of the sun. The sun is hot!"

Eekim gazed at me not unlike a psychiatrist evaluating an unpromising patient. I evinced a noncommittal shrug in what I thought to be a very eloquent manner. We rose and trudged to the cool shade of the trees as monkeys scattered to clear a wide area for us. I emphasized smooth, measured composure in my gait to contrast with Eekim's scampering, erratic digressions from a straight path.

"You'll notice that smart monkeys do not sit in the sun."

The condescending tone rankled and I tersely replied: "You sat with me."

"Yes," Eekim acknowledged, "but nobody said it was smart."

Upon reaching the shade I fell onto the cool sand with pleasure. Eekim sat beside me and asked: "What did you mean by saying all that stuff about the sun?"

"Oh," I flippantly replied, "merely attempting to define the larger concepts which face any salient mind during the journey through life."

"Yea, right." Eekim said. "But you might consider defining in the shade in the future. The sun seems to render you overly cryptic. Wisely is it written in the peels of my tribe: "The Big Banana gave us bananas, which are yellow. The Big Banana gave us tigers, which are yellow with black stripes. The Big Banana gave us the sun, which is yellow. This is probably important but until you figure it out just eat bananas, avoid tigers and stay out of the sun."

I could form no immediate reply so settled for watching the river with what I hoped was a knowing expression. This went on for quite a while but I was determined to make the little monkey curious. Enthralled as I was by the encounter, I felt I should attempt to get the upper hand. I do not know that I have ever considered the possibility of meeting a talking monkey, but had I considered it, I doubt that I would have thought it would go

5

like this.

Eekim fidgeted. I smiled to think he was getting nervous. I was sure that he would eventually reveal the reason he had sought me. Perhaps I represented some sort of messianic figure to them. Maybe I was to become a great teacher for the tribe. Possibly the monkeys looked to me for wisdom and enlightenment.

Eekim looked around at the other monkeys but I maintained my self-assured demeanor. Finally he leaned closer to me.

"Here it comes," I thought.

"You know you are in big trouble," he whispered.

BIG TROUBLE

While I was absorbing this revelation an old monkey shambled over, looked me up and down, and grumpily inquired: "Is this the one?"

Eekim rather unenthusiastically nodded.

The old monkey looked me up and down again. "Doesn't look like much!"

" None of them do," Eekim charitably observed.

"You know you are in big trouble," said the old monkey.

"I've been told that," I responded as cheerfully as possible. The old monkey's voice sounded familiar. "What's your name?"

"You don't even know names? My name, obviously, is Ooga and this is Eekim. He probably didn't tell you his name because he figured you were at least intelligent enough to recognize him. But you're not." And that was how I was formally introduced to Eekim and Ooga. I also realized that Ooga's voice had been the one which denounced my earlier attempt at flattery.

"What's my name?" I asked.

Ooga shook his head sadly: "You don't want to know. We'll call you whatever pleases you."

"My name is Josh."

"Yes," observed Ooga, "that is much more flattering."

"And he ain't joshin'!" interjected Eekim. Ooga and Eekim exuberantly laughed as if this was extremely funny. I had heard it before. They rolled in the sand in a veritable fit of amusement. Ooga then chased Eekim around and up a tree, down the tree, twice around me, then down to the river and back before settling down. Ooga possessed surprising dexterity for an old monkey. They continued chuckling together, somewhat rudely oblivious to my presence.

"What kind of trouble am I in?"

The chuckling immediately ceased. Ooga bared his teeth and emitted a clamoring cry in the typical expression of monkey laughter. "It is as plain as the nose on a monkey's face," he exclaimed. "You have a problem with civilization. We monkeys understand the term, we're just not sure how it can be applied to human affairs. So, to be more precise, you have a problem with the structure of living that your kind presumptuously call civilization."

"Your kind?"

Ooga glared at me. Eekim quickly but hesitantly interceded: "Well, you know....no undue offense,...uh,...human."

"I've always been proud of being human."

"Well of course you have," said Eekim while reassuringly patting me on the back. "Pride is a fundamental emotion one is allowed to experience during the course of existence. Pride contributes to one's sense of worth and is essential to the pursuit of accomplishments. All beings have pride, especially the most deluded and mistaken. One does not criticize the pride another feels, one merely questions the justification of pride in some species."

I may not be the most perceptive person in the world but I definitely detected sarcasm in Eekim's statement. He obviously reveled in word play and sugared his most vitriolic comments with a loquacious coating. Mildly acerbated, I inquired: "And what are monkeys proud of?"

Eekim laughed. "Of what are monkeys proud? Many things, many, many things. Monkeys are proud of their freedom, their social structure, their jungle, their bananas. We are proud of our progress, our poems, songs, and stories; our children, our future. Monkeys take pride in everything which is why monkeys do not destroy and abuse the world and call it progress. On a personal level, for instance, I took great pride in the creative path

7

I chose in walking here, compared to your rigid, direct line of march which seemed to declare that there was nothing interesting in the journey and the journey itself was merely an inconvenience necessary for the destination. But most of all, and this is relevant to your predicament, monkeys are proud to have no lawyers."

I was learning there was seldom room for argument with Eekim. When he made a statement it was simple, truthful and to the point. I shamefully admitted: "My species has lawyers."

"Yes, we know," somberly replied Ooga, and for the first time his voice was tinged with sympathy instead of contempt. "That is the reason we have sought you. The situation is extremely tragic but not incurable. Monkeys have watched the development of your kind for a long time. Humans have been exceptionally slow to evolve through the various fascist, feudal, royal, political and other power structures you indulge. Monkeys do not criticize your sloth as each species must progress at its own rate, no matter how retarded that progress may appear. However, the wisest of monkeys feel that your species will not be able to evolve beyond your lawyer system without some outside help. We are here to help."

"Why should you want to help?"

Ooga glared at me again.

Eekim once more smoothed the situation: "Well, I admit this altruism is more of a compliment to the superior nature of monkeys rather than any tangible value of which humans might be engendered. Your species is probably not totally devoid of all merit. There is, for example, your...um,...your,...well, your sense of humility, infrequent and underdeveloped as it is, shows promise. No matter what else is said of your race, every monkey appreciates those rare instances when one of your kind can achieve an appropriately humble outlook." Ooga reluctantly nodded agreement.

"I am overwhelmed by your praise," I dryly said.

"As well you should be," continued Eekim. "I am not totally or deceitfully stretching the truth when I say that monkeys still retain some minuscule hope that your species may, in the distant unforeseeable future, attain some small degree of respect."

"You're too kind," I admonished.

"Probably," Eekim enthusiastically responded. "It is an attribute of the monkey to sacrifice intellectual analysis to a more pleasing and wholesome vision of the heart. And who really knows? Your kind might be redeemed... someday... somehow .... maybe. It's at least a nice thought.

"You see," Eekim continued, "monkeys went through the same phases of social structures which humans have, are, and will be going through. It was long ago, during the eons when the most intelligent and gifted of your race were devoting their entire intellectual potential to discovering fire and making a wheel which was round. During those glorious millenniums of your development, monkey social progress paralleled what would eventually be human progress. Monkeys have faced the same problems as your kind, we merely faced them with supremely greater grace, alacrity and intelligence."

"Oh?" I interrupted. "And how long did it take you to go through fascism, feudalism and royalty?"

"Quite a while by monkey standards," admitted Eekim, his face slightly flushing with embarrassment. "The time varied, of course, but generally it took a week, ten days max, to evolve beyond the obvious fallacies of those systems. Fortunately, monkeys are educable and therefore did not have to repeat those mistakes a couple of dozen times before we learned. Those periods are immortalized in monkey history as The Gray Weeks. But the period in which your species is currently mired is comparable to the bleakest period of monkey history. It was a deplorable period which lasted for ninety days and is known as The Dark Months. Let me tell you a story:"

EEKIM'S STORY

Eekim cleared his throat and began: "In the beginning there was the jungle.

"The monkey tribe lived in the jungle and faced its advantages and disadvantages with general humor and happiness. The jungle was cruel, at times, but never in a sadistic way. The jungle was generous also, giving the monkeys what

9

they needed to live and prosper. Their prevailing attitude was that the jungle was good because it allowed the monkeys to live, and the monkeys were thankful for living an overall pleasant existence.

"Bananas rated as the greatest gift of the jungle. Monkeys recited poems, sang songs, and acted plays praising the banana. On many a sunny afternoon a rich cacophony of sounds arose from the jungle as various groups of the tribe indulged in blissful accolades to the banana. The various tributes were not mere noise but transmitted the spiritual and mystic association the monkeys felt. The monkeys really loved their bananas.

"The natural evolution of monkey passion for bananas led to the establishment of religions. The prevailing belief was that there was a cosmic Big Banana which had created the monkeys and put them in the jungle to live happy and fruitful lives. Another religion held that when a monkey died, after living a good life, the simian was reincarnated as a banana thereby perpetuating an eternal circle of existence. A similar religion stated that a monkey was the reincarnation of a banana thereby perpetuating an eternal circle of existence. The two religions gave birth to the perpetual and circular argument over which came first, the monkey or the banana. Although debates between the two religions were lengthy and, at times, very confusing as to which side was actually supporting what, there was general acceptance by most monkeys that it was at least a nice thought either way.

"Most monkeys possess a simple philosophy: Bananas are good, it is fun being a monkey, and anything which does not interfere with the relationship between a monkey and a banana is okay. Some philosophies were more detailed, such as the philosophy contained in the two-day long epic poem in which life is compared to the peeling of a banana, entitled: 'Ode To The Idea That Life Is Like The Peeling Of A Banana'. Some monkeys felt that the poem was too long and, once past the title, redundant. Many monkeys felt even the title was too long. It was the ingenuity of the original composer, however, to insert numerous banana breaks into the structure of the poem so that, in spite of length and repetition, it was a very popular opus. Even so, a more popular and shorter poem is entitled: 'Peel It, Eat It,

Do It Again'. The entire poem and the title are exactly the same.
"Into this veritable garden setting crawled an entity
which would destroy the monkey paradise. Its influence grew
slowly at first but it eventually became the nemesis of good
monkeys throughout the tribe.
"This unseen entity was pervasive and persuasive.
Around the entity grew a small cult of monkey followers who
began to take over the supply of bananas, a situation extremely
disconcerting to the average monkey.
"The monkeys involved in the takeover claimed they
represented the law by proclaiming: "We are 'Your Law'
Monkeys." 'Your Law' Monkeys, or yerlaws as they came to be
known, were at first tolerated by the monkey tribe. The typical
yerlaw was, after all, neither productive nor much fun to be
around. The only redeeming quality (and both redeeming and
quality are arguable) they possessed was the ability to speak
volumes of loquacious verbiage signifying nothing.
Occasionally yerlaws would cure insomniacs but more often
only irritated them..
"If these socially dysfunctional monkeys could find a
calling which kept them out of the way the average monkey was
all for it. After all, every monkey knew the difference between
right and wrong. It was wrong to attack or kill innocent
monkeys, it was wrong to steal bananas, and it was wrong to lie.
This was generally accepted as the sacred word of the Big
Banana. If monkeys followed these general principles
everything else could be worked out. So if the yerlaw monkeys
wanted to make a career out of something everyone already
knew, who cared?
"But then the subtlety of the yerlaw plan came to fruition
and the monkeys looked around and realized that the yerlaw
monkeys and their clients owned all the banana trees. 'This is
unacceptable!' they cried.
'No,' responded the yerlaws, 'it is legal.'"
"How did it become legal?" I interrupted.

FIRST INTERRUPTION
        I noted that Ooga had sat sulkily throughout Eekim's

11

narrative. He had occasionally looked at me in a questioning manner. This was followed by a deep sigh and a sad shaking of his head. Ooga then wistfully gazed into the distance. After a while he would repeat this sequence.

At my interruption Ooga emitted a short, disgusted "Harrumph", wearily jumped to his feet and purposefully wandered off.

I thought Eekim might also resent my intrusion into the flow of his story but he didn't. He merely stared at me for several long moments as if seeing me for the first time or not seeing me at all. Then he lazily scratched his head, his right arm and his left shoulder. Shifting his weight he quietly cleared his throat as if to speak. Next, he lazily selected a banana. With serene manner he calmly and slowly peeled the banana. After contemplating the banana peel for several meditative moments he slowly began to eat. Each bite was a ritual of enjoyment and Eekim smacked his lips with delight. After consuming the banana Eekim sat with a contented smile on his face. Then he turned to me and inquired: "Did you say something?"

"How did it become legal?" I repeated.

"Oh, yes. Well that is a strange part of the story. I was going to proceed in a logical manner but that may incur too great an effort on the part of my audience." Eekim smiled pointedly at me but I smiled pointlessly back. When it became obvious that I was not going to rebut the implied affront, he said: "Very well, I'll tell you how it became legal."

HOW IT BECAME LEGAL

"Monkeys had many uses for banana peels," Eekim continued. "They made hats and decorations out of them, and used them for runny noses and wiping their butts. The most important thing, however, was that monkeys had devised a sophisticated written language by carefully stripping the strings from the inside of a banana peel to form letters and words. This was very useful because the poems, songs and plays idolizing the banana could be passed from generation to generation.

"Now it had been observed that the yerlaws were accumulating piles and piles of banana peels. However, upon reading some of the peels from the piles, the average, intelligent monkey had dismissed them as gibberish. Some monkeys said: 'Oh well, if it makes them happy. After all, we all know the difference between right and wrong so what can it hurt?' A few monkeys were uneasy but since nobody understood the writing on the piles of peels no action was taken. Most merely considered it a shameful waste of good buttwipe.

"However, over time the piles of peels dictated the course of everyone's life. Laws were incomprehensible and banana peels were scarce. A popular saying was: 'I have to see my yerlaw so I can wipe my butt!' There were more graphic forms of this expression, such as: 'Yerlaws need all those peels because they are so full of monkey doo.' There were also more demonstrative maxims detailing exactly where yerlaws could put all those peels and many further described colorful and creative means of extraction."

"So yerlaws took over by accumulating a huge amount of banana peels?" I asked.

"In a manner of speaking," replied Eekim. "Keep in mind that the peels themselves were not so important as the preponderance of ritual and precedence which they embodied. The peels could have been considered merely symbolic of the real problem."

"Which was?"

"Yerlaws rendered a simple concept, that of right and wrong, into an overly complex and incomprehensible system of lore. For example, no longer was stealing wrong, it was a question of exactly what kind of stealing occurred, what kinds of precedence had been set which might or might not make it wrong, exactly which law in the colossal volumes of law had been broken, what procedure was proper so that the wrong could be addressed with the correct rituals, how to monitor the monkey jury so that their personal moral imperatives would not interfere with a proper, legal determination of guilt or innocence, and the amount of wealth an accused monkey could spend on legal defense. It was a study in meticulous extrapolations which became so complicated as to defeat the stated purpose. Of course, all this was a smoke screen because the real focus of the lore system was to exalt yerlaws. It was a classic example of

13

how a power system comes to exist solely to perpetuate and
expand its power.

"But these are disturbing discussions for night. It is
better to consider subjects like yerlaws in the light of day. I'm
going to munch a few bananas and find someone intelligent with
whom to talk before I go to bed. I'll continue my story
tomorrow," Eekim said and started walking into the jungle.

"Is that the way you say 'goodnight' to a new friend?" I
called after him.

"Of course," he laughed. "I don't believe in much *adieu*
about nothing." But he added: "See you tomorrow!"

Night falls quickly in the jungle. The hot afternoon sun
had disappeared and only a reddish halo of light above the tree
tops in the west indicated it had ever been there at all. The
deepening twilight warned of imminent darkness. A small but
cool breeze sprang from the river as birds ceased to swoop and
sought their nests.

BACKTRACKING

Later, I lay awake under the stars and thought about
Eekim.

One blatantly obvious observation was that he enjoyed
insulting me. I believed, however, that these insults were made
in jest rather than meaning any serious personal criticism. At
least, I liked to think that. I decided to treat his banter as a form
of intellectual sparring. As long as he didn't go for a knock-out,
I would roll with the punches.

I also observed that Eekim was an intelligent creature
with a simple and direct perspective. I reminded myself that
simple does not mean simplistic and resolved to be more
attentive to his conversation. It struck me with some surprise
that I should consider Eekim at least my equal and possibly my
superior.

"Well," I wryly thought, "I can be as simple as any
monkey." Perhaps this approach would also eventually impress
Ooga, whose insults were less superficial.

Finally, I observed that I was perhaps the first human
being to encounter a tribe of talking monkeys. Further, these
monkeys were evidently dedicated to helping my country

overcome the serious social problem presented by lawyers. I considered the impact this revelation might have and was struck by a premonition that great things were going to happen. I found this, personally, very disquieting.

My thoughts drifted towards how I came to be here.

I was on a canoe trip down the Big Piney in the Mark Twain National Forest in Missouri. The excursion was therapeutic in that I was attempting to reconcile a reversal of my relative fortune. The reversal was caused by a corrupt lawyer (please excuse the possible redundancy). The whole affair was, of course, drawn out over an extremely extensive time period and had slowly drained my optimism, finances, hope and will to live.

Nature has always been my psychiatrist. I am basically a well adjusted person with no major mental disorders other than lawyers.

My reasoning went like this: (1) the problem is well defined in that I had every conceivable non-violent crime perpetrated against me by a lawyer, (2) my course of action is clear in that there is no course of action possible because lawyers represent a closed system of which I am not a member, (3) I think I'll go stare at a tree.

Actually, I was going to stare at a lot of trees for a long time. All reports indicate this is a relatively mild reaction to an encounter with a lawyer.

I took comfort in visiting the Mark Twain National Forest. Samuel Langhorne Clemens said: "Hanging its lawyers would not correct all of this country's woes but it would be lots of fun and could do no harm to anyone." Sam was a pretty sharp Missouri boy.

So, anyway, I was on this canoe trip when I met Eekim. I don't know what a jungle full of talking, banana-swilling monkeys was doing in Missouri.

And then I fell asleep.

CHAPTER TWO

THE NEXT MORNING

I pointedly waited for Eekim beneath the cool shade of some banana trees. Evidently he was not an early riser because it took a while. At last Eekim, with a stalk of bananas on his back, strolled out of the jungle and sat beside me.

"There you are!" I cheerfully declared.

Eekim matter-of-factly replied: "I know that. But please feel free to keep me apprised of future developments."

I considered for a moment and decided that it was not a rebuke for stating the obvious but a clever response to a statement of the obvious. I casually examined Eekim's features and, though I am no expert at reading motives in a monkey's facial expressions, detected no guile or sarcasm; merely open-eyed playfulness.

"Would you like these appraisals at specific time intervals or only at important moments?" I inquired.

"Oh, keep them random," laughed Eekim. "Whenever the mood strikes you."

I nodded my head in agreement. Eekim and I smiled into the morning with a shared feeling that a bond was forming. It's funny the way a mutual joke can initiate a friendship.

"You're still there," I said after a time.

"But I am beginning to doubt the wisdom of perpetuating the situation."

My grin at this response was a reflection of Eekim's uninhibited smirk. I basked in that unique and special new-found-friend feeling. It's a mystic, kindred-spirit feeling which always makes me think of a seed which is just sprouting; a discovery of new and larger life experiences. The fact that I was talking to a talking monkey added to the feeling that this day was somehow special.

The sun continued to climb and its rays blossomed in the sky like a flower in spring. As its petals of light spread, the morning became the brightness of day and a feeling of rebirth and promise permeated our surroundings

"I hate to break the mood," said Eekim, "but we should discuss the lawyer problem in more depth. It's a shame to spoil a day with sordid conversation but Ooga instructed me to be your tutor."

"That was very considerate of him," I noted.

"I don't know," mused Eekim. "His exact words were: 'Try to make that moronic imbecile see the light. I don't have the patience!'"

I decided to change the subject.

"You know, I can't help but wonder if you're just an hallucination brought on by sunstroke," I said.

Eekim indignantly replied: "I can assure you that I am not an hallucination."

"Well, that's something."

"Not really," he countered. "An hallucination would assure you of the same thing. Don't worry, I have a feeling insanity may be an advantage when it comes to understanding your lawyer system. Shall we begin?"

"Might as well," I sighed. "Do you want to continue the story you started yesterday?"

"No. Monkey social evolution is not a perfect mirror for the human condition. Our progress was not the tedious process in which humans engage. The subject we should discuss first is one which monkeys did not encounter. Yerlaws were not tolerated long enough for a method of procreation or power inheritance to be a factor. This is not true of your lawyers. The first issue we must resolve is: What causes lawyers?"

WHAT CAUSES LAWYERS?
"Well, everybody wants justice," I conjectured.
"And what does that have to do with lawyers?" Eekim
retorted. "Everybody likes nature but we do not need biologists
to have it. Everybody likes the stars but we do not need
astronomers to have them. Lawyers do not cause justice. They
are merely the proprietors of the system which claims
responsibility for justice. Justice is less expensive than a lawyer.
Trust me on this."
"Okay," I conceded, "maybe law schools cause
lawyers?"
"Wrong again. Law schools are merely the tool for
ordaining lawyers. The question remains: What is the first and
primary cause of lawyers?"
"Well," I hesitantly forged onward, "people don't cause
lawyers, justice doesn't cause lawyers, Nature doesn't, the stars
don't, law schools don't....maybe lawyers..."
"Exactly!" proclaimed Eekim. "Lawyers cause lawyers.
There is no other possibility. I'm glad to see you are losing some
of the silly, preconditioned thinking which makes it impossible
for you to logically see things. Of course lawyers cause lawyers,
nobody else would do it!"
"That makes sense," I marveled.
"You bet it does. The first step towards solving a
problem is to recognize what exactly is the problem. Okay, we
have determined that lawyers cause lawyers, now we must
determine exactly how this self-perpetuating atrocity is
accomplished. How do lawyers cause lawyers?"
"Direct inheritance is probably the single most popular
method," I observed. "Progeny of lawyers inherit a law degree
the same way a child might inherit the family business. Lawyers
are always breeding more lawyers, which is a pretty disgusting
thought." I mimed an expression of involuntary retching and
heaved my shoulders.
"Please be objective," Eekim admonished. "You don't
see the repulsive thought of lawyer procreation putting me off
my bananas." He reached over and selected a banana. Quite

some time later, after the peel had been meditated upon and the banana consumed, Eekim continued: "We have now determined that many lawyers are conceived by one of the most primal acts of which a human is capable. This is not a necessarily despicable procedure but the involvement of lawyers does seem to contaminate the conception with a revolting taint. This, however, is irrelevant. Now then, how is the position of a lawyer transferred to offspring?"

"Well," I reasoned, "the position of lawyer is attained by acquiring a license to practice. This license is usually appropriated through study at a law school. It's rumored that law schools have excruciating entrance standards: one must have a superior intelligence, an exemplary history of social activity, or a note from one's lawyer daddy or lawyer mommy stating what a good lawyer you would be. I think that last thing is the most important. In some cases, however, a note from a well connected lawyer friend of the family will suffice. Occasionally, I guess, someone might become a lawyer on personal qualities alone."

This appraisal seemed accurate to me and I awaited Eekim's response with natural expectation of satiric commentary. I was not disappointed.

"So most lawyers are progeny of lawyers, and/or raised in a social environment which is conducive to an affiliation with lawyers. Hmm... This will do nothing to help your species resolve the question of heredity versus environment as the cause of integral defects in offspring. However, if the children of lawyers were isolated and raised in a moral environment it could then be determined if...."

"Wait a minute!" I interrupted. "We're not supposed to determine whether defective DNA or an immoral home atmosphere causes more lawyers. The lesser problems of genetics and environment can be addressed anytime. Let's stick to the problem of what causes lawyers in the first place."

"Quite right, quite right," said Eekim. "I apologize for the digression. So, there appears to be two kinds of lawyers: those who inherit their position by genetics or caste system, and those who are actually qualified to be lawyers. How do the two differ?"

19

"That's easy," I replied. "well-connected lawyers, whether by birth or affluence, tend to become involved in well-connected law firms. It's like show business, it's not what you know, it's who you know. At worst they inherit the clients of their mommy or daddy in the good ol' boys style and tradition of the family law firm.

"On the other hand," I continued, "a lawyer who makes it on personal qualities probably becomes an indentured servant of a major firm, a public defender, a prosecutor, an ACLU lawyer or a judge. I suppose that, occasionally, someone becomes a big time lawyer merely by possessing a cunning intellect and an amoral nature."

"Okay," Eekim eagerly said. "The solution is simple! We can begin solving the lawyer problem with the mandatory spaying or neutering of lawyers. It would be a very progressive first step."

"Now hold on," I firmly said. "We can't do that! A person could be sued for suggesting such a solution. Hell, why not just advocate the immediate execution of all lawyers?"

Eekim seriously pondered this question and then replied: "I give up. Why not?".

As I did not have a good reason, I decided to channel the discussion back to less litigious, albeit less expedient and less reasonable, methods of resolving the lawyer problem.

"We have not progressed far enough in our definition of the lawyer problem to propose solutions at this point," I righteously pontificated. "We are still in preliminary evaluation of the full scope of the problem. We must continue to define the primary cause of lawyers then, and only then, adopt a solution."

I looked at Eekim with an expression of a dissatisfied schoolteacher. He bought it. One for me.

"You're right." Eekim sighed. "I must apologize for my predisposition to directly attack a problem. I realize that humans enmeshed in an anal retentive lawyer system cannot simply do the right thing in the right manner for the right reason. Let us proceed to format a jurisprudentially acceptable solution. We have determined that lawyers, by way of heredity or socio-political connections, cause lawyers. But I would assert that the final analysis mandates a determination that the primary cause of lawyers is money."

"Well," I observed, "I've heard that lawyers are the highest paid profession in the country."

"Okay," said Eekim, "money is the primary cause of lawyers. Now, if money is the motivating factor, why would a lawyer desire to pass a practice directly to offspring rather than any randomly chosen morally defective person?"

"Probably natural distrust," I surmised. "A lawyer's secrets are better protected if kept in the family. There may be a tendency towards a philosophy that there is 'honor among inbred thieves'."

"Very good!" laughed Eekim. "If we accept the point that money causes lawyers, then all that is needed is to eliminate money from the justice system and, *quid pro quo*, lawyers will be eliminated."

"I don't think lawyers will allow that to happen," I said. "Remember, we are trying to reform a system which is controlled by the main factors in need of reform. Lawyers will not tolerate reforms aimed at a higher quality of justice if there is a simultaneous repercussion that lawyers will not procure huge amounts of money. Money and lawyers are inseparable. You said that when we started this conversation."

"That's right, I did," Eekim acknowledged with a weary sigh. "I see why it takes your kind so long to evolve, you always go in circles. Why is it so hard for humans to understand that the path to justice lies in wisdom, not greed? I knew talking about lawyers would spoil the day."

Eekim looked with less joy than usual at his ever present banana supply as if some of his natural vitality had been drained. He looked to the jungle where the sounds of happy, carefree monkeys filled the air. I swear he was trying to remember how to revel in such sounds and allow them to nourish his spirit. I guiltily felt that our discussion had robbed him of something very precious.

Being human, however, I was unaware of the iron constitution and resolute will of monkeys.

Eekim suddenly beamed with intense enthusiasm, scampered in an exaggerated and ridiculous dance around me and shouted: "Time for a banana break! Care to join me?"

21

THE BANANA BREAK

One of my fondest memories is of my first monkey-chaperoned banana break. Eekim explained rituals which were as complex as a Japanese tea-serving ceremony. Procedures observed for thousands of years were demonstrated: how to choose and share the best bananas, proper finger placement for grasping and peeling bananas, the 453 acceptable sitting and lounging positions, the 2,621 ways of smiling and their meanings. It was a veritable Kama-Sutra of monkey-banana relationships. It was also a very long break.

The one dominating rule; the one intractable, inarguable, non-negotiable, absolute rule was this: any rule can be broken if it results in laughter.

"The Golden Banana Rule, as we call it, is the most civilized of banana rules," Eekim proudly summarized. "It represents an axiom which, while negating all previously established rules and procedures, captures the essence of banana rituals. The true wisdom of the Golden Banana Rule is that it exalts the divine spirit of eating bananas above the monkey-made laws of eating bananas."

"So all the rules are actually meaningless?' I asked.

Eekim raised an eyebrow, flashed a quizzical expression across his face, nodded yes but said: "Not really. The Golden Banana Rule is, of course, the highest and most important rule. However, it is generalized and stipulates no references for behavior. The numerous procedures and rituals are designed to shed light upon tried and true methods of attaining an end. They are the means to the end and are therefore extremely important. The Golden Banana Rule establishes the goal while the procedures represent ways to achieve the goal. The procedures are subordinate, however, and will be modified whenever they conflict with the goal. The goal is never modified to accommodate the procedures. To put it another way: the Golden Banana Rule represents the whole purpose, the procedures represent the parts, and the whole is greater than the sum of the parts. Another translation of the idea is that the means must be justified by the end. This concept could also be paraphrased as...."

"I get the idea," I politely interrupted. Eekim displayed smile #1,424, which means: "I could go on like this forever but, if it pleases you, we can move on to something else".

"What you are saying," I continued, "is that the rules for enjoying bananas should never be allowed to interfere with the actual enjoyment of bananas. This could also be stated as: to enjoy a banana is to observe the rules whether there is one or not. Perhaps another interpretation would be: when in doubt, eat a banana. This could also be expressed as...."

"OK, enough," said Eekim, smiling #743, which means: "OK, enough". I shot back smile #1,424. Eekim fired off smile #322, which means: "it has been fun, but let's not milk it". I finished with a salvo of smiles #575, 576, and 577, which mean: "you're right", "sure", and "whatever". Dueling smiles is a favorite game during banana breaks.

"Bananas sure are great, aren't they?" Eekim asked.

It was a rhetorical question, of course, so I immediately responded with: "Have you ever heard of anything greater?"

"Who could have heard of something which does not exist?"

"If someone had heard of something which did not exist, would they have told us?"

"If it did not exist, why would they keep it a secret?"

And so on.

Dueling silly questions is also a favorite banana break game. It is a kind of monkey Zen exercise. For instance, to the question 'What is the sound of one hand clapping?" a monkey might respond "If one hand claps in the forest and no one is around to hear it, does it make any sound?".

OOGA INTERRUPTS

"Well, I hope you two are enjoying yourselves," grumbled a grumpy voice. Ooga merrily trudged through the undergrowth and stood in front of us with his hands on his hips and his eyes bouncing between Eekim and me, which gave the impression that he was shaking his head "no".

"Lawyers are running rampant, destroying your society, and here you sit munching bananas. No wonder humans are such decadent creatures!"

"We ask your pardon, O Venerable Wise One," Eekim somberly said. "But, if guilt is to be assigned, it is I who must bear the burden as it was, indeed, I who suggested we take a break from the sordid discussion of lawyers." Eekim gracefully bowed.

"Eloquently spoken," said Ooga, "now shut-up and listen." He joyfully stared at both of us at the same time, which is actually a very difficult thing to do, until he was sure he had our undivided attention.

"You," he said while pointing at Eekim, "have a job to do. You are to define the human lawyer problem and formulate an acceptable solution. Remember, you will continue to associate with this human until the job is done. That ought to be inspiration enough.

"You," he said while pointing at me," I do not expect anything from anyway but you could try harder to surprise me.

"Now both of you," he said while pointing at both of us with one finger, which is another difficult trick, "get busy!"

"Yes, O Wise One," said Eekim.

"Consider it done, sir," I said.

Ooga turned and testily strolled into the jungle.

"Nice guy," I observed.

"Heart of gold," added Eekim.

"Could be more upbeat," I postulated.

"Downright cranky at times," Eekim conceded.

"Get busy!" Ooga happily screamed from the bushes.

"Shall we get busy?" Eekim innocently inquired.

"It may be the most advisable thing to do," I acknowledged.

"Having decided to get busy," Eekim conjectured, "we must decide upon the most opportune time in which to get busy."

"There are myriad and sundry choices," I noted.

"How about RIGHT NOW!" Ooga cheerfully shrieked from the foliage.

"Perhaps right now?" I suggested.

"Perhaps, but is it wise to jump to conclusions without fully exploring every possible option," Eekim hypothesized.

"We should form a committee and study the problem to determine the most favorable course of action," I proposed.

"Don't make me come out there!" Ooga blissfully threatened from the flora.

Eekim sighed, I shrugged, and we got busy.

GETTING BUSY

The original location we had chosen for discussion had been open barren rocky ground, exposed to the sun, and not far from the rotten banana depository. The bleak surroundings, discomfort, heat and aroma seemed the perfect atmosphere in which to discuss lawyers.

We had endured this location for as long as humanly and monkeyly possible but after about thirty seconds we had opted to move to a cool, shady oasis with a pool of spring water and plenty of banana trees. Our reasoning was this: it is bad enough to discuss lawyers without masochistically subjecting ourselves to a hostile environment as well.

So we now returned to the site of our previous discussion and comfortably settled ourselves. (Dear reader, I would suggest you do the same).

"You know," Eekim thoughtfully said, "we may be making this too complicated. During the Dark Months of yerlaw rein, monkeys developed an expression which pretty much said it all: 'Yerlaws uck'. I think the expression would work for lawyers also."

"Lawyers uck?"

"Well, you have to say it fast so that the words run together in the vernacular tradition of the French *liaison*," Eekim advised.

"Lawyers uck?"

"Faster!" said Eekim.

"Lawyers uck? Lawyers uck? Lawyersuck! I get it," I laughed, "but somehow I don't think Ooga would be impressed."

"Your human faculty for stating the obvious never ceases to amaze me."

"Me too!" Ooga sarcastically yelled. The bushes to our right rustled in a very ominous manner. It sounded like something very big, very determined and very mad was coming our way.

"Okay," Eekim quickly said while staring wide-eyed at

the swaying vegetation. "We previously determined that lawyers are caused by other lawyers and that the entire lawyer power structure is predicated by monetary greed."

"Right," I hurriedly added while cautiously eyeing the bushes, which had settled down somewhat. "The logical next step is to determine the method by which lawyers operate."

"Correct," Eekim blurted, also eyeing the bushes, which were now almost still. "Having determined the cause and effect aspects of the lawyer problem, we can now proceed to formulate a solution."

"The end result of which will be to effectively eliminate lawyers and thereby make the world a much more pleasant place to live," I swiftly spoke while noticing that the bushes were now completely quiet.

"Then monkeys and humans can get on with the enjoyment and fulfillment of their lives," Eekim declared and then, while suspiciously looking around, whispered: "Do you think he's gone?"

"I don't know," I said while inspecting the shrubbery. "I'm not sure."

"You never will be!" Ooga gleefully yelled.

Eekim and I looked at each other. Eekim shrugged his shoulders and I sighed.

A SCATOLOGY CONCERNING THE METHODS OF OPERATION OF THE HUMAN SUBSPECIES LAWYER (*homo larcenus litigatus*) AND THE CONTRIBUTION OF SUCH METHODS TO THE DETERIORATION OF CIVILIZED SOCIETY

"How do lawyers operate?" Eekim asked.

"Mostly in secrecy," I began. "No one really knows what they do. Their language is shrouded in secret words derived from an ancient pagan society. Their methods are steeped in ritual and mysterious procedures."

"Black magic?" Eekim inquired.

"Nothing so innocent," I assured him. "Lawyers have imposed a caste system upon my country, and specifically my state, in which they are the hierarchy."

"What state are you from?"

26

"Missouri."

"Misery? Sounds appropriate for a region infested with lawyers."

"Yes. Well," I continued, "lawyers have perverted the concept of right and wrong to the point where you cannot be right unless you pay a lawyer a lot of money, and you are wrong if you are unable to pay. Justice is for sale, at exorbitant rates, and the only question is how much can you afford?"

"Hmm," mused Eekim. "Surely there were safeguards to prevent this sort of thing."

"Oh yes, but those safeguards were usurped by lawyers. Originally, the founding fathers of my country established three divisions of government to insure a check and balance system. Lawyers are technically in the judicial branch, but much of the legislative branch has been infiltrated by lawyers. Lawyers are also well entrenched in the executive branch as well, sometimes even attaining the leadership of the country. It is tragic but this has occurred twice in my lifetime. Lawyers who become President have brought such nefarious nicknames as 'Tricky Dick' and 'Slick Willie' to the forefront of American politics."

I choked with remorse and shame. Eekim sympathetically nodded and allowed me time to recover. After a while he gently asked: "Are there any other agencies involved in this travesty?"

"There is the American Bar Conspiracy, which represents the national conspiracy of lawyers, and each state has a similar regional gang. The Missouri Bar Conspiracy is the unholy alliance which operates in my region."

"What can you tell me about them," Eekim quietly probed.

"The American Bar Conspiracy seems to be mainly concerned with promoting the self-serving interests of lawyers and getting bent out of shape anytime anyone has the temerity, from their viewpoint, to criticize lawyers. Of course, given the public view of lawyers, this results in the ABC being bent out of shape most of the time."

"And the Missouri Bar Conspiracy?"

"About the same. I've had direct dealings with them and from my experience they exist to perform damage control

27

anytime a lawyer is accused of wrongdoing. They prefer to work in secrecy, or confidentiality as they call it. It is very effective for lawyers. In one year, of 20,000 lawyers practicing in Missouri, only eight were disbarred. That's an honesty rating of 99.96%. If one were to judge them by their own statistics then lawyers would appear to be moral and infallible to almost god-like proportions."

"I don't mean to offend you," Eekim carefully said, "but how do you know they aren't."

"Good question," I confidently answered. "In Missouri, we recently had an Attorney General (incidentally he was the lawyer son of a lawyer) who ran for Governor. He was later disbarred for scurrilous activity involving a public insurance fund. Dozens of other lawyers were implicated. A few of these were actually convicted (including at least one other father-and-son lawyer team). Anyway, the whole debacle was uncovered when one renegade honest lawyer, who I imagine has been black-balled by the legal community, gave testimony to a grand jury. Now then, if you consider that dozens of lawyers had to know what was going on, and only one lawyer took appropriate steps, then the integrity rating of Missouri lawyers falls to about 4%."

"Quite a disparity," Eekim said. "But I think you should remember that you're talking about the most powerful lawyers in your state, perhaps the average lawyer is not quite as corrupt."

"Could be," I admitted. "Who knows? The point I'm trying to make is that lawyers are in charge of investigating lawyers, and this is about as sensible as hiring a cannibal as a meat inspector. But you might be right, lawyers may get more disgusting as they become more powerful. My country has had a difficult time finding a high-placed lawyer who can pass muster to become Attorney General."

"Pitiful," Eekim agreed, "just pitiful."

"That's not all," I said, warming to my subject. "Lawyer ethics do not exist. The Missouri Bar Conspiracy will not disbar a lawyer unless he is convicted of a crime, and sometimes not even then. Ethics are supposed to represent a code of behavior which adheres not only to the letter of the law, but to the spirit of the law as well. However it would appear that Missouri lawyers must only stay below a certain level of criminality to maintain their right to practice law."

"I'm only playing the Devil's Advocate by defending lawyers," Eekim apologized, "but, since there are lawyers who get disbarred, doesn't the system work; at least in a very minimal and ineffective manner?"

"No," I sincerely replied, making an extreme effort not to take offense at the outrageous supposition that lawyers are not a totally amoral entity. "A disbarred lawyer can usually regain a license to practice law in a very short period of time, sometimes quicker than they can get out of prison. Also, a lawyer can move to another state and continue to perpetrate actions, with a clean slate, against innocent people. Therefore, and this is important, disbarment is more of a criticism of a lawyer's intelligence for getting caught rather than a punishment for having weak moral character or committing an offense. Disbarment effectively means 'be smarter next time and don't get caught'.

"What's extremely funny to me," I continued, "is that lawyers actually have malpractice insurance. Doctors have malpractice insurance which is extremely expensive, tens of thousands of dollars a year, but the average doctor will be sued four times in the course of their life. Lawyers, by comparison, are virtually untouchable. I've never heard of a lawyer being sued for malpractice. If you ever want a good laugh, call a bar association and tell them you need a lawyer to sue another lawyer. Lawyers continually sue everyone except lawyers; they sue doctors, businessmen, insurance companies, employers, workers, churches, homeowners, parents, schools, teachers, police, firemen, and people who have the audacity to defend themselves against criminals; but they seldom sue other lawyers.

"It really makes me wonder," I suddenly pondered, "what happens to the money lawyers pay for malpractice insurance. I've heard that The Missouri Bar Conspiracy has a sort of group insurance plan which covers all lawyers. Not only do they investigate their own profession, an obvious conflict of interest, but they are involved with the entity which would pay for any damage award, a second conflict of interest. Now then, if almost no lawyers are ever sued, what is happening to the money? Given the predisposition of lawyers to plunder insurance money to which they have access (remember the Attorney General) I imagine legal malpractice insurance money is being funneled to a few well-placed lawyers.

"I imagine the same thing occurs with Bar referrals," I added. "I imagine potentially lucrative cases are referred to the best old boys in the system. Young lawyers ought to wonder how the referral procedure actually works."

"Depressing, but we knew it would be," and Eekim smiled #1,729, which is a sort of grin-and-bear-it smile. "What other deplorable tactics do lawyers use?"

"Procrastination is a favorite tool. Lawyers operate a great deal like a scam siding company. They contract for work (except, of course, they never actually sign anything), show up, do just enough to get the job started, and then disappear. Eventually they show up and do a little more work. This pattern continues over an extended period of time until the job is finally finished. At this point their victim, whom they refer to as a client, is so glad for the situation to be at an end that there is no fight about cost or quality of work. Lawyers wear you down, wear you out and throw you out. The subtlety of their actions is an illusion created over time."

"Despicable, but we knew it would be," and Eekim smiled #1,730, which means "we've gone this far, let's get it over with".

"Probably the most detrimental impact of lawyers on society," I resumed, "comes from the operation of law practices as businesses. Business must cater to preferred customers. A preferred customer is a repeat customer. For lawyers, then, criminals are preferred customers because they represent repeat business. Why should a lawyer care if an innocent person does not receive a fair trial? An innocent person accused of a crime is somewhat of an anomaly and does not represent potential future income. But if a lawyer can get a repeat offender freed, that repeat offender will provide the lawyer with future business; not to mention great word-of-mouth advertising to the criminal community. Most precedents and technicalities are established in high-profile, million dollar defenses. However, these precedents are then used by lawyers trying to build a profitable business."

"I see," Eekim thoughtfully said. "The problem is you have no Golden Banana rule. You have no law which states what justice really is, and the letter of your laws are used to violate the spirit of justice."

"Exactly," I said with smile #1,111 (which, of course, means: "exactly").

CHAPTER THREE

OOGA SPEAKS

A monumental crashing of the underbrush suddenly sundered the serenity. The disturbance evoked impressions worthy of gods or demons. The vegetation violently swayed as though agitated by elemental forces of cataclysmic power. The very sun seemed to dim even though the clouds seemed to recede. The air pressure rose even though the barometric pressure diminished. Birds cautiously chirped as they headed for safety. Insects ceased to hum. Cosmic forces seemed to collide and burst. The whole world seemed totally rent asunder as if the unfathomable powers of another dimension prepared to make a material manifestation upon our physical plane.

Then, Ooga gracefully stumbled from the jungle with little bits of leaves and twigs stuck to his furry coat. He quickly brushed some of them away and then glared at Eekim and me as if daring us to make the point that some debris still adhered to his coat. I was not sure if twigs and leaves detracted from a monkey's dignity but did not feel like the question could be addressed at the current moment with reasonable expectation of a courteous response.

Having mounted a formidable display, in order to accommodate a dramatic entrance by Ooga, the world now seemed to return to its normal state if, indeed, it has one.

"What the hell are you doing?!!" Ooga uninquisitively

inquired in a voice which was the epitome of subdued accusation. He was so mad he was shaking

Mustering all my resources and instinct for survival in a situation which was attempting to make the quantum leap from intellectual discourse to actual physical confrontation, I squared my shoulders, looked straight into Ooga's eyes (which was difficult because each of his eyes seemed to be focused at angles which were mutually exclusive), cleared my throat, looked at my feet and then looked to Eekim. I was coming to depend on his innate ability to diplomatically handle any situation which arose. I counted on an aplomb of manner and an objective statement with which the situation could be diffused. I was confident Eekim would not fail me. He was my lifeboat, my parachute, my safety net.

Eekim remained silent although he did give me a sideward glance which conveyed the message: "Are you crazy! What do you expect me to do? That's one mad monkey!" Eekim can convey a great deal of information with just a glance.

Ooga majestically tramped back and forth, his hands behind his back, his eyes on the ground except when he accusingly fixed us with an incredulous gaze at which time I wished he was still staring at the ground. On the whole, it was an incredibly awkward moment.

"Now boys," Ooga condescendingly and charitably said, his voice edged like a guillotine, "I know no one is perfect." And he smiled at us with a smile which has no numerical enumeration but which I took to mean: "No one is perfect. You're not perfect because of what you've done. I'm not perfect because of what I'm about to do." It was rather ominous.

"But boys," he continued, "I'm here to tell you, you're doing a pathetic job. You've spent a day and a half on the lawyer problem and you're still playing word games with 'lawyers uck', have arrived at the astounding insight that lawyers crave money and power, and have determined that lawyers use procrastination, deception, procedure and secrecy to accomplish their goals. The Big Banana has certainly endowed you two with amazing powers of perception! Next you'll probably discover that the sky is blue, water is wet and air is invisible. Your mission was not to figure out that lawyers exist, but to figure out what to do about the damned things! Have you even got a clue?"

I said nothing, but looked at Eekim knowing he was my diplomat, my spokesman, my deliverer. Eekim looked at me as if to say: "Are you still looking at me?" I was beginning to understand that Eekim was, indeed, my equal. Damn the luck.

"Okay, human," and Ooga scowled at me as if to challenge me to comment on the way he had underlined "human", "I'm going to finish the story Eekim started, which is all you needed to know in the first place!"

Eekim, wisely in my opinion, did not meet Ooga's deprecating countenance. I, equally as wisely, did the same.

OOGA FINISHES EEKIM'S STORY

"Okay, you know the story Eekim started yesterday?" Ooga looked the question at me.

"Yeah," I replied as eloquently as possible.

"Very good! I was afraid I might be exceeding your mental ability."

I did not bother looking to Eekim for support, and he did not look at me as if to say: "I can't say anything supportive, we'll just have to grin and bear it. But for the Big Banana's sake, don't let him see you grin."

"To continue with the story," Ooga continued, "the evil entity, which by now even your mundane intelligence has figured out is yerlaws, or lawyers, took control of monkey civilization. Poor monkeys were punished, rich monkeys were not. The logic behind this was that poor monkeys often had to use a stick to steal, while the rich monkeys could merely juggle the strings on a banana peel. One was viewed as dangerous while the other was treated as a sophisticate. The fact which was conveniently being ignored was that the more rich monkeys stole, the more poor monkeys were picking up sticks. Any of this sound familiar?"

"I think it's like our S&L crisis," I replied. "About fifty groups of bankers, accountants and lawyers stole an incredible amount of money; about $4,000 from every man, woman and child in the country. It was all done on paper and was facilitated by contributions to politicians. When caught, however, almost none went to jail. Those that did were given light sentences in country club prisons. The Supreme Court even made a special ruling that 'lawyers and other professionals' could not be prosecuted under racketeering laws."

It was a rather long answer considering a simple "yes" would have sufficed but I was trying to make points with Ooga.

"Did your Supreme Court also declare that street gang members could not be prosecuted for crimes committed by the gang?" Ooga teasingly asked.

Eekim expectantly looked at me.

"Why would they do that?" I inquired.

"To protect their amateur status..." Ooga began.

"...until they could turn professional!" Eekim finished. Those two monkeys really got a kick out of that one. They were rolling in the dirt in hysterical fits of laughter. Several times they straightened up and I figured they were just about done but then one would burst out giggling and the whole thing started again. Nothing gets you off the hook quicker than a straight line although I didn't think it was all that funny.

I endured this display with smile #212, which means: "yuck it up boys, have a real good time; but it's really not funny'. One good thing, I realized, was that even stern old Ooga could not stay mad for long.

Finally, I did a quick calculation and said: "You realize that $4,000 is about 48,000 bananas." That got their attention. Money is a rather elusive concept to them but they understand bananas.

I pressed my advantage by sadly repeating: "Yes, it's true. 48,000 bananas were stolen from each and every person in the land."

"The Big Banana have mercy," cried Eekim. "We're sorry for laughing at such a tragedy."

"If I wasn't human, I might think it was funny too," I quietly commented.

"That's a lot of bananas," Ooga sadly said. "Imagine what taking 48,000 bananas from every monkey in our tribe would do. We'd be wiped out! Little monkeys would starve, we'd have to abandon our schools, no one would be singing or dancing or making poetry. Now I've never cared much for poetry, but I'd sure hate to lose everything else."

"We'd have to strip the trees of any bananas which were left. Pretty soon the trees would die. We'd have to live on the ground and then the tigers would eat us!" exclaimed Eekim. The little guy was really working himself into a panic.

"There are no tigers in Missouri," I reassured him.

"Right," Eekim quickly retorted, "pretty soon you'll be telling me there are no monkeys in Missouri."

I thought about that and decided perhaps I should find a more secure place to sleep.

"Your lawyer problem is worse than we thought!" Ooga said. "So, quickly, on to the end of the story: Monkeys looked around and perceived the situation. They conferred and came to the most reasonable and sensible solution. They were kind, goodhearted and generous monkeys who proceeded to slaughter the majority of yerlaws and their most prominent, corrupt clients. Monkeys took back their bananas, painted the survivors' butts blue, and put them to work." Ooga leaned back with a satisfied smile (I believe it was a hybrid of smiles #163 and #2,319 which mean: "that was a great story" and "did I do that well, or what?", respectively).

"That's it?" I incredulously inquired.

"You don't like it?" Eekim asked.

"Of course that's it!" Ooga gruffly proclaimed. "You were expecting miracles, maybe? You think the Big Banana is going to intervene for monkeys who won't even help themselves? Man, wake up and smell the bananas!"

"You don't negotiate with a monkeys who steal your bananas," Eekim seriously explained. "You either take the bananas back or you starve."

"Our ancestors took them back!" Ooga proudly declared.

"And we've kept them ever since!" Eekim fiercely added.

"The solution seems so final," I protested.

"That," said Ooga, "is the best thing about it."

BANANA WINE

"So what's the next step?" I asked.

"I think the human is a little tired," Eekim grinned at

Ooga.

"His mental processes do appear more retarded than usual," Ooga agreed.

"Perhaps he would be improved with a little refreshment?" Eekim suggested.

"True," conceded Ooga, "it would be difficult to unimprove him."

I was beginning to feel like I wasn't there because of the way those two monkeys were talking between themselves.

"Hey, I'm still here," I said.

"Yes," Ooga solemnly pronounced. "You are still here."

"My god, Holmes. You've done it again!" exclaimed Eekim.

"Elementary, my dear Watson." Ooga declared. "There is tangible empirical evidence that he is here: his awkward tracks in the sand, his somewhat gothic physical presence, his grating voice which keeps braying the obvious, the grotesque outline of his shadow upon the ground; all give testimony to the indisputable fact that he is, indeed, here."

They began laughing and rolling on the ground, of course. I wondered where those two had encountered Sir Arthur Conan Doyle's works. I considered the possibilities and was about to pose the question when Eekim abruptly stopped laughing (abrupt by monkey standards anyway, it had been less than two minutes) and said: "Come, human, you are about to be introduced into the joys of banana wine!"

This sounded like an interesting idea so I replied: "Oh, okay."

"We will revel in the joy of life."

"Okay."

"We will laugh and joke and celebrate our existence!"

"Okay!"

"We will probe and mock the very mysteries of the universe!"

"Okay!!"

"We will decide your destiny!"

"O...What? About that last part..." I protested.

"Come," invited Eekim while pulling me along a small path bordered with small, yellow flowers, "all will be revealed."

"Did I say I wanted everything to be revealed?" I asked. "I don't remember saying that."

Ooga, still laughing and pawing the ground, yelled: "Don't let him drink so much he befuddles his mind."

"Unlikely," Eekim shouted back.

"Good point!" yelled Ooga.

"I may have expressed a desire for knowledge," I said as Eekim continued to lead me down the path, "but I'm sure I never said I wanted everything revealed. Are you sure you don't have me confused with someone else? I'll bet that's it! Someone else said they would like for everything to be revealed and you've merely gotten the two of us confused. People are always saying I remind them of someone they know. Once, a couple of years ago, there was this...."

"What are you so worried about?" Eekim interrupted. "We're just going to have a few drinks."

"Is that all?"

"Yes."

"Then what," I confusedly asked, "was that part about deciding my destiny?"

"Are you worried about that? That's nothing," Eekim glibly said, "just an expression. Everyone is always deciding their destiny with each move and choice they make. Right?"

"Well, right," I hesitantly agreed.

"So this isn't anything different than what you're doing all the time. Right?"

"Well, right."

"So what's the problem?"

Somehow, Eekim made it all sound a little too innocent. Granted, destiny was going on all the time and everything one did or did not do contributed to its fulfillment. On the one hand, the destiny I had personally pursued had always been an attempt to avoid destiny. It was, of course, a pretty self-defeating endeavor. On the other hand, it had kept me out of a lot of trouble. On the other hand, trouble seemed to find me anyway. On the other hand, I only had two hands and had already exceeded their capacity.

"What the hell," I thought, "I could use a drink." It was my last clear, coherent thought for a while.

"Ah, here we are," said Eekim.

We had emerged into a small grotto. It was dimly lit with what little sun filtered through the dense jungle canopy. Pleasingly dark and pleasantly cool, it had a very comfortable ambiance. Monkeys were lounging around the place. Most of them cast curious, semi-friendly glances our way; a few stared.

"Just be cool," Eekim quietly said to me, "they don't see too many humans around here." Then louder: "Banana wine for my friend and me!"

The monkey who brought our wine sat two clay mugs before us. He briefly and noncommittally appraised me. "We don't get many humans in here."

"So I've heard," I said.

"He's a friend of mine," Eekim evenly said.

Their eyes met for just a moment.

"Well," said the bartender monkey, "I don't put bananas on my family's table by insulting a monkey's friends. Enjoy." And he hurried off.

"He's all right," said Eekim, "he's just naturally suspicious because you're human. Relax, enjoy the wine. Let me make the first toast: 'To Destiny!'"

We clanked our mugs together and drank. I imbibed a deep draught. The wine was surprisingly good; it was sweet without being sugary, tart without being sour, and light while possessing substance. It was a perfect embodiment of every elusive, contradictory characteristic ever ascribed to wine by even the most sophisticated connoisseurs. Also, it left a subtle but amusing banana taste on the palate.

The first initial warming in my stomach began and I felt a resilient glow start to flow through my body. I finished the mug and felt its spiritual reinforcement. This was powerful stuff. I immediately decided to drink as much as possible. As I stated earlier, my last coherent thought was previous to this decision.

"This is great wine!" I said to Eekim in particular and everyone in general. Several monkeys raised their mug in a gesture of agreement and the initial tension caused by my entrance seemed to dissipate.

"Please," I shouted, "bring us a jug of this fine beverage."

The barmonkey hustled over with that irascible hustling movement that only monkeys possess, filled our glasses and set the large jug beside us.

"You like the wine?" he asked loudly.

"I love the wine!" I yelled.

"He loves the wine!" he shouted and danced away with his hands over his head. Several monkeys cheered and everyone else clapped their paws or nodded their heads. I took a great swallow and beamed to the crowd.

"You know," I said to Eekim. "This destiny thing isn't really so scary. It's going to happen anyway. Right?'

"Right," said Eekim, and his little monkey face brightened another degree as he raised his mug.

"I mean, the great thing is that I do have a choice. I can accept what lawyers did to me, or by Big Banana, I can fight back! What would any self-respecting monkey, or man, do?"

"Fight back," Eekim cheered.

"Damned right, fight back! There's really no other choice." And I raised my mug and drank. "Besides, Ooga already outlined what must be done. Massacre the worst, take back the bananas, paint their butts blue, and put 'em to work."

"That's right!" Eekim exclaimed. "Worsacur the mass of 'em, take the backnanas ba, blue butts their paint, and work 'em to put."

I looked sharply at Eekim. He seemed to be getting drunk. His body mass was obviously more vulnerable to the effects of banana wine than was mine. He slouched, his expression dazed, and I noticed he was getting blurry around the edges. But his spirit was in the right place so I toasted his sentiments, whatever they were.

"You're cute!" said a voice in my ear. I looked around and into the eyes of a female monkey who had inconspicuously become attached to my shoulder. "New in town?"

"Well, yeah, I guess," I stammered. I didn't know how to react.

"Hey Rhia," said Eekim.

"Hey Eekim," said Rhia, which I guess was the name of the girl monkey who had taken a liking to me. "How you doing?"

"Oh, real good," said Eekim, straightening up. "My
friend and I were just having a little wine."
"Your friend's cute," said Rhia.
"You're drunk!" said a voice from the crowd.
"So are you," yelled Rhia.
"Oh...right...." said the voice.
"Well," Eekim thoughtfully said, "I wouldn't say he was
cute,..exactly...he does have that washed-out, abused, repressed
look, but he's a human, they have lawyers, it comes natural."
"Oh you poor thing," said Rhia. She gently stroked the
back of my neck which combined with the wine to send little
tingles up and down my spine.
"You know, I'm a poor thing too," Eekim tried.
"But you aren't plagued by lawyers," I said. Eekim
glared at me and I smiled #452 at him, which means: "gotcha".
"You know," said Eekim, slightly slurring his words, "I
might be sorry I taught you all those smiles."
"Me too," I admitted, "it's a lot of numbers to
remember."
"I think you've got a cute smile," said Rhia to me.
"Which one?" commented Eekim, rather bitterly I
thought.
I decided this had gone on long enough. Here I was
losing my best monkey friend over a monkey floozy and all I
really needed to do was confront my destiny. I was here to take
on lawyers. I was here to secure the future for the children, to
repulse the repulsive entity which had taken over my country
(Did I mention the chronology of my coherent thoughts?).
Apathy had been my inevitable but unsatisfying defense
for far too long. And I had drunk far too much wine to stop now.
"Friends," I said while rising and realizing with
amazement that I was so much taller when standing, "there is no
denying that I am human."
A few whistles and catcalls accompanied this
announcement.
"But I am here to tell you that, as a human, I have been
forced to endure trials and tribulations which you would not wish
upon a dog!"
Dogs are good.

41

"I live in a world which suffers from LAWYERS!!"

"No!", "Say it ain't so!", "Big Banana have mercy!", and "Poor thing!", the last from Rhia, echoed through the crowd.

"Yes, it's true; but, I say to you: 'Not for long!'"

Cheers erupted from the crowd. I noticed Eekim was smiling again although I couldn't make out which number it was.

"Yes, I am indebted to the wisdom of Eekim and Ooga for telling me the story of your courageous ancestors who eliminated their yerlaw problem by utilizing the very direct solution of eliminating yerlaws. I have formulated a plan and I will do the same thing for my species!"

More cheers.

"Yes! I will worsacur the mass of 'em, take ba the backnanas, blue their paint butts, and work 'em to put!"

There was a great deal of clapping, hooting, hollering and other spontaneous outbursts of positive reinforcement. The crowd began to chant the words. A few monkeys grabbed sticks and began beating out a rhythm. We formed a Conga line and began dancing around the grotto, singing:

"Worsacur the mass,
take the nanas,
blue butts their paint,
put work to 'em,
Uh huh, Uh huh."

Eekim, in particular, exhibited boisterous and energetic gyrations which were a marvel to behold.

"That's one spunky, funky monkey," I thought to myself with what passed for clever observation at the time.

We undulated around the grotto like a boisterous snake with about sixty left feet, no singing talent and very little sense of direction. None of the trees were safe and we careened off all of them. We stumbled, danced and crawled for at least four dozen renditions of the chant. Every monkey had a mug and I was drinking directly from the biggest jug I could find. Finally, I led the revelers to the path where we came face to face with Ooga, his arms were crossed across his chest and a very bemused expression adorned his face.

The singing, dancing and drumming immediately stopped. The grotto suddenly became eerily quiet. Eekim was supportively by my side, being held up by Rhia. I decided to bluff my way through. I swaggered up to Ooga and flung my arm around his shoulders.

"Ooga! Ol' buddy, ol' pal. So glad you're here!"

"You are?"

"YessIyam," I slurred, "and are you going to be proud of us! We've figured out what to do!"

"Yes, I heard," Ooga said with an bemused tone. "You're going to 'Worsacur the mass, take the nanas, blue butts their paint, put work to 'em, Uh huh, Uh huh.' Is that correct?"

"Well, yeah."

Somehow it had sounded better with a chorus.

"Close 'nough for jazz," Eekim declared.

"Right!" I said. "The details can be worked out later."

"Very good!" praised Ooga, "Then you can start tomorrow. We'll get your canoe ready and you can shove off at first light. I am so glad you are fully prepared to take on lawyers."

"Here, here," shouted Eekim.

"Wait," I protested. "I don't think I'm fully ready. Eekim really did most of the work and I just sort of went along."

"Here, here," yelled Eekim.

"And the details," I said. "I should stay here until strategic and tactical details can be decided. I don't think I could properly plan without Eekim. He's been my guide, my mentor, my inspiration.

"Here, here," bellowed Eekim.

I was beginning to wonder if he could remember any other words.

"No, no," Ooga amicably disagreed. "You really must begin your journey tomorrow. But, I can understand you considering Eekim indispensable to your mission. He is such a helpful individual."

"Here, he,....uh oh," Eekim was very suddenly a much more subdued little monkey.

Ooga addressed the crowd: "All in favor of Eekim accompanying the human in his quest to free the world of lawyers, signify by saying 'Here, here'."

"Here, here!" boomed through the little grotto.

43

"Well, that's settled," Ooga pleasantly declared. "Don't stay up too late. Big day tomorrow."

Ooga wheeled and practically danced down the path. It was the first time I had seen him truly happy and I didn't like it one bit.

Eekim gave the crowd a nasty look: "Thanks a lot!"

"You're welcome!" boomed back.

Eekim shook his head and muttered: "Sarcasm is wasted on drunk monkeys."

He turned on me like a marksman sighting the target.

"This is all your fault!" he accused.

"Welcome to my destiny," I affably said while filling his mug. Eekim sighed and I shrugged.

"I'm sure things will look much brighter in the morning."

THE MORNING AFTER

I woke-up naked on the beach. The burning sun was scorching my skin in places it had never had the privilege to scorch. Sand fleas had found their way into recesses of my body that I had seldom explored. My tongue had the texture and size of an old tennis ball. My closed eyelids glowed a brilliant red from sunlight trying to force its way into my skull. My brain had melted into the sand and I could feel it in a warm, scummy puddle beneath my head. I decided to lay there and savor the moment.

Eventually the persistence of the sand fleas won and I decided I might be more comfortable in the river. As an added incentive there was, of course, the possibility of drowning.

I rose unsteadily as my head exploded in an incredible fireworks display which would have been enjoyable under better circumstances. I looked around for several minutes and located the river (good thing it was right in front of me). My joints felt like they needed lubrication as I awkwardly shambled to the water's edge, pausing every few steps to reaffirm my balance. As gently as possible, I fell in.

After several more minutes I began to feel a little better; which is like saying that had I been a rock, I would have begun to feel a little softer.

"Good morning!" shouted Eekim with an exuberance

44

which compelled me to consider the moral ramifications of throttling a monkey. It was fortunate for him that I would have had to move to actually reach him. I was suddenly aware of how amusingly frail his neck was.

"Aren't you afraid of crocodiles?"

Some vague, disturbing memory seemed to play hide-and-seek in my mind. I pondered for a while, I noticed some deep scratch marks on my chest and arms, and the pieces slowly came together. "Eekim, didn't I wrestle a crocodile last night, a big one, until it managed to escape?"

"Yeah. Except it was a log. And it really wasn't very big. But it did manage to escape."

"Oh," I dejectedly said.

"Nothing to be ashamed of," Eekim consoled. "It was a hell of a fight! After all, you thought it was a crocodile. Actually, it was a very brave thing to do."

"You're just saying that to be nice."

"Of course, it's my job. We're partners. I couldn't very well solidify our relationship if I started talking about what a jackass you were for fighting with a muddy old log, now could I?"

I recalculated the distance between my hands, if I stretched them out, and the ridiculously fragile area between his shoulders and head. Although the act would still require too much effort, I filed mental notes (range, required pressure, duration of enjoyment), for future reference.

"You slept on the beach again last night," Eekim scolded. "Didn't I warn you about tigers?"

"I figured the probability was so small as to be impossible. I've never been very lucky."

"My, my, we are feeling depressed today," Eekim cajoled.

"We are also feeling naked, where's my clothes?"

"Rhia will bring them back to you in a minute," he replied.

Rhia? I suddenly had a feeling of trepidation. What exactly did I remember about last night?

"Um,...Eekim? Did Rhia sleep alone last night?"

"Of course not. She told me how wonderful you were.

She said it was because of you that she had the most exciting night of her life," and he gave me a conspiratorial wink.

"Oh my god!"

"What?" said Eekim, a puzzled expression on his face quickly turned to laughter. "You think,...you and Rhia,...man, you have an inflated ego! Rhia said you were wonderful because you kept telling her what a great guy I was. Because of you, she found out for herself, in a big way, what a great guy I am."

"Who has the inflated ego?"

"Just the facts," said Eekim, his face beaming.

Rhia, a huge, irritating smile on her face, came skipping down to the river and cheerfully shouted in a painfully loud voice: "Good Morning!" (I noticed her neck was even more petite than Eekim's.) "I brought your clothes back, all nice and dry. You know, you really shouldn't try to sleep in wet clothes, you could catch your death. Eekim and I made you undress, lucky for you."

I could have died in my sleep. But I didn't. Yep, that was my kind of luck.

"I'll see you when I get back," said Eekim, looking into Rhia's eyes.

"Oh,..Eekim honey, "she sweetly said, "no one thinks you're coming back. You're going to confront lawyers and all you've got is one lousy human to help you. No offense," she said to me.

"None taken," I assured her.

"But,...last night..." Eekim began.

"Oh, we'll always have last night," and Rhia strolled to the jungle. "No matter what else happens, we'll each have the wonderful remembrance of our special time together."

"Well, apparently you'll live to remember it a lot longer than I ," Eekim despondently observed.

"Maybe," said Rhia with a twinkle in her eye. And she disappeared into the trees.

Eekim stood, somewhat stricken, and stared after her. His posture was one of intense dejection and loss. A kind word, now, was what he needed most.

"Just the facts," I said instead.

"Shut up," Eekim testily replied. "And please get

dressed. Humans are even uglier without their clothes."

Eekim had already gotten a hold on himself and was back to insults and general mockery of my human condition. Monkeys possess a resiliency which is, at times, profound. They bounce back almost immediately. It's a true axiom "It's hard to keep a good monkey down". It's inspiring. In fact, I was inspired to find a two-by-four and really test that axiom. Unfortunately, there were none handy.

"Hurry up and get dressed, you oversized lump of furless flesh," Eekim encouraged as he walked downstream along the bank. "The canoe is over this way. Come on, we're already late because of you."

"Come here, Eekim, there's something around your neck!"

"No there's not."

"There could be."

"Be serious!"

"I am serious," I muttered while cracking my knuckles. But I finished dressing, tied my shoes and followed after him.

THE BIG FAREWELL

The canoe sat low in the water, probably because of all the bananas piled from one end to the other.

"We'll never make it in that!" I protested.

"Of course we will," corrected Eekim. "The good thing about packing a lot of bananas is that the load decreases as you go along. We'll have to be a little careful at the start is all."

"But you didn't even pack my gear!"

"I did too. It's spread out on the bottom so the bananas stay dry. We'll probably take on a little water at the start, so it was the only logical thing to do."

I was too hungover and miserable to argue. Eekim scampered to the front of the canoe. "Get in and push off," he commanded.

I did, and we sat in the middle of the river. Eekim gave me a pleasant, blank stare for a few moments and then admonished: "Don't just sit there, mate, start paddling."

"Okay already."

I reflected that, in my current state, I was like putty in

his hands. I started to get mad and then realized it might not be the worst arrangement. If I had been putty in my own hands I probably would have dropped myself.

"There they are," Eekim pointed at a half-dozen monkeys who walked to the bank, waved quickly, yelled "Bye" and walked away.

"Quite a send-off," Eekim proudly said while peeling a banana.

"What? They made almost no effort at all."

"Well, that's only natural," Eekim explained. "They really don't expect to see us again so why waste the effort? Considering the likelihood of success of this little venture, it was a gala *bon voyage*."

"Humans say longest good-byes when they know they'll never see each other again," I noted.

Eekim laughed: "Humans sure are funny, aren't they?"

"The funniest," I agreed. "You know, I guess Rhia gave you a very intimate good-bye."

Eekim stopped chewing, a highly unusual occurrence. His face brightened: "That's right!" He then thoughtfully masticated for a moment. "You know, I'll bet you sweet Rhia can't wait to see her big Eekim again."

I didn't say anything but I didn't think she could wait either.

"How about a banana, first mate?" and Eekim tossed me a banana even though there were about eight dozen within easy reach.

"Thanks, Captain."

I ate it even though a banana was the last thing I wanted. Eekim smiled #941, which means "we're in this together, we might as well make the best of it". I smiled back #378, which means "here we go".

And so we set off on our journey. In my opinion, two of the most improbable, reluctant, and inadequate heroes on the most impossible mission of all time. On the positive side, no one really expected us to succeed anyway.

CHAPTER FOUR

LADY JUSTICE

By late afternoon my back was aching, my arms were tired, my vision was blurry, I was profusely sweating, and my stomach felt like it was waltzing at a square-dance festival. My head thumped in time to both beats. On the whole, I felt much better. I began to have hope that concrete confirmation of my mortality was not imminent.

Eekim had watched my progress throughout the day and had reveled in such comments as: "What a beautiful day!", "Isn't that sky something?", and "Don't you just love the way this canoe rocks back and forth, back and forth, as we float?".

I refused to make any comments and silently allowed Eekim to indulge his sadistic wit. This seemed to please him.

Our progress was slow. Finally, we stopped to camp. Eekim carefully supervised the unloading of the bananas. Afterwards, he seemed to lose interest in camp preparations. He gracefully lounged, munching bananas, while I made camp and built a fire. I strung a rope and hung wet articles, which included practically everything, out to dry. I lit my lantern, turned it to low and hung it on a tree in readiness for the approaching night. I fixed burgers and beans for dinner, and savored the meal as if it were a delicacy. I particularly enjoyed the way it tasted nothing like bananas.

When camping, I always put a couple of two-liter plastic bottles, full of frozen water, in my cooler. Although they take up space, the cylindrical ice blocks keep the cooler cold, preserve the ice cubes I pour on top of everything, and provide ice water during a trip. I pulled one of these bottles from my cooler, settled on my still-damp blankets and relaxed.

"I've been thinking," Eekim casually stated.

"I was hoping you had been," I replied. "It would be a shame to just waste all that time when you're doing nothing."

"It's my job," Eekim laughingly defended. "Who was it said: 'Eekim is my guide, my mentor, I need his help.'? Who got me assigned to this expedition in the first place?"

"I don't know," I cheerfully lied, "but his judgment is certainly questionable. He should be locked up."

"He might be some day," Eekim said in a way which did not seem at all foreboding at the time. "What I was thinking, however, is that we may be able to simplify our mission. If people did not expect justice, they would not be disappointed in your lawyer system. Instead of changing reality to meet expectations, we could change expectations to accommodate reality. It's a more pragmatic approach."

"What's your idea?" I asked.

"We start with your symbol of justice. You know, the blindfolded lady with the balance and the sword. As I see it, this implies that your justice is blind, unable to read her balance scales, and as likely to cut the innocent as the guilty if she starts swinging that sword. This means your system is blind, unbalanced and dangerous. So far, so good. Right?"

"Well," I considered, "I think she is blindfolded, instead of wearing dark glasses, because there are none so blind as those who will not see."

"Whatever," Eekim resumed, "she can't see either way. But what if we enhanced her to more completely represent the lawyer system? For instance, earplugs would convey that not only is justice blind but deaf as well. And she should be sitting because lawyers do not stand for justice, a plush recliner would be appropriate. We could pile gold at her feet to illustrate the cost of lawyers. What do you think?"

"Thirty pieces of silver would be more appropriate," I mused. "It took you all day to come up with that?"

"Of course not! Contingency planning is my strong suit, I always have back-up plans and ideas. My other idea," Eekim proudly continued, "is to remake the statue so that she is being gang-raped by a pack of lawyers."

"Although not inaccurate, that is far too graphic for Americans," I explained. "We like nice, clean symbols in which we can believe. Besides, it would be rather sexist, there are women lawyers too."

"What would you suggest?" Eekim asked.

I thought for several moments but not about the statue. Lawyers had taken my money, my hopes and future. The bitter taste of bile rose in my throat whenever I thought about them. I had found that I could not just philosophize or joke the situation away. I could not stare at enough trees to become content. I was not worldly or sophisticated enough to rationalize just walking away, glad that I at least had my health. The old spirit of the Missouri feud had slowly started to heat in my veins. It had simmered for some time and I felt it come to a boil. Lawyers had declared war and the only question was whether I would fight or submit. I decided, then and there, that I would at least make a battle of it. To the hilt with a twist!

"Any ideas?" Eekim impatiently asked.

"The only thing I would change," I said, "is that I would like to see Lady Justice with her mouth open."

"To symbolize the endless babble of your lawyer system?"

"No."

"This isn't something erotic, is it?" Eekim asked with genuine interest.

"No," I said with a solid voice which seemed more than my own. "I want her singing."

Eekim sharply looked at me and held his gaze for several moments. He finally said: "You're serious again, aren't you?"

I merely looked at him.

"You are! Damn! I was hoping we could just sort of hang around the river for awhile and then go back and tell the tribe we had done our best." He seemed very dejected for a minute. "Oh well," he brightened. "I've got plans for this too."

We listened to the river as the night grew dark. The stars twinkled overhead. It was very quiet and pleasant.

"Josh?" Eekim whispered. "Why do you want to make her sing?"

"Because," I said in that same ethereal voice which was more than mine, which even the stars seemed to hear on a quiet Missouri night by the river, "it ain't over until the blind lady sings."

RECONNAISSANCE MONKEY

Eekim woke me during the night. "There's something out there!"

I rolled over and peered into the darkness. "Of course there's something out there. We're by woods along a river, there's always something out there."

"I mean something strange."

"Stranger than us?"

"Not with you here. Listen!"

Then I heard it, a feeble rustling with a very soft squeaking sound. A look of recognition suddenly flitted across Eekim's face. He tentatively raised his head, emitted a similar squeaking sound and quickly ducked behind me. I wasn't sure whether he viewed me as protection or merely something expendable to place between himself and possible danger. The squeak was repeated, louder, and directed towards us.

Eekim's face became resolute. He squared his little shoulders and began marching into the woods. "Come on," he commanded. "Follow me."

"Lead on, McDuff," I said while scrambling to my feet and sleepily stumbling after him. I struggled through the woods and tried to keep him in sight. Finally he pulled up and stopped while surveying the area in front of us.

"You sure make a lot of noise," he quietly criticized.

"Was I supposed to be sneaking?"

"It never hurts."

Once more he emitted a short squeak and was immediately answered by something close in front of us.

"This way," he said.

I followed, quickly looking around for a rock or club. Then I decided that if Eekim was not afraid there was no reason for me to be.

We emerged into a small clearing. About ten feet in front of us was a monkey. It didn't take a paramedic to know he was not long for this world. He had been shot, there was blood covering his paw which he held to his side.

"Squeeky!" cried Eekim as he ran to one side of the wounded monkey. I followed and knelt on the other side. "What happened?"

"They shot me," Squeeky solemnly declared. "Not much time,.....brought you... these,.." and he handed Eekim some banana peels.

"What are you doing here?" Eekim pleaded

"Ooga sent me ahead,....to scout for you,...read,...the peels." Squeeky managed to focus his eyes on me for a moment. "Is this...the human?"

"Yes," said Eekim.

"Ooga,...was right.....Doesn't,....look,....like much," Squeeky said with his last breath.

We buried Squeeky where he had fallen. It was a nice, shaded clearing above the normal high-water mark. We stood in silence above the grave.

Eekim respectfully intoned: "Squeeky, this is good-bye. You were a good monkey, you'll make a good banana. It's at least a nice thought."

We arrived back at camp as the day dawned. I packed the canoe while Eekim studied the peels which Squeeky had sacrificed himself to deliver. When I was finished I sat down beside Eekim. He continued to study the peels.

Eventually he said: "Well, the peels are kind of messed up. I don't mean to sound critical of Squeeky but they could have been delivered in better shape. Store-bought bananas are barely legible at best. The first part is garbled and I can't make out most of it. The part I can read says: '.....plan ready.... everything is go.... monkey...man ...must be stopped...... remember: Today Missouri. Tomorrow the Country. After a long, leisurely vacation at a tropical resort: The World!'"

"Sounds like a rich lawyer's schedule," I commented.

"Do you know what this means?" asked Eekim.

"That Missouri lawyers have a plan to expand their power base to control and subdue not only the state and the nation but to eventually master the world!" I exclaimed.

"Worse," Eekim gravely said. "They know we're coming."

SO MUCH FOR SUBTLETY

The canoe gently bumped the river bank and Eekim scrambled out. We were about half a mile from the take-out point where my car was waiting.

"Here's the plan," said Eekim. "They're looking for a man and a monkey, so I'll cut through the woods and join you when you leave. We'll have to dump the bananas here, may the spirits of my ancestors forgive me, so you won't look suspicious. Just load up and get out of there. Act casual and nonchalant. Don't attract attention, be subtle and inconspicuous."

"I think I can handle it," I mildly declared.

"Yes, well, I'm sure you can," Eekim doubtfully agreed. "Just be careful."

We unloaded the bananas and I paddled down river. I looked back and waved at Eekim. He waved his paw and quickly disappeared into the trees, a small stalk of bananas on his back. Personally, I thought we were being a little melodramatic.

I beached the canoe and brought my car down to load my gear. My car is a '76 Cutlass Supreme, a very good car except it's a little beat-up. I call it the "Spirit of '76". It's a big car and there was plenty of room in the trunk for all my gear. I put my cooler in the back seat.

"Spirit" at one time, had vinyl on the back of the landau top but I tore it off when it got ragged and painted that portion black. I never have understood why anyone would put material on the outside of a car. It makes as much sense as upholstering the exterior of a house. "Spirit" had about 100,000 miles on a 260 baby V-8 and was still going strong.

I drove the hundred yards to the canoe rental area. It was a small, yellow building with canoes piled by one side and an old truck with a canoe trailer parked on the other. I pulled up in front and got out.

A late model Mercedes sped up to the building and skidded to a halt behind my car. Two immaculately groomed and dressed men were inside. The driver rolled down his window and yelled: "Hey, I was going to park there!"

"I was here first," I irritably retorted, "there's plenty of other places." I pointed to the rest of the area in front of the store where there was room for at least half a dozen cars.

"That's not the point," said the driver. "I had decided to park in that spot, which establishes my right-of-way in the matter. You have rudely usurped my chosen parking place in a callous and premeditated violation of my constitutional right to free access in a public parking zone."

Remembering Eekim's advice I responded, with as much subtlety as possible: "Screw you."

The driver slammed his car in reverse, braked, slammed the car into forward and skidded to a stop beside my car. It was quite a display but mainly resulted in raising a lot of dust. The driver got out, slammed his door and stormed up to me. His companion approached in a calmer manner.

"You're asking for a lawsuit, did you know that?" he sneeringly inquired.

"Now Bill," the other one said to the driver. "We're just here to ask a few questions. I'm sure this gentleman did not mean any personal affront."

"Okay Mark," said Bill. "I'll drop the lawsuit."

"You see how a little friendliness and cooperation can ease a situation," Mark said while coldly smiling at me.

I remained impassive, looking at them. "You guys are lawyers, aren't you."

"That doesn't prove anything!" Bill defensively stated.

"Guilt by association," added Mark, "is specifically inadmissible as definitive evidence of lawlessness. Likewise, a man cannot be construed as guilty by factor of his membership in a group regardless of the reprehensible moral nature of said group."

"Have you been on the river?" asked Bill.

"I might have been," I answered.

"Did you see anything unusual?" asked Mark.

"Not until I got off the river," I responded while eyeing

them meaningfully.

"That's it!" said Bill. "I want to sue him. Let me sue him. That will teach him!"

"As you can see," smoothly said Mark, "my associate is rather excitable and vindictive. However, this would not affect the validity of a legal action, nor would it impinge upon his veracity in the documentation of actionable claims. I feel legal action can be avoided if a little consideration on your part, in the form of information, could be extended. Did you see any unusual wildlife, like, oh, I don't know, say, just for example, monkeys?"

I pretended to think for a minute. "I did see a log which had a remarkable resemblance to a crocodile."

"Did you see any monkeys?" asked Bill in his usual, perturbed manner.

"This is Missouri," I laughed, "there are no monkeys in Missouri."

"Objection," said Bill to Mark, "the witness is not on record as an expert on the fauna of Missouri. His testimony is inadmissible."

"Since I'm not an expert," I evenly said, "then there is no point in answering any further questions."

"Are you two bothering my customers again?" Cecil, the owner of the canoe rental, had come outside. He was not a big man but he had that solid, imposing presence of most country people.

"Certainly not!" said Bill.

"Certainly are!" I contradicted.

"Now, now," began Mark, "we were just inquiring as to river conditions. My associate and I are considering renting a canoe from this fine establishment which is open for public business and which, therefore, cannot refuse service to paying customers based on race, religion, creed, nationality, sex, age, and a number of other parameters including political or occupational affiliations. I believe we'll inspect that canoe by the river to ascertain if it meets our requirements."

They started moving to the car.

"Let me sue them," pleaded Bill. "I can sue both of them with one hand tied behind my back!"

"That's the problem with life," Mark wistfully said, "so many people to sue, so little time. But we have more important business. Let's look at that canoe."

"I'll bet we find something. I'd bet a year's dues at the club."

"Indeed, Mr. Ispadded," said Mark, "shall we draw up a contract to document the wager?"

"I never sign anything, Mr. Eddeck," replied Bill. "Gentlemen's wager?" and he held out his hand.

"Verbal agreements are virtually impossible to litigate," noted Mark.

"Prudent decision, counselor."

And they drove off.

CECIL

"Damned peckerhead lawyers," muttered Cecil as we went inside. "They been nosin' around here for weeks now. Don't know what they want. Sounded like you were holdin' your own with 'em."

"I guess," I modestly said.

"I seen 'em do it before. They buffalo a lot of people by pulling that 'good lawyer, bad lawyer' routine and threatenin' to sue. Didn't fool me a bit. Knew it was an act right from the start. Anyone with half a brain knows there's no such thing as a 'good lawyer'."

"Not if they're breathing," I commented.

"Right," Cecil laughed. Cecil had been looking me over as we talked, almost like he wanted to tell me something but wasn't sure if I could be trusted. We settled my bill for the canoe and supplies.

"Did they threaten to sue you?" I asked.

"Oh yeah. That scrawny one, Bill, said he was going to sue me 'cause my dust was gettin' on his car. I told him it sure as hell was my dust and he better not leave with it or I'd have him arrested for stealing. I didn't, of course."

"It's at least a nice thought," I ventured.

Cecil quickly looked at me and broke into a smile so big I thought his face would break. Motioning for me to wait he went to the back room and returned with a sack, the contents clinked.

"This is a favorite with us locals," he said, winking as he pulled out an unlabeled wine bottle full of crystal pale amber liquid. "We barter with some of the 'natives' for it. It makes a great cocktail. No charge."

"Banana wine! Great! I know somebody who'll be very happy to see this."

"Better hurry," Cecil said. "Them lawyers will be comin' back pretty quick."

I took the sack and left.

"Lawyers uck," Cecil called after me.

THE GETAWAY

With the wine safely stored in the back seat by the cooler, I pulled away. In my rearview mirror I noticed the Mercedes coming back from the river. Mark was excitedly talking into a car-phone and Bill was glaring and pointing at me. I nonchalantly gave them a gesture which is usually translated into words which seem to indicate a blessing of sexual bliss but is never bestowed, or received, with courtesy.

I floored the accelerator and "Spirit" sped away. The Mercedes didn't follow.

I slowed after I reached the first bend and passed under some trees overhanging the road. Eekim, with his bananas, swung through the open passenger window.

"How did it go?" he asked.

"Pretty good," I said.

"Yes, I heard. I was in the bushes until you went into the store. 'Screw you' was a particularly subtle remark."

"They're lawyers," I defended. "They expect such a response from normal people. Anything less would have been suspicious."

In the rearview mirror I saw a new, black, souped-up truck with over-cab spotlights, huge tires and customized high-suspension swerve onto the road. Once stabilized, it powered forward and quickly gained on us. This in itself seemed rather ominous but the thing which most instilled a disquieting sense of danger in me was the individual leaning out the passenger window with a rifle leveled in our direction.

"We've got company!" I said and floored it.

Eekim whirled and looked out the back window.

"This is all your fault!" he accused. "'Be subtle', I said. 'Be inconspicuous', I said. But do you listen? No! Do you stick to the plan? No! You say 'Screw you' to the lawyers and flip them off! What a stupid, undisciplined furless human you are!"

"Actually," I said while negotiating a curve, "I think they found something in the canoe. You didn't leave any muddy paw prints around did you?"

Eekim seemed to pale for a moment, if monkeys are actually capable of that.

"Well," he matter-of-factly stated, "this is no time to be blaming one another. I wish we had some wine."

"What? You want to offer them a drink?" I incredulously asked.

"Yes, that's exactly what I would like to do," he righteously replied.

"It's in the back," I sighed while whipping the steering wheel to keep "Spirit" from spinning off the road. "Sorry, but I forgot the cheese and crackers."

"Cheese is bad for the digestion," observed Eekim as he dove into the back seat.

The passenger in the big, black truck was now firing off rounds at appropriate times. The road here was bumpy and very curvy so, fortunately, there were few appropriate times. Still, I found it unnerving.

"Should we chill the wine?" I caustically asked. "It's above room temperature in here." I was beginning to sweat.

"It's perfect," said Eekim as he jumped into the front seat. He had worked the cork out of the bottle.

"Spirit" was holding its own against the truck only because the dirt road had a lot of curves. I was raising so much dust braking for a curve, skidding, and then taking off that the driver of the truck couldn't see. The high suspension of the truck also made it top-heavy and it had to slow more for curves. The truck swiftly gained on any short straight-away. The periodic sound of rifle-fire continued to increase the element of tension in the situation.

"Excuse me," said Eekim as he leaned over and bit my

shirt and then ripped off a section.

"Sorry I forgot the napkins," I grunted.

"You're only human," Eekim graciously responded. "Although," he regretfully added, "napkins would have been a nice touch."

"Spirit" rounded what turned out to be the last curve. A long straight-away confronted us and I stomped the accelerator.

"We're in trouble!" I yelled.

"Got a light?" asked Eekim.

I fumbled for my lighter as the black truck took the curve and double-barreled after us. I could hear the truck's engine kick-in above the roar of "Spirit". I threw my lighter at Eekim.

"We're in trouble!" I yelled again. It was no longer a spontaneous comment but still seemed to capture the essence of the moment.

A bullet shattered the rear window. I instinctively ducked even though I immediately realized that the bullet was already spent. "Ducking a bullet" is just an expression not an actual physical possibility. A bullet either hits you or it doesn't. However, I have never felt shamed by my actions, either then or now. I scrunched lower in the seat and peered over the dash to steer.

Eekim had lit the shirt-tail rag which he had stuffed into the bottle. The fire briefly flared inside of the car and then Eekim leaned out the window, yelled "Cheers!", and threw the flaming bomb at the truck. The bottle exploded on the windshield and the front of the truck was immediately engulfed in blue and white flames. It ran off the road and hit a tree with a crash which abruptly reduced its momentum to zero.

I stopped the car and we got out to watch. The truck exploded in a fireball which sent an ugly, black cloud spewing into the air. I had no doubt there were no survivors.

"Cecil said it made a great cocktail," I commented.

"An unpretentious wine, amusing but powerful. Best when consumed in moderation," said Eekim.

"Alcohol is a major cause of automobile accidents," I added.

"Wisely is it recorded in the peels of my tribe: 'Monkeys

do not grieve when a tiger dies'. Let's go."

We got back into the car and headed down the road.

"How much alcohol is in that 'monkey shine'?" I asked.

"Just enough, my friend, just enough."

THE GETAWAY, PART II

"Do you suppose those were the guys who shot Squeeky?"

"I hope so," Eekim cheerfully replied. "Hey, do you hear something?"

There was a staccato whiffing sound which was growing louder.

"Sounds like a helicopter." I looked around trying to spot it. "Probably saw the smoke from that truck and came to take a look."

"Don't you think that's a little unusual?"

I glanced at Eekim. The episode with the truck must have really shook him up. He was scared of everything now. The poor little guy was actually shaking. I was about to calm him by explaining that helicopters were not all that rare a sight when the first missile exploded in front and to the left of us.

"Highly unusual!" I agreed and once more hammered the gas pedal.

The road was another stretch of straight lane with no turn-offs. There was a field to one side and woods on the other. I panicked because there was no way to evade or outrun that chopper. The second missile struck close behind us and to our right. "Spirit" lurched with the concussion.

"They're getting our range!" I shouted.

"Here's the plan," Eekim shouted back. "If they miss again, slam on the brakes and swerve the car! Stop in the middle of the road."

I didn't like the sound of that, "if they miss"?

"What if they don't miss?" I yelled.

"Then we won't need a plan."

The next missile exploded right in front of us. Dirt and dust covered the windshield as "Spirit" bounced over the crater. I hit the brakes, slid into a three-quarter spin and stopped.

"Hang your head out the window," Eekim commanded.

"Play dead!"

I followed his instructions while he climbed into the back seat. I could hear him rummaging in the cooler. My head was tucked under my left arm and I was hanging out the window. I ruefully considered that if I got killed the last thing I would smell would be my own armpit. After several days on the river it was not a pleasant thought.

The helicopter circled overhead while Eekim clambered onto the back of my seat. He started pouring something on my head.

"Ketchup," he explained. "Whatever happens, wait here and don't move. That's the plan, got it? Wait here and don't move! Not too complicated for you, is it?"

"Got it," I mumbled into my pungent armpit.

The chopper settled in the field to one side, about forty feet from the car.

"Wait. Don't move," Eekim repeated and scrambled out the passenger window.

I peeked over my arm and saw two men in fatigues get out of the 'copter. They leveled what appeared to be standard issue Soviet AK-47 assault rifles at me and slowly advanced. Both were grinning.

"This the guy that's so dangerous?" one of them commented. "Doesn't look like much."

I was getting tired of these negative personal evaluations.

"Hey, can I shoot him a couple more times?"

"Later, our orders are to get that monkey."

Eekim began screeching somewhere behind the car. Both men swiveled and opened up with full automatic bursts. A blood-chilling animal scream pierced through the noise of their weapons. After emptying their clips, both reloaded.

"Come on. I think we got him." They ran behind the car.

"Here's blood. He can't be far. Let's go." The two men disappeared into the woods.

I couldn't move for a several minutes as sadness washed over me in waves. I looked up and the area was quiet. Sadness evolved to anger.

"Those bastards shot my monkey," I softly swore. "They're going to have to pay!" I wiped the ketchup off my face. Stealthily, I ran to the helicopter and opened the engine compartment. I pulled every wire I could find. I then looked around the small cabin. A web belt with a nine millimeter semi-automatic and a pouch of loaded clips caught my eye. I took it.

I ripped out the radio's microphone and shoved it into the pouch. I noticed a small ammo box and found it stuffed with grenades. After straightening the pins on two of them, I lodged them under the pilot's seat. I ran a wire from the pins to the closed door. I climbed out on the gunner's side and was jogging to the car when Eekim came skipping out of the woods.

Eekim saw me, and his eyes got big and his jaw dropped. He put his paws on his hips and started tapping one foot. "What part of the plan didn't you understand? 'Wait' or 'Don't move'?"

"Come on," I said.

As he climbed into the car, Eekim laughed: "Those guys will be following a trail of ketchup for hours while we just drive quietly out of here."

"Right," I said, and gunned the engine and laid on the horn. I stopped down the road where we could still see the chopper.

"Great, just great," Eekim said to himself. "You follow instructions like an idiot but compensate by acting like a moron the rest of the time.

"They're going to chase us," he excitedly continued. "Which means they will kill us! Is there some part of this progression which escapes your comprehension?"

"I sabotaged the engine."

"They can still call for back-up! Are you unfamiliar with a modern device known as the radio? It probably seems very mysterious to you but it allows people to communicate almost immediately over great distances."

I reached into the pouch and handed him the microphone.

"Oh. So what are we doing here?"

"Wait," I instructed, "don't move."

The two men ran out of the woods. One of them pointed

to us and they ran to the chopper. The gunner jumped in on his side, the pilot opened the door on the other. The first explosion produced an intense conflagration which was followed by smaller booms as gas tanks, ammo and various explosives detonated. The top propeller flew fifty feet into the air and then gracefully tumbled end-over-end until it stabbed into the ground.

I looked at Eekim and grinned: "When I make a whoopee cushion, I do it right."

Eekim gazed out the window, and then glanced back at the fire. He turned to me and conversationally asked: "So, how do you like the plan so far?"

CHAPTER FIVE

BY THE WAY

"Any damage?" Eekim asked.

We had driven several miles and turned into a narrow lane. I had pulled over to the side to inspect "Spirit". Nothing was leaking underneath and nothing was obviously broken or dangling; there were only dents and scratches which may or may not have previously decorated the body.

"Just the rear window, I guess." I started cleaning broken glass out of the back seat.

An old red farm-truck, with accents in black primer, approached behind us. Eekim quickly disappeared so I kept picking up glass, minding my own business and ignoring the truck. I could feel the driver looking the situation over. The truck parked in front of "Spirit".

A young woman got out of the truck. She was a vision of youthful country loveliness with blonde hair to her shoulders, a pink cotton shirt, cut-off blue jeans, and boots. She wore a baseball cap which advertised a feed store. Among my many reactions was the melancholy admission that I was pushing forty.

"'Lo, problems?"

I pitched the last of the loose glass into the sack with the wine bottles. My rear window gaped with a grapefruit size hole in the middle of a frame of spider-web cracks.

"Yea," I answered. "Guess a rock flew up and hit the

glass."

"Really?" Her expression and tone of voice questioned whether it was my habit to say idiotic things all the time or was this a special occasion? "Must have been some rock to fly up there. Did you notice what color its wings were?"

That's the trouble with dumb blondes, you see them all the time but they're never around when you need one. I didn't really mind that she wasn't a dumb blonde. I loved to have stereotypes shattered. It reaffirms my belief that we know very little about the world around us. I liked it that way. If we knew more, we would be "smart" enough to do that much more harm.

I had told Eekim, while floating down the river, that "the only thing men and women need in order to understand one another is a balanced, logical and honest view of themselves and others."

He had commented that this "precluded any reasonable expectation that men and women would ever understand one another."

In the final analysis, I had long ago accepted men and women as equals although I was still unsure which sex should feel more insulted by this condition. But, I digress.

"It had yellow wings, a red belly and a blue crest," I finally said. "I've never seen one like it before. I'll have to look it up in my Rockwatcher's Guide when I get home."

She ignored my glibness. Her eyes were dark green and they didn't miss much as she looked over the car. She started tracing something with her finger in the dust on the trunk.

"You should drive slower on dirt roads," she commented. "You're liable to tear the bottom out of this thing."

"Well, it seemed like the thing to do at the time," I said. "Wait a minute, how did you know I'd been speeding?"

She gave a short laugh. "I've got four older brothers, I know what a car looks like when it's been driven hard. The dust settles on it differently." She looked up and thoughtfully frowned, "and it feels tired."

Great, a girl with emotional empathy for a car's well-being.

"Do you live around here?"

She laughed again. "Well I guess so. You're in our

driveway."

"Oh, well, I just pulled in here to clean up some of the glass."

"No problem. Come on up to the house. I have some friends who own a salvage yard, we can give them a call. They might have a windshield to replace this. The house is about a mile down the way, follow me." She turned when she reached the truck. "Everyone calls me Nicky, short for Nicolette. What's your name?"

"Josh."

"My dad wouldn't want me bringing strangers home. Come on Josh."

I noticed the picture she had drawn in the dust. Considering the medium it was a very accurate and artistic portrayal of a turkey . I briefly considered whether she had intended it as a personal commentary.

I started the engine and waited just a moment to see if Eekim would climb through the window. He didn't so I figured he had listened and would meet me later.

SAM

I followed Nicky to a two-story, white farmhouse. She indicated I should park in back beneath the shade of two towering oak trees. As I walked to the front Nicky was talking to an old man in overalls and workshirt. A weathered and worn straw hat was perched on his head.

"Dad, this is Josh," Nicky introduced me. "Josh this is my dad."

"Good to meet you, sir." I don't usually call a man "sir" unless he wears a uniform and is in the process of stopping me for a traffic violation. The old man's manner neither demanded nor requested respect, but he exuded an air which silently declared it as the only appropriate approach.

"Sam," said the old man as he held out his hand. He did not try to crush my hand in his firm grip but I had few doubts that he could have. When I met his eyes all doubts vanished. He looked at me through steel-blue eyes which left the impression that whatever he decided to do would be done. His expression was not stern, however, but evaluating. He was sizing me up and I had the uncomfortable feeling the he was not totally unamused.

"Nicky said a rock flew up and broke your back windshield."

"I guess that's what happened," I sheepishly answered. The credibility of the "flying rock" theory was not enhanced by repetition.

"Strange," said Sam. "I heard of rocks falling from the sky, they call 'em meteorites. And I've heard of rocks being thrown, happens all the time. But I've never heard of a rock jumping up from the ground and flying."

"Freak accident?" I tried.

"More than likely," agreed Sam in a tone which implied both the accident and my conception could be described as such.

"I asked Josh to stay for supper," Nicky said. "I'll get it started."

She quickly turned, before any objections could be raised, and ran into the house. This left Sam and me alone.

I cleared my throat after a minute: "I appreciate you and Nicky helping me."

"You can thank my daughter," Sam stated. "I'm just going along because there's no use standin' in her way when she decides to do something. She's too soft-hearted, always bringin' home some hurt or sick animal which needs tendin' to." He pointedly looked at me.

"She's a beautiful young woman, inside and out," I said, not taking the bait but, instead, offering some of my own.

Sam did not argue the compliment.

"Yep," he feigned disgust but could not disguise his pride, "every boy within a hundred miles chases after Nicky."

"Well," I said, "the boys around here aren't too stupid are they?"

Sam laughed, a deep rolling sound like the echo of thunder in the mountains. He straightened immediately but I could tell from the twinkle in his eye that he was pleased. There are few ways to more favorably impress a father than complimenting his children.

"Well," Sam said after a few moments. "If you're stayin' for supper you'd better get cleaned-up. No offense, but you smell worse than most of the poor, dragged-out critters Nicky brings home."

R & R AND THE FARMER'S DAUGHTER

A good, long, hot shower cleanses not only the body but rejuvenates the soul. I was sorely in need of both. The dirt and grime from the last several days ran down the drain in brownish-gray water. I washed away the filth from the river, monkey partying, high-speed chases, brushes with violent death, confrontation with murderers and conversation with lawyers. I felt reborn and refreshed.

I put on my last clean pair of jeans (I always take a change of clothes when camping, which I leave in my car), a green T-shirt and sneakers. I was reluctant to even touch the clothes I had worn but gingerly stowed them in my stuff-bag. I combed my hair and, because of Nicky, took more notice than usual of my receding hairline.

"You look much better," Nicky smiled when I came downstairs again.

The aroma of delicious food filled the air.

"I smell better, too," I grinned while sniffing the air. "Either that or your cooking promises to be exceptional."

"Flattery will get you nowhere," she laughed. "Dad's already at the table. I made his favorite." The sly glance she gave me made me think that "Dad" now had a bill to settle with the cook. "By the way, my friends can fix your window in the morning."

"Great, thanks."

Sam looked up as we entered the kitchen. The table was piled with fried chicken, mashed potatoes, gravy, corn on the cob, salad and bread. Large glasses of iced tea crowded among the platters, bowls and plates.

"It's my favorite, thank you Nicky," he said. His voice sounded happy but there was a plaintive quality to it. Sam, also, was aware that he had been encumbered with some unnamed debt.

Dinner conversation enlightened me as to the state of affairs with the family and the farm. Nicky's brothers no longer lived on the farm but had settled into their own families. Sam served in Korea and had farmed the rest of his life on land which once belonged to his father. Sam's wife, Mary, had died several years ago. Nicky was twenty-four, a few years older than I would have guessed. One of their neighbors was digging a new well, and another was thinking of adding-on to his barn. Summaries of the livestock and crops were reviewed. The weather, a critical concern to farmers, was discussed at length.

"That was great," I praised, finally pushing my chair back after three helpings and glowing with the contentment which good food produces. "I've haven't had a meal this good for a long time. Thank you."

"You're welcome," said Nicky. She began to clear the dishes and I started to help. Immediate rebukes fell upon me, in mock anger, for insulting the hospitality of the home. Cheerful explanations informed me that a guest in this home did not do the dishes and such action would not be tolerated. She implied that failure to accept the arrangement would be considered an insult to herself, her father, her heritage and her dignity as a hostess. Mock threats implied that further failure to behave like a proper guest could result in serious physical harm.

Sam, enjoying every second of it, merely sat and smiled, eyebrows raised, through the tirade. I awkwardly looked around for some avenue of retreat.

"Let's go sit on the porch," Sam finally said. I was grateful for the escape but suspected he had intentionally delayed the suggestion in order to prolong his enjoyment of my predicament..

The porch was cool and fresh air lightly stirred in the evening breeze. The sun was almost completely down, only a faint glow remained in the west. It was that time of night when darkness seems to increase, in measurable quantities, every few minutes. Sam lit a pipe and puffed with satisfaction.

"Never argue with Nicky," he advised, "you'll lose."

"Do you speak from experience?" I asked.

"Of course," he answered, unperturbed. "Nicky is extremely independent, probably one of the reasons she's not married."

"She had to be independent, growing up with four

brothers."

"That's part of it," he agreed. He settled into the quiet reverie of a man savoring a cherished memory before telling an often repeated story to new ears. "I was there when Nicky first discovered her spirit. She was about five, and she and the boys were playing in the front yard. Eddie, my oldest boy, was about fifteen. He was supposed to watch the kids and kind of baby-sit them. He was busy and Steve, my youngest boy who was about eight, was teasing Nicky. Well, she was squawking and started yelling at Eddie to make Steve stop. She kept yelling and finally Eddie told her: 'Stop whinin', it'll make you a better person." Nicky just shut up for a minute, and stared at Eddie with an amazed look on her face. Then she got up and toddled over to where he was kneeling on the ground and popped him right in the nose with her fist. 'Don't whine,' she said, 'I'm making *you* a better person.'"

I chuckled and Sam joined in, a man glad to share the story with someone who could appreciate the humor.

"His nose bled pretty good," he continued. "Needless to say, Eddie rode tight rein on future teasing. But you should have seen little Nicky. She just kept staring at Eddie's bleeding nose and then looking back at her tiny fist. I think it was the first time she discovered that she could change things, that she didn't have to just sit back and whine if she didn't like something. She went around for days, making a fist just so she could look at it. But she never whined about anything after that, and she never tolerated anything she didn't like. She had learned to take action."

"Does she still punch people?" I asked.

"She doesn't have to," Sam laughed. "She's too intelligent to have to hit folks. She's good-hearted but she can twist anybody around her little finger."

"Which reminds me," I said, "I think you're going to owe her for that meal tonight." I enjoyed telling him this.

"Oh, I know," he resignedly said. Then he grinned and looked at me like an old cowboy who has been bucked off a horse and sees a tenderfoot climbing into the saddle. "I noticed you ate quite a bit."

He enjoyed telling me that.

71

THE NEWS

Stars came out, lightening bugs flashed their brief messages, and crickets and cicadas chirped and buzzed. Sam and I formed a small audience entertained by the wonder of Nature's simple theatrics. After a while, we went inside to watch the news and weather. I settled into one of the large, comfortable chairs which, along with the TV, comprised the main furniture of the living room. Nicky brought in bowls of ice cream. Several stories of regional interest were reported then the announcer transferred to an earlier, on-the-spot, report.

"This is Bob Richards, and I'm standing on the scene of a tragic accident which occurred earlier today. The smoking wreckage behind me is what's left of a helicopter which apparently crashed and burned. Two lives were lost in the accident. Police are investigating."

"In a bizarre twist, a wrecked truck was found a couple of miles from the helicopter. The truck apparently ran off the road, hit a tree and burned. Two bodies were also recovered from that accident."

"I have with me two individuals. Mr. Bill Ispadded and Mr. Mark Eddeck, two lawyers on vacation, who have given information to the police. Gentlemen, what did you see."

"Actually," said Mark, "we were not witnesses to the actual events which precipitated these tragedies. However, we are aware of an individual who was in the area at the time. This individual was extremely disagreeable and acted in an extremely suspicious manner. He was openly confrontational and reacted just short of violence to innocent questions which we posed."

"That's right," agreed Bill. "We have conferred with the Sheriff to the effect that this individual <u>may</u> be involved in the transportation of bootleg liquor and that he <u>may</u> be in the company of an illegal and unregistered monkey. There's no telling what other despicable activities he <u>might</u> be engaged. In light of recent events he should <u>possibly</u> be considered armed and dangerous. Honest citizens concerned with the protection of their families and home <u>maybe</u> should arm themselves and be prepared to deal with this <u>apparent</u> maniac."

"We are not advocating that this individual be shot on

sight, we are merely of the opinion that a reasonable person might consider it to be the only realistic option," continued Mark. "As attorneys, we are responsible for....strike that.... As attorneys, we are aware of the limitations of the police in dealing with violent criminals."

"Thank you, gentlemen," resumed the reporter. "And now, we talk with Sheriff Dan Tolling. Sheriff, what do the police think happened here?"

"We are just beginning our investigation," said an irritated officer, looking distastefully off-camera to where the lawyers stood. Dan Tolling was a big man on the slim side of fat. He wore a large black Stetson, sunglasses, and chewed the stub of a cigar.

He continued in a blunt, no-nonsense, competent voice: "We have two incidents which may or may not be related. The helicopter contained two bodies and a quantity of firearms and explosives. There were shell casings from automatic weapons by the road near the wreckage. The truck contained two bodies and firearms. A semi-automatic rifle, which was thrown from the crash, had been recently fired. Shell casings were found in the road behind the truck. We would like to talk to an individual, identified only by first name as Josh, who is driving an older-model blue Cutlass. We merely want to talk to this individual to see if he knows anything. There is no, I repeat, no reason to consider him as armed or dangerous. He is not a suspect at this time. We would appreciate this individual contacting the Sheriff's office. There is no reason to panic, and there is no reason for citizens to arm themselves." Dan Tolling gave one more disgusted look off-camera, and walked away.

"We'll keep you updated as events develop. This is Bob Richards."

The rest of the news and weather followed but I didn't hear any of it. My chair had become a whirlpool and I was being sucked into the vortex. My head was spinning from the confrontation with my recent actions. Of course I couldn't just walk away from attempts on my life; the police were involved, lawyers were involved, there were bodies, questions to be answered. And, I shamefully realized, I had naively placed Nicky and Sam in possible danger.

73

Nicky looked at me several times but didn't say anything. She gathered up the bowls, mine was half-full of melted ice cream, and headed for the kitchen.

Sam had watched the news, the special report, and the weather with equal, dispassionate interest. He slowly got up and switched off the TV. Standing in the middle of the room he observed me for a moment and then said: "Nicky's never been wrong about a man, woman, or animal. She's gifted that way. You're welcome to spend the night. She made up the upstairs bedroom at the end of the hall. We'll talk about this in the morning."

MIDNIGHT RENDEZVOUS

There was nothing to do until morning so I went to bed. The mattress and clean sheets seemed like the ultimate in civilized luxury after so many nights of sleeping on the ground. I decided to get a good night's rest and deal with my problems in the morning. I slipped into a blissful repose, feeling safe and content for the first time in a while.

The scratching sound repeated. It had slowly penetrated my dreams until I could no longer maintain the throes of glorious unconsciousness. I glanced at the luminous hands on the clock which proclaimed the time as 12:15. The room was dark, the area outlined by the open window was black. The scratching sounded like something softly grating against the screen. I got up and cautiously peered into the night.

"Wakey, wakey, O Mystic One," whispered Eekim.

"Cut the crap," I irritably mumbled, unhappy about being awakened. "What's up?"

"I thought you might be interested in my plan for tomorrow, O Mystic One," Eekim giggled.

"No. And why are you calling me 'O Mystic One'."

"Well, in my tribe, when someone claims to see flying rocks the only two options are: (1) they have had a religious experience, or (2) they have gone completely bananas. I am giving you the benefit of the doubt although I have not totally rejected the second possibility." He smiled #298, which means: "you're never going to hear the end of this".

"It could have happened," I quietly protested.

74

"Sure," laughed the little monkey, "and humans might fly out of my butt! Now, here's my plan...."

"No," I interrupted, "here's my plan. Tomorrow morning I'm going to get my window fixed, then I'm going to the sheriff's office and explain everything."

"Well, it's been nice knowing you," Eekim sadly said. "I should have attached more credence to that second option. I'll come and visit you at the asylum."

"Look," I patiently and somewhat righteously retorted, "I've done nothing wrong. I'll just go in and tell exactly what happened. I'm going to rely on truth and honesty."

"You call that a plan?" Eekim was incredulous. "You're going to explain to someone who wears a badge that you ran into a bunch of talking monkeys and got drunk on banana wine and then found out Missouri lawyers are involved in a conspiracy to take over the state, the country, and the world. These lawyers, knowing you were aware of their plan, then sent a truck and helicopter full of vicious killers after you but you were able to blow up both of them. Then a beautiful girl came to your assistance. They'll never buy that last part!" Eekim sarcastically finished.

Actually, although his last comment was a cheap shot, he made a pretty good argument.

"Okay, so there are a few details to work out. Maybe I won't tell the whole truth," I said. "Don't worry, I'll think of something."

"With what?" Eekim questioned. We glared at one another but Eekim's features softened and his expression became one of genuine concern. There were small tears in the corners of his eyes. "I feel terrible, this is all my fault!"

"No," I comforted, "I've made a lot of mistakes."

"Of course," Eekim evenly replied. "I meant I should never have tried to talk to you at night when your mind is obviously more dysfunctional than usual."

He flashed a particularly sneering version of smile #924, which means: "Sucker!", and vanished.

LOOKING BACKWARD THROUGH THE REAR

WINDOW

I rolled out of bed at 6:30 the next morning, quickly dressed and went downstairs to the kitchen. In spite of the hour I felt a renewal of spirit. There's nothing like a farm to give one a feeling of wholesomeness and belonging. The early hour merely added to my sense of purpose, as if rising early signified my ability to meet and solve my problems.

"There you are, sleepyhead," greeted Nicky. "I thought you were going to sleep all day."

"It's 6:30!"

"Oh, don't apologize," said Nicky. "You're a guest, you can sleep as late as you want. I kept some breakfast warm for you."

I mumbled "thanks" as Nicky set a plate of eggs, biscuits, and bacon before me. I slowly ate, considering my options for the day. At the end of my meal I was still undecided as to which facts to relate to the sheriff and which might be better left unmentioned. I certainly could not explain about Eekim, Squeeky, Ooga, the other talking monkeys, getting drunk on banana wine, or the plot by Missouri lawyers. Without these elements, of course, the story consisted of two groups of rampaging gunmen in a truck and helicopter, who, for some unknown reason or reasons, tried to kill me.

"Well," I thought, "it beats the hell out of 'flying rocks'." I decided to run the story by Sam to get an objective opinion.

"Hal and Stan, my friends from the salvage yard, should be finished with your window," said Nicky.

I thanked her again for breakfast and went outside to see how much the new glass would set me back.

Stan was a red-headed guy about thirty-five years old. He displayed a huge grin which I immediately categorized as his permanent expression. Hal was a little younger, with coal-black hair and a dour expression. Together, they reminded me of the smiling/frowning theater masks used in stage productions.

I made small talk with them. I asked if they had any problems installing the glass (no, they could handle anything to do with a car), commented on the excellent work, their consideration in coming out so early to fix it, and how much it would cost me.

"There's no charge," Stan happily said. "We did it as a favor to Nicky. Otherwise you'd had to've come to the yard, pull the glass yourself, and install it yourself. And we'd have stuck it to you on price, seein' how you're not from 'round here."

"Most folks," Hal sourly added, "would do anything for Nicky. She's a very special girl." He managed to make it sound threatening.

I thanked them for their help, and told them I would tell Nicky how lucky she was to have such good friends. This pleased them. Stan's huge grin got bigger and his eyes twinkled with delight. Hal's grimace melted to a steady frown. They expectantly looked at me as if I should have more to say. I thanked them again.

"Nicky's a special girl," Hal repeated. He continued in a menacing tone: "Most folks think that anyone who even says a wrong word to her oughta be shot down like a mad dog."

"That's right," Stan cheerfully agreed.

I explained that I was just a stranger to her. She had helped me because she was a very good-natured, warm-hearted individual. I was too old for her and she deserved someone truly special, someone worthy of her.

They just looked at me.

I further explained that Nicky was the most unique and special young woman I had ever met. My life had been enriched by meeting her, my faith in mankind restored. The very existence of such a woman proved that there was yet hope for this old world. I would be forever grateful for her assistance.

They nodded as if I was on the right track.

I launched into a long soliloquy on every virtue she possessed, idolizing her as the epitome of the human spirit at its best. She was like a goddess to me, and I would gladly sacrifice my life and soul to spare her even the smallest of hurts. I could die a happy man since having the privilege of looking upon her divine countenance. And I probably should die for I was not worthy to crawl the ground upon which she walked.

"And don't you ever forget it!" threatened Hal, apparently satisfied.

"That's right," Stan jovially concurred.

They got into their truck, a gangly hybrid reconstructed

from about a dozen different models. Honking a good-bye to the house, they rumbled off in a cloud of dust.

While inspecting the glass, I noticed that someone had written "Josh" and drawn an arrow to the dusty outline of the turkey. The handwriting was, not surprisingly, suggestive of an ape's penmanship.

DRESS REHEARSAL

I wiped out my name and rubbed my hands on my pants.

"Not very flattering," commented Sam, who had come up behind me.

"Oh, I don't know. Wild turkeys are very smart, Ben Franklin wanted them to be out national bird."

"True," admitted Sam. "But domesticated turkeys are stupid, they'll drown in a rainstorm from looking up with their mouths open. Aren't you domesticated, Josh?"

"Yes," I confessed, "but I've never drowned in a heavy rain. Of course, I usually try to be indoors when it's storming so maybe I haven't really been put to the test."

Sam chuckled and then looked at me with appraising eyes. This seemed like a good time to rehearse my story for the sheriff.

"Sir, about the news last night, what happened was...." and I narrated the sequence of events minus all references to talking monkeys, lawyers and plots. There were obvious incongruities with these limitations but I maintained my total bewilderment at the sequence of events. I was an innocent man caught up in a chain of circumstances which was totally beyond my understanding. Finishing with the sincere hope that these strange happenings could be explained by the police, I emitted the deep sigh of a man unburdening himself of the truth and, overall, I thought my act was very convincing.

"If you don't want to tell me what happened, just say so!" admonished Sam. "Personally, I think your 'flying rock' story is more entertaining. It's also shorter and every bit as believable."

With a snort, he headed for the house.

THE VOICE FROM ABOVE

"Very nice," said a voice in the tree, "your plan is going extremely well, considering its source."

Not looking up, for fear that Nicky or Sam would see me talking to the treebranches and have further reason to doubt my veracity, if not my sanity, I replied: "That's a pretty strong statement coming from an illegal and unregistered monkey."

"Possibly, possibly," mused Eekim, "but consider our relative situations. While no one believes <u>in</u> me, no one <u>believes</u> you. And though I may be illegal and unregistered, at least I am free while, my friend, your chances of remaining unincarcerated diminish with every passing moment. The only real question in regards to your imminent disposition is whether or not your cell will be padded."

"Probably," I sighed, "but what else can I do?"

"Fight! Resist!" Eekim urged. "You don't have to live a life of quiet desperation and spineless capitulation. Make a stand! Where is the spirit of the man who shouted: 'Massacre the worst of them, take back the bananas, paint their butts blue, and put them to work!'?"

"You're right," I declared, inspired by Eekim's words. The passion of the Missouri feud returned. "I've been thinking too much, it's time for action! I'll go in and tell the whole truth, about you, the other monkeys and the lawyer plot."

"Excellent, just excellent," Eekim bitterly intoned, "why settle for half-bonkers when the full-tilt bozo option is available."

"One cannot fight falsehoods with less than the full truth, it would ultimately be a self-defeating approach," I pedantically noted.

"That's logical," Eekim conceded, "for whatever that's worth."

He continued with the sincerity of a social worker trying to dissuade an emotionally disturbed child from an inadvisable course of action: "Still, don't you think it might be a good idea to have a back-up plan, just on the off-chance that your strategy flounders like a beached whale? Wouldn't that be good? Yes, that would be good. I excel at contingency planning. Perhaps I should formulate a Plan B, just in case it's needed. Yes, that's what we need. A plan which can be implemented at any time and which has the advantages of assessing realistic possibilities, anticipating probable occurrences, and actually has some potential for success. Does that sound like a good idea to you?"

"Whatever," I said. "Formulate your plan. I just don't want to hear about it."

"Great!" Eekim enthused. "That will preclude unreasonable objections and I will be spared the tedious burden of explaining subtleties. I like it! We sure make a great team, huh?"

I irritably glanced up but Eekim was focused on examining the structure of the bark of the limb upon which he was perched, an activity which suddenly captured his entire interest. I ignored him back but it wasn't very satisfying since he had ignored me first.

WE'RE OFF; MOST PEOPLE WOULD THINK SO, ANYWAY

Nicky bounced out of the house and climbed into the truck. She pulled up beside "Spirit", scooted to the passenger side, and said: "Hop in, you can drive."

"Wait a minute," I protested, "you're not going with me."

"No," she soberly responded, "you're going with me."

"Can we talk for a minute?" asked Sam. The screen door slammed behind him as he came out on the porch.

With an exasperated glance at Nicky I climbed the three steps to the porch.

"She can't go!" I told Sam.

"It's not your decision," and he added in a defeated voice, "or mine."

"Look, I know you don't believe my story, and maybe it wasn't the whole truth, but the fact remains this could be dangerous. There are people trying to kill me!"

"Doesn't matter. That's exactly why she thinks she should go with you," he explained. "The people chasing you are looking for one man, driving an old blue Cutlass. They're not looking for a man and woman in a beat-up farm truck."

"It's still dangerous!"

"What isn't? Look here, I'm her father, but I can't protect her all her life, which is why I'm not going to try. She's a grown woman and she's responsible for her own decisions. She needs to start living her own life."

"Getting killed isn't much of a start."

"If I thought that would happen neither hell nor high-water could keep me from going," he coldly replied. "But I think it's safe enough. I've got to show her that I can trust her instincts or she never will. I can't let her spend the rest of her life shackled to me. I can't let that happen. She's too soft-hearted, in my opinion, but she needs to follow her own feelings. She believes in you."

"She believed my story?" I hopefully asked.

"I said she was soft-hearted not soft-headed!" he scolded. "She believes in you, but she doesn't believe you. Still, she's never been wrong about anyone." After a pause, he softly added: "Josh, please don't make her wrong this time."

"She'll head back as soon as we get to the sheriff's," I promised.

Sam nodded. I grabbed the confiscated pistol out of "Spirit" and hopped in the truck.

"I don't approve of weapons like that," called Sam.

"Me neither," I called back.

"Don't worry, Dad," Nicky yelled while patting the pump shotgun mounted in the back window.

Sam smiled and looked at his feet, which started shuffling. He didn't look up until after we were gone.

CHAPTER SIX

ROAD HAZARDS

Rattling down the road in the truck, I glanced into the rear-view mirror. I was neither totally surprised nor totally thrilled to see Eekim's grinning face. He had obviously stowed-away before our departure. He energetically waved, danced, blew me a kiss, made faces and flashed the thumbs-up sign. I swerved to keep the old truck out of the ditch.

"Most people look forward when they drive," Nicky commented. "Is something back there?" She turned around.

"Nothing important," I assured her, Eekim had ducked out of sight just below the window. "Scoot over to the middle, I want to show you something."

"That's not a very smooth approach," warned Nicky. "I haven't heard a come-on line like that since early highschool."

"I'm serious. I want to tell you the truth about what's happened." I tapped the window and motioned Eekim to join us in the cab. Nicky doubtfully appraised me but moved a little bit closer.

Eekim swung in the open passenger window and yelled: "Howdy!"

Nicky shrieked, threw her arms around me and practically jumped in my lap. I would have to thank Eekim later.

"This is my partner," I explained to a speechless Nicky.

Eekim shrieked at her which made her jump even closer to me. I would have to buy him some prime bananas or something.

"Strange greeting ritual," Eekim commented, "even for humans. Are the females of the species always so negatively emotional, one might say 'rude'?"

"Sorry," stammered Nicky. "I was just so surprised. A talking monkey! And we all thought Cecil was just drinking too much of that banana wine of his. Pleased to meet you, my name's Nicky." It was amazing how quickly she regained her composure.

"Nice meeting you Nicky, I'm Eekim. I'm the brains of this outfit," he proudly boasted. "Josh, there, is the muscles, so I guess you can be the hysteria. Well, our little group is rounding out nicely, each member contributing their own unique qualities. Don't you think?"

"Yes, I do," Nicky firmly said. "I think you enjoyed startling me, and," slapping me on the arm, "I think you enjoyed it."

I briefly considered that startled and speechless were very desirable characteristics in a woman but decided it was not the time to open up for group discussion.

"Furthermore," continued Nicky to Eekim, "although you obviously contrived to put me at a disadvantage with your entrance, our friendship is not going to progress until you put a lid on that ego of yours."

Eekim stared wide-eyed at her for a minute: "Josh, you really know how to pick 'em. I bet you read a lot of women's books."

"Is he always like this?" Nicky asked, ignoring him.

"Not at all," I said. "He has a warm, lovable side which peeks through on occasion. But most of the time he's much worse."

"'Et tu, Brutus?'" quoted Eekim.

"Easy, Ceasar," I commanded. "The whole story is this...." I related the entire tale up to this point. Eekim found it necessary to interrupt every few sentences with insights, observations, and perceptions which he claimed were "essential to the proper understanding" of events. I found this difficult to believe as most of his comments were self-aggrandizing in the least and some were outright fabrications. However, I managed to tell the tale in a reasonably cohesive manner.

Nicky sat quietly when the story ended. "So lawyers plan to take over the world and apparently they will stop at nothing, even murder. Well, that's much more believable than flying rocks or mysterious gunmen. But, you only have this little monkey's word for what was written on the banana peels. Are you sure he's reliable? He could just be leading you on a wild goose-chase for his own amusement."

I seriously considered the possibility.

"Great, just great," muttered Eekim. "She's not only rude and hysterical but she makes up for it with indefensible attacks on the veracity of an innocent, some might say valiant, monkey who has done nothing except risk his life for the safety of her society. What about the lawyers at the canoe rental? What about the gunmen? What about the lawyers, on the news, suggesting citizens shoot Josh on sight? Besides, if I wanted to make fun of Josh I wouldn't have to lead him on a wild goose-chase. I could do that in the comfort of my jungle and with the support of my tribe." Eekim evinced a very convincing sulk; his little arms folded across his chest, his lower lip slightly protruded and his eyes fixed straight ahead.

"I trust Eekim," I said. "I often find him irritating, but I trust him."

"Sorry," Nicky apologized to Eekim. "This is all so new to me. I had no right to question your character. You're obviously a very intelligent and noble individual." She tweaked his left ear and crooned: "Cute too."

Eekim's sulk melted like ice in hot coffee. He tried to maintain a frown but it is impossible to frown and blush at the same time.

"Perhaps I misjudged you too," he said with smile #374, which means: "you're not so bad yourself". "Wisely is it written in the peels of my tribe: 'Unquestioning trust is not a tribute to the recipient, but a flaw in the giver.'"

"Stop the truck!" Nicky suddenly yelled.

I hit the brakes and skidded to a halt.

"What's wrong?" I asked, looking around.

Nicky just sat there as if she was thinking. Her head kept turning as if she was listening to something. I heard nothing but the sound of the engine.

"Sometimes I have feelings," she said. "Premonitions."

"I knew you were going to say that," Eekim moaned.

"We can't go any further, we have to get off this road. Oh, I should have been paying more attention, it may be too late." She was genuinely frightened, her face was pale and she was trembling.

"I'll scout ahead," said Eekim, "switch to Plan B." He popped out the window and disappeared into the brush on the side of the road.

"What's Plan B?" Nicky asked, her voice barely under control.

"I don't know," I confessed. "But I'm sure it's a good one."

Sitting in the middle of the road, I tried to comfort Nicky. I explained that everyone has feelings at one time or another but they don't always mean anything. After all, it was probably just the excitement of meeting a talking monkey which had made her feel jittery. I told her to look around, there was nothing wrong, it was just another summer day.

"On the other hand," I said while slamming the truck into forward and stomping the gas, "you may be right."

I had looked behind us and had seen the black Bronco purposefully approaching at a speed which raised a large cloud of dust. I was considering the pistol and the shotgun when we rounded the next curve. Slamming the brakes, we fishtailed to a stop before a black van and helicopter in the middle of the road.

A dozen armed men in fatigues, far too many to fight, converged on the truck. The Bronco had blocked any retreat to the rear. Two men approached each door and dragged us from our seats. An officer-type in a black beret marched up.

"Look," I tried to bluff, "if this is about the National Guard picnic last weekend, I'm really sorry about the watermelons. They were supposed to be delivered ice-cold. Now I admit it was unfortunate but I'm sure we can work something out. How do you feel about cantaloupes?"

It was pretty lame but it was all I could think of. I

looked forward to hearing Eekim's critique. Actually, I hoped I lived long enough to hear Eekim's critique.

The officer in the black beret merely grinned and made a motion with his hand. Chloroformed rags were immediately pressed to our faces. As consciousness faded, I thought: "Man, these guys sure like black."

CROSS-EXAMINATION

I woke in an unlighted room as dark as a lawyer's soul. I could not have seen my hands in front of my face even if they hadn't been tied behind my back. The hard, wooden chair to which I was tied had been selected for convenience of confinement rather than consideration for physical comfort. I was thirsty, sore, cramped, and had a headache from the chloroform but, on the whole, I was elated at being alive.

I had seen numerous movies in which the hero feigns unconsciousness in order to gain information about his captors. Also, I could use the time to plan my escape. I remained quiet for about two hours, watching, listening and planning. I reluctantly abandoned this approach when it became obvious that it was very dark, it was very quiet, and all my plans for escape revolved around freeing myself from the chair (an unlikely development).

"Hello, anybody there?" I called.

Immediately an observation panel, in what I assume was the door, slid open and a pair of eyes peered in. A flashlight shined in my face and I blindly blinked into the light. The panel slid shut.

I inventoried the newly acquired knowledge of my situation. There's a door about ten feet in front of me, it has a sliding panel at eye-level and a guard is stationed outside. Although I felt good about gaining the information I felt bad that it offered no perceivable strategic opportunity. I remained tied to the chair.

Another movie-inspired tactic occurred to me. Perhaps I could deceive my guard into rendering assistance.

"Help!" I screamed. "I'm having a heart attack!"

That panel slid open, the beady eyes looked in, a gruff voice yelled: "What?"

"My...my heart..." I gasped. "I think....I'm dying!"

"Good. Hurry it up, I don't like standing out here." And the panel slid closed.

Upon reflection, it occurred to me that the fake dying ploy only worked for the bad guys, in the movies, who could play on the sympathy and humanitarianism of their captors. Good guys could not count on these qualities as motivational factors in the behavior of their abductors. I found little solace in this revelation.

I whiled away the time by breathing. Every so often I would test the ropes around my wrists. They remained tight while not cutting off circulation. A good deal more rope confined my ankles to the chair legs and my upper body to the back of the chair. I developed a grudging respect for whoever had tied those knots, they obviously took pride in a job well done. I was bound as tightly as a lawyer's briefs.

A bare light bulb blinked on overhead. A key rattled in the lock of the iron door and it swung open. In walked a fashionably dressed man in a tailored three-piece suit, silk shirt and tie. He carried a leather briefcase and exuded the fragrance of expensive cologne. His hair was perfect.

"And how is our guest of honor?" he considerately asked in a voice which declared he couldn't care less.

"Great," I said. "I've been on the go a lot lately and this has given me a chance to catch up on my sleep. I appreciate your hospitality but, now that I've enjoyed a nice nap, I really must be going."

"I'm glad you do not take the situation any more seriously than I do." He looked at me with malevolent detachment, the way a small, malicious boy might observe ants being fried under a magnifying glass.

A shiver went down my back in a way which would have prompted my grandmother to ask if someone had stepped on my grave. In this case, however, my reply would have been that it was more like someone dancing.

He grabbed the other chair in the room and raised it threateningly above my head. Chuckling, he set the chair down backwards and straddled it, his chin resting on his arms. He was about two feet away, his black eyes peering into mine with detached amusement. I became more keenly aware of the ropes binding me. It was not the optimum position from which to confront a sociopath.

"Now then, Josh, I would like you to answer some questions," he coldly smiled. "Where's the monkey, Josh?"

"What monkey?"

"Now Josh, you're not being very smart. Believe me, you do want to be smart. We have you, Josh, and we have your girlfriend. Need I recite all the possibilities inherent in the situation?"

"Where's Nicky? What have you done with her?"

"She's fine, she's nearby. I'm glad to see that you care about her, it should make things so much simpler. Where's the monkey, Josh?"

He talked in a quiet voice, almost musical in quality. I had read somewhere that it is good to get a psychopath to speak the name of the victim, that this established the victim as a human being in the mind of the perpetrator. I had no illusions it would work in this case. This guy enjoyed saying my name in a manner not unlike a cheerful eulogy. (I realize that I have referred to this individual as both a sociopath and a psycopath. I know the two states are not identical but feel that he represented a horrible hybrid of the two. First impressions are lasting ones.)

"I don't know where the monkey is. He got away just before we were stopped."

"Ah, I see. Where did you meet this monkey, Josh?"

"Uh...I don't remember."

"Josh, let me explain. I don't care about you or the girl, you're just innocent victims of a diabolical plot. I only want the monkey. I'm sure you're aware of the unusual nature of his kind. We've dealt with them before. We don't like them going around and telling nasty stories about lawyers. We must put a stop to them. Won't you help me, Josh?"

"If I help you, you'll let the girl go?"

"Well, of course, Josh. You too." His smile convinced me he was lying. "I only want the monkey."

LIKE FATHER LIKE SON

I considered my options, which didn't take long.

Fortunately, we were interrupted by a young man. He strolled into the room like a royal prince, lofty and privileged. His suit was of the finest cut and material, diamond rings and a gold watchband glittered. However, he made a greasy, almost slimy, presentation in spite of the material finery. Black hair plastered to his skull proclaimed that no amount of washing or blow-drying could conquer its lipoid nature. A thin mustache adorned his upper lip. Oil from his skin seemed to seep through his clothing. He had an aura about him but it wasn't internal in origin, it was merely light reflected off an oily surface. He was short and had an overall slovenly appearance.

"My son," the older man proclaimed, "the leader of the New World Order."

"Pleased to meet you," I lied.

"He doesn't look like much," the son said as his black eyes peered right through me. "Father, I've just been to see the girl. I want her, before we get rid of her."

"Oh, the impetuous and amorous nature of youth," sighed the man, smiling. "I wish you hadn't asked me in front of Josh."

"He doesn't count," replied the son. "I know what you've taught me: no witnesses, no evidence, no crime. God, I love the law!"

"Is it any wonder I've spoiled him," said the father, with a patriarch's pride. "You know, he broke every law in the book before entering law school and was never once brought to trial, never even had charges filed against him. He's extremely gifted."

"Aw, Dad, I owe it all to you. A couple of times I only got off because of your political connections."

"Don't be modest, son. It's all part of The Game and we're winning, that's all that counts." He sighed: "It doesn't matter how many graduate from law schools, there are still only a few truly talented lawyers who fully understand how to use the law. Of course, we have to admit a lot of students just because of scholastic achievement. Our law schools suffered terribly when we had to expand enrollment, just to avoid criticisms of elitism, to include intelligent students. We're graduating more lawyers than ever but most of them just don't have what it takes.

Of course, when they get into the system they either learn or fall by the wayside. Would you believe," he said to me, "that if intelligence was judged, my son could not even have gotten into law school."

"Disgusting," I said, wisely choosing not to explain why.

"It certainly is," he continued, "he mastered every lawyer trick in the book before he graduated and he's invented a few since. You're looking at the originator of the 'Crack-back Blind Side Settlement' for which he is a legend among lawyers. A blind settlement is one where the parties not only agree to settle but also agree not to publicly discuss the settlement. Well, my son devised a way to only inform his clients of 50% of the settlement and then he took 40% of that, also, as his fee. Brilliant, just brilliant! They can't teach that kind of talent in law school!"

"Certainly not," I agreed.

"Dad," said the son, "it's almost time for my speech."

"I'll be there," replied the father. He proudly watched as the little greaseball exited the room. "He makes me so proud," a small tear had formed in the corner of his eye. When he turned to me, however, his face was suddenly void of all emotion, his smile returned: "Now then, what am I to do with you?"

"Um...where do you get the goons, the guys in khaki fatigues?" I desperately wanted to change the subject.

"They're former clients. Murderers, thieves, rapists and other people we have rendered services to, which is why they're still walking around. You would be surprised at the number of criminals who are not financially successful enough to afford a proper defense to prove them innocent. It has long been a dream of mine to somehow find a way to justify getting low-income criminals proven innocent. We make money off the rich lawbreakers, but it is nice that the poor criminal can now be provided a niche in which they can serve lawyers. My dream is becoming a reality.

"The criminals we utilize are amateurs, of course. If you really want to abuse the law you must first learn it. If you want to rob a Savings & Loan you don't use a gun, you become the manager. But, amateurs have their uses. They provide their services for services rendered, if you will. Who better to

90

organize and make use of their talents than lawyers?"

"You can trust them?"

"Of course not," he seemed surprised. "We recycle. There seems to be no end to them. A new crop is springing up all the time. The first duty of the new ones is to, how shall I put it, terminate the old ones. Needless to say, the retirement plan is rather cursory. It works out very nicely. And it's no worse than they deserve. They are the criminal version of 'hire the handicapped'.

"Now take my son, for example. He has a natural talent for murder, rape and robbery but he didn't just get by on his natural charm. He took the time and trouble to learn the law so that he could make the most of his talent. That kind of motivation and pride in oneself is what separates us from the amateurs."

"Should you be telling me all this?" I hesitantly asked, hoping we were forming some sort of bond of which I was totally unaware.

"Why not? Through my son's indiscretion, I certainly have no hope of deceiving you into cooperation. So, it's all moot. You certainly look intelligent enough to figure out what comes next."

"Maybe I'm not as smart as I look," I tried.

"Josh, you almost have to be," he laughed.

THE SPEECH

"You know my name, what should I call you?" I asked, trying again to initiate some sort of relationship which might influence a delay in on my untimely demise.

He shrugged: "It doesn't really matter. My name is Mr. Oney, but you can call me Lars. I feel we know each other well enough and, considering the situation, we must become friends quickly or not at all."

"I hope we can become good friends, Lars," I said with some degree of truth. "And what is your son's name, that distinguished and regal personage who just left?"

"Phillip," his chest swelled. "Everyone calls him Phil. He claims it makes him appear more accessible, more like an

91

average, honest man. It's a big advantage to gain someone's trust before you screw them to the wall."

"That's very wise," I noted. "That's probably why lawyers are so successful. They possess an innate, sophisticated cunning which is beyond the grasp of a common man like me. Lawyers are so complex and innovative, I only wish I could learn more about them."

"Do you?" he seemed pleased. "Well, my son is about to give a speech of great professional and historical importance. Perhaps you would care to attend?"

"I'd be honored," I humbly replied. This was my chance! I had endeared myself to Lars by praising his son and his profession. His pride obviously provided a chink in his armor. If I could ingratiate myself to him further, perhaps I could effect an opportunity for escape. Already I felt friendship emanating from Lars.

"Every man deserves a last request," he smiled.

I reconsidered. Perchance a lawyer's definition of friendship differed slightly from mine.

Lars called the guard. A burly misanthrope entered and untied me. I massaged my wrists and commented on how grateful I was to have the ropes off. He immediately retied my hands behind my back.

"One of the basic rules of lawyering," smiled Lars. "Once you tie-up someone, keep them tied-up."

"A prudent maxim," I reluctantly admitted.

I was beginning to feel a certain inadequacy in my ability to handle captivity. I had seen a lot of movies where the bad guys untie the good guy and let him wander around until he can figure out how to escape. It struck me as blatantly unfair that my captors could be so ignorant of the direction the course of events should be taking. Maybe their career goals restricted their social life to an extent which prohibited viewing movies as a pastime. Or, maybe they watched different movies than I did. These thoughts did nothing to promote a surge of optimism in my evaluation of my present predicament.

We exited the room. Directly across from my door was Phil, standing on a wooden box, leering into the slot on the door.

"Now Phil," his father gently criticized, "there'll be

plenty of time for that later. Hurry up now, it's time for your speech."

Phil hopped down and scurried off with the athletic prowess of a cockroach.

"Kids," chuckled Lars. "You gotta love 'em."

"Is Nicky in there?" I asked.

"I envision no problem with you knowing that."

"Can I see her?"

"I perceive no harm in that."

I started to move to the door but Lars laid a restraining hand on my shoulder.

"You said I could see her!" I protested.

"No," he firmly replied. "I said 'I perceive no harm' in you seeing her. I also perceive no benefit. Listen very closely when talking with a lawyer. Come along."

We walked down a dimly lit corridor. Lars began telling me about his son's latest case.

"It was open and shut, really. There was a fur wholesaler who was charged with arson in a warehouse fire. The prosecution had a strong case but my son was able to prove beyond reasonable doubt that the fire had not been set. Minor jury tampering and bribing of witnesses provided a solid foundation to support a brilliant defense. It was a very profitable triumph of justice. Phil got half the insurance money and two-thirds of the furs which were supposed to have been destroyed. He'll probably include some sort of sales pitch in his speech."

"Is that what this speech is all about?" I inquired. "Hawking insurance fraud furs?"

"Not at all," smiled Lars. "I told you it is of professional and historical importance. The fur scam is mere serendipity. I love it when good things happen to lawyers. Ah, here we are."

We entered a balcony overlooking a large auditorium. The place was filled with men and women attired in conservatively ostentatious styles. Most had briefcases or file books by their chairs. The yellow glaze of legal pads, poised in every lap, gave testimony to the seriousness of the affair.

The stage had one spotlight which shone upon the centered podium. Four flags, hanging from pikes, adorned the stage. The first was the Missouri state flag, the second was the

93

United States flag, the third depicted the world, and the fourth pike bore a gold dollar-sign on a green background. All the pikes had little statues of Lady Justice at the top.

A pudgy man made a short speech introducing Phil. Phil briskly strutted onto stage and stood before the fat man. Phil extended his right arm, palm outward in a shoving motion, and declared: "Sue." The obese man thrust out his arm in a similar pushing gesture and shouted: "Them all."

To this day I cannot remember the details of the speech. Phil was an impressive orator, with frantic gestures and impassioned pleas. His voice carried through the auditorium with the conviction of a fanatic. His entire audience sat mesmerized by the performance. Some of the phrases I later recalled were: "....glorious destiny....two-thousand years of legalities....Masters of the Rat Race.....further land deals like the S&L's.....mansions with bigger, better, and more living rooms....today, Missouri. Tomorrow the Nation. After a long, leisurely vacation at a tropical paradise: The World!"

Phil manipulated and worked the audience into a frenzy. By the time he was finished they were filled with a conquering obsession and a lust for power and money.

"And remember," he added. "I still have some very good deals left on minks, sables, white baby seals and foxes."

The fat man stood and yelled: "All hail our glorious furrier!" He thrust out his arm: "Sue!"

The crowd jumped up with military precision, their eyes were glazed and their faces shined with a fanatic glow as they extended their arms and replied: "Them all!"

"Sue!"

"Them all!"

"Sue!"

"Them all!"

Phil grabbed the dollar-sign flag and began waving it. "To the glory of the fourth pike! The two-thousand year pike!"

The exuberant celebration might have gone on for some time but for the sudden and piercing warning signal. It droned like an air-raid siren, or the melt-down warning used in nuclear reactors, or the loudest telephone busy signal you ever heard. A female voice, as cold as a lawyer's heart, came over a loud speaker: "Attention! Attention! We have just received notification of an industrial accident. Medical teams are insufficient to properly handle the situation. Nearby hospitals are expected to be pushed beyond capacity. Nearby fire units have contained the area of immediate danger. Computers project 1,214 potential lawsuits, some of which may even be legitimate. This is not a drill. Repeat, this is not a drill. Pilots have been given coordinates. Report to stations."

"This is perfect," murmured Lars. "What timing."

The fat man on the stage yelled: "This is it! This is what we've trained for! 1st and 2nd Elite Lawyer Airborne Divisions will go in first as shock troops and establish temporary offices. The 4th, 5th, and 6th Criminal Lawyer Brigades will eliminate resistance. The 6th and 7th Insurance Litigator Battalions will immediately move in with research and background support. Paralegals will initiate and maintain supply lines. Legal secretaries will establish communications. Come on people, move it!"

The auditorium cleared out quickly. Lars and I were left alone. His face shone with religious fervor.

"This is great!" he said. "Can you imagine the cosmic coincidence of having an industrial accident just at this moment?"

"It is hard to believe," I admitted.

Lars smiled knowingly but said nothing.

BACK TO THE MINES

Lars led me out of the auditorium as the Neanderthal in olive drab fell in behind us.

"You know," I suggested, "it's a shame no one recorded that speech for posterity. When your new world order is established, it would do much to document the sequence of events and place them in historical perspective."

"Who cares?" Lars abstractly inquired.

"Such a documentary would be incomplete," I continued, "without a biography of Phil and, of course, his father who so carefully nurtured and guided his development."

"Perhaps you're right," Lars reconsidered. "Most lawyers are, of course, almost totally incapable of writing anything which can be read and understood. Occupational necessity, you understand."

"I've done a little writing," I casually mentioned.

"Have you? Well, by all means let's stop by the library. I'm sure you'd be interested in the sort of literature a lawyer reads. Our real literature is a far cry from those endless numbered tomes you see in every law library and which nobody touches. They could be bound on all four sides and nobody would notice. They're merely window dressing to provide the illusion of complexity and meticulous research. Here we are."

The library was a luxurious room with deep carpeting, stuffed leather chairs, foot stools and those tacky, brass, green-globe reading lights. One shelf of books adorned a wall. Among the titles were: *EVERYBODY OUT OF THE POOL: A Guide To Packing A Jury, ETHICS: What They Are And Why They Are Obsolete, JUSTICE: A PRICELESS COMMODITY, and how to bill for it, AND JUSTICE FOR ALL: A Lawyer's Manifesto on the Financial Benefits of Dragging Every Man, Woman, and Child in the Country Through the Court System, LIES, DECEPTION, AND THEFT: A Lawyer Primer, A LAWYER'S GUIDE TO THE ADVERSARY SYSTEM AND AVERAGE CITIZENS, It's Us Against Them,* and *NO WITNESS, NO EVIDENCE, NO CRIME: Legal Advice for Professionals.*

"Amazing," I marveled, "I see you've authored this last book."

"Yes," he replied with great modesty for a lawyer, "from a legal standpoint it's the greatest story ever told. I taught my son to read with that book. He quoted the title earlier."

"I thought it sounded familiar, catchy title. So," I said while looking around, "why don't we find a pen and some paper, maybe get something to drink, and I'll just sit down here and get started on that book about you, your son, and your glorious dream. If I work diligently I may be able to finish a draft of the first chapter by morning. Let's see, is that everything? Oh yes, by the way, I suppose you'll be wanting to untie me so I can write?"

"Of course," Lars graciously agreed. "But first, Josh, where did you meet the monkey?"

I tried to make my voice seem very important: "That's

not important now, we must fulfill our obligation to the progeny of the world by recording your life's history. We mustn't risk even the smallest detail being forgotten while we pursue mundane and trivial matters. All pursuits pale to insignificance compared to this majestic endeavor. It is possibly the single most important undertaking in the entire world. Now, if you'll just untie me, I believe we're ready to start. This is exciting, isn't it?"

"Forget it, Josh." Lars didn't sound excited.

"I can't just forget it, this could go down in history as one of the greatest, no, make that THE greatest literary accomplishment of all...."

"Forget it, Josh." Lars firmly said with no hint at all of excitement in his voice. "I'm a lawyer, Josh, and one thing I know is bullshit. If we were in a court of law, I would play The Game with you for years or until my client's money ran out. But this is the real world, Josh, and I just don't have the time. I'm very disappointed in you. I was starting to like you. Aside from tying you up, imprisoning your girlfriend and threatening your life, I've treated you like my own son. Well, I tried." He motioned to the guard: "Take him to his cell. We'll try more persuasive means, later."

I felt pretty low as we walked to my cell. Our footsteps echoed through the labyrinth halls with the hollow ring of a lawyer's laugh.

I wanted to strike out at someone and hurt them. "That's a nice eyebrow you have there," I said to the guard. "If your hairline ever recedes you can just comb that eyebrow back over your head and no one will notice."

My grandmother had always told me: "If you can't say something nice, don't say anything at all."

The guard must have been given the same advice by his mother because he didn't say a word. He did bare his teeth in a savage grin. And he did repeatedly slam me into the walls, slap me about the head and kick me several times as he escorted me to my cell. I made a mental note to try to remember other wise sayings my grandmother may have imparted to me during childhood.

As the gorilla-like guard flung me to the floor at the last

turn in the corridor I saw Phil come whistling from the other direction. He carried wine, flowers and some candles. He stopped in front of Nicky's cell and motioned for the guard to unlock it. He winked at us before going in. The guard made a very low gurgling sound which I assumed was his version of laughter.

The guard pushed me towards my cell. I heard a squeak as the door opened. I lightly stepped over a small object on the floor. I turned in time to see the guard's left foot slide out from under him. He managed an extremely uncoordinated jack-knife in midair which resulted in his head striking the concrete floor with a dull thud. He didn't move.

"That old banana peel trick gets them every time," said Eekim. He grinned at me: "They always fall for it!"

I had forgotten about the old sidekick-to-the-rescue routine often used in movies. I suddenly felt more confident that movies had provided a proper foundation for dealing with this situation.

Eekim grabbed the keys from the guard and removed his bayonet from its scabbard. I noticed the area around the guard's head

"That's pretty good concrete," I noted. "Look, no cracks."

"Well, old buddy," Eekim beamed as he cut the ropes. "I'll bet you're pretty glad to see me."

"Actually, I had the guard right where I wanted him. Another second or two and I was going to make my move."

"Sporting of you to plan to take him with your hands tied," observed Eekim as he cut the ropes which bound me. "What was your plan? Talk him to death?"

"Something like that," I laughed and suddenly I couldn't act nonchalant anymore. I grabbed Eekim and hugged him. "Yes, I'm extremely glad to see you."

"Now don't get any ideas," Eekim said. "Eekim is all male monkey, no weird stuff."

"Come on," I urged, breaking the embrace and taking the knife which had brass knuckles on the hilt. "Nicky's just across the hall."

I burst into Nicky's cell and came to an abrupt halt. She

and Phil were seated at a small table covered with a white linen tablecloth. Two candles were lit, champagne was chilling in a bucket of ice and an assortment of premium vodka, bourbon and gin were available on a nearby portable bar. Steak and lobster were laid out on the table. Her cell was carpeted in deep shag with antique paneled walls, indirect lighting and tastefully selected paintings. There was a four poster brass bed, with an elaborate hand embroidered comforter, in the corner.

"Nice place," I said while looking around. "My cell was much smaller."

Phil growled and attacked me with a steak knife. I fell to battle with the courage which belongs only to the righteous of soul and pure of heart who are better armed and much bigger than their opponent. He didn't stand a chance. I parried his thrust, kicked him in the balls and then cold-cocked him with the brass knuckle hilt of the bayonet. The blow carried him onto the bed where he lay quietly.

"Eekim!" Nicky squealed and hugged the little monkey.

Eekim hugged her, saying: "Now don't get any ideas. Eekim is all monkey male, no weird stuff."

One of the candles had fallen and flames engulfed the tablecloth. I picked up one of the linen napkins and attempted to extinguish the blaze. However, my efforts merely succeeded in fanning the flames higher.

"Well, I tried," I said, a lilt of hypocrisy in my voice, "but it's burning out of control. At least it will make a nice diversion."

The small fire sputtered so I fanned it a little more before tossing the napkin into it for fuel. I poured the contents from the more potent distilled spirits around the room.

"We should get out of here," Eekim advised.

"What about him?" Nicky asked, her voice edged with concern.

"Wisely is it written in the peels of my tribe: 'When the tiger burns, the monkeys break out the marshmallows.' Besides," Eekim casually added, "this whole place should explode any minute now."

Nicky gave him a blank look before realization dawned in her expression. "Why didn't you say so?" she tersely asked.

"I did," Eekim defended. "Confinement has done nothing to sharpen your intellect. I tell you something and you immediately question why I didn't tell you. You're not really making a lot of sense. Have you suffered some type of head injury? Maybe you're in shock? Perhaps it is just...."

"Save it," I interrupted. "Let's get out of here."

"Now Josh, here, has a firm grasp of the priorities," Eekim said while leading the way.

Nicky and I followed Eekim through a maze of corridors and halls as dark and twisted as a lawyer's logic. We took numerous detours in our roundabout exit which, Eekim assured us, were necessary to avoid guards. Finally we came to a round shaft with a metal ladder leading up.

"Air shaft," explained Eekim, scrambling upward. Nicky and I followed at a less agile pace.

Emerging from the shaft into a clear night I took deep breaths of the sweet, fresh air. What I had originally assumed was a warehouse was actually an underground complex. A few camouflaged air shafts, like the one we had climbed, dotted the otherwise nondescript field. A small hill, or huge mound, was on the other side of the field.

A large, hidden door slid open in the mound and two medium-sized passenger jets emerged. They taxied down a runway, which was painted to look like a part of the field, one behind the other. The lawyers were apparently very anxious to get to the scene of the industrial accident.

Halfway down the runway the first jet suddenly skidded, sparks shooting out beneath its belly. The second jet rammed into it and both exploded in an inferno which lit up the night sky. We stood silhouetted by the light of the raging firestorm.

"Amazing," commented Eekim. "Funny how small things, like lugnuts on a jet's wheels, can be so important."

"The value of safety inspections should never be underestimated," I noted.

"There must have been a hundred lawyers on those planes," said Nicky in an awed voice.

"Do you really think so?" I asked. "Or are you just trying to get me to smile?"

"It's a shame we don't have any marshmallows," Eekim

said.

TIGER, TIGER, BURNING BRIGHT

Deciding our position was too exposed by the light of burning jet fuel, we jogged toward the trees at the edge of the field. Before we got there, however, the ground trembled with shock waves. A rolling rumble pulsed from the bowels of the earth. The air vents erupted in geysers of fire and debris. We flung ourselves to the ground as dirt and rubble rained down upon us. We waited, with trepidation, for the holocaust to abate. A series of booming roars pealed beneath the ground, great rents were torn in the earth and flames leapt forth. It was not unlike a scene one might envision as Judgment Day. Finally, with one great, final blast, the maelstrom ended.

"They sure had a lot of explosives down there," said Eekim as we shakily got up and brushed ourselves off. We continued walking, on trembling legs, to the trees. We sat beneath a large oak and watched the field. The jets continued to burn, fire still spouted from some of the blackened air vents and one huge crack in the earth glowed with a wavering light.

"Congratulations, boys, I didn't think you had it in you!"

We turned and saw Ooga and a band of a dozen, or so, grinning monkeys. Some of the monkeys had smears of soot on them and a few sported singed fur, indicating they had barely escaped the fire.

"Ooga!" I shouted. "What are you doing here?"

"Merely engaging in a little gorilla warfare," he quipped. "Well, human, I figured you were inadequate for the task and, as usual, I was right. Of course, the odds were with me since I was betting on your incompetence." His manner switched gears from caustic to genteel. "And what is the charming young lady's name?"

Funny, I had never figured Ooga for a ladies' monkey.

"Nicky, this is Ooga," I introduced them.

"I didn't expect to find such exquisite beauty this side of Heaven," crooned Ooga as he gently kissed Nicky's hand.

"Ooh, I like him!" Nicky laughed.

"It is, indeed, fortuitous that we were able to rescue you from the clutches of those litigating savages. Although Eekim

101

could have expedited the matter," Ooga glanced my way, "by ignoring inconsequential and expendable details. By the way, my dear, I regret to be the one who must inform you, but Josh is not a wealthy man."

"I didn't think so," said Nicky, somewhat confused.

"Really? But it's the only logical explanation for finding such an exquisite creature as yourself in his company." Ooga sighed: "I don't believe I will ever truly understand humans."

"Well," Eekim brightly said, "I can't wait to get back to the tribe, lay around in the shade and eat bananas. I guess my work, here, is done!"

"Guess again," Ooga sternly corrected. "Granted you have done admirably well on the first part of your mission, with invaluable assistance from my associates and me, but you still have much to do. Remember? Massacre the worst of them, take back the bananas, paint their butts blue, and put them to work."

Eekim groaned.

"Here comes the cavalry," I said while thinking this was another time-honored tradition of movie rescues and escapes.

A line of flashing lights, sirens wailing, sped down the road next to the field. Police cars, ambulances, and fire engines roared to a halt, and uniformed men and women got out and surveyed the destruction. As there was no one to arrest and no one to receive medical attention, the firemen took charge. A man in a fireman's coat and yellow helmet began barking orders through a megaphone. There was a great deal of confusion as the firefighters were unused to battling fires beneath the ground. So, they focused their attention on the jets.

"Stay here, Nicky," I cautioned. "I'll go talk to them."

As I started out, I heard Ooga ask: "Does he do crazy things often?"

"All the time." Eekim answered.

They both sighed very loudly, making sure I would hear. I ignored them and continued walking.

I covered the hundred yards to the road. The firemen were busy but the cops and paramedics were mainly standing around trying to figure out their place in the situation. I strolled out of the darkness, they stared at me with surprise and disbelief in their faces.

"Hey guys!" I waved. "Man, am I glad to see you!"

FOREBODING FULFILLED

A week later I was still in jail.

Upon reflection I shouldn't have been too surprised. I mean, here these guys were, at a scene of massive destruction, and they were just doing what they were trained to do. The paramedics administered first aid even though I assured them I was not hurt. And the cops arrested me.

The charges against me were somewhat vague. Technically, I was arrested "on suspicion", but I was never informed of what. When I asked Sheriff Tolling about it he merely shrugged and said: "On suspicion of having something to do with whatever the hell happened out there."

It wasn't the most eloquent of accusations but I could kind of see his point. At the time of my arrest there was still the business with the truck and helicopter. Sheriff Tolling offered to let me use the phone to call a lawyer but I didn't hold it against him.

I had divulged nothing about the sequence of events. My previous experience with attempting to concoct believable versions of my battles with lawyers and their murderous lackeys had convinced me of the futility of modifying the truth to produce a credible story. I firmly held to silence, claiming complete and utter ignorance of all that had transpired.

Sheriff Tolling had been initially irked with my refusal to supply details about the events. However, his manner softened during the week and he became philosophical about the whole matter. As he put it: "Look, I'm just a country sheriff trying to do my job. We've identified the bodies of 167 lawyers and 213 assorted murderers, armed robbers, rapists, and various other perpetrators in the wreckage; not counting the four in the truck and helicopter. Any way you look at it, this has been a major victory for law enforcement."

It probably had not hurt that the truck and helicopter had been eventually traced, through various dummy corporations, to Eddeck and Ispadded; the two lawyers from the canoe rental. They were unavailable for questioning as they had been present at the underground complex on the fateful evening. That night, referred to as "The Night of the Great Wiener Roast" by deputies, received a great deal of media attention. Ominous questions were raised as to what exactly had happened but the public reaction could only be described as thankful. Popular opinion held that whenever so many lawyers and criminals got together it had to mean bad news for honest citizens.

For once, the media seemed willing to allow the public a sense of triumph without attempting to dig up a sordid side to the story. Of course, numerous questions were asked about the association of so many lawyers and felons, but it all boiled down to conjecture as no facts were forthcoming.

The Missouri Bar Conspiracy denied any knowledge of the event. The Bar made one public statement: "Whatever brought these lawyers and criminals together will probably remain a mystery. It is beyond doubt, however, that whatever the role of the lawyers was, it was certainly honorable, noble, and respectable." This statement was often quoted as indisputable proof that the Missouri Bar possessed a highly developed sense of humor and that lawyers could tell a joke with a straight face.

Suggestions by The Missouri Bar that the flag be annually lowered to half-mast as a national day of mourning were met with an enthusiastic groundswell of public support that a National Holiday be declared. Although neither suggestion was enacted, a peculiar local celebration developed during the years ahead, culminating in a symbolic Wiener Roast in which 167 hot dogs (dressed in small three-piece suits with little briefcases attached) were thrown into a fire until thoroughly charred. Area ministers often utilized analogies of the "purifying fires of hell" in sermons during this week of celebration. The festival's fireworks, of course, took on a special meaning for jubilant spectators.

After seven days of incarceration I lay awake on my bunk, trying to decide my next course of action while mentally reviewing the many movies I had seen which featured prison escapes.

I concluded that any knowledge which lawyers' may have had concerning my mission had been destroyed with the fire. Not one lawyer had even so much as requested to see me, there had been no intricate legal maneuvering to force my testimony or transfer, and there had been no attempts on my life. I welcomed the indifference as an omen that my breathing was not the object of plots targeting its immediate interruption. I tentatively reviewed my previous plan of telling the truth.

A scratching sound emanated from the chicken wire which covered the bars on the small window to my cell. I stood on the chair and whispered into the night: "We've got to stop meeting like this."

"Well, if you'd stick to my plans we wouldn't have to," grinned Eekim. He was hanging upside down by his tail, his little fingers clutching the chicken wire. He smiled #672, which means: "I'm having fun, are you?".

"No one told you to surrender to the authorities, did they?"

"Well, no," I admitted, "but it seemed like the thing to do at the time. Did Nicky get home all right?"

"Oh sure," Eekim assured me. "I took her to the truck, it was still beside the road where you were captured, and she drove home. She's a very discriminating young lady, she had much to say about my ingenuity, courage and resourcefulness."

"Did she say anything about me?"

"Yea, she thought surrendering was a dumb idea too."

"Well," I cleared my throat to disguise a minor surge of dismay and changed the subject. "What's the plan for getting me out of here?"

"Don't worry," Eekim said, "it's all set. You'll like this, it's very simple and easy to understand. We merely wait until they get tired of keeping you locked up. When they unlock the cell and release you, you start walking away and then you keep going."

"Sheer genius, how did you come up with that?" I slightly sneered.

"Look," Eekim seriously replied, "I'm a law-abiding monkey and I would just as soon official law enforcement agencies remain unaware of my existence. It's one thing to take on lawyers, it's quite another to be listed in every cop computer in the country. My appearance would not be very easy to disguise, you know."

"I suppose you're right," I conceded.

"It shouldn't be long before they release you," he reassured me. "That's why I'm back. I figured I'd be here when you greet the world once more as a free man."

"That's very considerate. Where have you been?"

"Oh, I took a week and went back to the jungle. You should have been there! I was welcomed like a hero and treated like a king! The shadiest trees, the best bananas, lots of wine and singing and dancing. It was great! Rhia was extremely happy to see me. She asked about you, she worries about you."

"What did she say?" A week in jail had left me starved for any tidbit of concern by a female for my well-being, and I had fond memories of my encounter with Rhia. Although she was a monkey, she had a very full-of-life, exuberant quality which somehow transcended species differences. I would probably always think well of Rhia.

"She said: 'Whatever happened to what's his name? That guy that got stinking drunk. I worry about him!'."

I immediately recanted my earlier feelings: "That slut, that bitch, that....."

"Careful," Eekim evenly said, "you're talking about the primate of my dreams, my simian sweetheart."

"Sorry," I said, realizing my reaction was truly out of line. "I guess I'm getting a little stir-crazy."

"It's an interesting variation of the other forms which you tend to exhibit," Eekim noted. "Don't worry about it. After all, you're only human." Eekim smiled #1265, which means: "I like you in spite of your faults. But definitely keep working on those faults."

I wanted to make some sort of conciliatory remark to smooth the awkward moment. Eekim had always been vulnerable to flattery.

"Hey, you did a great job on that guard in my other cell! Where'd you get the banana? And how did you get there?"

"You know I hate to brag but it was sheer genius, wasn't it?" Eekim laughed. "Well, after those humans captured you, I hitched a ride on the back of the black Bronco because it was last in the convoy. I jumped off when we got to the complex. Ooga already told you that we've had that place under surveillance for some time, so I hooked up with the monkeys already there. Then we contacted Ooga and planned the sabotage. My job was to save Nicky, and you if possible, while other monkeys took care of the jets and wired the explosives which were already on hand. The lawyers already suspected our presence and there were lots of traps around, baited with bananas. I merely disarmed one, several in fact, ate the bananas and kept the peel which I used against your guard. A special commando monkey squad intercepted the saboteurs at the industrial plant and then phoned in the phony catastrophe report. The rest is history."

"And while I languished in prison you went off for a week of partying," I mused.

"Languished in prison," Eekim scoffed. "Until we were sure you were safe from lawyers, we figured it was the best place for you. I told Nicky to stay away, for her own safety, in case lawyers tried to kill you."

"Very considerate."

"What are you complaining about?" Eekim was incredulous. "You're lucky to be alive! And you've had a week of rest, relaxation, free room and board; all at taxpayer expense. You're not entitled to that, you know. You're not really a criminal," he accused.

"Maybe I'm just an ingrate," I said. "Seriously, I'm still considering my original plan. What do you think of my telling Sheriff Tolling the complete truth about what's happened."

"Well," Eekim surmised, "that's one sure way to stay out of trouble."

"You really think so?"

Eekim shrugged: "Of course. What kind of trouble can you get into when you're sedated and wearing a straitjacket in a room with padded walls? Look, I know it goes against your nature but don't do anything stupid. I'll see you when you get out, jailbird." And he was gone.

AND ON THE EIGHTH DAY...

On the eighth day of my confinement I opened my eyes and was greeted by the familiar sight of the stained bottom of the top mattress in the jail bunkbed in which I had been sleeping. I morosely contemplated that God had created the universe in seven days while I had spent the previous week idly incarcerated. I know I'm not God, but I still felt like I had wasted my time.

I glanced around the cell and noticed a formidable addition. A rather unkempt and disreputable individual stared at me from the other bunk in the cell. He looked to be about twenty-five years old, a little over six feet tall when standing, and a lean 220 pounds. He wore tattered blue jeans and a dirty gray shirt. Stubble from several days growth made his face appear dirty and his hair was tousled and greasy. Piercing black eyes hinted of potential danger.

"Good morning, cellmate," I greeted. Friendliness, I quickly decided, might be the best approach.

"Mornin'," he gruffly replied.

After an awkward moment of silence I decided introductions might be in order. "My name's Josh."

"So?"

"Just thought we ought to get acquainted. It's kind of a small cell for two strangers to share."

I had heard that, with certain mentalities, friendliness is interpreted as weakness. The man's posture, even sitting, uncomfortably resembled a predator preparing to pounce on prey. I kept my voice calm and indifferent: "Doesn't really matter either way."

I focused my attention on the ceiling, and meticulously began to count the cracks. Then I catalogued the various spider webs and assigned names to the arachnids which inhabited them. After that, I mentally recited the ABC's a couple of times, and then began to aimlessly count numbers. I never looked at the man although he continued to stare at me from the other bunk. When I reached 2,465 he sighed, leaned back, and relaxed.

"My name's Maurice," he declared. "And I don't tolerate white boys making fun of it."

"Wouldn't think of it," I truthfully replied. "Make yourself at home, Maurice. I'd offer you a beer but I haven't been able to get to the liquor store lately."

He laughed at that, which I took as a positive sign. My

experience had shown that a sane man, even a "tough guy", was much less likely to beat you to a pulp if he was laughing. Crazy men, of course, were a different matter. But, Maurice appeared relatively normal, just a little rough around the edges.

"What're you in for?" he asked.

"I'm not really sure. Been here a week now, but they haven't charged me with anything. I'm being held on suspicion."

"Suspicion of what?"

"Just a general suspicion that I may have done something and that, whatever I may have done, it was illegal."

"You need a lawyer," Maurice advised.

"I had one once. I don't ever want another one."

A puzzled expression crossed Maurice's features: "You involved with drugs?"

It was my turn to look puzzled: "I drink a little, but that's all. Drugs take your money, destroy your spirit and ruin your life. I don't need drugs, lawyers have done all that for me."

"I know what you mean," Maurice laughed again, this time more easily than the first. He launched into a verbal tirade which would have embarrassed a scurvy buccaneer. He began by calling lawyers every name in the book and when he finished the book he added a few more chapters, footnotes and glossary. Ranting and raving, he ascribed every disgusting and perverted act as the unnatural preoccupations of lawyers. He made allegations against their parentage, their methods of conception and their rightful place in the food chain. This lasted for about ten minutes then, having warmed up, he issued a long soliloquy on lawyer tricks, lies and thievery. The main themes of his speech involved frequent repetitions of phrases which incorporated words such as: money-grubbing, greedy, heartless, amoral, hell-bound, good for nothing, overpriced, conceited, lying, rich, self-serving, two-faced, and a host of innovative obscenities (the recitation of which I will spare you, my respected reader). I found it impossible not to like the guy.

Maurice finished and paused to catch his breath. His dark eyes fixed me with a defiant glare as if daring me to disagree. I, of course, had no intention of doing so.

"You got that right," I commented.

I waited for Maurice's breathing to return to normal and

for his blood pressure to lower from a homicidal level. While waiting, I decided to try my story out on Maurice. He would certainly be a receptive listener.

"Listen," I began when his pupils were no longer dilated, "my trouble started when I took a canoe trip...." I told the whole story: Eekim, Ooga, Rhia, Squeeky, banana wine, lawyers, their plot, Nicky, the truck, the helicopter, and the underground complex.

When the tale was told I leaned back with my hands behind my head and waited for his reaction. He stared at me for several minutes and then slowly got up. Without taking his eyes off me he stealthily crept to the cell door. Banging a tin cup on the bars he started yelling: "Guard! Guard! Get me out of here!"

Personally, I thought this a bit melodramatic.

This reaction should not have been totally unanticipated but still caught me by surprise. I lowered my arms and would have attempted to better explain the situation. At my slightest movement, however, Maurice whirled on me with the wild look of a desperate man prepared to defend himself to the death. I froze and merely stared at the opposite corner of the room, trying not to further excite him.

The guard arrived and Maurice whispered to him. The officer looked at me in disbelief and said: "Him? He doesn't look like much!"

I was coming to accept this phrase with a kind of indifferent superiority. A lot of people were sure going to a lot of trouble to kill me, capture me or lock me up for me not to be much.

Maurice frantically whispered again.

The officer carefully unlocked the cell. Jingling his key ring as if it were a voodoo totem which could ward off evil spirits the guard nervously looked over his shoulder at me as he escorted Maurice away.

I spent the next two hours pondering my attempt at honesty and how irritating it was for Eekim to be right all the time.

Sheriff Tolling strolled, whistling, down the hall and stopped in front of my cell: "Come on, we have to talk."

The sheriff acted cheerful and casual but I noticed he kept his baton handy and maintained a cautious three pace distance behind me as we walked to his office. He motioned for me to sit down and eased himself into the chair behind his desk. His fingers lightly drummed the handle of the baton which he had placed on top of his desk.

"How'd you do it?" he asked.

"How'd I do what?" I asked back.

"You know, how'd you spot the officer we planted in your cell? You sure had him going with that wild story you concocted. He really thought you were crazy. You did spot him, didn't you?"

"Yea," I admitted, "that's it, I spotted him. It was just a hunch."

"That's what I thought," laughed the sheriff. "You don't look smart enough to've figured it out. Just a hunch, huh? Well, can't win 'em all."

A knock at the door was preceded by the entrance of a spit and polish state patrolman. His slightly menacing black eyes surveyed the room.

"Hello Maurice," I greeted.

"Actually, it's Bob," he corrected. "Well, Josh, you suckered me on that one. How'd you spot me?"

"Like I told the sheriff, just a hunch. You did a good job of acting. That speech you gave on lawyers was very convincing."

"Thanks," said Maurice/Bob. "In undercover work it's always best to go with the truth whenever possible."

"Josh," the sheriff genially stated, "I guess we owe you an apology. You should have told us you knew Nicky. After Bob told me your story I gave her a call. She vouched for you and that's good enough for me. You're free to go. Sorry to have locked you up but you must admit the whole thing is a little out of the ordinary. I gotta say, I admire the way you refused to associate with lawyers while you were in jail. That showed some class."

"No real harm done," I said. "Nicky vouched for my story?"

Maurice/Bob and Tolling immediately broke into loud

guffaws. I joined in, the thought of not delaying my release uppermost in my mind. The laughter slowly ebbed and the sheriff wiped a tear from his eye.

"Enough, Josh, I'll bust a gut," he chuckled. "Nicky vouched for you and she explained that you liked to tell crazy stories just to pull a person's leg. She told me the one about the 'flying rock', that's a doozie! Mind if I use it?"

"Feel free," I offered. "And sheriff, speaking of feeling free...."

A few minutes later I walked out of the station. Fresh air smelled wonderful compared to the sour sweat, urine and sanitizer aroma which had permeated my cell. The stimulating energy of sun on my flesh convinced me I was capable of photosynthesis. I know it is physically impossible to derive nourishment directly from sunlight but perhaps the feeling was spiritual in nature. It was very enlightening. I experienced that infrequent, mystical, it's-great-to-be-alive feeling. I stretched and, remembering Eekim's advice, started walking and kept going.

Nicky pulled up to the curb in the red and black primer truck: "Hey stranger, new in town?"

I reached for the door handle and joked: "Young lady, you shouldn't associate with ex-cons like myself. What will people think?"

"Like my Dad says: 'I'll worry about what people think when they start'," she laughed.

Eekim grinned from his hiding place on the floorboard: "Welcome back, partner!"

CHAPTER SEVEN

MONKEY BUSINESS

The curtain rises on the lighted stage. Nicky makes her appearance to thunderous applause. Her sequined costume, a low-cut tuxedo top with bikini bottoms, accentuates her sexual appeal in a tastefully tantalizing manner. Top hat and high heels contribute to her natural statuesque beauty. Applause increases as she bestows her charming smile upon the audience.

She has the innate ability to make everyone think she is smiling just for them. Her empathic relation to an audience is so strong that she has been known to receive standing ovations merely for smiling. Tonight's crowd is less overtly responsive although the cheering continues for several moments while Nicky postures and poses. She has developed a number of artistic, but provocative, gestures and movements to fill the time when the audience expresses appreciation.

As the applause subsides she steps to the microphone. Her crisp voice amplifies throughout the theater and quiets the audience as if they are listening to an oracle of mystic origin. Static tension creates a magical atmosphere.

"I'm sure you've all heard of captive audiences, but few acts have created such controversy as to precipitate incarceration and legal actions in some of the most prestigious jurisdictions of the legal system," she announces. "Truly, they are captive performers! Here they are, ladies and gentlemen, straight from their last courtroom appearance, out on bail, and awaiting future subpoenas. I give you Monkey Business!"

I carry Eekim on stage amidst enthusiastic applause. My suit is tailored after the style popularized in Samuel Clemens' day; long coat, baggy trousers, white shirt and large, black bow-tie. The formula for our stage appearance is carefully calculated: Nicky represents the modern, the female, and the graceful while I represent the historical, the male, and the common. And, of course, there is Eekim.

Tonight he is garbed in a bright purple shirt with a haphazard pattern of day-glow bananas, glaring green pants and luminous yellow sneakers. Many patrons in the audience, in an action which has become one of our trademarks, immediately don sunglasses. Together, we represent a triumvirate of impressions: the male, the female, and the animal; the past, the present and the outlandish; the common, the graceful, and the unfathomable.

Adhering to our traditional stage entrance I sit in the chair, with Eekim in my lap, at center stage and say nothing. Eekim stares at the audience with his wide-eyed, mannequin grin which has graced the covers of most popular magazines. He keeps staring until twitters of laughter begin, chuckling follows and finally contagious laughter spreads throughout the audience. It has been written that Monkey Business is an act which "gets more laughter and applause while walking on stage than most acts get while walking off".

With a flourish Nicky unwraps a piece of bubble-gum and pops it into my mouth. I chew for a few moments while Eekim keeps the audience entertained by making faces. I blow bubbles as he begins telling the first joke:

"A blind bunny and a blind snake meet one another. As both are blind, they decide to feel one another to determine what they are. The snake feels the bunny and says: 'You're furry with long ears, and a cotton-tail, therefore you must be a bunny.' Then the bunny feels the snake and says: 'You're low-down, cold-blooded, slimy, and speak with a forked tongue; therefore you must be a lawyer.' In anger the snake fangs the bunny, injecting the bunny with poison. Then the snake strangles the defenseless bunny until the last essence of life has fled its twitching body. Ironically, these actions merely increase the similarity between the snake and a lawyer. The moral to this story is: No matter how low a form of life it is, never insult another creature by calling it a lawyer."

Okay, so it's not exactly a new joke, but it does have a few new twists and the audience loves it. Eekim's unique style and facial expressions could probably elicit laughter even if he was reading from a telephone book. As one supportive critic said: "Eekim's inimitable delivery and embellishments boldly take jokes where no joke has gone before." That line isn't exactly new either, is it?

Nicky places a cigar in my mouth and offers me a light. I heartily puff smoke as Eekim starts the next joke:

"A lawyer died. He went to hell, of course, and when he got there the demons gave him a big parade and the keys to hell. The lawyer was overwhelmed and asked Satan: 'What did I do to deserve all this?' 'Well,' said Satan, 'we don't often get somebody who lived to be 647 years old.' 'But I was 62 when I died,' replied the lawyer. 'Oops!' said Satan. 'We must have added up your billing hours. Don't worry, it happens all the time. Since you're a lawyer, we would have given you a parade and the keys to hell anyway. Glad to have you!'"

Halfway through this joke Nicky takes the cigar and, with distasteful expressions, puffs away. Although we had never billed Monkey Business as a ventriloquist act, people naturally assumed that was what it was. While never claiming this as the actual case we did nothing to dissuade the perception. Some cynical observers had once conjectured that perhaps Nicky was the ventriloquist, hence the cigar smoking.

Eekim tells a couple more jokes while I blow up a balloon and Nicky licks a popsicle (a favorite part of the act for imaginative and easily excitable males in the audience), and finally both of us play kazoos while Eekim sings a ribald song entitled: "Lawyers and Other Social Diseases".

After tumultuous applause we immediately launch the next part of the act, a rapid-fire question and answer session. Nicky and I ask questions and Eekim delivers the punch line:

"How many lawyers does it take to screw in a

lightbulb?"

"One. The client holds the bulb and the lawyer screws the client around."

"How do you cure a lawyer?"

"The same way you cure a ham."

"What's the difference between a lawyer and a prostitute?"

"One will screw you for money and is a known to carry every conceivable social disease and the other is, relatively speaking, a respectable business woman"

"What do you call a lawyer on a fishing boat?"

"Bait."

"What's the best thing about giving a lawyer a ride in a hot-air balloon?"

"Lawyers can't fly."

"What do you call two lawyers on a submarine?"

"Flotsam and jetsam."

"What's the difference between Dracula and a lawyer?"

"One is a soulless spawn of the devil which prolongs its evil, perverted existence by sucking the life out of innocent victims and the other is a fictional character created by Bram Stoker."

"What's the best thing about inviting a lawyer to Thanksgiving dinner?"

"You can practice on the lawyer before you carve the turkey."

"How do you know when a lawyer is lying?"

"Their mouth is moving and noise is coming out."

"What's the difference between lawyers and bats?"

"Bats are <u>warm</u>-blooded bloodsuckers."

"Why do trials take so long?"

"Lawyers usually get paid by the hour."

"What's big, black and looks good on a lawyer?"

"A body bag."

"What's a lawyer's dilemma?"

"Slipping and falling on his own sidewalk."

"Why did the lawyer commit suicide?"

"A sudden surge of social responsibility."

"What's the difference between lawyers and maggots?"

"Lawyers dress better."

"What's the best thing about being marooned on a deserted island with a lawyer?"

"No witnesses."

"How do you call a lawyer?"

"*SUE-ey! SUE-ey!*"

Eekim gives such an animated impression of a pig farmer calling his animals that this is the end of this segment of the show. The audience takes up the call and "Sue-ey! Sue-ey!" rings through the auditorium for several minutes.

Our audience has been referred to as "those people in our society who suffer from 'lawyerphobia' (the intense dislike and distrust of lawyers)", which could explain our sold-out performances.

There have also been numerous, scholastic papers written on the Monkey Business phenomena. Most conclude that the popularity of the act is due to three factors: (1) the hilarious antics of Eekim, (2) the choice of material; not so much the humorous nature of scripts, but the choice of an almost universally despised profession as the target for the jokes, and (3) the resilient nature of the human spirit in choosing laughter over despair when faced with an insurmountable travesty such as lawyers.

Eekim may have said it best: "Lawyers, if you can't beat 'em, you can still laugh at 'em. Of course, it would be more fun to beat 'em if you had a good stick."

The final part of the act is audience participation. Eekim takes questions, from the audience, which invariably concern the legal profession. We developed this improvisational portion of the program to counter accusations that the "dummy" must contain some type of recording device and that "its" conversation was merely a broadcast of a sound track. I believe it was the first time a "dummy" had ever been accused of lip synching. It was a fortunate ploy as this had become the most popular part of the show.

An elderly lady asks: "Why is verbal lawyer bashing so popular?"

Eekim pauses, thinking, and responds: "Because physical lawyer bashing is still illegal. Enlightened members of our society, however, are working to change these misguided laws."

A young man asks: "What is the function of lawyers in society?"

Eekim brightly answers: "Lawyers are the only thing standing between good people and criminals. Of course, the sooner we eliminate the middle-men, the sooner we can deal with the real problem."

A man in a beige sweater queries: "What should lawyers be paid?"

Eekim replies: "Lawyers should be paid what they're worth. Unfortunately, this would increase the number of welfare and food stamp recipients."

A college-age girl asks: "If a client is screwed by his lawyer, does the client have any options?"

Eekim quips: "Yes; unfortunately, they are all illegal."

A slightly tipsy woman inquires: "Is there any alternative to hiring a lawyer?"

Eekim smiles: "Lotteries offer better odds and the decisions are quicker. Instead of wasting money on a lawyer, buy lottery tickets!"

A little boy stands and asks: "What is justice?"

Eekim patiently explains: "In this country, it is anytime two or more lawyers make a lot of money. This is the only consistent and dependable feature of our system. I, personally, apologize to your entire generation for this disgusting state of affairs. You deserve better. We all do."

The boy nods and sits.

A scholarly woman, hair tied in a bun, asks: "It's been noted that our court system is clogged with silly, frivolous lawsuits. Why is that?"

Eekim responds: "There are a lot of silly, frivolous lawyers out there."

An overweight man inquires: "Why are they called Attorneys <u>At</u> Law."

Eekim gives this one some thought and says: "Well, there's no doubt it is poor English. This, of course, is in keeping with the lawyer tradition of utilizing incomprehensible language in order to project a mystique of sophistication. However, I personally believe it is derived from the phrase Attorney Outlaw. Originally, it was as accurate a descriptive as the redundant phrase: Criminal Lawyer."

A pompous, well-dressed, innately disagreeable, balding man rises. Nicky, who has been selecting the people asking questions, flashes a prearranged signal. This is unnecessary as the man is obviously a lawyer. Clearing his throat, casting a disdainful look at the audience as if he is ashamed to be in the midst of such average, common people, the man asks: "Aren't all your jokes merely insulting, rude, and insensitive cheap shots?"

Eekim seriously ponders the man and replies: "Of course! Keep in mind that we are talking about lawyers here. It's not as if the subject matter deserves anything better."

The lawyer, as has happened many times, refuses to sit down and blurts out: "Your act does nothing but degrade a fine profession!"

Eekim innocently surveys the audience and states: "We don't degrade the lawyer profession. We don't have to. Lawyers have already done that for us."

The audience, which has been laughing during the exchanges, senses the mood shift with the current inquisitor. Silence descends on the auditorium. Eekim confronting a lawyer is one of the treats our audiences look forward to.

I raise my eyebrows at Nicky as if to say: "Here we go again." Nicky shrugs as if to reply: "They never learn, do they?"

The man's face grows red with frustration as he proclaims: "Lawyers deserve respect!"

Eekim shoots back: "Lawyers get respect. Of course, they only get it in a court of law where there are armed guards and threats of jail to keep people from expressing their true feelings. On second thought, maybe that means lawyers don't get respect even in a court of law. Maybe it's merely a situation where disrespect cannot be shown. Perhaps the best a lawyer can hope for is a police-state environment where disrespect can result in imprisonment."

The man shouts: "It's insults like that which are making lawyers insensitive and thick-skinned!"

Eekim laughed: "Really? I thought the thick skin was Mother Nature's way of telling us lawyers would make great suitcases."

Loosening his tie, the man declares: "For your information, lawyers have guided the development of the political and social systems of this country!"

Eekim agrees: "That's true! But have you taken a good look at our political and social systems lately? I guess we should consider that a confession!"

Several members of the audience rise and begin advancing towards the man. A subdued mumbling passes through the audience: "He's a lawyer! He's a lawyer!"

"People, please!" Eekim pleads. "No violence, do not abuse that man. He acts like a lawyer, so God knows he deserves it, but do not allow yourselves to be pulled down to his level. In this country a man should be innocent until proven guilty, instead of innocent until proven poor as is the current state of affairs. But the fact remains, there is no definite proof that he is a lawyer. Don't hurt him!"

With grumbling and threatening stares the advancing individuals retake their seats. Of course, neither Eekim nor I really care if a lawyer falls prey to the whims of an outraged mob. This would merely be an example of social progress in action. We have had far too many experiences with lawyers to maintain any sympathy for them.

However, a fight had occurred at a previous performance and the lawyer had sued us for "inciting a crowd to riot and perpetrate injury" upon himself." We argued, in court, that the lawyer had brought it on himself by being silly enough to declare himself as a lawyer in a public place. The lawyer, in order to disprove our contentions, repeated his actions in a bar, a fast-food restaurant, on a street corner and at a country club. This resulted in three public beatings and it is rumored that the kitchen staff of the country club performed subtle but creative atrocities on his meal.

Although the suit was subsequently dropped we wish to avoid any similar situations.

Eekim begins the chant which signals the end of our performance: "Lawyers uck! Lawyers uck! Lawyers uck!"

The lawyer, pointing at me, makes a final effort by declaring: "Why does your monkey hate lawyers?"

"Because he's no dummy!" I retort.

I enjoy this as one of the few moments when I am not the "straight man" in the act although the audience, of course, doesn't get the whole joke.

The crowd laughs and joins in the chant which gains momentum and volume. The pompous, balding man storms out of the auditorium and the audience expresses appreciation of this by increasing the decibel level.

Nicky, Eekim and I take our bows to jubilant applause and exit the stage.

BACKSTAGE

Eekim and I relaxed in our dressing room while Nicky went into her "reconnaissance meditation". She really does have psychic abilities and she has continued to develop her special gift. It's the only reason we are alive.

Lawyers made numerous attempts on our lives after the destruction of their underground complex. As these attacks seemed focused on me, we had concluded that all information on Eekim had been destroyed in the fire. Nicky predicted their plans for assassinations and we then took proper steps.

At first we merely avoided confrontations with the killers the lawyers sent after us, but when attempted attacks continued we started setting up the assassins for arrest. The lawyers eventually decided there was too much chance that one of their lackeys might talk and the attempts ceased. We still, however, maintained our guard and that is why Nicky periodically took psychic evaluation of our surroundings and immediate future.

Fortunately, lawyers almost always sent a hired killer after us because lawyers never do their own dirty work unless it can be accomplished on paper or by verbal deception. They prefer to leave physical dirty work to their hired criminal help. Nicky had found that she was almost totally unable to "read" lawyers, although she did quite well with normal people and even murderers.

The only really close call we had experienced was when a lawyer made an attempt on Nicky's life. That instance occurred when Nicky was waiting in the lounge at one of the hotels at which we stayed. A charming, good-looking young man had made her acquaintance at the bar and offered to buy her a drink. Nicky accepted because she could read no bad intentions in the man. She almost took a drink before she realized that not only could she read no bad intentions, she could read nothing at all. She distracted the man, whom she realized was a lawyer, and switched the drinks.

We never found out what sort of drug was in the drink but a half-hour later the man was babbling and swinging from the light fixtures. Psychiatrists later evaluated him as permanently mentally impaired and forever incapable of coherent thought patterns. He now has a thriving law practice in St. Louis and is considering a political career.

Nicky explains her power in vague terms. She claims she has no telepathic ability, that she doesn't "read" minds. She also claims that she doesn't really have empathic ability to the extent necessary to explain her precognition. She maintains that her power lies in the ability to commune with the spiritual world of souls, which enables her to determine future events. This seems as reasonable an hypothesis as any and it does explain why she can't read lawyers.

Nicky came out of her trance and blinked several times as if she were waking. She needed more time, and deeper meditation, when gazing into the future than she did when taking a quick read on the present.

She looked at us and smiled: "All clear. Everything should be okay for the next couple of days." After a pause, she lamented: "We were kind of hard on that lawyer in the audience tonight. He was really upset."

"Wisely is it written in the peels of my tribe: 'When the tiger cries, the monkeys laugh.'" Eekim quoted.

"You know what they are capable of," I added.

Nicky was most vulnerable to her sympathetic nature, what Sam had called her "soft-heartedness", when she came out of a trance. It was as if contact with the spiritual world made her more aware and regretful of the callousness of this one. Her gentle nature longed to bring some of the beauty of that world here.

However, this is the material world and if something is to be done here it must be accomplished in physical terms. Lawyers will not be changed by dreaming or wishing. Like my Dad, in a crudely eloquent way, used to say: "Wish in one hand and shit in the other and see which one gets full first."

Eekim and I were supportive on these occasions. Nicky was often full of doubt when she came out of a trance with an "all clear" appraisal. It was as if she were facing a pivotal internal moral dilemma. When the message was danger, however, she was as firm and decisive as anyone fighting for their life.

"Every historical instance of social progress has pissed-off some group of wealthy, powerful people," I said. "Some people profit from injustice, otherwise it wouldn't exist, and those people don't like the system to change."

"We can't turn up the heat on the lawyer system without a few fingers getting burned," Eekim added. "Tonight, we may have angered one lawyer, but we made hundreds of people laugh. It's a reasonable sacrifice."

He calmly lit a cigar, an action which usually angered Nicky and brought her out of her melancholy malaise.

"That thing stinks!" she scowled unmercifully at Eekim.

Eekim had developed a taste for the cigars we used in the act. We had reached the compromise that Eekim would only smoke them on the roof or, occasionally, when important matters were discussed.

"Yes, it does," he admitted. "It's too bad. Aside from the smell, the ashes all over the place, the smoke in the eyes, the infrequent burn holes and the health hazards; they're really quite enjoyable. But, as we agreed, I can smoke on special occasions."

"They'll kill you," Nicky ruefully added.

"My dear," Eekim calmly retorted as he puffed on the cigar and exhaled a couple of smoke rings, "after living among humans for almost a year now, that factor must be posted in the 'plus' column."

"Cynic," Nicky grumbled.

"Optimist," Eekim laughed.

"What's the special occasion?" I interrupted. I knew full well that the debate which was brewing could go on for hours without resolving anything, as it had many times before.

"Well, it's like this," Eekim slowly said. "It's time to break-up the act. We set out to raise money for our operations against lawyers and we've done it. It's time to move on and actually do something constructive. Don't get me wrong, I like insulting, degrading, affronting and slamming lawyers as much as anybody. But you have to admit that aside from having a real good time, providing an outlet for public outrage through humor, and provoking every petty lawyer around (in other words: all of them); we're really not accomplishing much. It's time for Phase Two. It's time to paint their butts blue!"

Eekim confidently grinned at us and puffed his cigar so that the end glowed cherry red.. Nicky and I exchanged bewildered expressions.

"Would that be turquoise or electric blue?" I asked.

"I've always been partial to cerulean," Nicky joined in. "There's nothing more relaxing than a deep sky-blue color. Although indigo is very nice too."

"I could get some color charts from the paint store," I suggested. "I'm sure we can find just the right shade and hue. That'll be the difficult part. After that, all we have to do is grab some paint brushes, line up the lawyers, have them drop their pants and bend over. Do you think it will be necessary to give them two coats?"

"Wouldn't spray paint be easier and more sanitary?" Nicky teased.

"Make fun if you will," sighed Eekim with an exaggerated, weary expression. "It should be obvious that we cannot literally paint their butts blue, so we are left with the option of symbolically painting their butts blue. Tell me, Josh, why do you think monkeys painted the butts of yerlaws blue?"

"Red would look too festive? You got a good deal on the paint? Tribal crafts project? So a blue moon was a less infrequent occurrence?"

"To identify them!" Nicky interrupted, precluding further theories I was developing.

"Exactly!" Eekim agreed. "To identify them, shame

them, and punish them. By identifying them, they were naturally shamed and the public took care of the punishment. That's what we must do to the lawyers in your society. We must identify them so they can no longer walk around disguised as normal human beings. The shame and punishment will, naturally, take care of itself."

"So how do we do it?" Nicky asked.

"That's the part of the plan I haven't decided upon yet," Eekim admitted. "I suppose physical mutilation or shaving their heads is out of the question?"

"Our constitution protects everyone, including lawyers. An obvious oversight on the part of our Founding Fathers," I noted.

"Pity," said Eekim. "Well, I had three options prepared: mutilation, head-shaving or HOSTILE. Looks like it's HOSTILE."

"We're going to commit acts of violence against lawyers?" Nicky asked in disbelief.

"Not an unattractive option, considering it would certainly be justified," Eekim mused. "But no, I do not mean violence. I mean HOSTILE, or Hang Offensive, Sleazy, Treacherous, Immoral Lawyers Effigously."

"Effigously?" I questioned with raised brow.

"You know, in effigy. Symbolically. Like hanging a dummy of a losing coach after a big game. I had to bastardize the word a little to make it work, but I never hesitate to turn a noun into an adverb when it is appropriate. I really wanted to use the word HOSTILE, reminiscent of the legal term 'hostile witness'. If we're successful enough, maybe someday we can change it to Efficiently."

"That's a stupid idea," I blurted, "you've come up with some crazy ideas in your time, my little monkey pal, but this one redefines the term idiotic. If you think I have any intention of participating...."

"I like it," declared Nicky.

"It does have its good points," I immediately revised. "As I was saying, if you think I have any intention of participating in HOSTILE, you're absolutely right."

I hate myself when I do that. Sam had been right about

Nicky, she can twist anybody around her little finger. At times like this my self-esteem is equivalent to that of a pinkie ring, and not a very ornate one. I can't help myself. I feel extremely estranged in my battle against lawyers and Nicky is the only human person who knows the entire story and is on my side. Believe me, if a man can have only one person on his side then a beautiful, resourceful, intelligent, psychic woman is the person to have. On the whole, I have pretty much reconciled myself to the fact that, in circumstances like this, I am going to behave like a spineless, gutless, wimpy wonder. I'm a big enough man to recognize and accept this about myself.

Eekim has extensively criticized my wishy-washy behavior on numerous occasions. These occasions have always been when I sided with Nicky against him. At the present time, as my capitulation is in his favor, he is conspicuously silent about the merits of my malleability.

"Well, that's settled!" He declared in a triumphant, self-satisfied tone. "Let's celebrate! Wisely is it written in the peels of my tribe: 'When monkeys decide to hunt the tiger, they should cherish the time they have left on earth.'"

We returned to our hotel rooms where we broke out a couple of bottles of banana wine and ordered pizza. Eekim, of course, partook of his ever-present supply of bananas. With the gala solemnity of a last supper, we planned our campaign against lawyers.

HOSTILE

First, we established HOSTILE as a non-profit organization. We rented a small office in Sedalia, Missouri, the headquarters of the Missouri Bar Conspiracy although otherwise it's a nice town. Our telephone number was 1-800-SHYSTER.

With these unnoticed initial actions, we quietly declared war!

Our next step was less inconspicuous. Huge billboard ads appeared in St. Louis, Kansas City, Jefferson City, Columbia, Sedalia, Springfield, St. Joseph, Independence, West Plains, Joplin, and various other cities strategically located throughout the state.

The billboards cashed in on the notoriety of Monkey

126

Business. Most featured Eekim's smiling face and a short message informing people of the existence of HOSTILE. Typical billboard messages included: "This monkey knows better than to trust a lawyer!", or "When it comes to lawyers, it's a jungle out there!", or "Before you pay a lawyer even one banana, call Eekim! Eekim knows lawyers (he doesn't like them, but he knows them!)", or, simply, "Lawyers uck!". The billboards suggested interested people call 1-800-SHYSTER.

Phone calls poured into our small office. We added more phones and hired an office staff. Nicky supervised personnel. Her special talent proved invaluable as she weeded out incompetent applicants and also a few "plants" which were sent by lawyers to infiltrate our fledgling organization. The result was that we were blessed with an office staff of dedicated, honest and efficient personnel.

Mrs. Constance Miller supervised our phone staff. Constance was a very sweet, very proper elderly lady. She can only be described as a classy lady who embodied the epitome of the social graces. She was also an extremely vehement lawyerphobe.

The only "legal advice" we issued was: "never, ever, under any circumstances or for any reason whatsoever, trust a lawyer. Protect yourself with whatever means available and keep good records." This suggestion, of course, fell more under the heading of common sense than actual legal advice. But you can get into trouble offering legal advice if you're not a lawyer. They don't like people cutting into their pie.

HOSTILE's courteous phone staff explained to callers that we were not allowed to give specific legal advice, that what we were attempting to do was establish an informal civilian review board, outside of the bias and influence of the Missouri Bar Conspiracy, which could document, track, and dispense information about lawyers. We were also interested in setting up support groups for victims of lawyers. Callers were requested to give their name and address so they could be sent a questionnaire.

The questionnaire contained inquiries such as: "On a scale of one to ten, with one being inexpensive, five being reasonable, and ten being exorbitantly overpriced, rate your lawyer." (This is one question, at least, where lawyers were able to score an almost perfect ten). "On a scale of one to ten, rate the competence of your lawyer." "On a scale of one to ten, rate your confusion level about legal proceedings." (Another high score area). "Did you file a complaint with the Missouri Bar Conspiracy about your lawyer?" "What is your lawyer's name and business address?" "Please list friends and relatives who may be willing to fill out a questionnaire similar to this one...." Finally, being a non-profit organization, we asked for a small donation so that we could continue our good work.

The Missouri Bar Conspiracy was outraged after they purloined a copy of our questionnaire. Lawyers immediately issued a public statement which declared: "HOSTILE is a hate group dedicated to the destruction of the legal system as we know it. HOSTILE is using indiscriminate, mud-slinging, character assassination against every lawyer in the state. It is an organization dedicated to the destruction of the fine reputation of lawyers."

Our phone calls quadrupled. The Missouri Bar's statement succeeded in giving us free publicity, establishing the credibility of our group, and convincing people that we were a worthwhile, deserving organization. Donations poured in.

We established a data base from the questionnaire responses. Nicky used her unique ability to reject falsified responses. Most of these were sent by lawyers hoping to initiate legal action against HOSTILE.

In the very short time period of four months we were able to create a public opinion poll of every lawyer in the state, make those results available to the public, solicit donations to fund HOSTILE for several years and establish HOSTILE as the consumer advocate resource for the legal system.

We were extremely proud of our success. We had toppled the pedestal upon which lawyers had placed themselves, rendered them somewhat accountable for their actions and made the dream of justice a greater possibility for the average person.

Needless to say, we made enemies.

LAWSUITS, OR INJUSTICE REARS ITS UGLY HEAD
Eekim served as the official spokesmonkey for

HOSTILE. His status as ventriloquist's "dummy" rendered him the most unique public relations expert in the country. Only Nicky and I were aware of his true nature. To other members of HOSTILE and the rest of the country, he was merely an entertaining mascot.

Eekim enjoyed his status as a noncorporeal being and relished the spotlight into which he sailed. For instance, when HOSTILE unveiled its trademark (a gallows with a hanging stick figure carrying a briefcase) there was national TV coverage by the four major networks and cable. Eekim became even more of a national celebrity than he was during the heyday of Monkey Business. His was one of the most recognized faces in America.

Nicky, for her own safety, was reduced to relative obscurity. She was the most valuable member of HOSTILE because without her the rest of us would have immediately fallen victim to lawyer plots. Using her abilities, she protected the personnel of HOSTILE from physical violence and contrived litigation. Fortunately, lawyers never suspected her talents. I assume they are so enmeshed in the material world as to be completely oblivious to the spiritual. There's an old saying: "Your greatest strengths are also your greatest weaknesses."

And so it was that one day Constance knocked on my office door. "You're appointment is here," she stated in a genteel and cultured voice. "He's a lawyer," she added with disgust.

"Thank you, Constance. Show him in."

A man smoothly breezed into my office. He was dressed in a manner I was coming to recognize and loathe: expensive suit, expensive shoes, styled hair, expensive leather brief case, expensive jewelry, and a subtly overpowering cologne. The fact that he was sixty pounds overweight rendered his tailored suit into a rather satiric juxtaposition. Jowls hung loosely from his face and his chins were ever-changing in numerical composition. Sniffing once or twice, he surveyed my office with disdain. Sniffing a few more times, he quickly appraised me and was obviously unimpressed with my flannel shirt, jeans and no-name tennis shoes.

His expression declared that he had completely and realistically evaluated everything worthy of notice and was convinced of his innate superiority. This seemed neither to surprise nor disappoint him.

For my part I felt repulsed by the fashionably adorned porcine figure before me. A disagreeable, slightly sulfurous, odor seemed to loiter beneath the cologne. I wondered if it were possible to actually smell corruption (if so, it smells like insane cheese).

As is my habit, I tried to formulate humorous terms to describe this individual. "Those auditory lobes are a mystery," I thought. "Certainly they would make unsuitable silk purses."

"Pleased to meet you Mr. Wetwood," he sniffed while extending his hand, his voice void of conviction and his beady eyes sparkling. "I'm William Bilkem, from the Missouri Bar Conspiracy."

I grasped a soft, effeminate hand which demonstrated absolutely no animation and certainly no familiarity with physical labor. There was no constriction of muscles and no pumping motion. My hand recoiled of its own volition and an involuntary shudder ran down my spine. An inexplicable and haunting residue adhered to my palm and I hoped he was just using a hand lotion. A corpse could have completed the male-bonding ritual of a handshake with more success. I'm not the most macho guy in the world but when I shake hands with a man I like to feel that someone is on the other end.

"Call me Josh," I cheerfully invited, sensing that an informal, friendly atmosphere would put him at a disadvantage. I motioned for him to sit and inconspicuously wiped my hands on my blue jeans. I considered burning them later (my jeans, not my hands).

"Very well," he distastefully agreed, "and you may call me Will."

"What did you want to talk to me about, Willy?"

He glared at me to indicate he didn't appreciate the nickname and I smiled back to indicate I didn't care.

"So (he pronounced 'so' as 'sue') glad you asked," he began. "Josh, you've got a nice set-up here. You've struck a chord with the average person in this state and, even though you're critical of lawyers, we don't mind as long as nothing is actually done about the situation. We're used to criticisms, everyone's got at least one, but we're not used to anybody acting on those criticisms. Do you understand what I'm getting at?"

"No," I responded with a smile, "if you're getting at something go ahead and spit it out. I'm pretty sure I can understand it then." I used my best Ozarks twang and, as I anticipated, this seemed to further upset him.

He eyed me for a minute, sniffed, and continued: "Josh, lawyers do not mind if someone makes money off our justice system. That's what it's there for. However, we don't want people rocking the boat. This non-profit organization of yours, if properly managed, could make you a wealthy man. Do you know what I mean?"

"Sure," I brightly replied. "You mean: 'This non-profit organization of mine, if properly managed, could make me a wealthy man.'"

"Exactly!" beamed Will. "Everyone desires easily acquired wealth, that's why there are so many lawyers. Now then, all you have to do is play ball with the powers that be and we'll insure that you become a rich man. Just sell those buttons and bumper stickers of yours, rake in the money, and let us tell you the advice to dispense. That seems like a mutually beneficial arrangement, doesn't it?"

I was getting tired of his speech pattern, every spiel ended with a leading question. Nonetheless, I replied: "You mean all I have to do is ignore the principal upon which this organization is founded, steal the money which is donated for a good cause, and betray the people who have placed their trust in me?"

"That's all you'd have to do," Will affably agreed. "Just think of yourself as a prosperous servant of the judicial system. Just like me! Why, it'd almost be like you are a lawyer yourself!" He smiled as if he were paying me the supreme compliment and welcoming me into his brotherhood.

I considered whether polecats found other polecats appealing or if they just didn't have any other choices. If I accepted his offer, would I one day come to view Mr. Will Bilkem as a beautiful human being? The very notion of even possibly considering the potential contemplation of such a proposition was repulsively out of the question.

"Mr. Bilkem," I firmly stated, terminating the friendly

atmosphere, "I have no intention of betraying HOSTILE. I'm not in this for the money. I'm in it to reform the lawyer system."

He blindly stared at me for a moment, sniffed, and proclaimed: "I knew it, I just knew it! I could smell it on you the minute I walked in here. You have an unsettling and disagreeable odor of integrity about you, Mr. Wetwood. It is an odor which I have always found indicative of naiveté. This is the real world, Mr. Wetwood. Do you know what we will do to you if you persist in your actions?"

"I know what you've tried to do in the past. There are about two dozen people awaiting trial for attempted murder and various other charges."

"Yes," calmly admitted Bilkem. "None have been convicted yet, have they? Do you really suspect the legal system is insurmountable? Without admitting that I have any direct knowledge of any alleged attempts on your life, I must say that it will be extremely difficult, under current laws and procedures, to prove intent to commit murder when there is no body. You appear very healthy for a murder victim. However, I can assure you that the Bar Conspiracy does not intend you any physical harm. Alleged previous efforts in that area have been extremely misguided, mainly because you have an astounding quantity of luck and have avoided so many alleged attempts by so many alleged professional killers. How did you do it, anyway?"

"Maybe there's a traitor within your group," I suggested. "You know, a lawyer with integrity and character, one who will not condone murder."

"Extremely unlikely," Bilkem declared. "We have excruciating standards which are almost foolproof in weeding out undesirables." After a moment's thought, he hesitantly added: "Still, there are those rare, inexplicable instances where a lawyer has elevated the issue of morality above normal lawyer priorities."

By his painfully thoughtful expression I could tell that Bilkem was reviewing the involved lawyers and evaluating their trustworthiness. Invariably, one judges the character of others by one's own personal standards. Therefore, the contemplation of trust in others must be a very unsettling and unnerving adventure for a lawyer. I patiently allowed Bilkem to indulge his disquieting suspicions.

"Well, no matter," Bilkem finally said, shrugging off his troubled reverie. "The point I'm making is that we will deal with you in the courts, in our arena. Josh, do you have any idea what real power in this country is? Let me assure you, courts run this country and lawyers run the courts. Missouri lawyers are trying to maneuver into a position to more fully capitalize on this situation.

"Consider the S & Ls. Do you really think that $600 billion dollars could have been plundered from the Savings and Loan business without massive political and legal help? Do you think it was mere coincidence that about 50% percent of the S & L failures were in Texas, the same state George Bush claimed residence? Do you think it was pure chance that his son Neil was involved in the El Dorado Savings and Loan failure? Do you think there is nothing unusual in the Clintons' involvement with a Savings and Loan failure? Do you think the Supreme Court was doing its duty when it declared that RICO, a law which was designed to combat white-collar racketeering, could not be applied to 'lawyers and other professionals' during a Savings and Loan trial? Do you think the S & L questions will ever be answered when so many members of both parties are culpable? That's power! Unanswered questions demonstrate power. I think Adolf Hitler said it best: 'No one will ask the victor if he lied.' We're winning, Josh. What's the average person going to do about it? Vote? Once both parties are involved, does it matter who they vote for?"

Bilkem was making a very strong point. If voters only have two realistic options, and they are both the same thing, is there really any option? As Samuel Clemens said: "Congress is the only distinct criminal class this country has. It cannot be mere coincidence that 97 percent of Congress are lawyers."

"Look at it this way," he soothingly continued. "Lawyers are the power in this country. We control the courts, the legislature, and, quite often, the Presidency. Missouri lawyers merely want more opportunity to participate and get a bigger cut. How can you fight us?"

"With HOSTILE action," I smiled, admiring the wisdom of the name Eekim had chosen. "Lawyers are obviously worried

133

or you wouldn't be here. I'm going to fight with the things you fear most: public opinion, information, and accountability."

"You're nothing but a little self-serving egomaniac," Bilkem accused and sniffed, "you're no better than us! You're filled with the grandiose self-image as a crusader. Why, you're nothing more than a self-righteous troublemaker! You're drunk on a feeling of importance and power because you have established an organization critical of lawyers. Big deal, anybody could have done that! But you have a very sobering experience on the horizon. Soon, you'll be in the lawyer arena. Do you know what happens there?"

"Lawyers win?" I questioningly answered.

"Every time!" He steadfastly asserted. "You'll walk into an arena where you are alone, you'll be facing laws made by us, interpreted by us, and enforced by us. You'll be the lone gladiator and you will be unarmed! The coliseum will be filled with your enemies, the spectators will be armed foes, and the judges will have already given the 'thumbs down' judgment. Your defeat is preordained."

"At least I'll make a fight of it," I resolutely stated.

In my mind, however, I suspected he spoke the truth. Lawyers enjoy an invincible, strategic advantage in their own arena. In my heart, though, I had the resolve of the Missouri feud. I wasn't fighting because I could win. I was fighting because there was no other choice. A man who will only fight when he can win is nothing more than an opportunist. The bravest men are those who have marched into battle knowing the battle is already lost, but also knowing the battle must be fought if the war is to be won. Courage is required to lose a battle in order to win a war! Maybe Bilkem was partially right, maybe I was getting a little carried away with myself.

However, I again said: "I'll make a fight of it."

"No you won't," Bilkem heartily laughed and his voice rang with vicious amusement. "We will shame and humiliate you first and then, and only then, we will destroy you! We have no intention of creating a martyr. Your name will not live as a rallying cry for the oppressed public. The same rabble of downtrodden malcontents who flock to your ranks now will cheer and throw stones as we drag your naked body around the coliseum! The public is fickle, Josh. They really don't want to defeat us, they merely want to defeat someone, anyone, so they can enjoy a feeling of victory.

"Be reasonable, Josh," Bilkem urged, switching back to tones of friendly conversation. "Messy publicity will not be good for either of us. It will mean fleeting embarrassment for us and permanent obliteration for you. Let's compromise. If you could be content with merely appearing to be a leader of reform then you could still enjoy all the advantages, and more, of a public hero. The status of an icon is very important, Josh. The great unwashed public does not need leadership, they merely require the perception of leadership to keep them happy. You, Josh, could be the instrument of that perception. Make people happy, make us happy, make yourself happy; that's what I'm offering you. Isn't that what life is all about?"

"First you threaten me with total annihilation if I oppose you and then you offer me assurances of happiness if I join you?" I asked.

"It is our way," he acknowledged, sniffing.

"What about the lawyer I hired several years ago? He lied to me, cheated me, and stole from me. I filed over a dozen complaints which were ignored by the Missouri Bar Conspiracy. You didn't care much about my happiness then."

"Of course not, you were just another individual. Don't you get it, Josh?" he inquired with amazement. "Individuals do not matter, they are powerless. Back then you were nothing more than a person. You were vulnerable to the whims of any lawyer into whose clutches you fell. But now you have the potential to become a public institution. You are poised on the verge of becoming a social power. It won't matter what you do, it will only matter what you can convince people you do. The old 'reality versus perception of reality' compromise. Give up the struggle to attain justice for the security of promoting the illusion that justice has been achieved. Take it from me, it's a lot more fun that way. We will allow you to publicly spout all the meaningless ideals you wish as long as you cooperate behind closed doors. It's either that or we'll crush you into the dirt."

"You have very charming powers of persuasion," I sneered. "But I can't help remembering that you have tried to have me killed on numerous occasions and failed. I can't help but think that your current threats may be just as ineffective."

"Although, of course, I have no idea to what you are referring, believe me, Josh, killing you is not the worst we can do," Bilkem seriously replied. "We can dissect you piece by piece in a courtroom, over many, many years, until there is absolutely nothing left. We can make your life a living hell of litigation! And, of course, we can completely drain you and your organization of capital. Ironic, isn't it, that an organization dedicated to opposing lawyers should have to hand all its money to lawyers in a futile effort to survive?"

"That would be ironic," I reluctantly admitted. "But wouldn't it be even more ironic if someone were able to smash the mirrors which reflect your illusions, or able to roll up your sleeves and reveal the hidden card? Wouldn't it be ironic if someone revealed the sleight of hand with which your cheap parlor tricks are performed? Or perhaps even I am too awed by your supposed power, maybe even I give you too much credit. Wouldn't it be ironic if all I had to do was shout to the public: 'Look! The emperor has no clothes!' And wouldn't it be funny if the public shouted back: 'You're right! Not only that, but he's got one ugly butt hanging out there!' You're not sophisticated enough to be a magician, you're just a well-dressed, street-hustling, con artist. Wouldn't it be ironic if all the individuals out there, whom you seem to consider your private pool of suckers, were able to unite and pull the rug right out from under you?"

"That would be ironic," he casually sniffed. "But it will never happen. Lawyers have attained a position of social leadership and responsibility. We are going to allow neither you nor society to interfere with our goals. We <u>are</u> con artists, and we <u>are</u> magicians, and we <u>are</u> politicians; and we're the <u>best</u>! You can't stop us! If that noble public, in which you seem to have so much faith, were going to become outraged enough to rise up against us, they would have done it long before now."

"It is long overdue," I conceded. "But maybe the time is ripe, maybe all the ingredients are finally ready to be combined to bring about your downfall."

"Impossible!" Bilkem declared. "We are invincible. We

are in complete control. We are the philosopher kings of Plato! We rule, and if your philosophy is different from ours either convert, endure, or perish. No one can stand against us!"

With amused introspection I contemplated: "And to think that, earlier, I was worried about getting carried away with myself."

"Josh, this is the Golden Age of Litigation," Bilkem said as if delivering a summary. "Missouri lawyers will be in a position to take advantage or, dare I say it, initiate the next great scam like the S & Ls. Don't get in our way!"

Bilkem ponderously rose to his feet and took a card from his pocket and laid it upon my desk.

"Think it over very carefully," he advised. "My private number is on this card. If I do not hear from you by ten o'clock tomorrow morning, I will file suit against you. Good-bye Mr. Wetwood."

With a final glance around my office he sniffed and haughtily strode out with his nose in the air.

"Don't let the door bang your ugly butt on the way out!" I called after him.

HOLD MY MESSAGES, HOLD MY CALLS, HOLD MY HAND

Constance politely knocked on my door a few moments later and entered with a pile of paper for my files. It was something she did every day but I knew she had timed this to see how I was doing.

"New membership lists," she explained. "My, that gentleman seemed very irritated. Of course, with some people it's hard to discern irritation from their natural outlook. Did you say anything to upset him?"

"He's just another flim-flamboyant lawyer," I said by way of explanation.

"Well, no wonder," Constance laughed. "Keep up the good work, boss."

She leaned over and patted my head in a motherly way. She is quite aware that I find this slightly annoying and totally embarrassing, but she is also quite aware that there is not a damned thing I can do about it except laugh good-naturedly. For a proper and dignified lady, she has an ability to tease in a way which is immune to the normal avenues of protest. And she doesn't tolerate moodiness.

"Constance," I said in mock reprimand, "I've warned you before about physical contact between employers and employees. There is such a thing as sexual harassment, you know."

"Whenever you're ready," she smiled sympathetically, "you find yourself a good lawyer and sue me."

"Very funny," I grumbled. "please hold all my calls. I'll be in conference with Nicky the rest of the day."

"For someone so concerned about sexual harassment you don't appear to be worried about what people will think when you lock yourself in your office with a very attractive female employee," she primly criticized.

"Constance, please, it's been a long day!"

"Don't whine," she sternly stated, wagging her finger at me, "and don't beg. You're the boss, act like one! Sit up straight at your desk, dear, and don't slouch."

"Hold my calls, shut the door, and get out," I firmly said.

"That's better," she praised. "That's the way a boss should act! A decisive, take charge sort of person. Shoulders back a little further, dear."

"Now, Constance!" I raised my voice slightly.

"Well!" she said, acting miffed, "I never! You know, there's a thin line between a decisive personality and a dominating tyrant."

"Thank you, Constance," I said politely. "That will be all."

She smiled pleasantly and promptly turned to leave the office. When she reached the door she opened it enough for the rest of the staff to hear and said: "Very good, Mr. Wetwood. Don't worry, I'll take care of everything." She gave me a sly but friendly smile, flipped the lock on the door and shut it behind her.

Constance was a mystery to me. For a cultured and refined lady she had a very down-to-earth way of relating to people. She took seemingly random liberties and yet maintained a balance of socially acceptable behavior which baffled me. For instance, I was her employer yet she would tease me like a big sister might tease a younger brother, and I was just as helpless. For another instance, she liked for me to call her Constance and she would call me Josh in private. In front of the staff, however, she always referred to me as "Mr. Wetwood". It was one of the many things about her I did not fully understand. Well, okay, I understood it, but I wouldn't have bothered. I never cared much about appearances.

"Maybe," I thought, "that's why no one calls me cultured and refined."

Nicky and Eekim came into the office. The entrance to Nicky's office was through mine and the entrance to Eekim's office was through Nicky's. We set it up this way to insulate our secrets from the staff and the world. We had an open microphone from my office to both of theirs. This allowed us to have immediate access to one another without anyone else knowing the extent of our partnership. We were all immediately aware of what was going on, and could confer in private at any time. But as far as the world knew: I was the leader of HOSTILE, Eekim was a "dummy", and Nicky was a "private secretary" who performed the services of any other private secretary.

I admit that I, like anyone else with a little imagination, sometimes had a spontaneous, errant fantasy about that "private secretary" part. On the whole, though, it worked out extremely well. The only drawback was that Eekim continually complained about having to be carried in and out of the building in an extra large briefcase. You can imagine...

"Well, old buddy," said Eekim as he scampered to the top of my desk with a half-eaten banana in his hand, "you handled that pretty well. It would have been better if you could have somehow managed to paint the emperor's butt blue during that analogy, though."

"I was improvising," I defended. "I didn't have time to work out every detail."

"It's at least a nice thought," Eekim adamantly maintained.

Nicky slumped into a chair: "I can't believe we're going

139

to get sued!"

"Really?" I laughed. "I'm not even a little bit psychic and I could have predicted that! It's the only logical thing which has happened to us so far. If you piss-off lawyers, they will sue you. That's as predictable as the sun rising in the morning."

"Sure," agreed Eekim. "The guy with the funny-looking little ears speaks the truth. You really didn't see this coming?"

"No," she replied.

"Wisely is it written in the peels of my tribe," quoted Eekim. "'When you slap the tiger, you will soon be running a very important race.'"

"But I didn't see it coming," Nicky said in an exasperated voice. "Don't you understand? It's my job to look out for you two!"

"Hey, you have," I said. "We'd have been dead several times over if it hadn't been for you. But now we're safe. Lawyers won't try to kill us anymore. They think they have us right where they want us; in the courts. We're safe!"

I smiled #439 at Eekim, which means: "help me, our friend needs support".

"That's right!" Eekim enthusiastically agreed. "Wisely is it written in the peels of my tribe: 'The only place a monkey can hide, and be sure the tiger cannot eat him, is in the belly of the tiger'."

I grimaced at Eekim and smiled #1822, which means: "is that the best you can do?". Eekim smiled #111 back, which means: "give me a break, I can't be wise all the time".

"So what do we do?" Nicky asked, weariness evident in her voice.

We were all a little tired from a year on the road with Monkey Business and the months of hard work with HOSTILE, but Nicky had borne a heavier burden by feeling responsible for everyone's well-being. She needed a break.

"Lawyers won't kill us now. Why don't you take a vacation and visit your Dad? It will give you a chance to rest up, and you can keep up your psychic surveillance from there. Eekim and I can handle the preliminaries."

"That's right!" Eekim positively stated. "I don't know if I've ever mentioned this before, due to my modest nature, but I possess quite a knack for strategic planning. In fact, perfect planning which accounts for all possible contingencies and strikes boldly into the face of the enemy in such a manner as to insure victory is my forte. I am possibly the world's greatest strategist. And the funny-looking guy with the big nose, here, can probably be of some minor help. We can't fail!"

I smiled #376 at Eekim, which means: "you're laying it on a little thick aren't you?". Eekim flashed #787, which means: "do you want my help or not?". Nicky smiled #963, which means: "don't you two ever get tired of all these smiles?". Eekim and I both smiled #2, which means: "no".

Nicky sighed: "Well, I'll go home for a while. What are you going to do?"

"I'm glad you asked," Eekim grinned, "because I don't have the faintest idea. But it is exactly the question which we need to deal with first. What are we going to do? Well, we must first postulate a general strategy, and then proceed to work out tactical maneuvers while accounting for all possible variations in events which may develop. Shouldn't be too difficult. The first step is to realize that being sued is the most predictable thing which has happened. Therefore, the most strategic response from us is..."

"The most unpredictable!" I interrupted with a flash of insight.

Eekim looked at me with a blank expression and sadly shook his head: "An obvious example of why some are born to lead and," fixing me with a disappointed gaze, "some are born to follow. In short, you are wrong, Josh. We, also, do the most predictable thing. But, and this is the brilliant part, we do it in the most unpredictable manner!"

"That's the same thing as what I said!" I protested.

"An excellent example of the difficulty in explaining the subtleties of strategic planning to the layman," Eekim noted. "Your plan would call for us to do something awkward and ineffective, like write a book or something. My plan says: if lawyers want to sue us, we let them. But we let them do it our way."

"And 'our way' is?" inquired Nicky.

"Bilkem said it himself," Eekim continued, "lawyers

141

don't want a lot of messy publicity. In other words, lawyers want to have their own private circus. Confidentiality is their greatest weapon. People can't object to what they don't know about. My plan says we let them have their circus but we make it a three-ring extravaganza and the entire public is invited free of charge! We'll sell souvenirs! We give them 'The Greatest Show On Earth', complete with..." indicating himself, "...enthralling animal acts and..." gesturing to me, "...hilarious clowns."

"Thanks a lot," I mumbled.

"I like it," said Nicky.

My acceptance of the plan, by this comment, was universally recognized by all. I was not ashamed.

"And," Eekim demurely added, "if we need a shapely acrobat in a tight-fitting, revealing costume, we can call on you. You'll be our ace in the hole if we need it."

"Sounds like a plan," Nicky said. "Are you going to hire a lawyer?"

"Too risky," Eekim commented. "None of them are trustworthy. No, we'll have to do this ourselves. It would be a strategic blunder to employ a lawyer to battle the lawyer system."

"True," Nicky conceded. "I guess it's something we must do for ourselves. It reminds me of a quote: 'A slave is anyone who waits for someone else to free him.' We can't wait for a lawyer to free us from the legal system."

"That's good," I commented. "Pretty sharp for a country girl."

"Country and stupid are not synonyms," she blandly replied. "Anyway, it sounds like you two have the situation under control. I'm going to get my things and head home. Call me if you need me. And I'll let you know if I sense any danger."

We exchanged good-byes and Nicky left the office. I stared at Eekim for a minute while he cheerfully ignored me.

"Why did you have to act like my suggestions were idiotic," I demanded. "You just took charge and treated me like a fool."

"It was necessary," Eekim plainly declared. "Nicky had to know I was the leader and that the plan was in competent, intelligent hands. Otherwise, she would never have taken a much needed vacation. You do want what's best for Nicky, don't you?"

How could I argue with that? Granted, the conclusion formed a nonsequitur which was unsupported by the premise, but the desired result had been effectively achieved.

Eekim and I planned strategies, counter-strategies and tactics for the rest of the night. I must admit, he is a perfectionist when it comes to planning. I had a few glasses of banana wine while we completed the details. It was four o'clock in the morning when we finished.

"Well, I guess that's it," concluded Eekim. "Not a bad night's work, if I do say so myself."

"One more thing," I corrected.

I pulled out Bilkem's card and dialed the number.

"Hello," a sleepy voice answered after only twelve rings.

"Mr. Bilkem, this is Josh," I said, feigning a rather defeated voice. "I've thought about everything you said, and I only have one question."

"Yes, Josh, what is it?" he asked, excitement evident. "Have you carefully considered your options."

"Yes, I have, Mr. Bilkem. And I was just wondering, do you prefer cerulean or indigo?" I asked and hung up.

Eekim laughed so hard he rolled off the desk.

"A brilliant tactical maneuver!" he chortled from the floor.

CHAPTER EIGHT

PRELUDE

A lot has happened since Chapter 7.

To begin with, Nicky had spent several months on the farm with her Dad. She had returned once more full of enthusiasm for our mission.

We had also hired a computer/electronics genius.

And HOSTILE had continued to function in spite of numerous motions by the plaintiff, the Missouri Bar Conspiracy.

This small miracle was accomplished in an unexpected manner. Although we had originally decided not to use the services of a lawyer it had become apparent that mere innocence, honesty and intelligence were insufficient tools when dealing with modern courts. One must know how to play the game. Fortunately, two lawyers volunteered their services to the cause. This was astounding as it proved that two Missouri lawyers possessed an honorable personal code of ethics, which were two more than I had suspected to exist.

Of course, the two lawyers refused to actually represent us, or appear in public with us, or be associated with us in any way whatsoever. They supported reform but would not risk destruction of their professional status, their families or their clients. They were quite aware of the potential for retribution. Our meetings were clandestine and they acted as advisors only. The advantage was that we could check the advice of one with the other. With legalities, as with medicine, it is best to get a second opinion if you can afford it.

The two lawyers were unaware of each other's existence and each would have been skeptical that another decent human being could have achieved the status of lawyer. They insisted on using code names and we never did discover who they really were. With their assistance, we were able to play the suit, counter-suit, motion, counter-motion, tort and retort legality game and keep HOSTILE going.

About a month before the trial, Nicky had insisted we hire an individual by the unpretentious name of Melvin Potts. Melvin was an electronics and computer genius who did everything from improving the programming capabilities of our data base system to fixing the automatic coffee maker so that it made a really good cup of coffee. He also installed a foolproof security system and routinely de-bugged our offices, which made Nicky's job much less demanding.

I remember interviewing Melvin for the job. He entered my office wearing blue jeans, sneakers and a plain, gray T-shirt. Sitting in a chair with a very casual, almost over-relaxed pose, he leveled a bored, washed-out gaze at me. He seemed somewhat lifeless with mousy hair and nondescript features. When I met his gaze, however, I was shocked to see sparkles of lightening flash in his eyes. The synapses of his brain had to be firing with gigawatt power to produce such an effect.

"Tell me about yourself, Melvin," I began.

"My name is Melvin Potts. I make things work better," he said in clipped tones which abruptly stopped. The conversation flowed into the forthcoming awkward silence like the splash of a rock at the bottom of a well. You know the feeling: you drop a rock down a well and anticipation builds as it falls. Splash! And then a feeling of disappointment when nothing else happens. "This guy's deep," I wryly thought to myself.

"Nicky says you're very good with computers and machines," I attempted to continue.

Melvin noncommittally shrugged.

"Are you?" I inquired.

"I improve things," he vaguely responded.

"Uh huh," I glibly acknowledged to fill the ensuing silence. In the back of my mind I heard another "Splash!".

I noted that the top of my filing cabinet needed dusting and there was a paper clip on the floor. For the first time, although I care little about interior decoration, I observed that the carpet could better match the color of the walls. I noticed the broken coffee-maker, with four or five file folders stacked on top, on a small table in the corner.

"Can you fix that?" I asked, pointing.

Melvin's nose slowly traced an invisible line from my finger to the coffee-maker and the disarray of files. He impassively surveyed the situation for a long moment.

"Do you want it to hold more files?" he asked.

I laughed, glad for a bit of humor to ease the clumsiness of the interview. I felt that at last we were beginning to establish a rapport. I was still laughing at his amusing comment when our eyes met and I realized that he wasn't joking. I immediately covered my social *faux pas* by indulging in a spontaneous coughing fit.

"Excuse me," I apologized when it passed, "I must have swallowed wrong."

Choosing my words very carefully, I explained: "No, I don't want the coffee-maker to hold more files. I want to know if you can make the coffee-maker make coffee."

"It's not nearly as challenging a project, but sure, I can do that," Melvin stated. He rose and went to the corner, set the files aside and picked-up the coffee-maker. "I'll have it back to you tomorrow morning."

Without further comment he headed for the door. I started to protest that the interview wasn't over and that I hadn't meant for him to go fix it right now.

Then I reconsidered and let him go.

MY COFFEE POT

"Good morning, Constance," I greeted.

"Good morning Mr. Wetwood," she smiled. "That nice

146

young man you interviewed yesterday is installing your coffee-maker in your office."

"Installing?" I said with befuddled bafflement. "It's just a coffee-maker. What's to install?"

"That's what he said he was doing," she cheerfully replied. "Well, he said a lot of other things but they were too technical for me. He's quite an exceptional young man."

"Did you talk to him?"

"Oh my, yes," she enthusiastically said. "He's such an articulate and personable young man when he's not being technical. Although," she noted with a slight frown, "he's usually being technical."

With a sense of forboding I entered my office. On the small table in the corner stood a contraption which in no way resembled my former coffee-maker. It was larger and had a good deal more buttons and knobs. A tangle of metal protruded from the top.

"What are you doing, Melvin?" I skeptically asked.

"Just finishing up," he said. "I've installed a few computer chips so that everything is fully automated. I improved your coffee-maker so that it's voice activated. You can input specific preferences for coffee brand names, filter brands and mesh sizes, temperature, strength, sugar and creamer parameters, and portion size. It has a memory capacity for 64 specific coffees and 146 filter brands and mesh."

"I really wanted something rather simple," I said while eyeing the various buttons and dials.

"No problem," Melvin stated in a monotone voice. "Just pour a pound of coffee in here..." he indicated a bin, "the smaller bins are for different varieties of coffee. Sugar in here and creamer in here..." he pointed out two smaller bins on the side. "Most people don't add sugar and creamer to a whole pot of coffee but it's useful for making individual servings. The filters are stored here and automatically feed into the system as needed. You just say: 'Make Coffee', it will ask for any further information it requires."

"Then what are all the dials and buttons for?"

"I had to have tools," he patiently explained, "for completing the initial interface of the operating systems, setting the calendar and clock, and inputting the primary information systems. I also plumbed into your water pipes so you'd never have to fill it with water.

"That might be getting a little carried away," he sheepishly added, "but I wanted to make a good impression on my first project."

"Well," I tried to sound pleased as opposed to doubtful, "it certainly looks involved."

"Try it!" Melvin encouraged. "I've already filled everything."

"Make Coffee," I commanded.

"Brand, please," said an electronic voice.

"Mountain Rain," I said, reading the can. I proceeded to answer the other questions on filters, sugar, creamer, temperature, strength and portion.

"It will keep all your responses in memory," Melvin explained. "You never have to input new information unless something, like your brand of coffee, changes. Then it keeps a memory file on how different brands should be served and how they should be adjusted for different filters. For individual cups you must always specify black or cream and/or sugar."

I hesitantly tasted the concoction when the coffee was ready. It was absolutely perfect.

"This is great!" I exclaimed. "It's the best coffee I've ever had."

"I programmed an internal file on boiling procedures, filtration rate ratios and hot water to coffee contact formulations based on gourmet recommendations. I also programmed some extrapolations of my own origination," Melvin stated.

"This is the best coffee I've ever had!" I repeated after taking another sip. "Melvin, you're a genius!"

"Well, if that's all for now, I told Constance I'd improve the coffee-maker for the staff and visitors," he said as if asking permission.

"That's fine," I agreed. "By the way, Melvin, what's that metal thing on top?"

"That's a revolving file folder," he simply replied. "It's interfaced with the coffee-maker. Just say the name of a file and put it in the front slot. You can automatically retrieve the file by saying the name again. It's detachable in case you don't want your coffee-maker to store files anymore."

"I like it," I stated, truly impressed with his ingenuity and thoughtfulness. "You did a great job, Melvin. I'm glad you're on our side."

"Thank you," he said and headed out in his quest to improve the next coffee-maker.

A demanding knocking issued from the large briefcase I had carried. I shut and locked my office door, and opened the case. Eekim scrambled out, complaining all the way.

"It's about time!" he raged. It was fortunate that my office was soundproof. "I thought you might be content to share doughnuts and coffee while I suffocated in there!"

"The idea never occurred to me."

I tried to sound apologetic but made it a point to remember the suggestion at some appropriate future time. Actually, there were plenty of air holes in the case, a space for banana storage and a container of water. There was even a small, empty, sealable container for emergencies. Eekim could comfortably survive in there for some time. Still, if the holes were somehow plugged.....

Nicky arrived. I ceased indulging my imagination concerning the case and explained the wonders of the new coffee-maker-file-index machine.

"I told you Melvin is very good at his job," she smiled when I had finished.

The truth is, I grew to love my new coffee-maker. It was more like an electronic friend than a machine. "Good morning, sir. Coffee?" greeted me every morning when I walked into the office, thanks to the calendar/clock and electronic eye which Melvin had installed. It remembered my birthday and other special occasions, kept an appointment calendar and wished me a "Goodnight, sir." as I left. I used its file index almost exclusively for all active files because it was so efficient. After a while, I found myself confiding in my coffee-maker and telling it my inner secrets and feelings.

I soon discontinued this practice. You see, the drawback with the device became evident when I worked late in the office by myself. I would be concentrating on my work and then, suddenly, for no reason, glance nervously at the coffee-maker. I sometimes got the haunting impression that it was watching me. This was not unnerving in and of itself, but I also developed a sneaky suspicion that it was smarter than me and that it was silently critical of my every move. It embarrassed me to realize I avoided being alone at night with it.

THE NIGHTMARE BEFORE THE DAWN

The TV set was broken so the night before the trial I lay dozing in my recliner. In my sleep, I heard the doorbell ring and got up to answer it.

The man standing there presented a somewhat unusual appearance. It wasn't that he was funny looking or anything but I had never seen velvet coveralls or a silk work shirt.

"My name is Ralph," he said. "I'm here to fix your TV."

"Oh, good," I said. "Come on in."

"What seems to be the trouble?" he asked while gazing at the set.

"When I turn it on, there's no picture."

"Well, I'd say that's the problem," he wisely surmised and continued to contemplate the set.

"Aren't you going to take the back off and look at it or something?" I asked after a reasonable time had passed.

"Oh, I can't do that until Tom gets here," he replied.

At that moment the doorbell again rang and I opened the door to find another individual in overstated attire. This one had on cashmere overalls.

"You must be Tom," I greeted. "Come on in."

"Thank you," he said as he strutted past me. "Well, Ralph, we meet again. It looks like I got here just in time. Put those tools away."

It was then that I noticed Ralph had opened his snakeskin-covered tool box which displayed silver and gold tools neatly displayed in a velour-lined interior. The tools looked as if they were polished more often than actually used.

"Mr. Wetwood called me because his TV is broken," said Ralph.

"That's absurd," Tom replied.

"What's going on here?" I interrupted.

150

"Well, Mr. Wetwood, TV repairmen have taken a lesson from lawyers and we've adopted the adversarial approach to TV repair," Ralph explained. "You've chosen me to represent your interests in this matter and Tom was selected to represent your TV."

"My TV doesn't need representation!" I protested.

"I must object to your attempt to deny my client due process," Tom replied. "These are modern times and everyone and everything needs proper counsel."

"It needs to be fixed!" I yelled.

"You don't look like much, either," Tom calmly declared

"It's broken!" I bellowed.

"That's an unfounded accusation," he stated. "And there's no need to shout. I insist these proceedings be conducted in a civil manner."

"Perhaps you'd better let me handle this," Ralph said to me.

"You'll have to excuse my client," Ralph said to Tom. "The average layman just isn't sophisticated enough to appreciate the subtleties and technicalities of modern day TV repair. Well, shall we begin?"

"First we'll have to ascertain if there is actually electricity coming into this house," said Tom in spite of the fact that the lights were on. "Also, of course there is the question of whether or not TV stations and cable are actually supplying a signal. It must also be resolved whether there might be some type of phenomena, natural or unnatural, known or unknown, which may be interfering with the reception and thereby giving the appearance that the TV is broken. I will, of course, raise the question of competence on the part of your client and maintain that he is incapable of correctly operating a TV. The larger question which needs to be resolved, of course, is whether or not a TV is "broken" merely because it does not have a picture. Does a TV have a moral obligation to provide a picture merely because the whim of the viewer demands it?"

"You're nuts!" I yelled.

Tom leveled his gaze at me and said to Ralph: "I was afraid of this. In view of your client's behavior I'm afraid that

I'm going to have to raise the issue of abuse. I think I can prove that if, indeed, the TV does not work then it is due to a history of mistreatment which has impaired the TV's ability to function properly even though it really wants to. I feel I can establish a case for the "Battered TV Syndrome" and prove that the real victim here is the appliance itself."

"You're a raving lunatic!" I yelled.

"Please, Mr. Wetwood," said Ralph. "The client should never be abusive to a TV repairman. It's an insult to our profession and merely confuses the proceedings. That's my job. I can promise you that no matter how long it takes or how much it costs we will triumph. You will, one day, be able to claim your right to a TV which works."

Ralph picked up my TV and headed for the door.

"I suggest we appeal to a higher authority and proceed immediately to Steve's TV Repair," he said.

"You put my client down!" yelled Tom. "My client cannot be forced to submit to an examination without consent. This is barbaric!"

"Well," said Ralph. "Perhaps we can subpoena Steve to appear as an expert witness."

"I'll get my own expert witness," Tom threatened. "Besides, you only need an expert witness because you don't know what you're doing!"

"I take that as an insult," Ralph replied. "You don't have a case and you know it. You're just a money-grubbing repair truck chaser!"

"That's it, Ralph," Tom responded. "This is personal now! I'll see to it that this is the longest and most expensive repair job ever. I'll bury you with an avalanche of documents on schematics, maintenance and warranties. I'll take this case to the highest repair shops in the land. This is just the beginning!"

"You bastard!" Ralph shouted.

"Scumbag!" Tom retorted.

"This isn't right," I protested.

"Of course not," said Ralph. "The one thing we haven't mastered yet is how to get our money up front like lawyers. But don't worry, I'll send you a bill."

"So will I," said Tom. "Since my client is in your

custody and therefore subject to your protection I do hope you won't pursue a messy course of action such as refusing payment for proper representation."

Ralph and Tom proceeded down the walk with my TV. I realized that not only had I lost my TV but I was paying for two repairmen instead of one. I could also look forward to additional bills from expert witnesses and a parade of repair shop appearances.

"We should have thought of this scam a long time ago," Ralph laughed as they walked away. "TV repair has never been so easy or so profitable."

"I concur," said Tom. "I'm getting rich and I haven't actually fixed a TV in years. Hey, let's have dinner. I'm buying."

"You guys are crazy!" I screamed after them.

I was still screaming when I woke up in my recliner. I got up and threw my TV out the door. It was, after all, broken.

DETAILS, DETAILS

"This is it! Our day in court!" Eekim beamed from his perch on my desk. He had dressed in an ensemble conducive to the solemnity of the occasion: blinding red Hawaiian shirt with bold, yellow bananas, brilliantly luminescent blue pants and stunning purple paisley tennis shoes. He looked like a refugee from a Dali painting.

I wore my 1880's vintage suit and had added a Panama-style hat. I felt very fashionable in an outdated sort of way.

Nicky modeled her new business suit; a tailored light-blue jacket and dress, and pink satin blouse (no tie). Her outfit was accented with black high-heels and matching petite, yet functional, briefcase. She sported the black-framed glasses to which she had recently taken a liking and her hair was tied in a bun. I missed her costume from Monkey Business but this was probably more appropriate. At least it made it easier to concentrate on the business at hand. Sometimes.

We settled down to review our trial checklist with my coffee-maker. The electronic voice enumerated a long list of specific considerations such as: all vendors licenses procured?, vendors confirmed?, entertainers confirmed?, musicians confirmed?, electronics ready? (we made a note to check with Melvin), businesses contacted?, RSVP replies from HOSTILE members confirmed?, press contacted?, major networks contacted?, radio station remotes confirmed?, decorating committee on schedule?, last minute reconnaissance taken? (Nicky went into her office to complete this task), fireworks ready?, legal papers in order?, lovely fresh golden bananas of the highest quality procured? (Eekim's personal instructions).

Everything was on schedule and all systems were go.

"Ready partner?" Eekim asked.

"Ready," I replied. "I don't know why I'm nervous. I don't really have to do much."

"Yes," Eekim nonchalantly noted, "amazing how the plan worked out like that, isn't it? However, I have made the best possible use of our options and limited resources. Just stick to the plan for a change."

"Okay," I agreed. Looking to the corner of the room, I commanded: "One cup of coffee, cream and sugar."

Eekim paused from eating his banana and watched the machine. It had always fascinated him. The coffee-maker beeped a few times and then said: "Boss, you mentioned you were nervous. Might I suggest decaf with no sugar?"

"Very good," I replied.

Eekim smiled and shook his head in amazement. He playfully asked: "Don't you ever worry that it's after your job?"

I was considering the possibility when Nicky breezed back into the room.

"All clear," she announced. "They're not planning anything we don't already know about."

We all just looked at each other with excitement and expectation. We had prepared as best we could and were about to experience either a major victory or total defeat depending on how the dice rolled; even Nicky couldn't guarantee the outcome because of all the variables. But we had worked hard and had planned well. Anticipation rippled through the room and my knees suddenly felt weak and trembly. Nicky broke the tension by gathering us all together in a big hug. My knees still felt weak and trembly but it was for an altogether different reason.

From the door came a very polite and dignified knock. I

154

don't know how she does it and I can't describe it, but when Constance knocks on a door it is plainly obvious that there is a lady of culture on the other side.

Eekim froze in one of his "dummy" poses as I opened the door.

"Your limousine awaits," Constance formally announced but her voice slightly wavered and she was vibrating with excitement.

"Everybody load up," I said. "I'll get the 'dummy' and be there in a minute."

Eekim protested that he didn't want to get into the case until we arrived at the courthouse. I couldn't blame him for not wanting to miss out on a limo ride, so we agreed that he would keep up the "dummy" act in the car. I grabbed the case, put Eekim on my shoulders and headed for the door.

"Go get them, tiger!" encouraged my coffee-maker.

Eekim gave a startled shriek and stared in horror at the machine. "Some monkeys would say that's a bad omen," he said in a frightened voice.

"Coffee-maker," I commanded, "delete 'tiger' from your vocabulary.

It sat quietly for a moment and then cheered: "Give them hell, boss!"

"Better?" I asked Eekim.

"Much better. Luckily, I'm not superstitious," he said while crossing his fingers.

We marched to the limousine, and the chauffeur opened the door.

"Okay, troops," I said. "It's Showtime!"

THE DAY THE CIRCUS CAME TO TOWN

The limousine glided to a stop in front of the courthouse. The location for the trial was a small Missouri town which, in quaint fashion, had the courthouse located on the town square surrounded by retail businesses. The setting was perfect.

We had surreptitiously contacted downtown businesses and arranged a promotional extravaganza for the area. The merchants had been only too willing to cooperate in an event which would bring people to their stores. Many were having special sales to capitalize on the free publicity.

Signs were everywhere, but the most noticeable were the red, white and blue "Monkey Daze" banners which spanned every intersection corner. Fortunately, we had been able to keep the name of the promotion off all legal documents and permits which we had been required to file. Naturally, the HOSTILE name had not been associated with the promotion, which was officially sponsored by discreet members of HOSTILE who had established an *ad hoc* committee known as the Association of Professionals and Entertainers Syndicate.

Booths and small tents lined the sidewalk. Cotton candy, peanuts, popcorn, sodas, bananas, hot dogs and candied apples were sold at small carts. Other vendors sold pennants, hats, T-shirts, buttons and balloons decorated with messages such as: "Monkey Daze", "Lawyers Uck", "It's at least a nice thought", "It ain't over till the blind lady sings", "Support Justice, Stamp Out Lawyers"; as well as pictures of a singing Lady Justice and, of course, Eekim's smiling face. The HOSTILE trademark, the hanging stick figure with briefcase, was not used as this was a clandestine operation even though we were carrying it off in a rather overt manner..

There were numerous game booths which featured novelties such as The Ball Toss (knock down three "lawyer" pins and win a prize), Darts (hit the small, briefcase target three times and win a prize), Ring Toss, a modified crane game (the object was to manipulate the noose and hang a lawyer) and others. Prizes consisted of buttons, caps, pennants, T-shirts and a variety of stuffed monkeys.

A large, red-and-white striped tent stood inconspicuously but mysteriously vacant on one corner.

Clowns, magicians, jugglers and acrobats wandered around performing tricks, jokes and adroit feats. Each of the streets surrounding the courthouse featured music; there was a calliope, a "jug" band, a ragtime piano and a small jazz band. The music was kept low so as not to interfere with the dignity and austerity of courthouse proceedings. It would liven up when court was adjourned.

Some of the festival attractions spilled over onto the side

streets of the square. Two radio stations had large trucks parked nearby and were conducting live remote broadcasts. TV camera crews were already on the scene and newspaper reporters could be seen interviewing early participants.

I waved to a couple of beaming merchants and they returned friendly waves and smiles. Not only would they benefit from the growing crowds but a major portion of the concessions' profit was to be donated for downtown beautification. The advertisements for the event had been timed to hit in a last-minute media blitz. For eight o'clock in the morning there was an excellent crowd.

It promised to be an exciting three days.

VOIR DIRE

The first part of any trial, aside from the paperwork, is jury selection. I will not bore you, respected reader, with a full account of all the silly machinations of the modern trial. However, an account of the highlights must include at least some mention of the preliminaries.

Most of you, at some time or other, have been lured (by promises of pathetic wages and threats of contempt; sort of a rotten carrot and weighted stick approach) to participate in our legal system. You have dutifully shown up at the scheduled time and patiently endured the tedious judicial proceedings. You have looked around at the other people who have been called and have probably felt a certain amount of camaraderie with the other bored, confused and underpaid citizens. You are all there for the same reason, right?

In theory, yes. However, extreme options can be exercised during big trials. Fortunately, Nicky had supplied me with a list of six persons likely to share a bias against our case. The list included two names of contrived "plants" of the opposing lawyers.

The potential jury pool filed into the courtroom for jury selection. The judge was seated in his chair. Mr. Bilkem and three other lawyers, wearing smug expressions, sat at a table across from us. Nicky squeezed my hand and flashed a determined smile. Eekim quietly remained in his case.

Bilkem commenced, in a pompous manner which was

supposed to reflect complex efficiency but was more conducive to an impression of egotistical self-indulgence, to ask question after question of the potential jurors. This went on for almost an hour. His associates proceeded to ask questions for another half-hour each.

Finally, it was my turn. I rose and thoughtfully confronted the jury pool.

"I will be brief." I stated. "Is anyone here an idiot?"

"I object!" said Bilkem, anxious to assert his mastery of the situation. "Such a question is an insult to these people."

"Your honor," I replied. "Unless the plaintiffs are contending that idiots are suitable jury members, the question is legitimate. Also, it is not an insult to these people because I am merely asking for a self-evaluation, not making an accusation."

The judge, a middle-aged, tired-looking individual with premature gray hair, overruled the objection. Nobody raised their hand.

"Is anyone here not an individual willing to stand up for your rights and the rights of others?"

Bilkem started to jump up but one of his associates placed a restraining hand on his arm and whispered in his ear. Bilkem nodded and then smiled at me as if to say: "I'll get you later." Again, no one raised their hand.

"Is anyone here related to, or associated with, a lawyer?" I asked, and nobody raised their hand.

Nicky flashed me prearranged signals and I located the two individuals she had indicated by referring to the seating chart.

"Mr. Underhand, aren't you related to a lawyer?" I asked.

He flushed red and nervously replied: "Only by marriage, I thought you meant a blood relation."

"I see. Miss Skulk, aren't you associated with a lawyer?"

Her right hand raised and began primping her hair while her left hand involuntarily flexed in her lap, but otherwise she maintained her composure.

"I work for a lawyer," she calmly replied, "but I thought you meant 'associate' like a business partner."

"I see," I said, and gave each a long slow look. Then I

addressed the entire pool: "One final question. Is anyone here honest?"

Everybody raised their hand. Mr. Underhand and Miss Skulk received some curious and withering glances for doing so. "Thank you," I said and sat down.

People seemed pleased with the brevity of my interrogation, and I was hoping that my simple and direct method would be a welcome departure from the usual lawyer litany to which they had just been subjected for about two-and-a-half hours. The recalcitrant disclosures of Mr. Underhand and Miss Skulk would, I further hoped, begin to arouse their suspicious instincts. I wanted to develop a simple and direct jury which would analyze information and not take anything at face value merely because a lawyer told them to do so.

The jury pool was led out of the courtroom and we proceeded to the selection of jury members. Bilkem eliminated a few individuals, evidently for intelligence, honesty or other characteristics which he considered undesirable. I rejected the six names, including Miss Skulk and Mr. Underhand, on the list Nicky had provided me. We, therefore, secured a jury free of lawyer collaborators, sympathizers, subversives and spies.

Bilkem seemed rather disappointed at this.

TRIAL RUN

There has been some discussion of adopting a jury system using "professional jurors". I do not believe this is feasible. The only way to entice people to listen to lawyers is to threaten them with contempt if they do not cooperate. You could not pay enough for people to voluntarily do it. Besides, such a system would entail massive costs for therapy and rehabilitation for the unfortunate participants.

But, I digress.

Bilkem gave his preliminary address to the jury. It was a lengthy oratory which extolled the virtues of lawyers and their role in the legal process. He implied that the modern lawyer was the direct result of the vision and wisdom of our founding fathers and further extolled that any criticism of lawyers was tantamount to a treasonous usurpation of the American way of life. He explained that the Missouri Bar Conspiracy would not tolerate

159

such unpatriotic attacks, accused HOSTILE of destroying the reputation of lawyers by spreading malicious rumors, and demanded ten million dollars in damages. He sat and glared at me with a triumphant expression.

I rose and solemnly delivered my opening remarks to the jury: "The accusations of the lawyer for the plaintiff are, of course, bullshit."

"Objection," screamed Bilkem.

The judge pounded his gavel. "Mr. Wetwood, this court will not tolerate the use of profanity! Any further remarks like that and I will find you in contempt!"

"Your honor, may I approach the bench?" I asked.

The judge nodded. Bilkem rushed up and stood right at my shoulder as I conferred with the judge.

"Your honor," I humbly stated, "I apologize for any inadvertent and unintentional affront to the dignity of this court. I merely used the most appropriate word available to describe the situation. I am not a lawyer so I plead for tolerance of my lack of expertise. In order to comply with your directive I must inquire as to the judicially acceptable term for 'bullshit'."

"The court recognizes no such term," stated the judge.

"That explains a lot," I said and glanced meaningfully at Bilkem. I swear the judge almost smiled.

"Ladies and gentlemen of the jury," I resumed. "The plaintiffs have made a number of assertions which we will prove are fallacious inventions. The founding fathers of this country guaranteed us specific rights, among these are: the right to a fair and public trial, freedom of speech, the right to public assembly, and, as a last resort, the right to bear arms. As one of our early leaders declared: 'When faced with an oppressive tyranny it is not only a man's right, but his duty, to rebel.' We intend to show that lawyers represent such an oppressive tyranny.

"HOSTILE represents a patriotic organization," I continued, "which is attempting to reclaim and reaffirm the rights of individuals. HOSTILE has not destroyed the reputation of Missouri lawyers. Missouri lawyers have done that. HOSTILE has merely documented the disgusting decline in their respectability. Finally, we will prove that the Missouri Bar Conspiracy has filed a malicious and self-serving lawsuit. We ask for ten <u>billion</u> dollars in damages."

Our reasoning was this: if the dignity of lawyers could be priced at ten million dollars then the dignity of an organization of normal human beings, such as HOSTILE, must be worth at least one hundred times as much.

Gasps and murmurs filled the courtroom at the mention of the sum for which we were counter-suing. The judge banged his gavel for quiet and the noise subsided. The judge and the plaintiffs were already aware of the amount but did not, I believe, take it seriously. The jury, on the other hand, wore expressions of stunned disbelief. We had succeeded in getting their attention.

TRIAL AND TRIBULATION

Bilkem called his first witness, a Mr. Daryl Iction, one of the administrators of the Missouri Bar. Iction haughtily took the witness stand and proceeded to testify that lawyers were great, the Missouri Bar Conspiracy was great, and the legal system was great. He used a lot of flowery terms and expressions but that was the gist of it.

"Mr. Iction," I opened my cross-examination, "you work for the Missouri Bar Conspiracy and are a lawyer, is that correct?"

"Yes."

"You obviously have some self-interest in testifying that the Missouri Bar and its lawyers are so wonderful. Do you have any evidence to back up your claims?"

Iction cleared his throat: "Of course I do."

"And may we see that evidence?"

"Unfortunately," he squirmed, "the Missouri Bar Conspiracy is a highly professional organization which compiles its information under assurances of confidentiality. I am not at liberty to divulge specifics."

"Confidentiality? Isn't that the same as secrecy?" I inquired.

"Objection," protested Bilkem. "The witness is appearing as an expert on lawyers, not as a dictionary."

"Sustained," intoned the judge.

"No further questions, your honor," I said. "But I would

respectfully request that you relieve Mr. Daryl Iction of duty as a future witness."

"Overruled," said the judge.

"Worth a shot," I whispered to Nicky as I sat down.

The plaintiffs called a number of other witnesses and the testimony was about the same. The witnesses waxed loquacious about the truly outstanding virtues of lawyers and the Missouri Bar. I asked for any hard evidence to support their testimony. They said it was all a secret but they could attest it was true and asserted that they really were sincere and honest people. I hoped the jury could see the pattern.

Towards the end of the day Bilkem called his final witness, a Miss Creant, who was a secretary at the Missouri Bar Conspiracy. She was a lovely young woman with a likable and bubbly personality. Nicky had warned me about her. Bilkem hoped I would unfavorably impress the jury by confronting Miss Creant; an action which would appear brutish and ungentlemanly. Bilkem wanted the jury to sleep with that on their minds tonight.

Miss Creant testified, under questioning from Bilkem, that she worked for Mr. Iction and that he was a wonderful boss. She was positive that he was an honest and hardworking man who truly cared about people.

It really is helpful to have a psychic on your side. I turned Nicky loose on the witness. The contrast of the two women was obvious. Although both were very attractive, Nicky made Miss Creant look like a fluffy little airhead. This was appropriate.

"Miss Creant," began Nicky, "what do you do for Mr. Iction?"

"Oh, I'm his secretary," she enthusiastically responded.

"You have testified that Mr. Iction handles Bar Conspiracy affairs with honesty and professionalism. How do you know this?" Nicky asked.

"He told me," she coyly stated.

"You mean he talks to you about confidential matters of the Missouri Bar Conspiracy?" Nicky feigned incredulity.

"Oh, no," giggled Miss Creant, "we never talk about business. I meant he told me he was honest and caring and really concerned about the well-being of people. He told me he just wants what's best for everybody. In fact, he told me again just yesterday and again this morning."

"Okay. Let's see, you're his secretary. Hmmmm. How many words per minute do you type?" Nicky asked. I noticed Bilkem was suddenly holding his head in his hands.

"Oh, I don't type very well."

"Then you must be very proficient with a word-processor?" Nicky inquired.

"Isn't that like a computer?" Miss Creant replied.

Nicky gave her a look of disbelief at an angle visible to the jury.

"Miss Creant, what exactly do you do for Mr. Iction?"

"Well, sometimes I answer the phone, and sometimes I run errands for him, and I make his travel arrangements for his weekend court appearances. My schedule is really weird and I put in a lot of overtime with him on weekends. He says I stimulate his thinking, isn't that sweet?"

"So you accompany him when he travels for 'weekend' trials?" Nicky asked.

"Yes. But I don't go to court with him, he says I would be too distracting. Most of the time, the trials get canceled anyway," Miss Creant noted.

"Miss Creant," Nicky patiently inquired, "are you aware that courts do not schedule trials on weekends?"

"Really?" Miss Creant responded with a confused expression. "That's odd!"

"No further questions, your honor," smiled Nicky.

Bilkem was shaking his head and staring at the table in front of him.

The judge wearily banged his gavel and announced: "Court is adjourned until tomorrow morning. I am placing a 'Gag Order' on these proceedings, and they are not to be discussed in public."

I glanced at the jury and was reassured. If nothing else, we left them laughing.

TRIAL AND ERROR
The press mobbed us as we exited the courthouse.

Microphones were pushed at us and cameras flashed in our faces as reporters assaulted us with several questions all at once. I raised my hands for silence and, surprisingly, everyone quieted down.

"I'm sorry that I can't say anything about the trial," I announced. "The judge has placed a 'Gag Order' on the proceedings. A 'Gag Order' is not a description of the physical reaction to the legal system but, instead, a mandate to make no comment. I am not allowed to say that lawyers are lower than the regurgitated scum adhering to a wino's shoes, or that lawyers should be shot down like mad dogs! Since I'm not allowed to say these things, I won't."

Nicky and I retreated to the limousine, with its dark passenger windows, so Eekim could get out of his case. He blinked at the light, even though it was rather dark in the car, as he emerged.

"Are you okay?" Nicky asked with concern.

"Oh sure," Eekim replied. "I love being in a cramped, dark box all day and listening to dull boring legal arguments. It was a real treat."

"You're the one who insisted on being there," I reminded him. "And you know you can't sit and look like a 'dummy' all day."

"I've seen you do it!" he retorted.

"Boys! Boys! Please!" Nicky implored. "It's been a long day and we're all a little irritable. Let's relax! Tomorrow's another big day."

Eekim was succumbing more and more to Nicky's charms. She was one of the few people for whose feelings he actually cared. It was touching, really, to see the consideration he showed her. Of course, this meant that his sarcastic and critical side could be directed with more focus at other people around him. And since I was the only other person around him, I was his prime target. It was a burden I could bear.

"Nicky's right," Eekim brightly observed. "Josh," he scolded, "I'm surprised at you for tarnishing the moment with your petty little complaints. Have some dignity, man! Show some consideration for your friends' feelings."

"Sorry," I reluctantly apologized. "I'll try harder."

"You were great today," Eekim adoringly said to Nicky. "We all did great," she said, smiling at me. I felt better. Having reestablished our camaraderie, we decided to stroll around the square and enjoy the celebration. Eekim adopted his "dummy" persona, and we walked around talking to people, watching the excited children and listening to the music. Everyone was having a good time.

THE DAY AFTER YESTERDAY

Court promptly reconvened. Bilkem immediately jumped to his feet with all the agility his wide girth permitted.

"Your honor," he proclaimed in his deepest voice, projecting his words in a manner which would have inspired the envy of an accomplished Thespian. "Plaintiffs wish to protest the circus-like atmosphere which prevails beyond these courthouse walls. There are people partying out there. And items which impinge the dignity of this court are for sale. We maintain that a fair trial is impossible under these circumstances and ask for a continuance."

"Your honor," I responded. "Defense is confused by the plaintiff's motion. The events outside this courtroom cannot be used as an excuse for actions within it. The noise and celebration is subdued during court session and presents no interference with court proceedings. The jury is sequestered and not subject to any influence. Yes, there are people partying. Do the plaintiffs object to people having a good time? Yes, there are items for sale. Do the plaintiffs object to working men and women earning a living? If so, I would remind them that they are suing for ten million dollars and, in light of this, a protest would be somewhat hypocritical."

"Your honor," Bilkem pleaded, "there are too many people out there!"

"The Constitution guarantees every individual the right to a public trial," I countered. "If Mr. Bilkem will consult a dictionary I'm sure he will discover that 'public' means 'people'. The Constitution includes no provisions which indicate that 'too public' a trial is possible."

The judge surveyed the courtroom and announced: "Motion denied. The defense will now call its first witness."

I glanced at Bilkem and he thoughtfully stared back. I could almost see the little wheels turning in his head as he thought about some eventual retaliation. It was a little disquieting and I made a note to have Nicky take a psychic reading for any new developments.

"I call Ms. Constance Miller to the stand," I said.

Constance took the stand with penultimate dignity and grace. The sincerity with which she was sworn in was enough to bring a tear to your eye. The jury was visibly moved by her genuinely earnest manner. Not a few, I imagined, were reminded of a beloved mother, grandmother or teacher.

"Ms. Miller, do you work for an organization known as HOSTILE?" I asked.

"Yes, I do," she replied.

"And what does HOSTILE do?"

"HOSTILE is an organization dedicated to lawyer reform. It collects, compiles and distributes information based on sworn statements from individuals with direct experience with lawyers," she concisely responded.

"And is HOSTILE an honest and respectable organization?" I inquired.

"I told you I worked there," she firmly replied.

A lawyer might have asked for a more direct response to the question. I didn't. Her reply was a more eloquent expression of the truth than a direct answer. She had made the impression on the jury which I wanted.

"Thank you, Ms. Miller. No further questions." I said.

"The plaintiffs may now cross-examine the witness," advised the judge.

Bilkem rose and studied Constance for a moment: "Ms. Miller, do you like lawyers?"

"Absolutely not!" she declared.

"So you admit to a prejudice and bias with regards to the very profession you claim to objectively evaluate?"

"Absolutely not," she repeated.

"I beg your pardon. Could you explain how your intense personal dislikes could fail to influence your evaluations?" he vindictively asked. "Are you a saint that you could be so fair?"

"Young man," Constance chided, and everyone was

amused at the idea of addressing a middle-aged behemoth like Bilkem as "young man". It brought to mind the picture of an unruly child being scolded by his mother. I imagined Bilkem in shorts, dirty T-shirt, sneakers and baseball cap, with his plump face smudged by sweat and dust, his head hanging in shame under a motherly chastising; and forced myself to stifle a giggle.

"Young man," Constance repeated when courtroom twittering had subsided (I think she repeated the phrase because she enjoyed watching Bilkem's face get redder. Have I mentioned that Constance possesses a mean streak which she is able to exercise with impunity?). "If you would listen more closely, you wouldn't ask such impertinent questions! I don't make evaluations. The general public does that. HOSTILE merely processes, summarizes and distributes the evaluations."

"Your honor," Bilkem shouted in exasperation. "Permission to treat this individual as a hostile witness."

"Your honor," I interceded. "I'm confused. She is appearing as a witness for the defense, so, of course she is a HOSTILE witness."

Bilkem, his mouth hanging open, stared at me. Realization finally dawned and he irritably stated: "No, no! I don't mean HOSTILE, I mean hostile!"

"What?" I innocently asked.

Bilkem explained in an exasperated manner: "I don't mean HOSTILE witness as in witness for the defense, I mean hostile witness as in antagonistic."

"But HOSTILE is antagonistic," I confusedly noted. "That's why we have the hanging stick figure and briefcase for our trademark."

"Yes, yes," Bilkem irritably agreed. "HOSTILE is antagonistic, but what I mean is that the HOSTILE witness is also an antagonistic hostile witness."

"What?" I innocently asked again.

"Judge," Bilkem almost sobbed. "Do you know what I mean?"

"I think so," the judge slowly stated, "although you are representing your position with all the clarity of an Abbott and Costello routine. Mr. Wetwood, the plaintiffs are requesting permission to treat the witness as a hostile witness."

"Oh, I wondered what they wanted," I said. "Thank you for clearing that up, your honor. The defense maintains that the witness is not hostile, and would inquire if there are any legal procedures for asking permission to treat the legal counsel for the plaintiff as a hostile lawyer?"

The judge shook his head "no".

"Pity," I noted. "As an alternative, the defense maintains that it has known the witness for some time and nobody has ever had the audacity to accuse her of being hostile."

After only a moment's pause the judge declared: "Nor will I be the first. The bench instructs the attorney for the plaintiff to stop badgering the witness."

Bilkem didn't like it but he swallowed his pride (in my estimation a rather minuscule gulp), and continued: "Ms. Miller, the defense has continually asked for documentation from witnesses who assert that the Missouri Bar Conspiracy effectively enforces ethics upon its members. As a representative of HOSTILE, do you have any documentation to support accusations of misdeeds by members of the Missouri Bar?"

"Of course I do," Constance righteously proclaimed.

She signaled to a member of her office staff who opened the door to the courtroom. Six other staff members began carting in stacks of boxes loaded on two-wheelers. The boxes were left by our table and three of the staff brought in more boxes. "There are over a million pages of documents in these boxes," she said. "All are sworn statements by individuals who have evaluated the lawyers they hired."

Bilkem maliciously smiled: "I have a list of thirteen names here. I'll start with the first three. Do you know if those boxes contain statements from a Mr. Jack A. Napes, Mrs. Katy Tonic, or Mr. Dale E. Terious?"

He leaned on the witness box rail and malevolently grinned at Constance.

She returned his stare with a bemused expression. She waited long enough for his melodramatic pose to become ridiculous and he self-consciously backed off.

"I have no way of knowing the total contents of a million pages of documents," Constance admitted. "But it's funny you should mention those three names because I do remember *them*. In the early days of HOSTILE, we received several fraudulent complaints about lawyers which we assumed were submitted in order to compromise the integrity of HOSTILE and possibly provide a foundation for contrived litigation. After researching those three, we determined that Mr. Napes was a lawyer who had filed a complaint against his lawyer father, Mrs. Tonic had filed a complaint against her lawyer brother, and Mr. Terious had filed a complaint against himself using a fictitious client name; his handwriting matched. Those three files are in those boxes with notations as to why they were rejected as legitimate complaints. How did you find out about them?" She casually asked.

"That's not important," Bilkem awkwardly responded.

"Well," Constance laughed, "perhaps I can provide further insight. What are the other names on your list?"

"I'll ask the questions if you don't mind," replied Bilkem. He thoughtfully reviewed his list, retreated to his table to confer with his colleagues, looked over some other papers and announced: "No further questions."

I requested permission to re-examine the witness, which was granted.

"Ms. Miller, what precautions does HOSTILE take to insure the integrity of documents?"

"We require that all complaints and evaluations be accompanied by sworn statements of truthfulness," she explained. "We do this to prevent false accusations being made and, also, so that we can enter documents as legal evidence in court. Before we instituted such measures, HOSTILE received a little over a dozen fraudulent accusations."

"A little over a dozen," I noted. "Would that exact number be thirteen?"

"Yes," smiled Constance.

"And does HOSTILE make public the specific names of people who complain about lawyers?" I asked.

"Goodness gracious no," Constance exclaimed. "HOSTILE only distributes information in summary form."

"Do you have any explanation of how the plaintiffs would acquire a list of thirteen names, the same number as fallacious complaints submitted to HOSTILE?" I inquired.

"And how the three specific names mentioned would directly correspond to three of the fraudulent complaints?"

"I have no idea," she replied. "It does seem a rather curious coincidence, doesn't it?" Constance is a master of subtle voice inflection and her unassuming tone was less idle musing than condemning accusation. She didn't even have to mention the word "conspiracy".

"Thank you, Ms. Miller. No further questions."

I will spare you, esteemed reader, from extended narratives of the ensuing testimony. It was mainly concerned with technical questions about the methods HOSTILE used in gathering and compiling information. Several staff members offered statements concerning the integrity, honesty and efficiency of HOSTILE. The plaintiffs desperately sought some way to undermine our case but they were just fishing without bait.

THE DAY BEFORE TOMORROW

The sun rose on a beautiful day. Birds were chirping as small, fluffy clouds floated across the pure, cerulean sky. It was a day perfectly made for accomplishing something productive or merely for enjoyment. Unfortunately, we were going to court.

"We should go over the plan again," said Eekim as we rode to the courthouse. Today it was just the three of us in the limo so Eekim was not in his case.

"We've already gone over it several times," I replied. "My part is pretty simple and then the whole thing gets turned over to you."

"It's that first part I'm worried about," Eekim retorted. "I still think we should review the plan so that everyone, no matter how simple their role, is fully aware of what is expected of them."

"C'mon guys, save your arguing for the trial," Nicky scolded. "We have to maintain control, work together and follow through. Now get with the program."

Eekim was not about to argue with Nicky so he sulked and stared out the window. I didn't sulk, of course, but I also stared out the window on my side. Out of the corner of my eye I could see Nicky looking back and forth at the two of us.

Finally, with a sigh, she said: "The only thing that can screw this up is if we don't stick together. If we allow lawyers to divide us, they will conquer us. Everything has gone great up to this point. We can win if we just don't allow our egos to interfere."

"My ego isn't the problem," Eekim stated in a voice oozing with benign objectivity. "It's the second banana over there who has the ego problem. If he would just cooperate a little more with the brains of the outfit I think we would all feel more confident."

"All right, all right," I capitulated.

So we went over the plan again, reviewed the contingencies and tactics again, and everyone including an irritating and abrasive talking monkey were friends again.

"That's better," Nicky cheerfully said. "The only reason you two pick at each other so much is because you're so much alike."

Eekim and I stared at each other with disbelief in our faces. Both of us wore expressions which plainly bore the telltale signs of disagreement and insult at the outrageous observation Nicky had just made. I could see the little wheels turning in his head as he contrived some cheap shot he could direct at me and I began to form a cunning reply. However, for Nicky's sake, neither of us said anything. Soon everyone was laughing and joking again, but I couldn't help chuckling each time I looked at Eekim and considered how preposterous a thought it was that we were anything alike. I don't know why he kept looking at me and giggling.

We arrived at the courthouse. Nicky and I, with Eekim in my arms playing the "dummy", confidently strode towards the door. The streets and sidewalks were crowded with cheering people who burst into applause as we approached the entrance. The media had carried the news of our massive counter-suit and people were amused and supportive of the monumental amount.

Comments such as "Go get 'em!", "Good luck!" and "Nail the bastards!" rang out from all sides. Quickly the crowd united in a dignified yet exuberant chant of "Lawyers uck, lawyers uck, lawyers uck."

We reached the top step and turned to face the multitude.

171

I felt exhilarated, like I was some kind of hero or something. I felt Eekim's body go rigid as he subtly squared his shoulders and held his head a little higher. Nicky was the only one who maintained a relaxed composure and she waved to the crowd and then blew them a kiss. The resulting cheers were deafening.

Bilkem righteously glared at us as we casually sauntered into the courtroom.

"Inciting the rabble again, eh?" he quietly sneered.

"We prefer to think of them as the citizens of this country," I whispered back. "But you know what they say, 'if you've got it, flaunt it'."

Everyone settled down and court was brought into session.

"Now then," said the judge. "We have presented the evidence and examined the witnesses. We will now proceed with closing arguments."

"If it please the court," I said while rising to my feet. I was a little nervous because, after making such a big deal of the "simple part" I was to play, I certainly didn't want to blow it. "The defense would like to call one more witness."

"Objection!" shouted Bilkem. "This is an eleventh hour attempt to distract the court. What witness could the defense possibly wish to call? We've already cross-examined everyone in the HOSTILE organization."

"Well Mr. Wetwood?" the judge inquired.

"Your honor, with all due respect, I would like to put Eekim, my monkey, on the stand."

"Objection, objection, objection," Bilkem intoned. "Your honor, are you going to allow this farce on the part of the defense to continue?"

"I would like to see the defense and plaintiffs in my office at once!" the judge sternly commanded. "And Mr. Wetwood, I don't want to hear another word from you until we're there. You are dangerously close to contempt and you definitely do not want to try my patience."

Bilkem triumphantly grinned and stuck his tongue out at me (at an angle invisible to the jury). He strutted happily as he followed the judge into his chambers. I shrugged, picked up Eekim and tagged along. I paused at the door and Nicky conspiratorially winked at me.

"Your honor," began Bilkem. "We originally believed this was an open-and-shut case of one of the most serious crimes ever to confront the legal community; that is, the blatant and public criticism of lawyers. Through trickery and charlatanism, the defense was able to manipulate evidence and witnesses to make it appear that some valid points were possibly being made. However, this last tactic reveals the height and depth to which this farce can reach. Therefore plaintiffs demand a summary judgment, here and now, against the defendants."

"Do you have anything to say for yourself, Mr. Wetwood?" the judge grimly asked.

"No sir," I respectfully responded. "I believe I made it clear in the courtroom that my monkey has something to say."

"This is ridiculous!" screamed Bilkem looking up, with raised arms, as if he were appealing to the heavens. Actually, though, it would be more accurate to describe him as appealing to the fluorescent light which hung from the ceiling.

"Your honor," continued Bilkem. "Monkeys can't talk!"

"Your honor," I hurriedly said. "Much research has been done on the ability of apes to communicate and it has been established that they are indeed competent to communicate and understand human language in symbolic terms. Symbolic terms are, for the most part, what language is anyway."

The judge just stared at me in a manner which made it clear that he was attempting to control his anger and not rush to judgment about what I was saying. His expression further conveyed that he did not want to rush to judgment because he wanted to make sure his judgment entailed the worst possible consequences to which I was entitled. His expression even further conveyed that he was going to enjoy it.

"Your honor," pleaded Bilkem. "You're opening yourself up to a review by a board of inquiry. Monkeys are not capable of the highly evolved reasoning and cognitive abilities necessary to testify in a court of law. Besides, that 'monkey' is a dummy!"

"I would like to offer tangible evidence to contradict both those statements," Eekim suddenly said. He began to nonchalantly stroke his fur and casually added: "Humans can be so conceited when it comes to intellectual evaluations of other species. Besides, if dummies can't talk in court then you're out of a job, Bilkem."

Bilkem and the judge stared at Eekim in disbelief. Bilkem recovered first, pointed his finger at me and shouted: "He's a ventriloquist!"

"No I'm not," I replied.

Bilkem pointed at Eekim and shouted: "It's some kind of sound device, like a walkie-talkie!"

"The proper pronoun is 'he' not 'it'," Eekim said with a tone of affront. "And you're wrong either way."

"I'll rip its head off and then you'll see what I mean," Bilkem said while stepping threateningly towards Eekim.

I stepped between them and confronted Bilkem: "Don't you touch my monkey!"

Meanwhile, Eekim strolled the length of the table to the judge. "Your honor, could a walkie-talkie do this?" Eekim scampered about the room, climbed the drapes, jumped to the florescent light fixture before (or more accurately, under) which Bilkem had recently offered supplication, and performed a triple-somersault before landing on the table in front of the judge. It was just like the little show-off but I had to give him a 10 on execution, poise and degree of difficulty; he even pointed his little toes and stuck the landing without a waver.

"Okay, okay, so it's a real monkey," said Bilkem. "But that doesn't mean he," pointing at me, "isn't a ventriloquist."

"Your honor," Eekim regally stated. "Since there is a lawyer in the room Josh is not the most slothful mentality present. But still, I believe my intellectual prowess is sufficient to prove that my verbalizations are not the product of anyone present."

The judge merely stared, open-mouthed, at Eekim while Bilkem continued to bluster. "Okay, your honor, then that means that it's a real monkey, granted highly trained, but still...monkeys can't talk...which means...which means it's just a monkey... and...and it's got a walkie-talkie device implanted on it!" Bilkem beamed with self-satisfaction and confidence at this example of his deductive reasoning abilities. Unfortunately, for him, he was totally incorrect.

"I'll talk very slowly so counsel for the plaintiff won't get confused," said Eekim. "First, notice the precise synchronization of my lips with regards to the words I speak. Second, if I was a walkie-talkie, how could I know that the third book from the left on that bookshelf is bound with a blue cover, how could I know that the clock on the wall reads precisely 10:05 and 24 seconds, how could I know that the over-esteemed counsel for the plaintiff is now pacing back and forth with his hands behind his back and a face as red as a beet?"

Bilkem shook his head and then his face lit as inspiration supplanted rage: "Your honor, even if he's a real talking monkey, a point I'm not fully conceding, but even if it's true there are no precedents, provisions or statutes pertaining to testimony by a talking monkey and therefore plaintiffs ask that the witness be disqualified."

"Your honor," said Eekim. "I believe there is a constitutional guarantee of freedom of speech involved in this issue."

"You little twerp!" shouted Bilkem. "The Missouri Bar doesn't care about your freedom of speech. You can say anything you want. We're merely concerned with who is allowed to listen to you."

"Your honor," Eekim said in a soothing yet beguiling manner which I knew from experience was irritating Bilkem to no end. "Freedom to listen is implicit in the freedom of speech. Besides, what difference does it make where the truth comes from? The purpose of the court is to arrive at the truth, therefore the presentation of the truth is much more important than who presents it."

"What in the hell ever gave you an idea like that?" yelled Bilkem. "Your honor, you see what kind of radical, blasphemous ideas may be entered into the record if you allow that monkey to testify!"

"Your honor, if you will indulge me for just a moment," said Eekim. "I would like to point out some of the more intangible aspects of your decision. First, when the world finds out that I'm a real live talking monkey, I'm going to be a star. Children, parents, the scientific community and the media are going to have a field day. Now, you're coming up for reelection. How would you evaluate your chances of staying in office until retirement if you rule against the superstar of the moment?"

"That's blackmail!" interrupted Bilkem.

"As opposed to threatening the judge with a board of inquiry?" Eekim asked.

"Shut up Bilkem!" commanded the judge. He then turned to Eekim and cordially said: "Go on. You're beginning to interest me."

"It's not as if your decision is final, after all," said Eekim. "Everyone is well aware of the potential for the decision to be appealed. The question is: 'Do you want to be known as the tyrannical judge who crushed the testimony of the world's only known talking monkey, the hero of children and the darling of the media; or do you want to be known as the judge who allowed an extraordinary witness to testify in an extraordinary case so that justice could be achieved?'"

The judge pondered the question for a few moments. He looked at Eekim, he looked at me and then he looked at Bilkem. While gazing at Bilkem a shadow passed over his face and he said: "What the hell, I never did like lawyers anyway. That's why I became a judge. Okay. The monkey testifies and don't say a word Bilkem!"

Bilkem shut his mouth which had opened at the first indication of where the decision was going.

"Thank you, judge," said Eekim. "I'm sure you won't regret your decision. We're going to have some fun now!"

"You know," smiled the judge. "I believe you're right."

MR. EEKIM SPEAKS

I gave Nicky a thumbs-up as we entered the courtroom. Eekim had resumed his "dummy" pose (we wanted maximum shock-effect when he spoke for the first time in public) and I placed him on the witness stand. An errant thought passed through my mind on the incongruity of calling it a "witness stand" when the witnesses were always sitting in a chair.

"Eekim, would you please tell the court what your role in the HOSTILE organization is?" I asked.

Eekim maintained his "dummy" pose for a few moments

while the courtroom audience twittered with laughter.

"I'd be happy to," said Eekim as he abruptly broke out of his "dummy" act. Startled gasps filled the room and a general rhubarb of comments and exclamations filled the air, drowning out Eekim's further statements. The judge allowed the commotion, which bordered on subdued hysteria, to continue for a short time. He then pounded his gavel for quiet.

"I admit this development is quite startling," he began with calm understatement. "However, it does appear that a talking monkey is, indeed, about to offer testimony before this court. In light of the unusual circumstances the court is willing to extend understanding for the outburst from the spectators. However, the court has ruled that the testimony of this witness is admissible. The talking monkey, identified as Eekim, will therefore be extended the same courtesy as any other witness. I will have the courtroom cleared if there are any further interruptions."

The crowd immediately settled down because no one wanted to miss what was about to transpire. I think the fact that a talking monkey had suddenly appeared produced a sort of mesmerizing effect which helped to silence any comments. Shock is a very effective tool.

Eekim thanked the judge and then continued with a summary of his involvement with HOSTILE. His version of that involvement was somewhat grandiose but, knowing Eekim, I had expected that. When he finished, the crowd could no longer contain their excitement and burst into applause. Bilkem jumped to his feet to protest but the judge tolerantly smiled as his protestations were drowned out by the cheering.

Eventually, the judge pounded the gavel for quiet. "The plaintiff may now cross-examine the witness," he said.

Bilkem ponderously rose to his feet and maneuvered his bulk around the table; quite a feat in itself. He stared at Eekim for a few moments while Eekim smiled back with a bemused expression on his simian features.

"Mr. Eekim," he began, "it is certainly very extraordinary to find a talking monkey testifying in a court of law. But extraordinary is no substitute for expertise. Could you please tell the court the extent of your knowledge and formal training regarding the practice of law?"

"Oh, I have little real knowledge of the law and absolutely no formal training," Eekim cheerfully admitted.

Bilkem pounced: "Then by what right do you claim the audacity to criticize and judge lawyers?"

"I may not know the law," said Eekim. "But then again, nobody knows the law. Lawyers have to specialize in various fields because law is too complicated for anybody to understand. Even in their specific fields lawyers can seldom give a straight answer to a question because the law is so obtuse. I can only say that if the law were capable of being understood then I would understand it."

"So you admit total ignorance of the system you criticize, just as I expected," beamed Bilkem.

I probably could have objected to the comment but I figured Eekim could handle the situation. Bilkem was digging a deep hole if he thought he could denigrate the star of the moment.

"By what right then, do you set yourself up as judge, jury and executioner of the reputations of lawyers of the state of Missouri?" Bilkem asked.

"Because I know the difference between right and wrong," Eekim contended. "Laws exist to serve justice, not the other way around. As such, lawyers exist to serve justice. Too often, however, I see laws existing to benefit lawyers and justice is not even a consideration."

"Are you putting yourself above the law?" Bilkem inquired.

"It would be more accurate to say that current human practices have placed the law beneath me," replied Eekim. "I respect and serve the concept of justice so, naturally, I must reject lawyers and their system."

"But essentially, aren't you trying to foment a rebellion against the legal system of the United States of America?" Bilkem accused. "Aren't you, essentially, a rebel and an insurrectionist against the Constitution of this country?"

"Essentially, no," Eekim casually responded. "The Constitution is a very fine piece of work, by human standards, and probably represents one of your species' crowning achievements. All I'm trying to do is bring the legal system, from its current deformed state, back into line with the ideals of that worthy document."

"But if you accept that the current system is the result of 200 years of logical interpretation and refinement of the Constitution," crooned Bilkem, "then you must accept the current legal system as a more refined and evolved representation of the intent of our Founding Fathers!"

"Well, if someone believes that first part, they'll accept almost anything," Eekim noted. "It is possible for something to be both logical and nonsensical at the same time; just take a look at the current legal system. I personally believe the Founding Fathers of this country neither anticipated, nor would they accept, your current system."

"Mr. Eekim, you are spouting treason!" yelled Bilkem.

"No I'm not," said Eekim. "I'm using the most sacred tenants of the Constitution to accomplish reform, not rebellion. At the heart of the Constitution is the ideal that the people must be informed, they must be free and they must be in control. The current lawyer system operates in such a manner that it cannot be understood, it often operates in secrecy, people are at the mercy of the lawyers who represent them, and people are unable to have any influence on the actions, techniques and outright immorality of lawyers."

"It's not a perfect system," admitted Bilkem. "But it's the best system humanly possible!"

"No it's not," mused Eekim. "It's the best system lawyerly possible. Which is exactly the point of HOSTILE. We contend that if better humans were selected as lawyers, then the legal system would naturally improve."

"I've never heard such nonsense before in my life," sighed Bilkem. "One final question. You're the brains behind lawyer reform and the HOSTILE organization, and you're just a monkey, right?"

"No," said Eekim in a condescending tone. "I'm the brains behind HOSTILE and I'm a very intelligent, honest, sincere talking monkey who has come to help humans overcome a depraved system. I'm also very handsome. And you're just a lawyer."

"No further questions, your honor," Bilkem coldly said. "The witness may step down," instructed the judge. "We will now hear summations. Mr. Bilkem, are you prepared?"

"Yes, your honor, I am," said Bilkem. He assumed a very studious pose before the jury and stared into space as if lost in deep thought. He then spoke for hours about the dignity of lawyers, the dignity of the court system and the value of justice. He ended with a tirade against HOSTILE; the audacity of anyone, particularly a talking monkey, voicing criticism of lawyers; implied that lawyers were god-like and above reproach by mere humans (or monkeys); and reiterated the plaintiff's demand for ten million dollars in damages.

When Bilkem finished he strode to his chair with the air of a triumphant Caesar. He sat and stared at me with that righteous glare of impervious superiority which lawyers have cultivated to a fine art.

I rose and cleared my throat: "Ladies and gentlemen of the jury. I will be brief." Many of the jury members were visibly pleased with this statement.

"The main issue here is whether lawyers should continue to enjoy absolute control over their own system," I continued. "The research compiled by HOSTILE merely constitutes a public information system so that the average citizen has some means of choosing the most competent lawyer available. It merely functions as a Better Business Bureau for lawyers. From the number of complaints we have presented, the need for such a review board is obvious.

"HOSTILE has not assaulted the self-proclaimed dignity of lawyers. We've merely compiled evidence which indicates that any such dignity is an illusion perpetrated by the fact that lawyers have a closed system. Lawyers have been able to project a perception of reality in which they are above reproach. HOSTILE has shattered that illusion by presenting a documented review of the actual reality. In short, HOSTILE has pointed out that the emperors have no clothes!

"But what is this trial all about? Is it about the criticism of lawyers? No, because criticism of lawyers occurs anytime the legal system is discussed by rational, objective people. Is the issue here freedom of speech? No, because lawyers obviously don't care what is said about them or they wouldn't act the way they do.

"Ladies and gentlemen, the issue is not our freedom of speech but your freedom to listen! Lawyers don't care if HOSTILE cuts down the tree of lawyer self-righteousness and greed, they merely want to make sure it is done deep in the woods when no one is there to hear the sound of it crashing to earth." (Eekim rolled his eyes at this metaphor but Nicky indulgently smiled.)

"The only thing of which HOSTILE is guilty is patriotism. HOSTILE has undertaken the tasks of informing the public about lawyer incompetence and chicanery, freeing the public of the tyranny of a closed legal system, and giving control of the legal system back to the people. That is why HOSTILE is being sued!

"This trial is nothing more than harassment by the lawyer community against an organization which is trying to restore fairness and accountability to a system which, because of the nature of attorneys, is out of control. We respectfully ask ten billion dollars in punitive damages."

The judge issued final instructions to the jury and they filed out of the courtroom.

Eekim turned to me as I sat down at our table: "Not bad for a human boy."

"Does that mean you're starting to think Nicky was right? That maybe you and I are more alike than either of us wants to believe?"

"I'll have to reserve judgment until I see a few more signs of independent intelligence and resourcefulness," Eekim replied. "After all, a lot of what you said was merely a repetition of what I expressed during the session in the judge's chambers. A gifted parrot could have done that."

"Well, that's true," I noted. "But I did come up with that analogy about the tree falling where no one could hear it."

"That's true," Eekim conceded. "But we were discussing intelligence and resourcefulness. What's your point?"

I sighed, Nicky shook her head, Eekim grinned and the jury filed back into the room.

The judge asked the jury if they had reached a decision

and the foreman responded "yes". The judge inquired if the jury had fully deliberated and considered the evidence (they had only been gone about ten minutes) and the foreman responded "to the full extent it deserved."

The judge asked for the verdict and the foreman responded: "We find for the defendant and instruct the Missouri Bar Conpiracy to pay ten billion dollars in damages."

"Your honor, this is outrageous!" stormed Bilkem. "We will appeal this to the highest court in the nation!"

The foreman shrugged and said: "We figured that too."

"Not too much of a surprise, huh?" agreed the judge.

"Your honor, throw this decision out or we'll immediately appeal," shouted Bilkem.

"Why is it," mused the judge, "that the least appealing people in reality are always the most appealing people in the court system? The decision stands! Court adjourned."

The courtroom immediately broke into cheers and the three of us were swamped with congratulations and praise. People pounded us on the back, shook our hands and generally clamored around Eekim. I crossed the room to thank the jury.

"Folks, you did a wonderful job. Thank you," I said.

Bilkem waddled over and fixed me with a threatening look. "This isn't over, you know."

"Well, Bilkem," I smiled. "Aren't you even going to thank the jury for being such good citizens by rendering the justice system invaluable service?"

"We have their names," Bilkem stated. "We know were they live." And he turned and stomped off.

The jury foreman laughed but then turned to me with a serious expression: "Speaking for the entire jury, we'd like to know how to go about joining HOSTILE."

THE GRAND FINALE

Later, Nicky, Eekim and I strolled around the square enjoying the festivities. News of the jury verdict was common knowledge by now and everyone was in a celebratory mood. The original hubbub over a talking monkey had settled down and most people maintained an awed and respectful distance from him. Everyone seemed content just to get a glimpse of Eekim.

Discovery of a talking monkey and the awarding of a monumental monetary judgment against lawyers left people in a kind of wonderland of fulfilled dreams. Almost everyone wore euphoric expressions of amazement and few wanted to dispel the magic. They only wanted to revel in the moment and enjoy.

Eekim kept people off-balance by waving and shouting things like "Hello folks!" and "Great party, huh!" He had already been interviewed by most of the media and the reporters had all hurried off to get their pieces on the air or into print.

We hung around and played some of the games. Nicky won a "Lawyers Uck" hat for hanging a lawyer at the crane game. We snacked and listened to music as night descended on the jubilant scene. Stars came out and a carnival atmosphere prevailed. The red-and-white striped tent continued to stand mysteriously closed at one corner of the square.

Suddenly, Bilkem lurched out from the crowd and confronted us. I could feel the presence of other people jostling forward to surround us.

"There you are!" he said with an inebriated slur in his voice. "You think you're pretty smart, don't you?" he asked while poking his finger in my chest. "Well you and that talking ape of yours have another think coming because you can't make a monkey out of me!"

"Can't make a silk purse out of a pig's ear," quipped Eekim.

Bilkem turned his glazed stare at Eekim but the little monkey stared defiantly back with an amused expression.

"I grow weary of your pseudo-civilized attempts to appear sophisticated," Bilkem sneered.

"And I grow weary of your pseudo-sophisticated attempts to appear civilized," Eekim retorted.

"Two points for Eekim," Nicky cheered.

Bilkem immediately turned on Nicky. She doesn't like confrontations of that sort and she took a step backwards and averted her eyes from Bilkem's bellicose scrutiny. Bilkem misinterpreted these actions as weakness and, true to his lawyer instincts, attacked anything which appeared weak

Bilkem stepped towards Nicky, brushed her hat off with a flip of his hand and said: "Shut up, slut!"

183

It was as if a cone of silence had descended on our little gathering. The music continued to play in the background but it seemed subdued, as if the volume had been turned down. The square was still lighted but our immediate area seemed bathed in shadows. Time itself had slowed and oblivious partiers floated by like people in another dimension.

"That was exactly the wrong thing to do," declared a grumpy voice.

"That's right!" agreed a cheerful voice. "It was definitely the wrong thing to say, too."

Hal and Stan grabbed Bilkem and hustled him away. The other members of HOSTILE, who had crowded around when Bilkem approached, provided cover and distraction. In his current drunken state and flaccid conditioning, Bilkem was unable to catch his breath to utter a protest. He was lucky to keep his chubby legs pumping to the pace of his abductors.

With his departure, noise, lights and time returned to normal. After a moment of shocked silence, Nicky asked: "Are you kidnapping him?"

"I prefer to think of it as making him an unwilling participant in the lawyer reform process," I replied. "Besides, when he insulted you and knocked your hat off, I considered him a volunteer."

"Wisely is it written in the peels of my tribe," noted Eekim. "The tiger laughs when it captures a monkey, so vice versa and louder."

I smiled #947, which means: "you ain't seen nothing yet."

"Let's go over to the red-and-white striped tent," I suggested. "I have a feeling the show is about to start."

The tent flaps rose just as we arrived. Inside was a large, Plexiglas tank filled with blue water. Bilkem, looking dazed and bewildered, sat on pedestal suspended over the water. A small platform beneath the water's surface allowed access to the pedestal. Bilkem was dressed only in a blue speedo swimsuit which complimented his flabby build in a revoltingly humorous manner. He looked like a hippopotamus in a jockstrap.

"Ladies and gentlemen," shouted Sam from a small stage to the right of the container. "For your amusement and revenge, we offer the chance to dunk a lawyer! Fifty cents a shot. Who will be first?"

I stepped up and paid my money. The target I aimed at was so large that success was virtually guaranteed. I wound up and threw the ball. A loud clang rang out as the ball struck the bull's-eye. The pedestal upon which Bilkem was seated immediately cut loose and he was dumped into the water. Cheers went up from the crowd.

Bilkem surfaced and the crowd gasped. He was colored blue!

"Since lawyers believe they are blue-bloods who are born to rule," shouted Sam. "We thought it would be amusing to make them blue-skinned also. Who's next?"

Eekim stepped up but Bilkem refused to get out of the water. He stood neck deep in the water and mouthed insults at me. Fortunately, I had taken the precaution of instructing Melvin to soundproof the Plexiglas container.

"What about my turn?" wailed Eekim. "Make him get back on the pedestal so I can dunk him!"

"Just a minute," I said. I had hoped the cold water would provide enough incentive to get Bilkem to cooperate. However, I had other contingencies prepared. I turned to where Melvin was making some adjustments on a hand-held gizmo. "Ready Melvin?"

"Ready," he said and stabbed a button.

Bilkem jumped two feet out of the water and then came down with a shocked expression. He stopped yelling and stood wide-eyed and mesmerized in the water.

"Hit him again, Melvin," I instructed.

Bilkem jumped again and this time scrambled onto the platform and then onto the pedestal. The platform had been constructed so that his now-blue posterior region was prominently displayed during the process.

"That's one blue butt," commented Eekim.

"Yes," I agreed. "He never did tell me if he preferred indigo or cerulean, so I opted for cerulean."

"You know," Melvin studiously noted. "I think I'll have the voltage properly adjusted in just a few more dunks. It should encourage him to regain the pedestal in minimum time while presenting no actual threat to his health."

"Yea, yea, whatever," said Eekim. "My turn!"

He nailed the target and Bilkem plunged into the water. As Melvin predicted, Bilkem regained the pedestal in an amazingly short period of time. He just sat there puffing for air with a resigned look on his face.

"Beautiful, just beautiful," said Eekim. "Wisely is it written in the peels of my tribe: "There is nothing as joyful as a caged tiger, especially if it's wet and unhappy."

Constance came strolling up to the tent on the arm of the judge.

"Young man," she addressed me. "We've been watching this display and I must warn you that it is very uncivilized to treat a human being in this manner!"

"You must have missed the announcement," I said. "That's the lawyer from the Missouri Bar Conspiracy. You probably didn't recognize him due to his current pigmentation."

"Oooh! Give me a ball, give me a ball," Constance excitedly pleaded. Sam handed her a ball. "You know, I used to pitch on the girls softball team."

"You want to give it a try, judge?" I offered.

"No," the judge solemnly said. "I've worked out a better deal." He handed five dollars to Melvin and Melvin gave him the electric box.

Constance hit the target, the bell clanged and Bilkem was immersed in the water. The judge pushed the button and Bilkem jumped. Before Bilkem could climb onto the platform the judge began rapidly pressing the button. Bilkem started bobbing and bouncing off the walls of the container like a steel ball off fast bumpers in a pinball machine.

"Wheee! This is fun!" yelled the judge.

Melvin and I quickly got the box away from him.

"Sorry, judge," I said. "But the idea is to teach him to climb back onto the pedestal, not bounce him around like a Ping-Pong ball in a wind tunnel."

"You have fun your way and I'll have fun my way," the judge replied. "But I suppose you're right. I shouldn't deprive other people of their opportunities. Damn, that was fun while it lasted!"

"You were pretty sharp to figure out what we're doing," I noted.

"Judges aren't necessarily stupid," said the judge. "We just seem that way because we're always dealing with lawyers. Besides, I knew Bilkem couldn't move that fast unless his shorts were on fire, so I figured there was some sort of incentive involved. My compliments."

Nicky, Eekim and I moved away from the tent so other people could take their shot. Unfortunately, the line quickly became so long that we didn't get another chance.

THE MORNING AFTER

Nicky and I were having coffee and reading newspapers when Eekim, yawning and scratching himself, came into the kitchen. He hopped onto the table and went through his morning ritual of carefully selecting a banana, slowly peeling it, momentarily meditating upon the peel and then devouring the banana with relish (that is, with a great deal of enjoyment; Eekim never put relish on his banana although sometimes he dipped it in honey).

Eekim then looked at me with an unfathomable expression. It may have been approval but I had seen that so seldom from him lately that I wasn't sure.

"You know, Josh," he began suddenly. "You did a pretty good job at the trial. The finale was a work of art! I did some thinking last night and I know that I've been difficult to get along with recently. It's been difficult to keep up that 'dummy' act and maintain my usual high degree of civility and charm for those around me.

"Your performance was great!" he continued. "I had anticipated that we would have to settle for a symbolic victory, but you actually painted a lawyer's butt blue! Not only that, but while monkeys painted only their posterior region you painted the whole damned thing blue. It was brilliant!"

"Thank you," I proudly replied. "I sincerely appreciate your compliment about my work and I truly sympathize with your recent predicament. I believe we are entering a new era in our relationship which will..."

"It's rude to interrupt," interrupted Eekim. "As I was

187

about to say, in spite of your momentary brilliance you should have consulted me. Your lack of foresight into the repercussions of your actions is amazing. You do realize, of course, that there will be severe penalties for abducting a lawyer and painting him blue. You have managed to sacrifice months of hard work for one night of temporary glory."

"Eekim's right, of course," said Nicky as she launched into the scene we had rehearsed. "It would take a genius to contrive a plan to paint a lawyer's butt blue with impunity."

"Which is exactly why I should have been consulted," Eekim proclaimed. "If you'll remember, and I assume that is one of the cognitive abilities which you still retain, we decided to symbolically paint their butts blue because of the difficulties of getting away with really doing it. If I was unable to come up with an appropriate plan, what made you think you could?"

"Well, Josh," sighed Nicky. "I have to agree with Eekim. It would have taken someone more intelligent than him to execute such a caper."

"I know," I said while faking chastised humility with all the sincerity I could scrape up.

"Let's see what you have wrought," Nicky said with a resigned but curious tone. She began looking through the newspapers I had earlier purchased. She emitted a convincing gasp and exclaimed in feigned bewilderment: "But, this is amazing! It's a miracle!"

With a sly smile she slid a newspaper to Eekim. Among the stories about the trial, the verdict, the award, and notice of a divorce filing by Mrs. Iction was a headline which read: **"LAWYER PLUNGES INTO DEMENTIA FOLLOWING DUNKING TANK EPISODE".**

The story featured a color picture of a dripping wet Bilkem fresh from the dunking tank. The caption read: "Mr. Will Bilkem, the lawyer who just yesterday lost a ten billion dollar verdict against the Missouri Bar Conspiracy, which many say was a long overdue judgment, apparently suffered some sort of mental breakdown after court was adjourned. Witnesses have testified that Bilkem volunteered to participate in festivities but Bilkem denies this. His credibility is further called into question by the fact that he claims to have been painted blue during his alleged 'abduction', 'incarceration', 'humiliation' and 'torture' in a dunking tank. The above picture, as well as numerous pictures and footage by other news agencies, clearly shows this is not true. This newspaper extends hopes and best wishes for a speedy recovery. One legal associate noted: 'Fortunately, there is no prerequisite for sanity in the practice of law. Therefore, Mr. Bilkem will remain unconfined and free to practice his profession.'"

Eekim looked up from the paper. Nicky and I were grinning at him.

"I think I've been set up," Eekim meloncholily admitted. "It's a shame when a partnership has two people ganging up on the third member. I've always had an 'all for one and one for all' attitude about our working relationship. Trust and loyalty are essential to an undertaking such as ours. I can't help feeling somewhat betrayed by the way you two withheld information and kept me in the dark.

"I'm particularly disappointed in you, Nicky," he gravely added. "I always figured it was you and me against him."

"Be that as it may," I said. "I believe you stated earlier that it would take someone more brilliant than you to formulate a successful plan such as mine."

"How did you do it?" Eekim asked. "Mirrors? Smoke? What?"

It did not escape my notice that he had changed the subject but I responded anyway.

"I used a pigmented formulation known as 'process blue'. It's a type of ink, used for editing, which does not show up in photographs. Also, it's a very nice shade of cerulean. Melvin refined the formula so it was harmless and washed off easily."

"I should have known Melvin was involved," said Eekim. "He's a bright boy. Well, now that that's settled, I'm free to enjoy another banana."

"Eekim," Nicky playfully said. "You're forgetting that you owe Josh an apology for your earlier remarks. I think you also owe him congratulations for his successful plan."

"Well," Eekim sighed. "I can see that I'm not going to be allowed to enjoy my second banana until this matter is cleared up. As usual, it's up to me to restore peace and put this partnership back on the level. Very well. Never let it be said that I don't give credit where credit is due."

Turning to me, he said: "Josh, your plan was brilliant. I didn't think you were smart enough to consult Melvin so that the job was done right, but you were. I apologize for thinking you were stupid enough to try something like that on your own. All in all, it was a victory for the organization and I'm very pleased that you have finally managed to make a tangible contribution to our goals. Let's hope that, against all odds, you'll be able to keep up the good work. Satisfied?"

Nicky and I both laughed.

"Well, I guess I'll have to be," I chuckled. "How could I not be satisfied with such a tribute? You're going to spoil me with such heartfelt sentimentality."

"You two are enough alike to be brothers," Nicky smirked.

"Brothers?" Eekim questioned. "I don't know about brothers. But, if Josh can continue to avoid his usual mental lapses and maintain this surprising degree of ingenuity then I might one day accept the idea that I could be his nephew."

I felt rather complimented by this until Nicky smiled at me and said: "I guess you know what that makes you?"

"Oh well," I said. "At least it's a nice thought."

Eekim smiled and innocently selected another banana.

CLASSY AND APPROPRIATE CLASSICAL-TYPE QUOTE

"You know," Nicky mused. "The whole episode with the dunking tank and painting the lawyer reminded me of Robert Louis Stevenson's 'The Portrait'. There's a passage that goes:

'I am a kind of farthing dip,
Unfriendly to the nose and eyes;
A blue-behinded ape, I skip
Upon the trees of paradise.'"

"That's fairly appropriate," I commented. "Lawyers could have helped to make the world a paradise, but instead became noxious, ugly beasts who merely use the world as their own private playground. And eventually, someone had to paint their butt blue to punish them."

"Right," said Eekim. "And we rose to the occasion, as a team, to accomplish that. But shouldn't that first line read 'farting dip'?"

"No," replied Nicky. "A farthing is a coin with little or no value. In the poem it means 'worthless'."

"Oh," said Eekim, nonplused at the correction and reaching for another banana. "I guess it works either way."

CHAPTER NINE

SUE BIZ

A couple of weeks later I was seated at my desk when I heard a commotion in the outer offices. My door burst open and a huge fellow, decked out in an outrageously loud purple suit, plowed into the room.

"I'm sorry, Mr. Wetwood," Constance said, flustered almost to the brink of her genteel demeanor. "I couldn't stop him and he wouldn't take no for an answer."

"Nobody stops me!" declared the colorfully attired individual. "And I don't know the meaning of the word 'no'."

"Should I call the police?" Constance more calmly inquired. She had quickly regained her lady-like control and put a stern warning into her voice. She also added an inflection which implied immense personal enjoyment at the potential sight of the intruder being hauled off by the police.

"Mr. Wetwood," said the chromatic aberration. "I require but a moment of your time to convince you that I am the most important person in the world as far as you are concerned."

He was six foot tall and fairly normal looking except for a cheap radiance to his skin and a streak of peroxide-induced white in his bouffant coal-black hair. He exhibited rather foppish mannerisms.

"I'll handle this," I nodded to Constance. "But check with the police and see if they have a car cruising in the area." She quietly closed the door.

"What's this all about?" I inquired of the prismatic presence.

"You don't recognize me?" the amethyst apparition asked in amazement. "Well, by all means allow me to introduce myself. I am none other than M.T. Blarney, lawyer extraordinaire for the downtrodden and suffering. Surely you've heard of my firm, 'The Greatest Sue On Earth'."

"Afraid not," I said.

"Really? I am amazed!" he exclaimed. "I run commercials on all the major networks. You don't watch much TV do you?"

"Not really."

"Pity," Blarney said. "Most of the downtrodden and suffering do. Oh well. I've worked tough audiences before. I'm here to offer you the chance of a lifetime! I can tell you're an intelligent man who doesn't waste time, so allow me to bottom-line it for you. 'On with the sue!' as we say in the business. I think you and your monkey have the potential to become one of the greatest courtroom acts of all time. Think of it! The money, the glamour, the notoriety, the money, the endorsements, the attention, the fame, the money, the glitz, the glitter and the glory of being the headline act and main attraction in the entire modern legal system! Can I get a 'Hallelujah' from you, baby!"

"No."

"That's good, that's perfect," enthused Blarney. "You have a wonderful persona for the courtroom; quiet, unassuming, no nonsense. I like it. The crying and sniveling acts are effective but every agent has one. Oh, the court camera is going to love your face, baby. You virtually ooze sincerity. Can you keep that up for long?"

"I think so."

"Great! Great!" he marveled. "The hardest thing about most acts is the sincerity schtick. But you're a natural. Oh! There's no business like sue business! It's in my blood. And baby, I can make you a star! What do you say to that?"

"What are you talking about?" I irritably inquired.

"That's what I like about you, baby," bubbled Blarney. "You don't mess around. You know that backstage, out of the spotlight, this is a tough business. There's no place for amateurs. I can tell you're a pro. I think we're going to get along wonderfully. Can I get an 'Amen' from you, baby!"

"No."

"Great! Just great!" continued Blarney.

"Are you a preacher or a lawyer?"

"Whatever works," admitted Blarney. "All lawyers are preachers, spin-doctors, psychologists, PR men, salesmen, con men, liars, actors or whatever else we need to be in order to manipulate peoples' thoughts and emotions. But let's talk about you.

"You see, what you need to make it big in this business today is a gimmick, something unusual. Something to 'WOW' the audience and bring standing ovations from the jury box. You've got that monkey-thing working for you, baby, so you're the hottest item in jurisprudence entertainment going! Punch my ticket and give me a front row seat, baby!"

"I think I understand part of what you're saying," I replied. "But Eekim and I have recently won a ten billion dollar court case. What do I need you for?"

"Exposure, baby, exposure!" shouted Blarney. "I'm thinking sequel, baby! Granted you've made a splash in your debut but without proper handling you could be a flash in the pan. You're on top now, but by tomorrow you could be a has-been. The public is fickle, baby. Your opening was stupendous and you have rave reviews and verdicts to your credit, but you don't want the show to close after just one performance. With my help, you could have the longest-running hit in legal history! You've got the talent to be one of the great ones, you only need the drive! Let me drive you, sweetheart!"

"I don't see..."

"Of course you don't, that's why you need me, baby," Blarney blurted. "You need to concentrate on your art and let me handle all the dreary details. I can make you big, Big, BIG! Any lawyer could get you some gigs, baby, but I can make you a star in mega-buck production numbers! Your name will be on the marquis in the biggest courts in the land." He burst into song with: "There's no business like sue business, There's no business I know..."

"Mr. Blarney," I said with all sincerity, "there's something I should tell you. Even as cynical as I am about the nature of the court system, my attitude does not do justice to the exploitive excesses of your proposition."

He stared at me with a blank expression on his face. "Save it for the act, kid." he said out of the side of his mouth. "This is M.T. Blarney you're talking to. I may be flashy on the surface but I have the same interest as every other lawyer in the biz. I know how to make money."

His effervescence returned as he crooned with sparkling eyes: "Who loves you, baby? I've already helped you in a few discreet ways, just because I want to see you make it to the top. Trust me!"

"Trust you for what?"

"C'mon, baby, work with me! Look at the big picture! You've got the monkey, you've got your secretary, and you've got that sincerity thing working for you. With me to put it all together in a marketable package, we're a sure thing! We pack the jury with animal lovers, men and motherly types. We can't miss!"

"Thanks a lot," I said. "But I still don't know what you're talking about. What are we going to sue somebody for?"

"So innocent, so pure," Blarney condescendingly smiled. "To sue or not to sue, that is the question. And the answer is 'Why not?' You have talent, but you're still a baby in this business. We don't really need a reason but let's throw some ideas against the wall and see if they stick. Let's say, for example, we sue all the cities with major zoos for keeping Eekim's 'relatives' locked up without a trial? Catchy, huh? It's got that certain pizzazz which every court case needs. Or, we could sue every animal act in the country for enslaving Eekim's 'relatives' in unfair labor contracts. Doesn't that send tingles down your spine? And how about all those animal experiments being conducted across the country? How does that grab you? And, of course, there's always things like residuals from all those 'Planet Of The Apes' movies. I'm telling you, that's just the tip of the iceberg. I'm full of ideas! I got a million of them! My philosophy is 'Sue them all, let God sort them out!' We're going to show this country that Missouri isn't the 'Sue Me' state for nothing!"

"'Show Me'," I corrected.

"That's the spirit, baby!" laughed Blarney. "Of course I'll show you. I tell you kid, with me as your agent you can't miss! Of course, I've been thinking about that Nicky girl. We may want to have auditions for that role. My casting couch is always available to new talent. If she wants her name in the credits, however, I'll be happy to reevaluate her performance during the tryouts. Now, the first thing we do is..."

While Blarney prattled about the visions of court cases dancing in his head, I called Constance on the intercom and asked her to send in Mr. Potts. Melvin shuffled in a few moments later.

I interrupted the purple specter and said: "Mr. Blarney, I'd like you to meet Melvin Potts, my technical wizard."

Blarney stared at Melvin before declaring: "No, no! The chemistry is all wrong. We can't use him."

"Melvin, activate the self-destruct sequence on the coffee-maker," I said. He shrugged and turned towards the machine and began fiddling with the adjustments. The self-destruct sequence was a special installation which he had added for cases of extreme danger. I figured the current situation qualified.

"Mr. Blarney," I said in my coldest voice. "My assistant is currently arming a device which will blow this office sky-high, which I prefer over listening to you any longer. I would appreciate your leaving so that your body parts are not mixed with mine when the event occurs."

Not to fear, concerned reader. Melvin had assured me that the device was completely safe. He had instructed me, therefore, only to use it when I was sure a bluff would work.

"It's ready," said Melvin. "There'll be a thirty-second countdown and then this place is history." His face paled. "I'll be going now. Any last messages for Nicky or Eekim?"

"No," I stoically replied.

I admired the way he was contributing a sense of fear for

his personal safety. He caught on quick.

"Okay. I'll get people cleared out of the front office and moved to a safe distance. It's been nice knowing you, Mr. Wetwood," he said.

That was a nice touch. And Blarney thought he couldn't act.

Melvin hurriedly exited and began shouting to the secretaries: "Listen up people! I've just armed the self-destruct on the coffee-maker. We have thirty seconds to get to cover. This is not a drill! Let's go!"

I overheard Constance remark: "Oh dear, I hope the poor boy knows what he's doing."

Chairs scraped and feet pounded as the staff sought cover. This was great! If I didn't know better, I would have sworn everyone was running for their lives.

The coffee-maker announced: "Self-destruct sequence has been initiated. Anyone partial to having their limbs attached to their bodies should immediately seek shelter at least fifty yards from this building. Event horizon in thirty seconds. Beginning countdown: 30...29...28..."

Blarney looked at me as if I was crazy: "Theatrics like this are unnecessary!"

"Mr. Blarney, I would rather die than continue this conversation."

"23...22...21..."

"Look, I understand that major talent is often cursed with a self-destructive nature, but this is ridiculous!" screamed Blarney. "If you want to die, I can arrange something much more spectacular and lucrative."

I just stared at him.

"17...16...15..."

"Think of your fans!" pleaded Blarney. "Think of me!"

I stared.

Blarney started sweating and threatened: "Don't toy with me kid! I know a bluff when I see one."

I stared. Blarney stared.

"11...10...9..."

We stared.

"7...6...5..."

Blarney blinked. "Sue be it! I made you and I can break you. You'll never work in this business again!" he screamed as he ran out the door.

"2..."

"Coffee-maker, cease self-destruct," I said.

"Whew!" said my coffee-maker.

I sat at my desk and congratulated myself on a successful bluff. I felt steady and solid as a rock.

Soon, Melvin poked his head into the office.

"Boss, is everything okay?"

"Why wouldn't it be?" I cheerfully asked.

"Well," Melvin slowly said. "It's just that threatening to blow yourself up is a pretty drastic solution to a lawyer."

"It all depends on your perspective," I replied. "Besides, you told me that device was perfectly safe."

Melvin shrugged.

"It's perfectly safe," he assured me. And added: "It'll never blow-up unless you want it to."

I froze like a statue at his words (Which, for those interested, is quite different from sitting like a rock. I realize both a statue and a rock are similar in composition but, in my current metaphor at least, their inner feelings are very different. One is solid and unmovable, the other is frozen and unable to move.)

"Melvin," I finally croaked. "I understand that you called it 'safe' because it would only blow-up on command. But if it would really explode, why did you tell me to only use it when I was bluffing?"

"Gee, boss. You don't really want to end up splattered on the walls, do you?"

He had a point. However, I couldn't help contemplating the irony of having my own private doomsday device as a defensive measure. Also, I couldn't help but feel that perhaps Melvin had failed to note the ambiguity of his instructions concerning "safe" and "bluff". I was about to lecture him on the matter but decided to have a cup of coffee instead.

"Decaf?" the coffee-maker inquired.

I noted that my hands were now unfrozen and were making up for their recent stolid performance by trembling and fluttering like leaves in the wind.

"Right. No sugar," I sighed. "And no explosives."

A MUSICAL INTERLUDE

We whiled away the next few months working at HOSTILE; forwarding the cause of justice, supporting the constitutional rights of citizens, and playing pranks on lawyers. We even helped Mrs. Iction with her divorce settlement. Wives of lawyers are renowned for getting the shaft when a divorce occurs.

One of our favorite pranks was to call a lawyer and say: "I know what you did to me and I'm not going to put up with it!" Then hang up. We weren't naive enough to think we could play on the moral conscience of a lawyer, but justified paranoia can be a powerful tool. Over time, many lawyers began to look less smug and secure.

During this time we also had one of our most unusual triumphs. It may have been partially inspired by M.T. Blarney's show business attitude towards the courts. Eekim, Nicky and I didn't want to take show business into the courtroom but we saw no reason not to take the courtroom into show business.

Nicky wrote the music and even included her old piece "Lawyers and Other Social Diseases" (from Monkey Business) among the musical numbers. She had a surprising range which included raunchy vaudeville, sleazy jazz, inspiring solos and, of course, love songs.

Eekim choreographed the dance steps. I think he enjoyed playing the tyrannical expert and continually complained that he had to tone down his artistic vision to accommodate a bunch of clumsy, awkward humans. The dancers, for some unfathomable reason, came to love him for the innovations and intricacy of the dances. I was grateful for his involvement as it kept the little monkey off my back for a while.

I wrote the script.

"Attack Of The Mutant Lawyers From Hell" opened with a scene in which the Devil, while whipping and lashing the damned, bemoans the fact that his job is too demanding. There just doesn't seem to be enough time to perpetrate all the horror he would like. He is, in fact, suffering from burn-out.

199

One of the demons suggests the Devil have a son which he send to earth to facilitate the fallen angel's goals.

And so it comes to pass that Sonny Saiton arrives on earth.

The plot follows the age-old pattern of the penultimate evil lawyer rising to power by stomping the living daylights out of every decent person he encounters. The hero battles Sonny Saiton and eventually wins with the help of an exorcism which sends the villain back to the depths of Hell. There is also, of course, the love angle with the heroine.

It's a tried-and-true formula which, while lacking originality, never fails to be a crowd pleaser. "Attack Of The Mutant Lawyers From Hell" received great reviews and remains one of the most popular musicals on Broadway.

A BODY OF EVIDENCE

Then one day, upon arrival at HOSTILE headquarters, we were greeted by several squad cars. Police and detectives were milling about. A detective in a shabby gray suit approached me.

"Are you Mr. Wetwood?" he asked. He was medium build with a swarthy complexion and conveyed an air of unhurried frenzy and relaxed stress. His voice was gravelly, probably from smoking cigars such as the one he now puffed.

"I'm Josh Wetwood," I replied.

He nodded as if it had not been a real question.

"Mr. Wetwood, we have a situation here which is somewhat serious. Late last night, or early this morning, a lawyer named Lou C. Fur was murdered not far from here. The body was discovered this morning by a mailman. The mailman was in shock until he found out the profession of the deceased. Afterwards, he reluctantly cooperated with authorities but was unable to provide any further clues or information.

"Now, Mr. Wetwood," continued the detective, his attention focused on my face, "I'm sure you understand that because of the nature of your organization and the proximity of the body, investigators must at least consider the possibility that you or someone in your organization may have had something to do with the murder."

"Are we suspects?" I asked with slight irritation.

"Mr. Wetwood," the detective declared, "because the victim was a lawyer I am forced to consider every decent citizen as a possible suspect."

"What do you want?" I defensively asked.

"We want to question you and your staff, and look around the premises."

"Don't you need a warrant to search the place?"

"Mr. Wetwood," sighed the detective. "This is a lawyer we're talking about. I could get a warrant to search the Vatican if I asked for it. The public can get shot to dollrags and it's no big deal, but let a lawyer get killed and suddenly every high-placed muckety-muck wants action now. Personally, every man on the force would rather be investigating a crime perpetrated against an innocent person. But we have our orders. Now, do you want to cooperate or do I need a search warrant?"

I glanced at Nicky who had come out of a quick spiritual reconnaissance. She gave a barely perceptible nod.

"We're always glad to cooperate with the police," I said.

The detective had noticed the exchange and turned to Nicky. "Miss, what do you think about all this?"

"'As ye sow, so shall ye reap.'" Nicky responded.

"I can understand that," he replied.

"What about you?" he inquired, pointing at Eekim.

"This is stupid," said Eekim. "Wisely is it written in the peels of my tribe: 'When a tiger is killed, do not postpone the celebration to look for the intrepid hunter.'"

I thought the remark could have been more in keeping with the official nature of the question, but the detective smiled and said: "I hear you! I've heard of the talking monkey and seen him on TV, but I never thought I'd meet him in person. This is indeed an honor. My Mrs. is a big fan of yours."

Eekim beamed and said: "I think it's obvious your wife has impeccable taste in monkeys and men."

Eekim can schmooz with the best of them when he wants. He and the detective exchanged compliments for a few moments.

Nicky and I conferred while the officers questioned and

searched. She had the foresight to check not only to make sure that none of our more exuberant defenders of justice had been involved but also that no evidence had been planted around our headquarters. In dealing with lawyers, we were well aware of the potential for being framed.

After several hours the officers appeared ready to leave. The detective-in-charge approached me again.

"Well, Mr. Wetwood," he said in his grating voice. "There doesn't seem to be any reason for us to suspect any of your people. Aside from a somewhat morbid curiosity as to how painful and slow the lawyer may have expired, they do not appear to be involved. We'll be in touch if we need anything else."

"Do you have any other possible suspects?" I asked.

"In a case like this?" he asked. "Oh my goodness, yes. I'm off right now to question a minister, a priest and a rabbi. They all preach about right and wrong so, like you, they definitely have a motive. I know the Bible says: 'Vengeance is mine, sayeth the Lord'. But what if one of them decided to do God's work? Their churches and synagogue are near here so, again like you, they may have had opportunity. And, of course, there's the family and associates of the deceased."

"What about his friends?" I asked.

"Excuse me saying so, but you wouldn't make much of a detective," laughed the detective. "The deceased was a lawyer, where is he going to get friends? No sir, associates about covers it."

"Well, what if you think another lawyer did it?" I persisted.

"Now that would be a toughie," he admitted. "After all, a lawyer would demand a jury of his peers. How are we gonna get a conviction without honest people on the jury?"

"Do you have any hopes for solving the case?" I asked.

"Oh sure, sure," said the detective. "Put yourself in the perpetrator's position. He's just killed a lawyer, what's the first thing he's going to want to do? Brag, of course! People will buy him dinner and drinks, introduce him to their friends and invite him to parties. I believe I'm looking for someone who is suddenly very popular."

An officer handed him his raincoat as he ambled towards a beat-up car. He opened the reluctant driver's side door and then turned back to me.

"Just one more thing, Mr. Wetwood," he said. "Have you ever heard of a man named Tom Window?"

"No."

"Probably nothing," he smiled. "Have a nice day."

I had a strange feeling that I would see the detective again but I never did.

LATER THAT MORNING

"Mr. Wetwood," Constance said over the intercom. "There's a gentleman here who wishes to speak with you. He says it's very important.

I paused and let the slight white noise of the intercom system linger. I really didn't want anymore interruptions because Nicky, Eekim and I had a talk show appearance scheduled for this afternoon.

The appearance was unique in that his particular talk show had grown with HOSTILE and reflected similar values and concern. Many of our members were avid fans. The show featured a semi-formal, round-table debate and discussion on the impact of the legal system on the average individual. It was called "Meet The Oppressed".

"Does he have an appointment, Constance?" I asked. I knew he didn't. I had put a pedantic tone into my voice to indicate that the answer to that question would also be the reply to whether or not I would see him.

Constance sidestepped the tactic by replying: "He's very insistent, sir."

Constance obviously thought I should talk to the guy. If I refused to see him I might undermine her authority with the rest of the staff (I didn't really think this would happen. Constance didn't depend on me for her authority. It was more likely that I would undermine my own position with her staff.). Besides, she had referred to him as a "gentleman" so he wasn't a lawyer.

I considered saying: "Very well, I've got a few minutes." I felt this was an adequate compromise. It acknowledge the value of her judgment while maintaining my authority. I was, therefore, postured as a man who, no matter how busy, would always take the time to be considerate of his staff's recommendations. I considered that the ramifications of this action might strengthen both Constance's and my position. Then I concluded that I had over-analyzed the situation and probably needed a vacation.

I opted for a more direct approach.

"What's his name?" I asked.

"Tom Window," she replied.

"Send him in," I sighed.

Tom Window fell into a category somewhere between clean-cut and rough-edged. His tanned face was outlined with longish blond hair which had that natural wind-blown look so often poorly imitated by people with blow-dryers. I reflected on my own receding hairline and considered that I might be a touch envious. I bolstered my ego by reevaluating my balding noodle as a shining trophy to hard work and dedication. I concluded that I definitely needed a vacation.

"What can I do for you, Mr. Window?" I formally asked. I inwardly winced at the implication that I was going to do anything at all for him. I should have said: "State your business" or "What was it you wanted to see me about" or even "I'm a busy man, bottom-line it for me". None of these expressions really fit me though. I resisted the urge to inquire if he had been doing any fishing lately.

He wore a blue-and-black flannel shirt, blue jeans and hiking boots. A small backpack was slung over his shoulder. White teeth were accented by a slight shadow of stubble on his cheeks. His clear, gray eyes had none of the glint of the fanatic.

"Mr. Wetwood," he began, "I'm surprised to find you still alive."

This struck me as a strange way to begin a conversation.

"You came to see me, Mr. Window," I reminded him. "So what could be so surprising? Do you often go to see dead men?"

"When they take on lawyers I do," he sadly smiled. "I've been to several of their funerals. And please, call me Tom."

"Okay, Tom. Perhaps you should tell me exactly what it is you're talking about."

"Well," he began. "My surprise at finding you alive has been a daily marvel ever since your career began. I've never known anyone come even close to lasting as long as you have while being so openly critical of lawyers. You must lead a charmed life."

"I've been lucky," I admitted.

"Lucky?" he laughed. "Shit, you're a walking miracle! I've buried friends who did nothing compared to you! It's one of the reasons we waited so long to contact you. We thought it might be a trap."

"We?" I asked with raised eyebrows.

Tom shifted uneasily and looked self-conscious for the first time since he walked in. His easy-going manner disappeared as he said: "We? Did I say we? I meant I."

Our eyes locked. He was lying, of course, and he wasn't very good at it. He knew I knew. But his eyes had that stern "it's for your own good" look I had often seen in my father's eyes when I was a boy. I decided not to push the issue and looked away.

Tom cleared his throat as he opened the backpack. "Josh, maybe it would help if I showed you something." He pulled out a small but expensive-looking tape recorder and sat it on my desk.

While plugging it in, he said: "The police have been here to see you about a lawyer named Lou C. Fur?"

I nodded.

"This tape contains excerpts from phone conversations which we...I mean I, tapped. The first voice is Fur. Please, just listen." He pushed the play button.

THE FOLLOWING WAS PRE-RECORDED
First Conversation:

Fur: "Burnem? This is Lou C. Fur. I'm representing E.Z. Mark in that potential suit against your client company."

Burnem: "Yes. I've been over the file and it seems the company does owe the money. I've talked to the company officials and they agreed that the only right thing to do is pay the money. I believe I've got a settlement offer which will be acceptable to your client.

Fur: "Well, it may be acceptable to my client but it's not acceptable to me. It's up to me to decide what is in whose best interests. Look, Burnem, how do you expect me to make any money if the company just pays up? You've got to fight this thing. You know the drill. You file motions, I'll file motions, Mark will eventually win and I'll kickback a percentage of the take."

Burnem: "Right. I make trouble for him, you 'save' him, and the schmuck is so grateful he forks out a wad to you. Wasn't that tactic originated by Phil Oney, back in our school days?"

Fur: "Yea. I miss ol' Phil. Remember how he used to get the cork out of a wine bottle with his tongue instead of a corkscrew? He was one of a kind. They killed the mold after they made him. Well, I guess it's all settled. Set up a lunch date with my secretary and we'll discuss the details."

Burnem: "How do I know I'll get my share of the take?"

Fur: "Look, if two school-chum lawyers can't trust one another to bilk a client, then what good is our profession? You remember our law school fight song don't you?" (Singing) "You take care of your client,"

Burnem: (Singing) "And I'll take care of mine,"

Together: (Singing) "When he's out of money
                           together we will dine."

Fur: (Laughing) "That song brings back memories. Don't worry. I'll gouge him for enough money that there'll be plenty to go around."

Second Conversation:

Fur: "Hey Art Ifice, how's my favorite client?"

Ifice: "Listen, Fur, you've got to help me. I've got the word that the expert witness the prosecution is calling to the stand is a real whiz. He could put me away!"

Fur: "With me on retainer? You think I'd let that happen to a steady customer? Don't sweat, Ifice, I'm going to use my 'humanity defense'."

Ifice: "'Humanity defense'? What's that?"

Fur: "It's my standard cross-ex of an expert witness. It goes a little something like this: I say: 'You're a human being, correct?' He says: 'Well, yes.' I say: 'Being human, you cannot be perfect, correct?' He says: 'Well, yes.' I say: 'Not being perfect, by your own admission, it follows that you could have made a mistake of which you are unaware. Correct? You have made at least one mistake in you life haven't you?' He says: 'Well, yes.' I say: 'I rest my case, your honor. By his own admission, testimony and precedence, this man cannot possibly be considered a competent witness against my client.'"

Ifice: "You really think it'll work?"

Fur: "It always does. I have a very polished speech for the summation in which I am outraged that someone imperfect would testify against you."

Third Conversation:

Fur: "Will O. Wisp? This is Fur. Look, I think I've got an airtight suit against the homeowner for you breaking your leg."

Wisp: "I hired you to defend me on burglary charges!"

Fur: "Oh, that part's no sweat."

Wisp: "No sweat? I broke their basement window!"

Fur: "Accidents happen."

Wisp: "I crawled into their house at two o'clock in the morning!"

Fur: "Well, of course you did. And it's to your credit that in spite of the late hour you wanted to check out the damage and make sure everything was safe."

Wisp: "I had a gun!"

Fur: "Who can blame you? It's a dangerous society we live in. Look, just because there are some questionable circumstances is no justification for leaving clutter around in an unlit basement where anyone coming through the window could injure themselves. You didn't deserve to break your leg! How dare they judge you just because you're not perfect!"

Wisp: "You really think you can get me off?"

Fur: "Before I'm done, you'll own that house."

Wisp: "What about the burglary charges?"

Fur: "Don't be silly. You can't be convicted of breaking into your own house. How's the leg coming?"

Wisp: "Fine."

Fur: "No it's not."

Wisp: "The doctor says I'll be walking on it in no time."

Fur: "You've got the wrong doctor. You need a specialist. I'm going to transfer you to my secretary. She'll set up an appointment for you. Now, you do what the doctor says, you know what I mean?"

Fourth Conversation:

Fur: "Ms. Anne Thrope? This is Lou C. Fur. I'm representing Don D. Drane in that negligence case."

Thrope: "Yes, what did you want to discuss?"

Fur: "To be honest, I'm having second thoughts about the validity of my position in the suit. You see, when Drane originally came to me I was touched by his story. Plus, I had my eye on a new Mercedes. To put it in a nutshell, I allowed him to talk me into taking only twenty percent of the settlement as my fee. Now, granted the guy has a valid case for pain and suffering damages since negligence resulted in him becoming a paraplegic, but what about my pain and suffering for being a lawyer? You see what I'm saying? Not only did I insult my personal dignity, and the dignity of my profession, by demanding too small a percentage, but I allowed a moment of tender-heartedness to interfere with my judgment about the best disposition for the case."

Thrope: "What, exactly, are you proposing?

Fur: "A solution to everybody's problems. I need money now, you need to reduce the liability for your client, and Drane needs to go through a trial so that he feels he has received his day in court. What I'm proposing is that you pay me one million dollars now, then we drag the suit on for years and eventually settle for $100,000 which I will magnanimously give entirely to Drane."

Thrope: "So my client saves almost ninety percent, but still pays over one million dollars?"

Fur: "Exactly. I'm prepared to offer you, personally, a sweet deal on my percentage of the take."

Thrope: "But we still go through a trial?"

Fur: "Oh, we'll spend years in court, but we'll do it the easy way. In fact, I've got a file from another case that is so similar about all we need to do is change the names, dates and

208

places on the court documents we'll file. We can generate about 1,500 pages of motions and cross-motions with no effort. By the time we're done, even another lawyer couldn't figure out what happened."

Thrope: "It sounds interesting. I'll need to discuss this with my client."

Fur: "You do that. Then contact my secretary and set up a lunch date so we can discuss the specifics."

Thrope: "Aren't you afraid your client will be upset?"

Fur: "The guy's a paraplegic. What's he going to do? Kick my ass? Besides, by the time we drag him through the court system for several years, he'll be glad to get what he can and get on with his life, such as it is. It'll serve him right for underestimating the value of a lawyer. It's a workable solution. The justice system isn't perfect, but God knows I'm doing everything I can.

Fifth Conversation:

Fur: "This is Lou C. Fur. Could I speak with N.D. Redd, please."

Secretary: "Just a moment, sir."

Redd: "Lou! How are you doing?"

Fur: "Just fine Newt. Hey listen, have I got a deal for you. One of my richer clients is setting up a will with a trust fund for their kids and grandkids. They're a cautious couple and they want to make sure that a good accounting of the money is made. Naturally, I thought of you."

Redd: "How much is the deal worth?"

Fur: "It's hard to say exactly but it's enough to be interesting. You'll have to trust me on that. A lot will depend on how creative your accounting procedures are. You interested?"

Redd: "Are you kidding? Ever since you defended my accounting firm, Redd, Inc., from mismanagement charges in that S & L case I've been wanting to work with you again. We do good things together."

Fur: "Well, this will be a little more complicated and not quite as lucrative, but we can't always have the luxury of working with government insured money. These aren't taxpayers with whom we'll be doing business. We'll have to be a little more careful."

Redd: "That's okay. I don't forget my friends. I remember, when you represented me before, how justice was served."

Fur: "Up on a platter?"

Redd: (Laughing) "Exactly! If you think we can do it, that's good enough for me."

Fur: "Trust me. Where there's a will, there's a way."

Sixth Conversation:

Fur: "Lou Dan Lascivious? This is Fur, I'm representing Sharon Demony in the divorce against her husband, Macon, whom I believe you represent."

Lascivious: "That's right. My client is offering a fair settlement because he doesn't want this dragged through the court system."

Fur: "Well, something has come up. My client wants it all."

Lascivious: "Mr. Fur, I'm sure you know the laws of this state won't support such a demand. There is such a thing as law."

Fur: "Of course there is law, but there are also lawyers to get around it. My client knows the letter of the law. She also knows the spirit of the law. She's willing to pay a much bigger percentage to take it all than your client is willing to pay in order to keep his share."

Lascivious: "Mr. Fur, that is not justice. That is simple arithmetic. Okay, how do we screw my client out of his money?"

Fur: "That's the spirit! As those great heroes of Texas said: 'Remember the Alimony'. I'll have my secretary contact your secretary and we'll set up a working lunch to discuss the details."

Seventh Conversation:

Fur: "May I speak with Justin Lowlife, please?"

Lowlife: "This is me."

Fur: "Justin, I have a job for you. I've got a very important trial coming up and I need some discreet influence with the jury. I figured you were my man."

Lowlife: "What's in it for me?"

Fur: "Well, this is a big trial. My client is very high up in local organized crime and politics. It could be your shot at moving up in the social circles."

Lowlife: "Why are you doing this for me?"

Fur: "Hey, I'm just naturally altruistic. I like to see people get ahead in life and make something of themselves. It gives me a warm feeling inside. Besides, you're my kind of people. Are you in?"

Lowlife: "Okay."

Eighth Conversation:

Fur: "Ben D. Rules? This is Lou C. Fur. I'm representing Abel Toby Framed on those stealing charges tomorrow. You'll be prosecuting attorney in the case, is that right?"

Rules: "I've been expecting you to call. I suppose you've looked at the evidence and noted that it's not all that strong. You probably figure I should drop the charges rather than go through a trial."

Fur: "Actually, I don't really care about the charges being dropped. I just don't want to go through a trial. I'm too busy right now. I want to plead my client guilty and get it over with."

Rules: "Are you serious? The D.A. was considering dropping the charges!"

Fur: "Well, that's the way it goes. If I don't have the time to properly defend him then he'll just have to do some time."

Rules: "Do you really think he stole the money?"

Fur: "Probably not. If he had, he could have afforded a lawyer to prove him innocent. What's your point?"

Rules: "Well, you're supposed to act in the best interests of your client."

Fur: "This is the best act I've got. Look, you're a prosecutor. All you need to be concerned about is your conviction record. I'm making it easy for you. Have we got a deal or not?"

Rules: "Well, sure."

AND NOW, FOR A LIVE REPORT

"That's very interesting," I said when the tape ended, "but I don't see much that's new or shocking. You've documented that one specific lawyer was a weasel. I assume you have other recordings to indicate that other lawyers have similar dispositions. But what's your point? You can't use that to get a conviction because it's an illegal wiretap. You might use it to persuade a few people that lawyers are corrupt, but do you know what the toughest challenge is when it comes to convincing people that lawyers are scumbags?"

Tom shrugged.

"It's finding someone who doesn't already know," I explained. "The second toughest challenge is convincing people they can actually do something about it."

"Maybe for you," Tom solemnly said. "For my people, the toughest challenge is to stay alive and healthy long enough to do something about it. We're on the run most of the time and in hiding the rest of the time. How do you do it? Lawyers know who you are and where to find you. How do you stay alive? Do you have supernatural powers or something?"

The conversation had turned dangerously close to the truth. Eekim, Nicky and I had agreed that, for her protection, her powers were never to be divulged to anyone.

"I'm just lucky," I stated.

Tom looked at me the way a perpetually hungry man might look at a fat man eating a seven course meal; a stoic mixture of envy and disgust.

"Yea, well, I wish you could share that kind of luck," he finally said.

"I can. Why don't you join us, Tom? Become a part of HOSTILE."

He gave me a lopsided grin and looked at me out of the corner of his eyes. "Actually, I came here to ask you to join us."

"Us?"

"Yes, us," he restated. "I'm not going to try and bullshit you. There's a bunch of 'us' who are actually doing something Josh. You know about Fur. He's not the first and he won't be the

212

last. We're not just bitching about lawyers and publishing little criticisms of them, we're taking action!"

"You're action seems a little extreme," I commented.

"Extreme? Extreme!" his voice raised. "I'll tell you what's extreme. Extreme is when there is no workable justice system because an entire profession is greedy, overpaid, corrupt bastards who have the power to police themselves and, instead, unite to form a union of smug sociopaths! Extreme is when you have to shoot a criminal's lawyer in order to have any hope of putting the criminal in jail. Extreme is when lawyers buy and sell-out their clients like cattle. Extreme is when the law can be twisted by every double-talking attorney until no one knows what is right or wrong. Weren't you listening to the tape? That's extreme! And it happens every damned day!"

"But Tom, what you're doing is..."

"What Josh? What is it? What was it with you and that big bonfire? Does it seem different because the lawyers I deal with are too clever to carry guns? Let me tell you, lawyers can cut-out your heart with a tort, they can put you on the rack with an obscure precedent, they can blow your brains out with a motion, they can choke you to death with an objection and they can torture you forever with appeals and delays. You know I'm right Josh."

I understood his point. I wished Eekim were here. That little monkey was honest and direct. He could bring a very wise perspective to a discussion. On the other hand he probably would have agreed with Tom. I once heard him quote the peels of his tribe, in their wisdom, as saying: "It is difficult to change a tiger's stripes while he is breathing."

"But what if you make a mistake?" I protested.

"You mean like offing an honest lawyer?" Tom scoffed. "What are the odds? Huh? Besides, lawyers refer to themselves as 'hired guns', it's about time they took some incoming fire. Innocent people have their lives destroyed by corrupt lawyers every day. So what if a few 'innocent' lawyers get hurt? There's no such thing as a perfect system, but if it has to be as screwed up as ours then we ought to make sure everyone gets their share."

"What do you call yourselves?" I ventured.

Tom glared at me for a moment but then his shoulders relaxed. He let out a deep breath and kind of chuckled: "I got pretty worked up there. It's an emotional issue." After a pause he calmly said: "We like to think of ourselves as unofficial legal corrections officers. I'll tell you one thing, Josh. We never ever take a chance on hurting a child or someone who isn't a lawyer. We consider it a war but we only attack the enemy. We are not cowards or terrorists. We call ourselves patriots. And we call ourselves dead.

"We don't have any illusions about our chances for a long and happy life. Most of us have already had our fate determined by a thieving lawyer so it doesn't really make too much difference. But lawyers shouldn't have so little respect for us as to leave us alive as if we're not even strong enough to do anything except whimper and cry until we die of despair. We have more dignity than that."

He smiled: "Realistically, of course, the reason lawyers don't kill all their victims is because it would show up statistically.

"But, like I said," he continued, "we consider ourselves patriots. Yes, we do want a revolution. We want a revolution which returns the justice system to the ideal upon which it was founded. This country was started by a revolution and that revolution needs to be refought today. Our forefathers foresaw the need for continual revolution. They gave us the vote so we could have a revolution every four years. They gave us an impeachment process so we could have a revolution more often if we needed it. I don't think they foresaw what a mess our legal system would become or they would have put in more safeguards. Or maybe they did foresee it and that's why we have the right to bear arms."

"You say we can have a revolution every four years," I noted. "So why can't we have a nonviolent revolution to combat the lawyer problem?"

He heartily laughed: "Josh, you're naive. Lawyers are sophisticated, organized and powerful. They can pervert any reform you come up with. The only thing that is going to make a lawyer think twice about screwing a client is fear. Most lawyers have absolutely no fear they will be punished. We're trying to change that."

"I can't join you," I flatly stated. "I have an obligation to the people who belong to HOSTILE. I am dedicated to the ideal that we can reform lawyers if people get together, work and have faith. I can't betray that principle. But I can invite you to join us."

Tom shook his head: "It's too late for that. I, too, am dedicated to principles. I don't have your talking monkey or your 'magic shield' so I had to make choices based on my reality. I wish it had been different but I don't regret my decisions. I'm a fighter, but I 'fight the good fight'."

He stood and placed the recorder inside the backpack.

"You know," he mused, "the first thing any tyrant does is make it illegal to oppose him. Lawyers won't allow anyone else to police their profession."

"Tom," I said while holding out my hand, "I hope we can join forces someday."

"It's at least a nice thought," he replied and firmly shook my hand. He looked me straight in the eye. "I don't think I'm long for this world but I think I might outlive you. I hope your magic holds."

With that, Tom relaxed his grip and walked out the door. He had a very noble manner for a dead man.

I didn't realize how his words, like the prophecy of a ghost, would come to haunt me.

MEET THE OPPRESSED

We sat under a glaring blaze of lights in a room unnaturally quiet except for the soft hum, only slightly more than a vibration, of machinery, cameras and electric current. It was hot with a dry heat but my skin was covered with a light film of perspiration. The hardwood table we sat around felt as friendly as a warmed skillet might if it was large enough to rest your elbows upon.

My eyebrows were dark with mascara, my hair (what there was of it) was stiff with spray and my complexion was bland with pancake make-up which made my face feel like it had been dipped in mud. I was afraid my face would crack if I smiled. After depleting my countenance of all character by the

215

application of a smooth, consistent layer of pancake the make-up girl had applied rouge to my cheeks to give me "that robust, healthy look". The mirror told me I looked like a corpse ready for a night on the town.

I had worn some make-up during the heyday of Monkey Business and I had been if front of cameras several times but this day was different. Before, there had always been interaction with the audience or reporters. Now, the whole thing seemed staged and intrusive, like being under a microscope beneath the scrutiny of unseen eyes. I felt as if I was just another prop on a stage where appearance outweighed substance in importance.

Even the tan, upholstered chairs were deceptive. They looked plush and comfortable but were constructed from a cheap material which crinkled with brittle little creaking noises every time I moved. Someone had the foresight to weave thousands of tiny, spiked, metallic shards into the fabric so that it itched relentlessly.

Around the table sat Nicky, looking engaging; Eekim, looking mischievous; several reporters, looking curious but prepared to shift to bored on a moment's notice; and Dr. Ruth Leslie Prosaic, a psychiatrist who looked as if she thought she deserved more degrees than she had while no one else deserved as many. She was dressed in a severe black business woman's suit with a white blouse and had the air of being a clinician's clinician. Her frizzy reddish hair came just over her forehead in front, just past her ears on the side and just over her collar in back. When our eyes met I was convinced she could tell me where every frizz and frazz on her head was, what every kink or twist meant and why it was important.

She dispassionately met my eyes, enigmatically smiled as if reading my thoughts and then let her gaze rise to my sparsely covered pate which had required an extra layer of pancake to diminish reflections from the lights. Her smile changed from enigmatic to condescending amusement as she looked away. I decided to take an immediate dislike to her.

The moderator for the event was a man named Luke Warm. He began by welcoming the viewers and introducing the panelists and reporters. Turning to Dr. Prosaic, he said: "Doctor, perhaps you could get us started by stating your

216

position on the lawyer problem."

"I'd be mildly delighted to do so," replied Prosaic. "The undesirable impact of lawyers on society has been a continuing problem throughout the history of this country. Lately, of course, the ramifications of the problem have become so immense that some type of cure must be found. The current state of affairs is that lawyers are allowed to control our legal system and, further, establishes their profession as the only authority with the ability to institute and enforce ethics upon themselves. Indeed, the obvious result is that the situation has grown so desperate as to resemble the chaos which would result if the inmates ran our asylums."

She looked expectantly at the reporters and then pedantically prompted: "That's a professional joke."

All the professionals in the room emitted charitable chuckles. I wondered if this was what was meant by "professional courtesy". Nicky rolled her eyes and Eekim mockingly laughed at the professionals.

"What is needed," continued Prosaic, "is a solution. But before a solution can be found the problem must be thoroughly studied by people educated and trained in the rehabilitation of social deviants. Mr. Wetwood, although he doesn't look like much, has attracted a lot of attention with his HOSTILE organization. Such an organization, which supports punishment for offenders, obviously appeals to laymen who desire a sense of revenge disguised as justice. In point of fact, however, his amateurish approach merely treats the symptoms and not the illness."

"I would like to respond to that," said Eekim. "HOSTILE was my idea, and it's a damned good one! We agree that lawyers are a problem and harmful to society, so how can you say that efforts to document and punish lawyer malfeasance is 'amateurish'?"

"I will explain it once more for the benefit of the talking monkey," Dr. Prosaic coldly replied. "HOSTILE treats the symptoms but not the illness. It is not enough to punish lawyers for being corrupt, incompetent, immoral and self-serving. We must determine 'why' they are corrupt, incompetent, immoral and self-serving before we can find a cure."

217

She gazed at Eekim with smug superiority.

"Come off it, lady," replied Eekim (Nicky smiled. I put my hands behind my head and relaxed. Eekim would take it from here. She really shouldn't have insulted him.) "Lawyers are the way they are because people have allowed them to be that way. Lawyers will stop being the way they are when people demand they stop."

"A typical monkey analysis of the situation," pooh-poohed Prosaic. "The clinical approach demands that we first define the root cause of lawyers. There are three avenues for statistical analysis which can be stated as..."

"Heredity, environment," interrupted Eekim. "And...and...something else?"

"Score two for the monkey," Prosaic derisively laughed. "Yes, genetics and social factors are two proper areas for inquiry. The third is the 'traumatic event theory' of human behavior. In simple words, the theory maintains that some devastatingly profound event can occur in a person's life which can turn them from a life of honesty and dignity to one of jurisprudence."

"What could cause that?" Eekim incredulously asked.

"We're not sure, that's why more study is necessary," responded Prosaic. "Even the simple explanations of genetics and environment are more complicated than they first appear. Many lawyers are the progeny of lawyers and, therefore, are raised by lawyers. It is difficult to isolate the distinctive effect of each factor. The issues are even more complex because they may be interrelated or they may originate with different factors.

"For instance, let's consider the genetic theory. Suppose we were to accept that lawyers are caused by some constituent of DNA. It would still be left to determine if the malady is a combination of substandard genes which promote a predetermined tendency to reduce the individual to a lawyer or if there is an aberrant DNA strand, which may lie dormant even in normal healthy people, which is then passed to some offspring like a genetic time-bomb waiting to explode. The second theory is more popular among professional psychiatrists because it would explain both a lawyer's predisposition to produce children who become lawyers and also the manifestation of the mutation within the general population."

"Hmmm...," considered Eekim. "I hadn't considered that."

"I know," smiled Prosaic. "Likewise, the environmental theory is two-fold. There is the possibility that lawyer parents, through interaction with their children, pass on attitudes and perceptions which can condemn the child to life as an attorney. Similarly, though different, it must be remembered that children of lawyers are often isolated from contact with normal children. The result is that lawyer offspring are forced into a peer group with children who come from similarly deprived moral environments. Having been raised in such an inadequate atmosphere the child comes to view the future as hopeless and inevitably turns to a life of litigation."

"What about the 'traumatic event theory'," asked Eekim with genuine interest.

"That theory is still being explored," replied Prosaic. "Many professionals in the field of psychiatry believe that no single event could be devastating enough to turn a rational human being into a lawyer. But the most espoused example is that of the law degree. Proponents of the theory argue that a person could still lead a respectable life even after being burdened with a law degree. The reason lawyers don't, these psychiatrists claim, is because lawyers are shunned by employers seeking honest, hardworking employees. Eventually, the lawyer resigns himself to nothing more than the pursuit of profitable cases. The awarding of the law degree, therefore, becomes the 'traumatic event' which acts as a catalyst for the degradation of ethical behavior in the individual.

"Most opponents of the theory hypothesize that a law degree in itself does not make a lawyer. The proof for this, they claim, is that you could award a law degree to dog and it would not immediately turn into a jackal. Both schools of thought are, of course, considered radical by mainstream psychiatrists.

"There is a related theory which is referred to as 'Cumulative Debilitating Behavior Pattern'. This theory suggests that a history of lawyer-like behavior, which includes lying, deception, and trickery; produces physical changes in the brain. Just as a lie detector can measure electrical impulses, proponents of this theory argue that these electrical impulses cause short-circuits in the neural net of the brain. It is hypothesized that a history of deception causes enough damage to the brain as to render it functionally unable to recognize or relate to the truth. It is an innovative theory and is still being explored."

"That's extremely interesting," said Eekim in a tone sounding like a saber sliding from its scabbard. "But what good is all your study and theories? HOSTILE has shaken the foundation of the lawyer conspiracy. People now have documented recommendations to aid them in finding the least objectionable lawyer to represent them. HOSTILE has made lawyers pay for their past misconduct with their reputation. Granted, it was a small price to pay but at least some of their debt to society has been collected. HOSTILE doesn't delude itself with the idea that we are making lawyers more ethical, but we are forcing them to be more careful. The result is that people are safe to walk the streets to the courthouse. We have formed a kind of 'Neighborhood Watch' program for our courts so people can sleep peacefully at night."

"You may have made lawyers more careful," taunted Dr. Prosaic, "but you haven't cured a single one of them. Just as thieves can figure out how to thwart a burglar alarm, lawyers will soon figure ways around your safeguards. The trick is to cure or rehabilitate them so that safeguards are unnecessary."

Eekim jumped up on the table and confronted the doctor with a steely glare: "And exactly how many lawyers have you cured?"

"As a matter of fact," Prosaic proudly announced, "I have brought with me today the first lawyer ever successfully converted into a moral human being. Like most scientific breakthroughs, it happened quite by fortuitous accident. Please bring in Mr. Ben Reformd."

Two medical technicians in white coats pushed an invalid in a wheelchair on-stage. The seated figure stared vacantly ahead, his hands lay limply in his lap. He gave the impression of not having moved in some time. One of the technicians wiped a trickle of spittle off his chin.

"We are very proud of Mr. Reformd," Prosaic beamed. "He is the first documented case of a lawyer who successfully and completely renounced his former immoral tendencies. He was able to achieve this breakthrough by way of a serendipitous head-on collision with a semi tractor-trailer. The accident necessitated the removal of 85% of his brain, but the unexpected upside is that he has been completely rehabilitated. He no longer feels the slightest inclination to lie, cheat or steal."

The reporters and Luke Warm broke into applause; even Eekim looked pleased. A couple of the reporters shouted things like "marvelous" and "amazing".

"Of course," explained the doctor, "the loss of brain tissue also rehabilitated Mr. Reformd from eating, drinking, talking, bathing and moving. Overall, though, my professional opinion is that it was a beneficial trade-off, both for Mr. Reformd and society."

More cheers from the reporters.

"By the Big Banana," swore Eekim. "Do you mean you favor 'curing' lawyers by lobotomizing them into drooling zombies?"

"The proof is sitting there before you," answered Prosaic. "Look at him. He will never commit another act of lawyer indiscretion for as long as he lives!"

Eekim stared at Prosaic and then glanced appraisingly at Reformd. After a moment he shrugged his shoulders and said: "Right! Works for me."

With a showman's intuition, Luke Warm broke in with the announcement: "We'll be right back to further discuss the question 'Lawyers, what the hell are we going to do about them?', after a few words from our sponsors."

Warm smiled at the panel and said: "Okay, we've laid the foundation in the first segment of the show. It's now question and answer time. We'll start with Mr. Ed Iter, followed by Ms. Carmen Tater and then Mr. Reed Allabotit. Please try to keep your answers brief so that everyone gets equal time."

"Time to match wits," Eekim said to Prosaic. "Would you like a few pointers?"

The doctor tolerantly smiled and replied: "I deal with disturbed mentalities all the time. Don't worry, I'll be gentle."

Eekim's gratuitous smile froze on his face, but he quickly recovered and casually observed: "Discussions with lobotomized patients may be challenging, for you, but I don't believe they have properly trained you to debate a highly developed intellect like mine."

"Actually," Prosaic icily retorted, "your vocabulary is larger than the average vegetable but I'm not convinced there is any substance in your statements."

"Why, you..." Eekim fumed. "I'll peel you like a banana!"

"What a quaint simile," Prosaic teased. "Abstract yet irrelevant. Does this obsession with fruit often interfere with your ability to intelligently communicate?"

Luke Warm broke into the exchange and announced: "We're almost ready to go back on the air."

The three reporters hurriedly scribbled new questions. A journalist thrives on controversy and their expressions had progressed from mild interest to carnivorous zest. There was no doubt the conflict would be exploited to the maximum.

I glanced nervously at Nicky. She was calm and tranquil, projecting a reassuring confidence. I decided her approach would be more appealing to viewers and frenziedly composed myself into a serene demeanor.

The prompter began a countdown: "And five, four,..."

"Witch!" hissed Eekim.

"Banana brain!" whispered Prosaic.

"One," said the prompter.

"Welcome back folks," effused Warm. "Our panel is now ready to accept questions. We will begin with Mr. Iter."

"I would like address a question to both Dr. Prosaic and Eekim and have them each answer in turn. Each of you have taken different approaches to the problem of lawyers. Perhaps you could each define the advantages of your approach and explain why you consider it superior to the other's. Dr. Prosaic?"

"The main point of contention between my esteemed colleague and myself is how we approach the premise of the problem," Prosaic began. "We both agree that lawyers represent a devastating malady which afflicts the social health of our country. But the question remains 'How do we solve the problem?'. I take an intellectual, scientific approach which is aimed at achieving a definite and total cure. My colleague, on the other hand, takes an instinctive, one might say primitive,

222

approach which relies on a political solution. Granted, the instinctive approach is appealing because it provides immediate gratification, but in the long run it does nothing to definitively reduce the lawyer threat to society. My colleague maintains his HOSTILE organization is successful because it has made lawyers more 'careful'. I remind my colleague that, as an example, in the search for a cancer cure we do not look for a treatment which makes cancer more 'careful', we look for a way to eradicate it.

"My colleague claims success because he documents lawyer atrocities," she continued. "I remind him that a disease is not cured merely by keeping count of the victims. I believe the presence of Mr. Reformd, the only lawyer in existence ever to be totally rehabilitated, is living proof of the superiority of my approach."

"Mr. Eekim," said Iter, "would you care to respond to this attack on your position?"

"Indeed I would," said Eekim. "The main advantage of Dr. Prosaic's scientific approach relies on the flexibility provided by ignorance. She fumbles around searching for the 'cause' of the problem. She says it may be substandard genes, or one mutant gene, or lack of parental values, or peer pressure, or some devastating trauma, or maybe a cumulative debilitating behavior pattern. She over-intellectualizes her analysis. I know the cause of the problem with justice in our society, it is lawyers. The problem is obvious and we need look no further. Dr. Prosaic confuses and complicates the issue by looking for the cause of the cause.

"I would like to use her metaphor of cancer to illustrate my point. How do we treat cancer? We cut it out, kill it, radiate it, poison it or medicate it. We don't tell a cancer victim that absolutely nothing can be done since we don't know what caused the cancer. We don't tell cancer victims to be patient until we find the cause of the cancer. We do what we can. Lawyers are a cancer, we must do what we can."

"Dr. Prosaic," said Ms. Tater. "How do you respond to a monkey who insinuates that your greatest strength lies in ignorance? And how do you feel about Mr. Eekim turning your metaphor around and using it against you?"

Dr. Prosaic smiled and said: "I will answer the latter prior to the former. The problem with using metaphors is interpretation. My colleague reinterpreted my cancer metaphor in a clever, albeit bestial, manner.

"However, he further claims that I ignore the 'obvious'. I believe he is guilty of even greater intellectual omission by ignoring the proof of my success, which is sitting propped-up in that wheelchair and drooling on himself."

Reed Allabotit asked: "Mr. Eekim, how do you respond to the accusation that you are nothing more than a beast who is incapable of recognizing evidence even when it is propped-up in front of you?"

"I'm glad you asked that," said Eekim. "I acknowledge that Mr. Reformed has been cured of his despicable lawyer inclinations. I recognize and applaud that accomplishment. But I don't see how Dr. Prosaic can claim credit since it was an accident in which she had no part. One of the requirements of the scientific approach is that results must be verifiable by repetition. Now, while I am positive that a large number of red-blooded, American truckers would gladly smash their eighteen-wheelers head-on into a lawyer's fancy automobile, I do not believe lawyers can be convinced to willingly participate."

"But we can build on this success," stammered Prosaic, flustered for the first time. "Perhaps we can discover exactly what parts of the brain malfunction to produce lawyer behavior. We could then remove those parts and still leave a lawyer in control of his bodily functions. If we could do that, then we could pass legislation requiring the operation upon completion of law school..."

"So!" Interrupted Eekim with a thin smile. "You'd have to rely, at least in part, on a political solution!"

"Not necessarily," Prosaic countered with agitation. "It may be possible to replicate the effect without surgery. An associate of mine, who is an expert in Behavior Modification, thinks that we could achieve the same results if we could compel lawyers to sit-down and shut-up for the rest of their lives."

"And what are the odds of doing that?" Eekim demanded.

Before Prosaic could answer, everyone's attention was

drawn to Reformd who had begun spasmodically twitching in his wheelchair. His movements rapidly progressed to uncontrolled convulsions as the attendants attempted to restrain him. His body became stiff as a board with a final seizure before collapsing in the chair. One of the attendants felt for a pulse and then sadly shook his head and placed a blanket over the inert form.

"You call that success?" Eekim asked.

"Scientifically speaking, he's still cured," Prosaic retorted.

"Well, yeah," Eekim conceded.

"And now, a word from our sponsor," said Luke Warm.

During the break the attendants tied Reformd to the chair with a discarded piece of electrical wire. They argued over who had to do the paperwork as they pushed him off the stage.

Dr. Prosaic, stricken with grief, muttered: "He had made such wonderful progress. Why did the bastard have to die now?"

"Maybe it's all for the best," Eekim comforted.

The prompter intoned: "Five, four, three, two, one."

"Welcome back folks," said Luke Warm. "That's about it for this show. I want to thank Eekim and his associates from HOSTILE for being with us. I also want to thank Dr. Ruth Leslie Prosaic, author of the new book ROOTS OF EVIL: A Study of Lawyers in Modern Society. Sorry about your patient dying like that, doctor."

"It's okay," sighed Dr. Prosaic. "The real drawback is that I'll have to experiment on rats now. I have some professional reservations about experimenting on higher life forms."

"I understand," sympathized Warm. "As always, I want to extend appreciation to members of the press for their participation. Next week, we feature Cal Les Dands, a Southwest Missouri farmer, who will combine a discussion of the admirable, chemical composition of lawyers with a presentation on the agricultural advantages of natural fertilizer. Until then, I'm Luke Warm and this has been 'Meet The Oppressed'."

"And we're clear," said the prompter.

AFTER THE SHOW

Nicky and Eekim preceded me to the dressing room after the show. As I turned the corner in the corridor I noticed Dr. Prosaic slip into our room.

I heard Eekim say: "Where's your broom, you old witch?"

I heard Prosaic say: "Go suck a banana little monkey. By the way, did you know that bananas are phallic symbols?"

I heard Eekim say: "That's hitting below the belt."

I heard a loud bang! I heard a crash! I heard Nicky cry out!

Fearing the worst, I broke into a sprint and charged into the room. Unfortunately, in my haste, I caught my foot on the doorjamb and tripped flailing through the doorway and then stumbled over a chair which sent me crashing against the wall and then sprawling to the floor.

Everyone was quiet for a moment.

"Thanks, Josh," Eekim broke the silence. "I was feeling clumsy until you arrived."

I looked up from the floor to see Nicky, Eekim and Dr. Prosaic looking at me with mixtures of amusement and concern in their faces.

"What happened?" I astutely inquired with as much dignity as possible for someone lying in a crumpled heap on the floor.

"I can explain," Eekim helpfully replied. "You charged into the room. Unfortunately, in your haste, you caught your foot on the doorjamb and tripped flailing through the doorway and then stumbled over a chair which sent you crashing against the wall and then sprawling to the floor."

"Thanks for clearing that up," I ungratefully replied while getting to my hands and knees as the first step towards regaining my feet.

"Mr. Wetwood, are you okay?" asked Prosaic with concern.

"No broken bones anyway," I responded as I stood up.

"Good," she acknowledged. "But that's not what I mean. Excessive clumsiness has often been diagnosed as a symptom of low self-esteem."

"Don't worry about it, Doc," Eekim commented. "His self-esteem is no lower than it should be."

"What happened just before I got here?" I asked, changing the subject. "I thought I heard a shot, a crash and a scream."

"Well," Eekim began. "I popped the cork on this bottle of vintage banana champagne, the cork flew out and broke that lamp by Nicky and then she kind of shrieked in surprise. I thought it was all very exciting until you made your dramatic entrance, then it all seemed kind of hum-drum by comparison."

"I think it was rather heroic that you were coming to the rescue," said Nicky. Bless her.

"Right. Bozo saves the day!" laughed Eekim. Damn him.

"Are we celebrating something?" I noticed champagne glasses sitting on a table.

"Nothing gets by this guy," Eekim quipped. "It's a much more accurate deduction than the one you previously made. You know, the one just before you came charging into the room where, unfortunately, in your haste you caught your foot..."

"I remember," I interrupted. "What are we celebrating?"

"Josh," Eekim proudly said. "I'd like to announce the newest member of HOSTILE. I signed her up just before the show. Do you remember Dr. Ruth Leslie Prosaic, or did you hit your head when you stumbled over the chair which sent you crashing into the wall and then..."

"I remember," I again interrupted. "But I'm somewhat confused. You two were just arguing on national TV. And I heard you exchanging insults just before I, uh... just before I entered."

"Let me address the latter prior to the former," giggled Eekim while glancing at Prosaic who merely raised her eyebrows, smiled and looked away. "Exchanging insults is a form of intellectual jousting. Among highly developed minds it is a way of sharpening verbal fencing skills. There's no way you could know that, of course.

"As to our conflict on national TV," he continued, "it was all for show. It would have been a boring broadcast if we had gone on the air and merely patted each other on the back.

227

Conflict is more interesting and ultimately served both our causes. There now, that's one less subject for you to be confused about. You now have more time to devote to other subjects."

"You see, we're really not so far apart," interjected Prosaic. "I've joined HOSTILE. And Eekim has agreed to collaborate on my next book, which is tentatively entitled: <u>KILL THE ROOTS: A Clinical and Practical Solution to the Lawyer Problem</u>. Do you understand what I'm telling you?"

"What do you think I am, an idiot!" I demanded.

"I've described you to her," explained Eekim with a laugh. "Your stunning entrance did full justice to my description."

"I still think it was heroic the way you came dashing in here," Nicky charitably reiterated.

I wished she would give it up. I appreciated the gesture but every time she said something supportive I felt more incompetent. How fragile did she think my ego was? I felt a little insecure that she didn't know I was more self-confident.

"Yea, yea, dashing, stumbling, whatever," grumbled Eekim. "Hey! Come on! This is a celebration. Let's pour the bubbly before it goes flat."

He quickly filled the glasses and passed them around. As he handed me mine, he said: "Here Josh, this will make you forget how clumsy you are."

"Really?" I doubtfully asked.

"Yes," Eekim assured. "But don't worry, I'll be here to remind you."

He smiled #637, which means: "What are friends for, anyway?"

CHAPTER TEN

ONE SMALL STEP...

Later that night Nicky, Eekim and I carried on with the celebration after returning to HOSTILE headquarters.

We were just polishing off our fifth bottle of banana champagne. I added the dead soldier to the small mortuary accumulating on my desk. Raising my glass in salute to the fallen five, I toasted: "Well done, noble warriors, you have served your country and your fellow man well. Rest in peace."

"That's it!" exclaimed Eekim.

"What's it?" asked Nicky.

"What the balding primate said," answered Eekim. "Serve your country! Look, we had some specific goals when we started out. We were going to 'Massacre the worst, take back the bananas, paint their butts blue and put them to work'. We had lofty goals, I agree, but that doesn't negate the fact that we have fallen short. We whacked <u>some</u> of the worst lawyers at the underground complex, we took back <u>some</u> of the bananas in the lawsuit with the Missouri Bar, we painted only <u>one</u> lawyer's butt blue and, through HOSTILE, have succeeded <u>somewhat</u> in putting them to work. We have much to celebrate, but we must also recognize that the job is only partially begun."

"So, what do you suggest?" Nicky asked.

"Our next step," Eekim proudly declared, "is to run for President of the United States of America."

"Our next step?" I inquired. "But neither Nicky nor you are old enough. And I'm not sure if a monkey can run for President anyway. Which means..."

"Congratulations on your nomination," Eekim grinned while shaking my hand. "I'm sure you'll make a fine President."

"I don't know anything about politics," I protested.

"That," Eekim proclaimed, "is your best qualification; philosophically at least. Don't worry, I'll handle the politics. I've always wanted to be a mover and shaker, it fits my dance style. Don't worry, with Nicky as your Press Secretary and me as your Campaign Manager you'll be a sure thing. Just follow the example of previous Presidential candidates: never tell a lie even when the truth would make more sense."

"That's a rather cynical premise," Nicky noted.

"Hey, we're running for President here, not opening a day-care center," Eekim argued. "C'mon, let's have a few words from the next President of the United States!"

"I'm not sure I want the job," I objected. "I don't think I'm qualified. I don't have any political experience. I don't like politics. All I know is I don't like lawyers and I want some sort of control put on them. Running for President is a stupid idea and we haven't got a chance in hell of making it work!"

Eekim blankly looked at me for a moment and then turned to Nicky: "Okay, as Press Secretary it's your job to put a positive spin on that. Clean it up and we'll use it for his acceptance speech.

He raised his glass to me and toasted: "Hail to the Chief!"

ONE GIANT LEAP...

Take my word for it. Running for President sounds ridiculously stupid late at night when you're in a good mood with a couple of bottles of champagne under your belt. In the light of day and with a clear head it sounds even worse.

However, Eekim convinced Nicky it was the proper

thing to do. He argued that with the current state of the country it was a question of "evolution or revolution". His basic argument was that we either grabbed the reins of power and guided the country to a new course of action or we must be prepared to just sit back and watch as the country continued to decline with the inevitable erosion of social structure and resultant chaos and revolt.

I thought his argument was a little melodramatic. Still, it was hard to look around at the current state of affairs and contend that he was completely wrong. When Nicky bought into his plan, needless to say, so did I.

"Beautiful," crooned Eekim. "With the three of us working together we'll be unstoppable. Now let's get down to business. Josh what are your best qualifications when it comes to being President of the United States?"

"I'm not sure," I admitted.

"He's never held any elected office," Nicky commented.

"That's good!" Eekim enthused. "A career unblemished by political corruption. Okay, what else?"

"I don't know," I brooded. "I'm not sure I've got the background for politics. I'm just an average man, my family wasn't rich or powerful. I'm not well connected."

"That's good too," Eekim declared. "This country likes to think that an average man has the opportunity to become President. We'll take it one step further and imply that an average man should become President. Okay, what else?"

"Josh can't stand lawyers," offered Nicky.

"Good, good," intoned Eekim. "An individual's respectability is defined as much by his enemies as his friends. Lawyer reform will provide the political basis of our campaign. That ought to be good for a lot of grass roots support. This is forming up nicely, don't you think? But we're still missing something. What is the best thing you have going for you? What's the one thing none of the other candidates have? What is the single most unique and attractive aspect of your success?"

"Charisma?" Nicky tried.

"Honesty?" I suggested.

"It starts with 'E'," Eekim hinted.

Nicky and I exchanged a knowing glance.

231

"Energy?" I playfully guessed.

"Enthusiasm?" Nicky teased.

"Entelligence?" I joshed.

"I've been around here too long," he said with a scowl. "You two are starting to take me for granted. The answer is obviously me! Eekim! The one and only talking monkey! The scientific miracle, hero of children and darling of the media. I don't like to brag, but I'm the most popular, modern hero to walk this planet in centuries. If these were less sophisticated times, I would have been declared a god by now."

"It's amazing you can maintain such a humble outlook," Nicky dryly commented.

"It is, isn't it," Eekim agreed. "Just another one of my admirable characteristics. Now then, I've outlined some campaign slogans for your approval. Here they are: 'Eekim, A Tough Monkey For A Tough Job', 'Never Send A Man To Do A Monkey's Job', 'Sometimes A Monkey Has To Do What A Monkey Has To Do', 'Eekim, A Monkey Of The People', 'Josh Wetwood, The Monkey's Choice', and 'Elect Josh Wetwood Because Eekim Will Be His Right-Hand Monkey'."

"Those slogans seem to be mostly about you," Nicky observed.

"Let's go with our strengths," commented Eekim.

A HEARTBEAT AWAY...

We spent some time working out the platform for our campaign for the highest elected office in the country. Eekim and Nicky began the immense task of forming an organization which could take on the political machines which currently determine candidates and elections. It was a monumental task which I tired of quickly.

The organizational and managerial requirements were immense. I could understand why those best suited to serve could seldom get selected to be elected. Fortunately, Eekim possessed a natural gift for intrigue and strategy while Nicky excelled at management details. Constance kept track of the organization and Melvin developed computer software to track demographics. They soon expanded HOSTILE to a point where it was an ever-growing juggernaut of political support.

They did let me choose my running mate.

And so, a few weeks later, Tom Window strolled into my office, casually sat down and said: "I heard you wanted to see me."

"Yes," I replied. "How old are you, Tom?"

"Thirty-six."

"Have you ever been convicted of a felony?"

He smiled: "Not yet."

"Have you ever been charged with a felony?"

Again he smiled: "Not yet."

Well, that was as good as the qualifications of most of our Presidential candidates.

"Do you have any skeletons in your closet?"

"Josh, you know I'm a suspect in the suspicious deaths of at least one lawyer."

"Yea, I know. But is there anything in your past that is disreputable? Anything the American people would be offended by?"

"I don't lie, cheat or steal, if that's what you mean," Tom replied. "What's this all about?"

I cleared my throat and said: "Well, Tom, you've got to be aware that we are currently organizing to make a run for the Presidency. I was wondering if you want to be my Vice-President."

His eyes popped open and he erupted in laughter: "You've got to be kidding! Josh! I'm wanted for questioning in a couple of killings!"

"I don't see that, in itself, as a problem," I replied. "You merely take a hands-on approach to reform. There are very few saints in politics. Elected officials maintain our military, send troops into battle and keep the police in this country armed and ready to protect us. Just because they wear suits doesn't mean they are any less responsible when the trigger is pulled. If anything, they are more responsible.

"The world is not a nice place," I continued. "We don't need wimps in office. We need fighters. We just need to make sure whose side they're on. As you told me last time we spoke, you 'fight the good fight'."

"But why me?" he asked.

"Well, for one thing," I chuckled. "With your reputation for integrity and, shall we say, 'fatal criticism' the public will be assured of my honesty. With you at my back I would be a fool to enter into any morally compromising arrangements."

"Sort of a lethal Jiminy Cricket?"

"Something like that," I agreed. "Not that I intend to do anything wrong, but you never know how the trappings of power might warp a man's judgment. I believe you would provide more solid spiritual guidance than three ghosts at Christmas."

"The dickens you say," Tom laughed and then added: "Well, it's an interesting proposition. I assume that if you're willing to choose me as your second then you're not going to shy from controversy."

"Absolutely not," I guaranteed. "Tom, I have no intention of becoming a career politician. I am not going to make compromises merely so I can make political allies and be assured of getting elected to another office. I'm going to accomplish certain goals and get out. I have no intention of spending the rest of my life on the public dole as a career politician."

"Interesting," Tom reiterated. "And what exactly is it you want to accomplish?"

"Some basic reforms," I answered. "Basic reforms which everybody except our politicians recognize. First, of course, we need lawyer reform. I propose to establish a national version of HOSTILE. We'll have to call it something else so I was considering 'The Better Lawyers Bureau'. It would be a publicly funded and politically untouchable lawyer review board."

"You think you can get that passed?" Tom asked.

"Not as it stands," I admitted. "But it's a viable compromise position. Eekim and Nicky both agree that we should establish a strong front and be ready to fall back to that as a compromise. It's one of the fundamental tactics of negotiation, as Eekim has informed me. He tells me one should always demand more than you know you can possibly get, then compromise back to what you really want. So, we'll also be asking that lawyers be placed on probation immediately after graduating from law school. Granted, we probably won't be able to get that passed because a law degree is only circumstantial evidence of the intention to commit a crime. But at least it's a nice thought. We also want a law which says a person cannot become a lawyer if one of his/her parents is a lawyer or even closely related to one. We'll also be favoring free pens for lawyers."

"Free pens?"

"Well, if they're good enough for pigs they're good enough for lawyers," I explained. "We'll probably have to compromise on that one too. Pity though, it would be easier to regulate lawyers if they were all in one place."

"I like it," Tom commented. "What else you got planned?"

"The second plank of our platform is called the 'Domestic Treason Act'. The country is fully aware of the dangers of agents in this country selling us out to foreign powers, but we don't have any laws that handle selling us out to domestic powers. Well, we have a lot of laws but they seem impossible to enforce. Just look at the S & L travesty. There are laws but we don't seem to be able to get convictions in court. The 'Domestic Treason Act' establishes that any <u>betrayal</u> of the public trust is a serious crime. Anyone who deals with taxpayer dollars, including everyone from bankers to school boards to government contractors to politicians, would be held accountable under the law. 'Betraying the public trust' would include stealing, gross mismanagement and even plain, simple lying.

"As an example, when a senator lies to Congress he would be guilty of Domestic Treason because he is paid with taxpayer money. The view we take is that he is lying to the American people. We don't want anyone to do that anymore.

"A lawyer would also be held accountable under this law because he works in a taxpayer funded system. He is a guardian of the public trust to ensure that individuals can get a fair trial. <u>Betrayal of the public trust</u> will be a term which encompasses a wide range of professions and will include any act which can be construed as contrary to the best interests of the public. Lying will be a crime sufficient to get a conviction. Terms like 'misleading Congress' will be prosecuted as lying. 'Misrepresentation' will be prosecuted as lying. We're not going to play games anymore.

"The next time something like the S & L crisis occurs," I emphasized, "we want people punished. Actually, average people were punished the first time. What I mean is: we want the people who are responsible punished."

"The next time?" Tom asked.

"There'll be a next time," I said. "There were hundreds of billions of dollars stolen from the American people. Hardly anybody went to jail and those that did didn't stay long. We need laws which guarantee easier convictions for white-collar and political crimes. Next time, we need to set an example of what it means to betray the American people, not demonstrate how profitable it is. C'mon, we sold off an entire generation in that scandal. What are kids supposed to think? What are elderly people supposed to think? What's a working person supposed to think? I think we all think the same thing: it sucks!"

"We definitely think alike," Tom commented.

His genuine amusement at the proposition of being my running mate had gradually ebbed into reserved interest. He still appeared skeptical but also evidenced a willingness to consider my offer. I don't mean he was convinced. When our eyes met it was clear he still thought it was all a joke, but there was a modifying feature to his expression which indicated it was a joke in which he might like to participate.

"You got anything else?" he asked.

"I've got a corollary to the 'Domestic Treason' law," I answered. "It's called 'Economic Reparation'. If convicted of 'Domestic Treason', a perpetrator, or perhaps just plain traitor would be more descriptive, would be subject to monetary punishment. For instance, a politician caught with his hand in the cookie jar..."

"Actually," Tom interrupted. "I never liked that phrase. It makes it sound like a politician is just a misbehaving little boy. It's too cute. It's kind of like 'misleading Congress' or 'misrepresentation'. You need to call it what it is."

"You're right," I agreed. "Okay. When a politician is caught stealing or abusing his office he would be subject to monetary damages as well as a jail sentence. The amount of the fine could be several times the dollar amount of the actual transgression or the total amount of money and benefits he had received while holding public office, whichever is greater.

"The result of these laws will be to allow the American people to successfully prosecute and punish transgressions by individuals who hold a position involving public trust. The yardstick for measuring the seriousness of economic damages involves a concept we call Economic Murder. An individual who works for minimum wage, $4.25 an hour, forty hours a week, fifty-two weeks a year for forty-five years will earn $397,800. Anyone in a position of public trust who steals that amount, if found guilty, will be condemned to Economic Execution. They will have their money, savings and property forfeited; and they will be put in a work program which pays minimum wage for the rest of their lives. There will be lesser penalties for Economic Rape, Economic Assault and Battery, Economic Mugging, and so on. Criminals are not more respectable merely because they don't have to pick up a weapon. Our programs will make it easier to convict white-collar and government criminals. And it will ensure that the punishment fits the crime. We're just plain tired of getting screwed. In the inner circles of HOSTILE, our program is called the 'strip and whip' approach."

"Catchy," Tom noted. "You think you have any chance of making it work?"

"There are some obvious obstacles," I admitted. "Recent history in this country has shown the fallacy of allowing amoral social groups to police themselves. Look at Congress. Look at lawyers. If respect were wind, the combined force of those two groups wouldn't put a small ripple in our flag, it would hang limp from the pole."

"Awkward metaphor," Tom said.

"Nicky and Eekim will write the speeches," I countered. "But you get the idea. We also need to come up with a new type of jury which can effectively deliberate justice when either of those groups are involved. We're still working on details. But one thing is certain, protection will be of paramount importance. Tampering with such a jury will be considered extreme Domestic Treason. It will be a capital crime. It's harsh but it's necessary. Throughout our history men and women have sacrificed their lives for the honor and dignity of this country. It is neither cruel nor unusual to demand the same from our enemies. Individuals who work themselves into positions of trust and responsibility, and then use those positions to betray us are not just our enemies; they are our worst enemies."

Tom sat with a whimsical smile for several minutes and contemplated my words. Finally he said: "Okay, I've heard enough. Sign me up."

A TIGER BY THE TAIL

Our political campaign showed more promise than we could have hoped. Public support continued to grow, contributions poured in and polls indicated that we had a viable chance of putting an independent candidate in the White House for the first time.

Eekim and Nicky campaigned like fanatics and quickly became popular heroes. One could not watch a news show, open a magazine or read a newspaper without encountering their pictures and comments on something or other. Their notoriety overshadowed mine to a large degree. Eekim was fond of pointing out that this was probably for the best.

Tom was cleared of any wrongdoing in the case of Lou C. Fur but the public harbored a suspicion that he had somehow been involved. This was of great benefit in validating his worthiness to be Vice-President.

Yes, everything seemed to be going according to plan.

One of the maxims wisely written in the peels of Eekim's tribe is: "Tigers admire silly monkeys who think the world is one big bunch of bananas." A shorter version of this observation is: "Tigers find foolish meat the sweetest."

And so it was that one day I walked into HOSTILE headquarters to discover Constance and the staff already hard at work. I had a hard time keeping track of all the plans and obligations a Presidential campaign entailed. My usual routine was for Constance to give me a summary of the day's activities.

I walked into my office, accepted the automated greeting of "Good morning, sir." from my coffee-maker, ordered a cup of Mountain Rain and awaited her report.

She came bustling in a few moments later, exclaiming:

"Of all the times for him to take a vacation!"

Thinking it was probably one of her staff, I casually asked: "Who?"

"Who do you think?" she demanded. "I have to cancel two appearances and three interviews all because that little monkey of yours needs some 'rest and relaxation'. My foot! He's gone off to dally with that little trollop of his."

I felt a twinge run down my spine.

"Eekim went to see Rhia?" I asked. "When did this happen?"

"Last night," she replied with disapproval in her voice. "Here we are in the midst of a big campaign. We have obligations and commitments, schedules and appointments. But the first time that little floozy sends him a love-letter he's off gallivanting around like some playmonkey!" Constance became excited at times but always quickly regained calm control. She asked: "Do you think you could handle his interviews today?"

My feelings went in the opposite direction of hers. My previous tranquillity evaporated into flustered concern. I ignored her question and asked: "Rhia sent him a love-letter?"

"He found it when he went through his mail late yesterday," Constance explained. "Now we have an interview at..."

I rushed from the office with alarms ringing in my head.

Constance admonished my retreating form with: "You're not going on vacation too? You know, you're not President yet!"

THE MAD DASH

I jumped into "Spirit" (my '76 Olds) and headed for Cecil's Boat and Canoe Outfitters. The drive was a mad race down the highways of southern Missouri. Speed is a funny thing, the faster you want to get somewhere the slower the trip seems no matter how fast you are traveling.

Telephone and utility poles did not zip by as if viewed in fast-forward on a VCR. They didn't fly by at all. Instead, I had an unsettling feeling of deja vu every time I passed another one, as if I were passing the same one over and over again.

Eventually, I began to calm down a little. After all,

Nicky had detected no danger or she would have warned us. In spite of her busy schedule, she continued to perform her "psychic reconnaissance" to make sure that everyone within the HOSTILE organization was safe. This safeguard had proved invaluable on numerous occasions.

Still, there was the unsettling fact that Nicky's excursions into the "world of souls" could not detect the direct action of lawyers. She could discover the intentions of normal people with even a bit of conscience, but nothing about lawyers themselves.

Fortunately, lawyers seldom performed their own dirty work. Nicky's success in thwarting the murderous schemes of their criminal underlings had eventually convinced lawyers of the futility of violent actions. Lawyers seemed to have resigned themselves to battling us with the more conventional weapons of deceit and destruction which are currently referred to as the legal system. Attorneys would even smile, in public, at us and even address us with the same empty, meaningless civility which constitutes their concept of decency.

But, as Eekim often said: "Wisely is it written in the peels of my tribe: 'The tiger's smile hides large teeth.'" What if lawyers had decided to bare their fangs?

However, sustained panic is an emotional state which is difficult to maintain. It is too tiring and frustrating; it also gets boring after a while. I alternated removing my hands from the steering wheel and wiping them on my pants leg until my palms were dry once more. I forced myself to grasp the wheel in a hold which less resembled a death grip.

I mentally forced myself to relax. I rationalized that I was doing everything possible and should save my energy in case it was needed later.

Everything has just happened so fast for so long, I told myself. A tribe of talking monkeys, a psychic woman, capture by a paramilitary group of psychopath lawyers and the fortunate destruction of their underground complex, arrest and jail, on the road with Monkey Business, the establishment of HOSTILE, the much publicized trial with the Missouri Bar Conspiracy, painting a lawyer's butt blue, a doomsday coffee-maker, a patriotic rebel, and now a campaign for the Presidency of the United States. It all seemed slightly unreal.

Perhaps it was just the overwhelming nature of it all. The totality of it finally culminating in the possibility of attaining the highest office in the country. The journey to this point had been one great roller coaster ride, and now that the ride was over I still retained a feeling of rapid and curvaceous motion which made stillness seem not normal.

Or possibly it was like the feeling one gets when one has been on a boat fishing all day and has become accustomed to the rolling waves. Afterwards, the ground feels insubstantial and rolling because leg muscles continue to try to adjust even though the waves are no longer there. One knows the ground is not moving but one also knows that it feels like it is.

Or maybe it was like waking from a long and vivid dream. The feeling of dreaming persists for a while like an audible echo of the subconscious. I had noticed that the first sense I employ upon emerging from an unsettling dream is not sight but sound. I wake and find myself listening for confirmation that the dream is over and only then opening my eyes to verify the fact.

Dwelling on thoughts like these provoked a suspicion that perhaps it had all been a dream. Using the age-old test of this theory I pinched myself. I could feel it. Then I wondered if I had only dreamed I had pinched myself and felt it.

Spirit's engine crooned like a precision machine in fast idle as I raced down the road. Hal and Stan had taken a special liking to the old car and took special pride in keeping the old warrior in top condition. I felt a surge of confidence from listening to the tuned engine's sound. The sturdy mechanical melody of the machine finally chased the doubts from my mind. This was no roller coaster or boat ride or dream. My monkey might be in trouble and neither hell nor high water was going to stop me from helping him. I felt more solid than I had in my entire life.

Speeding along I tried to figure out an alternative explanation for what had happened but could not. Something was definitely wrong with the picture. Rhia had sent him a letter? It just didn't make sense. A banana peel I could've understood, but a letter? It didn't fit.

EEKIM

Cecil was standing on the porch and squinting into the bright afternoon sun when I arrived.

"Have you seen Eekim?" I anxiously asked as I got out of the car.

"No," he answered with a worried look. "But something's wrong. There's been more lawyers on the river than maggots on a road-kill."

"I need a boat," I said quickly. "Not a canoe. I'm going upriver quick and I need a motor."

"You can borrow my fishing boat. It's flat-bottomed," he said as we headed for the landing. "You want me to come with you?"

"Thanks, but no," I replied. "You stay here in case Eekim comes along. What were the lawyers doing on the river?"

"I don't know," he scowled. "They were here first thing this morning wearing camouflage, three-piece Armani suits and Gucci combat boots. They left just a little while ago. But something is very wrong. I've never seen a happier pack of lawyers."

We got the boat into the water and I yanked the starter cord on the motor.

"You be careful!" yelled Cecil. He stood and watched as I made my way against the current until I was out of sight.

I knew where I was going. It was the place I had first met Eekim. There was a small stream which flowed into the larger river at that point and I was sure I could find the landmark.

All the way I kept watching for some sign of the little monkey along the banks. As I rounded every bend in the river I shut the engine off and called his name several times. My disappointment mounted as each time I was met with only silence.

After several hours I thought I spotted the small tributary. I eased the boat into the bank, got out and then pulled it further onto the ground to keep it from floating away. I went ahead and tied a rope to a tree just in case.

I surveyed the woods beside the river. If Eekim's tribe was still here I figured they would have heard the motor and come to investigate.

Nothing.

I listened for any sounds which might indicate their approach but all I heard were the songs of birds, the buzz of insects and the usual rustlings of the breeze in the tree leaves. I hesitated to call out. This was my last and best hope for finding Eekim and the thought of failure was devastating.

Finally, I cupped my hands to my mouth and yelled "Eekim" three times. Between each yell I waited a few seconds to see if there was any response. There was none. I started yelling for Ooga and Rhia but again received only a silent reply.

With frustration bordering on desperation I screamed: "Hey! It's me, Josh! Is anybody here?"

Frantically I looked around. This had to be the right place.

Maybe the tribe had moved, I told myself. Or maybe Rhia was meeting him somewhere else. Or maybe...

I didn't want to consider any other maybes as forboding welled up inside me. I went crashing through the brush and forest shouting "Eekim! Eekim!" until there was no breath in me. I stumbled through the dense undergrowth in a frantic search for signs of Eekim or the tribe. I found nothing but tangled vines and thick vegetation over which I twice tripped in my haste. My skin was torn in a dozen places from thorns and branches as I stood panting and sweating, almost ready to admit defeat. I slapped a mosquito on my arm and then looked up and saw it.

The path to the grotto, where I had first tasted banana wine with Eekim, was dimly visible through the foliage just in front of me. I was in the right place after all.

With a triumphant "Whoop!" I stumbled to the path. That's why no monkeys were around, I told myself. Monkeys are too smart to come running and sweating just because some human calls to them. They were all relaxing and drinking wine in the cool grotto as would any sensible person. They knew I would come to them.

As I raced down the path I enjoyed thinking how much fun Eekim would have ridiculing me for my condition. He'd be reclining beneath a tree with a jug of wine in one arm and Rhia in the other and he'd look up at me and say: "Hey, look what the tiger dragged in!"

I chuckled to myself, as I jogged along, anticipating the wisecracks he would deliver at my expense. I didn't care. The first thing I would do is give him a big hug. I knew he'd respond with something like: "Don't do that! What's my girl going to think? By the Big Banana, I didn't know even humans could be so sweaty and smelly!"

Bursting into the grotto I spread my arms wide in triumph and with a big grin on my face I declared: "I'm here!"

The grotto was empty. Broken jugs lay scattered around the clearing and the smell of spilled wine filled the air. The comfortable reclining areas were wrecked with leaves and branches thrown around in disarray. The ground was scarred with deep grooves and prints of heavy-heeled boots.

"Human, as usual, you're a day late and a banana short," said a faint voice.

I looked to the sound and was momentarily elated to see Eekim with his arms flung wide as if he were preparing to return my embrace. Horror replaced joy as I realized that Eekim's back was against a tree and his feet were not touching the ground.

They had crucified him.

Numbed to the bone and reeling from the sinking feeling which overwhelmed me I rushed to his side.

"Hold still," I cried, "I'll get you down."

I fought back the tears which were blurring my vision. I had to see in order to help him.

"Damn those bastards!" I cursed, knowing anger would be a more effective emotion than sorrow in dealing with the situation.

"Don't touch me," Eekim weakly said. "It's no use. I'm done for."

"Hang in there little buddy," I sobbed. "You'll be all right. The first thing we need to do is get you down. I'm not going to let you die."

My voice cracked at the last word. But I summoned every last ounce of resolve in my soul, stilled my shaking hands and choked back my grief and tears. I was determined to save my friend.

"It's no use," Eekim calmly, almost peacefully, said. "It's over. It's all my fault. Wisely is it written in the peels of my tribe: 'The monkey who stalks the tiger must see forwards and backwards at all times.' Now my tribe is scattered. They'll regroup and go into hiding, but lawyers left me here as a warning. I just wanted to stay alive long enough to see you. I knew you'd come."

"You can't die," I pleaded.

"Not my choice," said Eekim. "You'll be all right. At least you saw through this last trick. You're a good person for a human. Just be careful and keep up the fight, that'll be my revenge. Tell everyone I fought at the end. Wisely is it written in the peels of my tribe: 'When cornered by a tiger it is better to be remembered as a valiant warrior than a submissive snack.' And, even though it usually works the other way around, take care of Nicky. I really like that girl."

Eekim was fading fast. I saw that he had hung on long past the time of his death just to say good-bye. I thought back to the words he had said over Squeeky so long ago.

"You're the best and wisest monkey I ever met," I solemnly intoned. "Eekim, you're a great monkey, you'll make a great banana."

"It's at least a nice thought," he whispered.

Eekim's head rolled to one side and a final shudder shook his body as his soul fled to a more hospitable world. Intense admiration was my first reaction. How had such a small body held such an immense and great spirit?

The smile frozen on his face, as I had learned so long ago, was #2,621. It's the final smile which every noble monkey aspires to conjure at death. It means "it was all a nice thought."

THE LONGEST JOURNEY

I don't know how long I sat there crying.

It was dark when I carefully removed Eekim's body from the tree and walked back to the boat. I gently laid him inside and motored downstream to Cecil's.

Cecil gave me a sheet to wrap him and a box to hold him on the drive home.

I arrived in the early morning hours.

It was the longest journey of my life and I don't remember a thing about it.

THE END

It was raining when I arrived at HOSTILE headquarters. The sky itself was shedding tears over the death of my brave monkey friend.

Nicky's car was in the parking lot. I figured she had used her powers and already knew about Eekim. I knew she was in there crying and feeling like it was her fault for not foreseeing this tragedy.

I wanted to rush in and comfort her but I didn't want to leave Eekim's body in the car. I grabbed the box in my arms and ran through the rain to the door. Fortunately, it was unlocked and the alarms had been turned off so I was able to go directly to my office.

Nicky's arms were folded on my desk and her head was resting on them. She looked up with reddened eyes and a tear-streaked face as I entered. I set the box with Eekim's body on a chair and went around the desk to her.

Even though she looked as if she had wept for hours, she stood and we embraced for a long time while she cried into my shoulder. I kept saying things like "There, there." and "It's okay." I said a lot of other things, equally meaningless, in an attempt to comfort her. I hoped the sound of my voice would be a comfort because I knew my words were not.

Nicky eventually began crying: "It's all my fault."

"Nonsense," I said in my most soothing voice. "You didn't do this. Eekim didn't blame you. You've been able to save us all several times, but you can't hold yourself responsible for everything. You can predict the future but you can't always control it. Ease up on yourself. This isn't your fault, don't do that to yourself."

"That's not what I mean," she said. "I mean I should have told you."

I had no idea what she was talking about. Before I could ask a voice said: "What a touching photo opportunity."

Startled, I looked up to see M.T. Blarney entering my office. Behind him were Will Bilkem and another man. The three were still wearing their designer fatigues. Bilkem was unmarked but Blarney had a gash on his forehead and the other man had a black eye. Eekim had not gone without a fight. All of them carried guns which they pointed at us. All of them were grinning.

I edged Nicky behind me. "Get out of here!" I yelled at the three of them.

"You're not a very congenial host," Bilkem admonished. "Especially after all the trouble we took to arrange this meeting. Let's see, I believe everyone here is acquainted except for our associate. Mr. Rob N. Pillage, I have the extreme pleasure of introducing Josh and Nicky. I believe the corpse in the bed-sheet shroud over there is Eekim. No need to get up, Eekim," he laughed.

"What in the hell do you want?" I demanded.

"We've got what we want," Bilkem chuckled. "In fact, we have more than we want. There's one dead talking monkey, there's one soon-to-be-dead Presidential candidate, and there's one young lady who will get to live if what we heard before we entered is true. Are you really psychic, my dear?"

"Wouldn't I have seen you coming if I was?" Nicky spat at them.

"Well, as your former employer here said, 'you can't be expected to always control the future just because you can see it'," Bilkem thoughtfully replied. "This HOSTILE organization of yours would not have survived this long without some sort of supernatural help. No, no, I believe there is adequate evidence to say you do have a very unusual gift. At least enough evidence to justify further investigation."

"Look, you've killed Eekim and you've got me," I said. "That's all you need. Nicky is no threat to you, let her go and I'll come quietly."

"You can't plea bargain for a reduced sentence without having something to offer," Pillage jeered.

"That's right," agreed Bilkem. "We don't need your cooperation. I asked for it once. Do you remember that? But no, you had to play the high and mighty reformer. Well, see what your temerity has wrought!"

"Let her go," I tried once more. "If she was psychic she

would have known this was coming."

"Not necessarily," said Bilkem. "She may have useful abilities even if she is not infallible. Besides, we planned this moment well. Lawyers handle divorces, bankruptcies, wills, and any number of other traumatic matters. We are very familiar with how vulnerable an emotionally upset person can be. The little monkey served us well. You were both so upset that you left the alarms off. Did you know he tried to be brave at the end? But I'm afraid he screamed a little when the nails were driven in.

"God it's exhilarating to take a hands-on approach to work! I like working on paper and being the architect of a plan, but it's refreshing to actually pick up the tools and do the measuring and pounding myself. Fresh air, physical labor; I feel like a new man!"

Blarney loudly cleared his throat.

"But I digress," laughed Bilkem. "It's such a joyous occasion that I can hardly contain myself."

Behind me, Nicky lifelessly quoted: "Wisely is it written in the peels of Eekim's tribe: 'If you expect the worst of a tiger you will seldom be disappointed.'"

"Even if the girl isn't psychic she has other uses," leered Pillage. "I'm sure she can be persuaded to cooperate."

I tensed and leaned forward, ready to rush the three of them and try to give Nicky a chance. I knew it wouldn't be much of one but there seemed nothing else to do.

Nicky placed a hand on my back and whispered: "Don't. I have a better plan.

"Coffee-maker," she said. "Run emergency program Nicky One."

"Self-destruct program Nicky One now running," said the coffee-maker. "Revised timetable for explosion is ten seconds. Run now if you want to live. Commencing countdown. Ten...nine...

"Hold me," said Nicky. I pulled her to me and tried to smile #2,621.

"It's a bluff!" said Blarney. "That idiot pulled the same trick on me once before."

"Shoot Josh after the countdown reaches zero," Bilkem commanded. "We'll show this son-of-a-bitch how a lawyer bluffs!"

"We're not bluffing," said Nicky and held me tighter.

The lawyers laughed loudly at that.

They were still laughing when the coffee-maker exploded.

FINAL CHAPTER

Josh, Eekim and Nicky looked at each other with stunned expressions.

"Are we dead?" asked Nicky.

"I don't know," said Eekim. "I always believed that after I died I would come back as a banana. That was just a theory, of course."

"I don't feel dead," said Josh. "Then again, I don't know what dead is supposed to feel like. I feel good, though, as if a great burden had been lifted from me."

"Wait a minute," said Nicky. "Let's figure this out logically. Josh, you and I were blown up by the coffee-maker, weren't we?"

"The last thing I remember is the countdown reaching zero," Josh answered. "I don't remember the explosion or any pain."

"Maybe it happened too fast," suggested Nicky. "What about you, Eekim? Lawyers nailed you to a tree. What do you remember?"

Eekim furrowed his brow. "Strange," he said. "It seems like I can remember it happening, but I don't remember any pain. It just seems unreal, like a dream. Perhaps we just have a problem with death perception."

"Well," said Josh. "I don't see how any of that helps a whole lot." Looking around he asked: "Where do you think we are now?"

"Looks like somebody's office," said Eekim. "There's a desk, chair, computer, books, tables, pens, paper and assorted clutter around. Do you suppose this is God's office?"

"I would think God would be a better housekeeper," Nicky conjectured. "Besides, how would that explain the rods and reels and tackle boxes?"

"He's supposed to be a fisher of men," suggested Eekim.

"Yea, but what about this other stuff?" asked Josh. "A dart board, ballcaps, backpack, juggling balls, pictures out of a child's coloring book. A telephone? Surely God wouldn't need a telephone!"

"If He does," said Nicky, "I'd like to know which long-distance company He uses. I never did figure that one out."

"Maybe we're all just crazy," Josh suggested.

"I thought of that," said Nicky, "but considering the possibility would indicate a rational mind. Like they say, if you think you might be crazy it's a good sign that you're not."

"Yea, sure," Eekim sarcastically commented. "People who think they're crazy say that a lot."

"Well, do you think we're crazy or that we're really here?" Nicky inquired.

"The two are not mutually exclusive," said Eekim.

"Well, let's see," Josh pondered. "Maybe we all hit some kind of time warp."

"It wouldn't fit the formula for the secret of time travel which my tribe discovered long ago," Eekim disagreed.

"Monkeys know the secret of time travel?" Josh asked.

"Sure," Eekim replied. "Wisely is it written in the peels of my tribe: 'The secret to time travel is you can only go forward from one moment to the next.'"

I decided this had gone on long enough so I popped into the room with a cheerful: "Hi gang! How's it going?"

The three of them stared at me with perplexed expressions.

Eekim recovered first: "Who are you?"

"Allow me to introduce myself," I cordially smiled. "My name is Frank Sixfeet, and I'm the author of this book; the one in which you exist." I gave a polite bow.

"Book?" said Eekim.

"Author? I've been narrating the whole thing. I thought I was the author!" exclaimed Josh.

"That's what I wanted you to think," I said.

"Bullshit," said Eekim. He clenched his little fists and advanced towards me. "I'm not usually a violent monkey, mister, but you're really ticking me off! You better start explaining right now or by the Big Banana I'm going to..."

"Stop!" I commanded. "Shut up and listen." And, since I'm the author, he did just that. With a very puzzled expression on his face I might add.

Josh jumped up and yelled: "What did you do to Eekim?"

"Just a demonstration of my power," I explained. "Josh, go stand on your head in the corner for a minute." And, of course, he did.

"You bastard!" said an upside-down Josh. "You're going to pay for this! I'm going to..."

"And be quiet," I added.

Nicky had watched this with wide-eyed amazement. "I don't think I need a demonstration of your power," she said.

I smiled at her: "You were always the brightest of my characters. Wisdom, heart and beauty are all combined in you. You were always my favorite." I tenderly kissed her hand.

"Lecher!" Josh accused.

"Pervert!" Eekim admonished.

I sighed. An author has only so much control over his characters. I had told them to "shut-up" and "be quiet", but I didn't say for how long. Josh had finished the minute on his head and came to an upright position.

Oh well. It wouldn't have been very much fun if they did everything I told them to. An author is similar to a ruler. He has a great deal of power to shape the course of events but can never fully control his subjects. They must be free to make their own choices, otherwise they are merely lifeless puppets; animated but uninteresting.

An iron-fisted ruler will always fall. An enlightened leader merely points the way and allows others the choice of whether to follow. This allows his subjects the individual resources and freedom necessary to overcome obstacles along the way. In my own humble way I have tried to follow the path of an enlightened leader.

"I apologize for my little demonstration," I said. "Please, let's sit and discuss this as reasonable men and women and monkeys should."

"That's better," said Eekim. "I don't know how you made me shut-up for a moment, but the very idea that a human could create something as evolved and civilized as my monkey tribe is ridiculous!"

"I think he's telling the truth," said Nicky. "How else do you explain our being here after we died?"

"It's just so embarrassing," said Eekim while shaking his head in denial.

We all silently sat while the implications of the situation settled. I could understand how they felt. Their world had suddenly been shattered. All their preconceptions about who and what they were had suddenly been dissolved. Their very existence probably seemed trivial. Their integrity and worth no longer rested on a solid foundation. Their individual rights were suddenly seen as being controlled by an outside force. The very nature of basic morality, the simple questions of right and wrong, were no longer applicable. Reality, as they understood it, had ceased to exist.

I understood how they felt. I have been to court.

"You know," I gently said. "I tried to soften the shock of this revelation. Josh, you made several references to movies when you were captured by lawyers. That's close to the idea. You also addressed the reader on several occasions. And Eekim made a couple of references to books during your adventures. "

"That's right!" said Josh. "I remember now."

"I thought I was just being clever," Eekim sulked.

"But what about Nicky?" Josh demanded. "Eekim and I should have realized the situation, I can accept that, but you had no right to put Nicky through all this without her knowledge!"

I couldn't help but tolerantly smile at Josh. He was so protective of Nicky that he allowed his emotions to interfere with his reasoning. He just didn't get it.

"You just don't get it," I said. "Nicky has known all along."

"What? How?" he demanded with monosyllabic brevity.

"Josh," Nicky softly said while placing her hand on his. "Have you forgotten about my ability to enter the world of souls and see the future?"

"Well," stammered Josh. "That would, of course, explain how you knew. But why didn't you tell us?"

"You didn't want to know," answered Nicky. "You

might have had less resolve if you had thought you were a character in a book. I still care about you even if you are fictional. I was with you at the end, wasn't I?"

"Not so fast, human," Eekim addressed me. "You may think you're clever just because you can play god to characters you create, but I want to know 'why me?'. Why did you create me to be your little toy?"

"Eekim," I sincerely replied, "you weren't my 'toy'. I chose you more than created you. I needed a character who was extremely resourceful, gifted with superior intelligence, and the benefactor of a cultural wisdom higher than human standards. I chose you because you could capture the imagination of readers and captivate an audience with your antics. In short, I chose you because I needed a stalwart leader, a visionary, a monkey in shining armor. I wanted a character to illustrate the maxim 'you can't keep a good monkey down'. I needed a hero."

Eekim turned to Josh and Nicky and said: "Well, we certainly can't fault his judgment on that issue."

(He bought it. One for me. I was glad Ooga was not present.)

"What about me?" asked Josh. "Why did you choose me?"

"Because Batman needs a Boy Wonder," laughed Eekim. "Superman needs a Jimmy Olsen, the Green Hornet needs..."

"Don Quixote needs a Sancho Panza," interjected Nicky.

"Hey lady, I never chased a windmill in my life!" Eekim steadfastly declared. He then looked at me and tentatively inquired: "Did I?"

I shook my head.

"See!" he steadfastly declared.

"Seriously," resumed Josh, "what about me?"

"I think you were there to inspire others. Sort of a 'human see, human do' kind of thing," snorted Eekim.

"Well, that's essentially right, but I would have expressed it in a more dignified manner," I said.

"You're the author," acknowledged Eekim.

"You see, Josh," I explained. "I needed a human voice for this adventure. You are a man who was victimized by lawyers, yet you never gave up. You took up the feud. You never surrendered to the injustice, greed or incompetence of lawyers. You gave voice to the frustration, outrage and determination of the individual battling against an insane, indifferent and insensitive system."

"That's intelligent, inspirational and instructive writing," snickered Eekim.

(Everyone's a critic.)

"Seriously, Josh," I continued. "I needed you to exemplify the triumph of the individual."

"I guess I can live with that," conceded Josh. "Or whatever it is I do. Maybe it would be more accurate to say I can exist with that."

"It's a fine philosophical point," I admitted.

(Either way, another one for me.)

"What about Nicky?" asked Eekim.

"Yea, what about Nicky?" echoed Josh.

"What novel is not benefited by a beautiful, smart, sexy, charming, psychic young woman?" I asked.

"*Treasure Island*," quipped Eekim.

"It was a rhetorical question," I retorted.

"You know what I think?" asked Nicky while looking straight into my eyes. "I think you needed a woman with super powers to keep Josh and Eekim from getting crushed by lawyers. I also think you needed someone to be the pivot of their teeter-totter, one-upmanship relationship."

She does have deep, lovely eyes over which it is impossible to pull the wool. She smiled at me in a bemused, knowing manner. (Oh well, two out of three ain't bad.)

"But what was this all for?" asked Josh. "We're just fiction, so we didn't really change anything. The whole thing didn't make any difference!"

"On the contrary," I countered. "You made a major difference. After your deaths, the citizens of this country rose up and demanded a justice system to replace their antiquated, self-serving lawyer system. Tom Window became President and forced your legislative reforms through Congress. Monuments in honor of you three were erected in DC, state capitols and most large cities and towns."

"Wow! Really?" asked Eekim.

"Hey, I'm the author aren't I," I responded. "It really happened, in a fictional way of course."

"Exactly! It was still fiction!" Josh protested. "You just made it up!"

"You're making too much of the fact that it was fiction," I explained. "In the final analysis, does art imitate life or does life imitate art? I think they are both the same thing. We can create and mold both of them. Our civilization and our social systems are just things we created.

"To put it another way: the reality is that our legal system is just fiction. It was just made up. There is nothing God-ordained about it. Lawyers, unfortunately, have compromised the system. Just because everything which transpires in court is given a rubber-stamp of 'JUSTICE' does not make it so. It's the biggest, most powerful fiction around.

"Which, in a way, is good," I continued. "Because that means we can change it! We don't have to put up with sleazy, overpriced lawyers who pad their pockets off the suffering of others. Just as I created you and then recreated you after your deaths, the American people can recreate our justice system. It's such an obvious solution I'm surprised no one has thought of it before. As a people, we are probably too awestruck by the judicial mystique to realize that all judges and all lawyers are just employees. All we need to do is rewrite the job description."

"Frank, you sound pretty confident," Nicky noted.

"I am," I said. "Josh and Eekim did a lot of things I had not originally planned. They paved the way with concepts like the Better Lawyers Bureau, Domestic Treason, Economic Murder and Economic Reparation. Those are brilliant ideas! Not too shabby for fictional characters. That's what I'm talking about when I say that reality is not that much different from fiction. Both are our creations. We are in control. We can make change occur. All it takes is effort and willpower. We must merely act!"

"Frankly Frank, you make it sound too easy," mused Eekim.

"Nothing is easy," I disagreed. "Everything takes sacrifice. For example, although my chances of a fair trial were minuscule before I wrote this book, I'm pretty sure they are totally nonexistent now. Lawyers will fight truth and nail to keep their cozy little legal system unchanged."

"Aha!" shouted Eekim. "I know what it is. You're one of those humans with a martyr complex. That's why the lawyers crucified me! You want the glory of going down in flames to inspire the masses."

"You're exactly wrong, my furry little friend," I smiled. "There's an old saying that 'doctors bury their mistakes'. The legal corollary is 'lawyers incarcerate or impoverish their mistakes'. I have already been through the court system. I have already been martyred. Lawyers are smart enough to turn a person into an unknown and powerless martyr. I didn't like it. I consider myself an avenger who is trying to right the wrongs done to me and my country. And I'm trying to make sure that the children of this country are not similarly victimized."

"Aha!" Eekim again cried. "You have a savior complex!"

"Eekim, you're not being fair," said Nicky. "Since Frank created us, the only logical way to look at it is that each of us represents a part of him. If he has any complex at all, it's us. Josh represents the practical and intellectual side, I represent the emotional and intuitive side and you're the instinctive and irreverent side. The heart, mind and spirit. Josh narrated the story so I can only assume that Frank is more in tune with that part of his nature. That's why the book proposes a practical solution to the lawyer problem."

"Frank's pretty fragmented any way you look at it," muttered Eekim.

Josh looked at Eekim: "I don't know why you're complaining. You're the only one who got laid." This last remark carried a tone of envy and maybe a little bitterness.

"Can't stop a sex machine like myself," Eekim boastfully laughed.

"Actually," I said. "I wanted to respect your privacy. If Nicky and Josh had a sexual relationship, they might have been more than a little embarrassed and angry to find out the whole world had been witness to their intimate moments. You two are not exhibitionists, so I figured you deserved a little more dignity and respect than that."

"What about me?" Eekim incredulously asked.

"Eekim, you're an exhibitionist from the word 'go'," laughed Nicky.

"Gotcha!" Josh added.

Eekim stared at us for a moment and then shrugged: "That's true. But what I mean is: why weren't more details of my sexual exploits related? I can't help thinking that humans would have benefited from descriptive details of love-making sessions involving a virile and unrestrained simian stud such as myself."

"Perhaps there are some things people should find out for themselves," I suggested.

"True again," Eekim noted. "Besides, my amorous adventures might prove too potent for the frail, male, human psyche. Every man in America would be whimpering 'I can never measure up to Big Eekim'. You might develop a mass inferiority complex."

Martyr, savior, inferiority. All this talk of complexes was closely bordering on the real reason Nicky and Josh had not become romantically involved. Although they each developed characters of their own, it's true that they were based on parts of me. If Josh and Nicky had become lovers then the charge of narcissism would have been hard to deny. I wanted this book to be more than literary masturbation.

"I still can't get used to the idea that I'm fictional," said Josh.

"You worry too much, Josh," Eekim chided. "The way I see it, if I'm fictional then it relieves me of any personal responsibility. I can do anything I want and blame Frank. I like being fictional. I never felt better in my life!"

"You all may be fictional," I explained. "But that doesn't mean you don't exist. You have become part of the perception of reality. And if you never lived then you can never die. Doesn't that make you immortal? You have made some great proposals, Josh. I think Eekim expressed it best when he said to the judge: 'Isn't it more important <u>what</u> is said rather than <u>who</u> says it?'

"And as Mark Twain commented: 'Of course truth is stranger than fiction; fiction has to make sense.' You may be fictional, but you make sense."

"But what's the bottom-line?" Josh asked. "I understand that we triumph in the book. But what difference does it make in the real world?"

"Ah!" I said. "That is a story still in the making. We have given people some tools. It is up to them. They must act. The future is up to them to create."

"Good enough," said Eekim. "You got any bananas around here?"

LAST FINAL CHAPTER

I arrived at the rendezvous. It was a seedy, dimly lit little bar outside of Joplin, Missouri. The joint was smoky and the lamps all had that moonlight, glow effect they created in old movies by smearing Vaseline on the camera lens. I thought this was strange because this is a book, not a movie. "I Fought the Law and the Law Won" played softly but melodramatically on the jukebox.

As the waitress brought me a beer a voice behind me said: "I'll have a beer also."

The man sat across from me in the booth and we looked each other over. I saw a nervous individual with dark wavy hair. He was dressed in a leather jacket over a sweatshirt and wore blue jeans. His eyes were hidden behind dark glasses with black frames. I have no idea what he saw.

After the waitress brought him his beer, I said: "You're the man who called?"

"That's right," he said. "Allow me to introduce myself. My name is Frank Sixfeet, however I'll deny it if anybody asks."

"Mr. Sixfeet," I began. "You said over the phone that you were holding members of my family hostage."

"That's right," he said while looking over his shoulder. "Of course, I'll deny it if anybody asks."

"What do you want?"

"I want you to get this published," he replied and slid a bulky stack of papers across the table to me. The cover sheet said: **"IT AIN'T OVER UNTIL THE BLIND LADY SINGS (or, How The Monkeys Got Their Bananas Back)" by Frank Sixfeet**.

"The title is too long," I noted.

"Everyone's a critic," sighed Frank. "Do whatever you have to do."

"You want me to get this published?" I asked.

"That's right," said Frank. "I wrote it and now I'm going into hiding. I didn't abduct your family but I can get to them at anytime, so you must follow through with my instructions."

"This seems rather bizarre," I said. "And quite alarming since you are threatening my family."

"Did you bring the materials I asked you to?" he inquired.

"Yes," I replied. I got out the paper and pen I had been instructed to bring.

"Write down everything we've said," he ordered. "It must be documented!"

I scribbled away for a few minutes.

When I finished he leaned back and smiled: "That ought to give you a first line of defense in case lawyers attack you for printing my book. Every jury can understand a man protecting his family."

He winked at me behind his opaque lenses. "Keep writing everything down."

"So you don't really intend to harm my family?" I asked.

"Maybe I do and maybe I don't," he smiled. "I'll deny either if anybody asks. You must keep your defense intact."

I considered the possibilities and decided to hear him out.

"You said you would offer me four lines of defense," I prompted.

"Yes," he continued. "The second defense is more subtle. Just as in the book I reveal that Josh, Eekim and Nicky are all parts of me, you can claim that I am a part of you. If worse comes to worse you merely declare that you are a victim of a multiple personality and that your alter personality, me, is also afflicted with multiple personalities."

I nodded but thought: "They'll never buy that."

"Of course they'll buy it," laughed Frank. "It's a new and original defense. Lawyers aren't going to throw away something that valuable just because they don't like you."

"Hmmm," I pondered. He may have a point there. "And the third option?"

"The third option is that you plead insanity."

"Wasn't that the second option?"

"You misunderstand," Frank said. "I don't mean you plead that you're insane, you plead that the lawyer system is."

"Well, it's a valid point," I admitted. "But somehow I don't think a court will buy it."

"Ask for a jury trial," Frank advised.

"What's the fourth option?"

Frank shifted uneasily and once again looked over his shoulder.

"The fourth option is more drastic," he whispered. "As a final fail-safe to my identity I would have to insist that you simply run amok and shoot every lawyer in sight."

"That option doesn't exactly guarantee me a long and bright future," I surmised. After further consideration I said: "Still, it's something I've always wanted to do."

"That's the spirit!" encouraged Frank. "I knew I had picked the right man. Will you do it?"

"I guess so," I agreed.

Frank gave me a relieved smile and took a deep breath. He immediately seemed more relaxed. He got up and glanced casually around the place before leaning over and whispering: "Just remember, no one must ever find out who I am or discover my whereabouts."

He calmly walked out the door.

I glanced at the written record of our conversation, which was before me. After ordering another beer, I added: "This book is fiction. Josh, Eekim and Nicky are fiction. Frank Sixfeet is fiction. The legal system is fiction. I am fiction. Even you, respected reader, are fiction.

That's my story and I'm sticking to it."

Hey, I wouldn't lie to you.

What are you going to do now?

FINIS

Well, what Eekim, Nicky, Josh, Ooga, Frank and I recommend is that you submit the following to your favorite law-maker. The following is freely given in the hope that, together, we can do for lawyers what the Visigoths did for an arrogant, decadent, self-serving Roman Empire. It is free of all copyright protection. Distribute as you will.

Dear elected employee:

I will make this direct and to the point, something you may be unaccustomed to as a politician. This will take slightly more than thirty seconds which, judging from the usual communication I have from politicians, may overwhelm your attention span.

I think lawyers are out of control. Do you know anybody who controls them besides other lawyers?

I thought not.

Therefore, I would like for the following to be enacted:

(1) All lawyers must give the address and phone number (not a Bar association) where complaints can be filed. This must be incorporated on their business card and handed out to anybody who comes in their office.

(2) Anybody who hires a lawyer can complain about cost, competence or honesty.

(3) Results of these questions will be available to the general public. I would suggest that the phone number for filing complaints and the phone number for inquiries be the same. It will simplify the cards which lawyers must now provide. Hey, I'm always willing to be helpful.

We need a Better Business Bureau for lawyers.

I am your employer. This is your job. Get with it.

Sincerely,

A VOTER